While You Were Out

By

Gary S Burroughs

Poison Pen Publishing
A Gary S Burroughs Imprint

While You Were Out
First published December 2021
Re-edited 2023

Contact the author:

gary@wasteground.co.uk
www.twitter.com/g_s_burroughs
www.facebook.com/gsburroughsbooks

Acknowledgements

Starting a novel is hard. Finishing it is impossible. Editing it so that it is not littered with spelling mistakes and grammatical errors plumbs depths that no writer should be forced to endure. With this in mind I am eternally grateful to my sisters, Sue and Lynn, for shouldering some of that responsibility and saying kind words about my little book. I must also say immense thanks to my girlfriend, Katie, for knocking down walls in our house and making the finishing bit even harder. For the next book I'm going to build a shed in the garden and hide in there!

But, seriously, thank you.

Preamble

It was a small thing, but it bothered her. She was sure that the last time she had seen it, it had been sitting on the mantelpiece alongside an ornament they had collected together during their trip to Luxor. The statue of Horus still stood with its squat little beak pointing out across the room. But the ring had gone, and it bothered her.

He had given it to her when they first started going out. She was barely eighteen, and he had just celebrated his twenty-first birthday. It had been love at first sight, and the ring had been his declaration of everlasting union.

And then they had married, and she had become Mrs Elouise Ellington, wife of Paul Ellington. And they had been happy.

Then he became sick. It was a slow progression, and they barely noticed it at first, but slowly it worsened until he was a shadow of his former self, and he passed away, never having reached his thirtieth year.

The ring had kept her sane throughout his illness and for a long time after his death, and she had kept it on the mantelpiece so she knew where it was whenever she needed a pick-me-up. And then it had gone, and she couldn't find it wherever she looked.

She could have knocked it off, she supposed. She may even have vacuumed it up, but she had pulled the dust bag to pieces trying to find it.

Elouise sat in her small armchair and reached for the remote control to switch on the television, but her hand dropped to an empty coffee table. She looked over to a three-seater leather sofa she rarely sat on and saw it resting on the arm.

She frowned. It was odd, and it wasn't the first thing she noticed as odd, and she felt a lump develop in her stomach.

A missing ring. A remote control where she was sure she had never left it. An electric toothbrush not in its cradle. She always replaced it in the cradle. Didn't she? Then there was an empty milk container returned to the fridge. But, again, she was sure there had been milk in it when she left.

'Grief.' Her mother had told her. 'It does funny things to you. It stops you from thinking properly. It makes you do silly things. Things that are out of character. When your father died....'

They all said the same thing. It was grief. Give yourself more time.

She was sure it wasn't grief.

The ring bothered her. Of all the mysterious goings on, she couldn't believe she would lose her ring. Perhaps it had been stolen?

She opened her mobile phone and called the local police. Perhaps they could help.

***

Laura Hampshire sat at her dressing table and brushed her long, greying hair. She didn't mind the grey so much. She was still fortunate to have a full head of mostly dark hair, and the grey accentuated it rather than making her look old.

She was also pleased that she had retained most of her youthful figure, although age was beginning to tell in certain areas, but she dealt with them easily enough through finance or clothing.

She dressed for bed and slipped slowly beneath her bedsheets. It was early Spring, and the nights were still cold. She curled into a ball and waited while she warmed up. Then, when she was sufficiently comfortable, she reached out and switched off the light.

Sleep came quickly, but it was fretful, and she tossed and turned into the small hours. She got up around one o'clock to visit the bathroom and walked across her small landing in the dark, making the trip with her eyes half closed.

The smell woke her up. It was a masculine smell—a smell of male odour and deodorant.

And then it had gone almost as quickly as it arrived, and she chided herself for her fanciful notions. She had been dreaming, nothing more. This was her home. She was safe there.

***

Detective Constable Paton was shown to the kitchen, where he was handed a freshly made cup of hot coffee.

Mrs Elouise Ellington was very pretty, he mused and thanked her for the coffee. He spooned two large spoonfuls of sugar into his cup and stirred vigorously. A widow, she had said. Her poor husband had died very young. He thought it seemed such a shame that someone so young and beautiful should lose the love of their life before they had had time to live it.

'I understand you've lost some items of value?' He asked.

'Not lost, Constable,' Elouise declared firmly. 'Stolen.'

'And what has been stolen, exactly?' He asked.

'A ring.'

'A ring? Just a ring?'

'Not just a ring, Constable, but a ring given to me by my late husband. It has a great deal of personal value to me.'

'I see.' DC Paton said. 'And what would you estimate its actual value to be?'

'A few pounds.' Elouise said, realising that this would all sound silly in the cold light of day.

'Has anything else been stolen?' DC Paton asked, hopefully. He doubted there would be any promotion off the back of this one.

Elouise hunted in vain for the right words. In the end, she said, 'I realise that this may all sound a bit silly, Constable. And I did wonder whether it was right to call you our not. I don't want to waste your time, and I realise that nothing of great value has been stolen, but….'

DC Paton waited politely. He watched as the young widow struggled with the thoughts in her head.

'And I suppose you may call it grief or loneliness, but….'

'But?'

'But I'm sure someone has been in my house,' she said at last. 'They move things. Little things, things you wouldn't normally notice, I suppose, but which were put back in places that I know I wouldn't have done.'

'Such as?' DC Paton asked.

The milk. The remote control. Other things. The missing ring. She blurted them all out and saw how ridiculous it must have been to the policeman.

DC Paton copied his notes down in a small book. It did seem silly. Maybe it was grief. Grief did do stupid things to people. And she may have lost or misplaced the ring, and it wasn't really of great enough value to worry about, but still. He made positive humming sounds.

'Well,' he said, soothingly and with a good bedside manner, 'I certainly don't think you've wasted our time. I'm sure you've wondered whether or not you've moved these items yourself or perhaps mislaid the ring, but it's always best to be cautious in these matters.'

'But I don't suppose there's much to investigate, is there?' Elouise asked.

DC Paton closed his book and smiled. 'Not really, no. But there are certain things you can do to increase your security, just in case someone is taking the liberty of coming into your home.'

'I always lock my doors.' Elouise said.

'But they are old doors, if you don't mind me saying. Newer doors have better locks—the same with your windows. Little things like that can vastly alter your home security. And maybe some cameras?'

Elouise shook her head. 'I can't be doing with the hassle of installing CCTV. Not to mention the expense.'

'You don't need to spend a fortune,' DC Paton said. 'You can buy small ornament-type cameras that sit on your mantelpiece and let you log into them via an app. Do you have a smartphone?'

'I do.'

'The equipment's very cheap. Some people use them to watch the kids or the cleaners. Some like to watch their pets while they are at work. You can set them to alert you if there's any movement in your house. Here, let me show you.'

A quick search on the internet threw up a dozen different makes and types.

'Actually,' Elouise said, 'that's quite interesting. I may buy one.'

'It can't hurt,' DC Paton said. 'If nothing else, it will put your mind at rest. And if it ever records someone in your house, we'll have something to investigate.'

Elouise thanked DC Paton and watched as he strolled down her footpath. She held his card in her hand and wondered. Was it too soon? It had only been a year…. Was it time to get back on the horse?

She closed the door and returned to her computer. Five minutes later, she had ordered three little cameras for next-day delivery. She was curious to see what stories they would tell.

***

Sarah Finch's dark hair was tinged with purple and blue and fell in waves across her thin shoulders. Her skin was pale beneath the lightly perfumed bath water that cascaded over her body. She lay there in the hot bath and felt the stress wash away. She clipped the end of her nose and dipped her head beneath the water, coming up for air a few seconds later.

She wasn't sure if she had heard the noise or imagined it. Had a door closed in the house? She bent her ear to the door and listened, but all she could hear was the rain falling on the window and a television playing in a neighbour's house.

And then she heard it again. She couldn't quite make it out. Was it a door?

She called out, 'Hello? Is anyone there?'

There wouldn't be anyone there; she had changed the locks recently. Paul?

She sat up. 'Paul? Is that you?'

It couldn't be Paul. He was the reason she had the locks changed.

She waited to see if the noise came again, but it didn't. She sunk back into the hot water and closed her eyes.

She must have imagined it.

***

Laura Hampshire threw a gown over her nightwear and took the stairs three at a time.

There was someone in the house.

She had heard the footsteps outside her room as she had dressed for bed. Then a door opened further down the corridor. She felt the fear and the panic in her heart as the adrenaline began to surge through her veins. She opened the door to her bedroom slowly and peeked out. Then, seeing the corridor was clear, she made a bolt for the front door.

She banged hard on her neighbour's front door and pressed the doorbell. A light came on from within, and she waited as the lock was undone.

Richard Wilkins stood in his dressing gown and frowned at his neighbour. It was late, and he had just climbed into bed.

'Bloody hell, Laura, are you okay?'

She held out her arm and held his.

'I think there's someone in my house!' She exclaimed.

Richard sighed, but it went unnoticed. It wasn't the first time Laura had declared that there was someone in her house. He noticed that she was dressed and ready for bed, and he could make out her figure beneath the thin gown that covered her shoulders.

'Let me get my shoes on.'

They toured Laura Hampshire's home slowly and carefully. As much as Richard doubted his neighbour's motives, it paid to be careful. They walked around the front room slowly, and Richard held an iron poker aloft while Laura stayed a pace behind him. Richard noticed an empty bottle of wine on the table, and a single glass sat next to it.

She was lonely, he thought. And she was drunk.

They made their way upstairs, turning on all the lights as they went. Richard went into each room first, his poker held firmly in his hand. They opened cupboards and checked under the beds. Nothing.

When they had completed the search, Laura poured herself a large glass of scotch.

'Can I offer you one?' She asked.

Richard declined the offer and made his excuses. He looked over his shoulder as he left Laura's home and saw her watching his every move.

She wasn't unattractive, he thought to himself. Perhaps if she just asked.

***

Jane Wilson slept soundly in her vast four-poster bed. The wind blew fiercely outside, but it was barely audible beyond the double-glazed windows. At the foot of her bed was an opened suitcase with a handful of clothes neatly laid out inside.

Jane was an advance packer, finding comfort in preparing for a holiday and carefully planning which items to pack.

On a chair nearby was a pile of neatly folded items that she would pack at the last minute, and on her dressing table was a collection of recently purchased holiday essentials which included a pack of paracetamol, four bottles of factor thirty, replacement razor blades, tweezers, shampoos and conditioners and a truckload of moisturiser.

The excitement of her holiday had left her restless and unable to sleep, but a few gins had taken the edge off, and she had climbed into bed and fallen swiftly asleep.

Had she been awake, she still may not have heard him as he climbed the stairs or noticed as the door to her room was pushed open. Had she been awake, she may have smelt him, but she would have struggled to see him as he stayed safely in the shadows.

He stood at the foot of her bed and watched her. He watched as she slept.

When Jane Wilson woke up the following day, he had gone.

She showered, dumped a few more items into her suitcase, and got ready for work. There was just one more sleep until her holiday, and she felt it had been a long time coming. She couldn't wait.

***

'Get him, Buster! Get him!'

Richard Wilkins had returned from his walk as the evening light faded. Laura Hampshire was standing at the front of his house, pacing restlessly. He sighed. He always sighed when he saw her. She was beginning to grind his nerves.

'He's in my garden!' She had said, and together they made their way around the house.

Laura's garden was as long as a football pitch, although narrow, and bordered on one side by a small fence and fields and on the other by Richard's garden. As they rounded the edge of the house, he thought he could see a figure at the far end, making its way between the fruit trees.

That's when Richard Wilson loosed his four-year-old German Shepard.

'Get him, Buster! Get him!'

He knew all too well that Buster was bloody useless as a guard dog and more likely to slobber over the fleeing man, but he was big and made all the right noises. He took off towards the figure and growled and barked as he went.

They found Buster sitting at the garden's end, his way blocked by a hedge. Beyond the hedge was darkness, and Richard knew that what lay under that shroud of darkness was a quarter of a mile of fields which dropped down into woodland. The man had long gone.

Buster looked pleased.

***

DC Paton sat in a small front room drinking tea from what he thought was probably the lady's finest china. Sometimes all the old women wanted was a bit of company, and he didn't mind too much. This was what community policing was all about, and their cakes were rather lovely.

Clare West was about sixty, he guessed, but she dressed older.

'You see, I'm sure I could *smell* him,' Clare said. 'It was most distinctly a man's smell. Musty. Sickly sweet, if you know what I mean. And I don't have male visitors, so it was out of place, do you see what I mean?'

DC Paton nodded.

'You said some items have been stolen?' He asked.

'Yes. A few trinkets. Small items, really. Items you wouldn't notice were missing until you looked for them, and not convinced you hadn't just mislaid them, if you see what I mean. One does lose things as one gets older.'

'So what makes you think they have been stolen?'

'The smell.' Clare said firmly. 'I'm telling you, Constable, someone has been in my house.'

DC Paton flipped open his notebook. He re-read his notes from Elouise Ellington's report. *I'm sure someone has been in my house.* It was very similar, even to the taking of small items.

And then there was Miss Laura Hampshire. She had filed a report a few days ago that had certain similarities. She was on his list of witnesses to interview.

It was all very curious. Very odd. Very odd indeed.

***

Elouise Ellington drove her little car along the A34 towards the city. It was early afternoon, and she was late. She pushed her toe down on the accelerator and edged the needle toward eighty miles an hour.

She didn't like going fast, but it was dry, and the roads were pretty quiet. She passed a lorry on her left and sped towards her exit. Radio Two had taken to playing some odd music which pained her ears, so she reached down to the panel and scrolled to the next station.

90s drum and base filled the car.

Her mobile phone was sat in a small cradle which itself was attached to a vent. She looked at it as a notification popped up.

She never answered her phone when driving. Not once. Not even hands-free. She liked to concentrate on the road ahead. Even if it was an important call, they could wait five minutes while she found a lay-by.

But it wasn't a call but a notification from the security app she had recently installed.

Despite her best intentions, she was intrigued. One of the cameras in her house had detected motion. It was probably just a fly, but her interest was piqued. She reached over and swiped the screen.

The app opened, and she saw her front room laid out in full colour. But there was something else. Or, rather, there was *someone* else.

He was sat on her three-seater sofa watching the television.

She looked closer at the screen to see if she could recognise the man, but it was no one she knew.

Her eyes were glued to the screen. She looked up briefly, and to her horror, the landscape had changed. The road ahead was filled with cars with their brake lights lit up. She was going too fast. She was going way too fast, and they were way too close.

She stepped on the brakes, but it was too late. There wasn't enough time to stop. In desperation, she yanked the steering wheel sharply to the left and tried to avoid the collision.

She made it with barely an inch to spare, but now she was off the road and hurtling into the tree line. She made contact with a forty-year-old oak tree that sat barely fifty yards from the highway. Those that heard the collision said it was the worst noise they had ever heard.

Mrs Elouise Ellington was killed on impact.

Sarah Finch drew back her curtains, and glorious summer sunshine flooded her small bedroom. It was only early, but the heat was intense. The forecast was good too, and she looked forward to a long hot summer of lazy weekends by the river, evenings in the local beer garden, and romantic strolls in the countryside.

She felt better now. She and Paul had reconciled. It had been a mistake, and she had apologised.

At the time, it all made sense. She had a feeling that she was being watched. It was nothing concrete, just a feeling.

But it had been a strong feeling. And her father's watch had gone missing; she was sure of that. There were other things, too. Little things she couldn't quite put her finger on. Items that had been moved or taken and then put back.

Of course, she would accuse Paul. He could be pretty childish sometimes. And he was the only person besides herself with a key to her flat. He had denied it, of course. But she was sure it was him. She had even smelt his scent long after throwing him out of the flat.

It all stopped once she had changed the locks.

And then she found the watch. She hadn't remembered putting it there, but she couldn't remember not putting it there. Perhaps she had let her imagination run wild. She rang the local police station and told them she had found the watch. She cancelled the insurance claim too.

Then she apologised to Paul, and she had made it up to him the way he liked the most, and life had returned to some semblance of normality.

She stood at the window and drank in the smell of summer. She revelled in his scent, too. It still lingered in the room long after he had left.

She let the door close behind her as she stepped out into the street.

He watched her from her bedroom window, a hint of a shadow behind the nets.

***

Constable Sam Paton drew up his report and read through what he had written to check for errors.

It was all very odd, but there was little to say beyond the oddness. He had gathered up a collection of mysterious burglaries or break-ins and drilled deep into each to see if he could find anything of interest.

He dropped his report on his senior officer's desk, who read it in a perfunctory manner before handing it back.

'That's good work,' he said. 'E-mail it to the burglary coordinator.'

He wrote his name across the top of the report.

Detective Sergeant Phil Spencer, Burglary co-ordinator, Thames Valley Police.

Constable Paton typed a brief message and attached his report to the e-mail. But, of course, it would likely come to nothing as they so often did. And there wasn't anything there—nothing tangible, at least.

But still, he couldn't entirely escape that uneasy feeling that sat heavily on his stomach.

***

No one ever saw him. He stole through the night like a cat; his senses peaked, his nose sniffing out every dark corner, alley, and light that shone from curtained windows.

He kept to the shadows, dark lanes and the woods where no one went after dark. He moved through the darkness like a predator stalking his prey, hunting down their scent, sniffing out their weaknesses.

He flew like an eagle on the thermals of the wind; his eyes saw what others missed. A chink in their armour, an unlocked door, an open garden. Weakness. He hunted down their weakness and approached with stealth, moving towards them like a lion in the low grass.

And they never saw him.

One

It had already been a busy night. She was almost at the halfway point of her shift. Already that evening, she had dealt with five domestic abuse calls, three fights outside pubs, two burglaries, a sexual assault, a stabbing, and five road traffic calls, including one that had led to the closure of the M40, a missing child (fortunately reunited with its parents in quick time), three counts of driving off without paying and multiple hoax calls.

She glanced at the clock. It was almost ten o'clock. A coffee and cigarette were just a few minutes away. They would be the longest and most traumatic few minutes of her life.

On the wall in front of her desk hung a large computer screen that continually updated the call centre staff with the progress of their calls that evening. It had already surpassed the previous evening in the volume of triple nine calls, and the rate of calls seemed ill-inclined to diminish.

The emergency 999 button on her screen flashed. She answered it automatically, in the same reassuring voice she always used.

'Police emergency…'

Nothing. Silence. In itself, that wasn't unusual, but what was unusual was that the caller didn't hang up right away. Hoax calls usually ran in one of two ways. They instantly hung up or engaged the responder in a meaningless conversation that meandered nowhere in particular. Like most emergency call centres, they were prone to serial hoaxers, but something here felt different. She couldn't put her finger on it, but she felt the hairs on her neck stand on end.

'Police emergency… Go ahead caller…'

She was about to put the call down to another hoax and hang up the call when the voice came. It was a young voice. The voice of a girl. It was hushed, as though the caller had pressed her mouth tightly to the receiver and cupped her hands around the mouthpiece.

'He's… he's in the house….'

'Who is? Who's in the house?'

'I don't know… I…. I think he's killed them….'

She could sense the panic in her voice. The fear was tangible. She glanced up at the caller ID and breathed a sigh of relief. It was a landline number. Landline numbers were linked automatically to British Telecoms' database. They came with addresses. Mobile phones didn't. They were difficult to trace and nearly always took time. Time they didn't have. As she continued the call, she uploaded the information to a real-time emergency response form automatically linked to first responders in the field. She could talk to the girl while directing emergency services to the right place. She also pressed a high-priority button on her dashboard, alerting call centre management that a serious emergency was breaking.

Her fingers blurred as she tapped away on her keyboard.

22 Chatsworth Drive, Cherwell. Intruder on site. High Priority.

'Okay… I need you to stay calm. Where are you? Are you somewhere safe?' She could barely hear the reply.

'I'm hiding. Upstairs. In a bedroom cupboard.'

She uploaded the information almost as quickly as the girl was relaying it.

Caller hiding in an upstairs bedroom.

'What's your name, sweetheart?'

'Please hurry. I think they're dead. I think he killed them….'

She heard a faintly audible click as her supervisor joined the call. She looked across the room at where her supervisor sat and saw two managers gather around the screen. She typed more information into her screen.

Intruder on site. Possible assault. Proceed with caution.

'The police are on their way. You'll be able to hear them soon. We know where you are calling from. 22 Chatsworth Drive. We'll be with you soon.'

She looked across at her supervisor and felt her heat sink. Her supervisor was gesticulating frantically to an imaginary face while shouting down her telephone. The look on her face filled her with dread. Her supervisor turned and looked across at her, shaking her head as she went. She held up her free hand and splayed her fingers out. She clenched her fingers into a fist and stretched them out again. She repeated the action three times.

Fuck. Fifteen minutes.

Then her supervisor clenched her fingers one more time and slowly raised her fingers. Twenty minutes…

'The police are blue lighting to you right now. You should be able to hear them any second.'

The lie burned her soul.

Caller a young girl. High Priority. Intruder on site.

She didn't know what else to do. She felt a terrible sense of hopelessness.

'Please…. I can hear him. He's moving about downstairs.'

Then a sharp intake of breath.

'Please… He's coming… he's coming up the stairs….'

'Stay calm, sweetheart. We're coming. We're nearly there. Try and stay very quiet. I'll stay with you. You're not on your own.'

'He's in the room!'

'Okay. Stay very quiet. Don't make a sound. We're coming, sweetheart. We're nearly there….'

Then came nothing but the hiss of static and the sound of a young girl barely stifling a sob.

And then the scream. It was a scream that would haunt her for the rest of her life. It was primal, made of nothing but pure fear and terror. And then came the silence.

She listened carefully, trying desperately to make sense of the silence and grasp what had happened.

Then came the sound of breathing. Deep breathing. The deep breathing of a man.

She took a breath and steeled herself. 'This is the police…. whoever you are, you should know we are on the way. We're just around the corner.'

And then a click as the receiver was replaced. All she was left with was silence and a dark sense of foreboding.

Two

Lovelace knew she was dreaming. She knew it because her mother was cooking, and her mother couldn't be cooking because she was dead. And the reason she didn't try and wake herself up was because of the detail. Details she couldn't quite grasp in the light of day. Her mother's smell, for one. How the corner of her mouth rose ever so slightly when she smiled and the gentle, soft way she spoke. She yearned for it when she was awake and was grateful for it when she slept.

But there was a bell ringing. The bell was annoying, and she couldn't ever recall a time when there was a bell in the house. Or was it sirens? There would be sirens. She knew that. She remembered that. She didn't know about the bell, though; it seemed to get louder. And then things started to change. Well, not really things.. more the sense of things. She couldn't quite put her finger on it but felt a sudden overbearing sense of dread. And the ringing. Why wouldn't the ringing stop?

She turned and saw him there. He stood in the doorway, his entire frame filling it from side to side. He was in shadow, and she couldn't make out his face, but she knew it was him. She would know her father anywhere. Daddy.

Then there was fear. She was afraid. Daddy stood there in the doorway, not moving a muscle. He was holding a kitchen knife. She remembered the knife…

She always woke at that point. The dream never went any further, but the addition of the ringing was a new element. The ringing continued as she came awake and rubbed the sleep from her eyes. Finally, she rolled over and picked up her mobile phone from the bedside table. She had found the source of the noise. The time said 3:30. It was ridiculously early.

'Hello?'

'Detective Constable Lovelace?'

She smiled. That was the first time she had been called that since she had been promoted to Detective.

'Yes.'

'Sorry for the earliness of the call. DCI Graham. I'm sending a car for you. Can you be ready in half an hour?'

'Yes.'

'Good. I'll see you shortly.'

Click. Silence.

She knew that DCI Graham was a man of few words, but that was brief.

She slipped out of bed and straight into the shower. She felt an overwhelming sense of relief that she had spent the previous evening sorting out what she would wear on her first day. It took away the necessity to work these things out on the fly. Everything she needed was neatly folded on a chair next to her dresser. She showered, dried herself off, and dressed in less than fifteen minutes. Her hair was a different problem. It had always been a problem. It was one she shared with her mother. It mattered little what she did with her hair or for how long she did it, after ten minutes, it did what it wanted, and that usually meant looking a little scruffy, as though she had just got out of bed. She brushed it quickly and tied it up in a ponytail. It was long, auburn hair, and despite the fact it irritated her that she could do so little with it, she liked the scruffy look. But today, it would be neat and tidy for an hour or so.

Twenty minutes after the phone call, she was waiting outside beneath an unlit streetlamp on a street that had been plunged into total darkness. Local authority cuts had seen overnight lighting switched off, and the world had become a much darker place. It felt odd to be out so early and not in uniform. She had always enjoyed the

24

night shift as a Police Constable. The world at night was a different place, with different players.

It was warm, too. Recently, the thermometer had risen sharply, and the needle had pushed into the late 80s. Unfortunately, the forecast was for a lot more of the same. Even in the early hours, it was becoming difficult to escape the humidity.

She was pondering this when she heard the throaty growl of a V8 in the distance. She knew about cars and couldn't mistake that sound. It grew steadily louder as the driver weaved through the streets until she saw lights on the windows of a house further up the road. Then, as they got brighter, she saw the nose of a dark Jag pull up at the junction. It edged out of the junction, and she could feel the engine's grunt as it pulled up beside her. The passenger window inched downwards, and the driver looked out.

'DC Lovelace?'

'Yes.'

He flipped open his warrant card. The face matched the driver. A pretty face. Slightly older in the flesh, with a hint of grey around the ears.

'DI Luton. Get in.'

She opened the door, and a wave of icy air blew over her, bearing as it went the smell of fresh coffee and, if she wasn't mistaken, the faint aroma of cigarettes. A glance at the fingers on his right hand showed yellowing around the tips. She smiled. It was a basic and straightforward observation, but the detail pleased her.

'I bought you a coffee. Black. There's milk in the bag and some sugar if you want it.'

'Thank you. Black's fine.'

She took a sip. It was still fiercely hot. She wound up the window and sat back as he powered the car out of her street and out of the city. The air in the vehicle was a blessed relief verging on the too-cold. The coffee was strong, but the taste and odour were uplifting.

'My name's Steve, by the way. Only the boss is the guv'nor. Everyone else is first names only. No rank.'

'Lucy.'

He looked across and smiled. He said, 'I know,' and she felt the words meant so much more. People always knew her. Or at least, they thought they knew her. Maybe she shouldn't have kept her childhood surname. Perhaps Uncle Mike had been right. She smiled inwardly. No, she said to herself, Uncle Mike was never right.

Luton nodded over his shoulder, 'The iPad's for you. Your login code is the last six digits of your warrant number. It's uploaded with everything you need to know. It's got its own sim. There's access to the Police National Computer and most of the other databases you'll need. Don't lose it.'

She reached over and picked the iPad up. It had a leather cover that folded out into a stand.

'Where are we going?' She asked.

'It's about twenty minutes outside the city. Residential area mostly, surrounded by fields. At about ten o'clock last night, Abingdon contact centre picked up a 999 call from a house at the edge of the town. The caller claimed that her parents had been murdered and that the killer was still in the house. It took nearly thirty minutes before the first responders got there.'

'Shit. Why so long?'

'Busy night. There were two rapes, a violent assault in the city centre and a fatal stabbing. The Major Investigation Team were called to this job around 10:45. We've been sitting on our hands since then, waiting for Scenes Of Crimes to turn up. They should have done their preliminary walkthrough by the time we arrive.'

'Were they dead?'

Luton nodded.

'The victims were Sara and Tom Parkes and their daughter Molly. The parents were found in the kitchen. By the look of it, they disturbed an intruder at the house when they got home. It didn't go well for them.'

'They had been out for the day?'

'Yes. Drayton Manor Park. You know, the theme park. They had been there since 9 am that morning, arriving home, we think, just before ten.'

'How do you know?'

'It's on the pad. The long and short of it, I logged on to the mother's Facebook page. She pretty much shared everything. It's all there. The first responders wore body cams so you can get a good look at the crime scene. I warn you, though, it's pretty brutal. Mother and father were the victims of a blitz attack. They didn't stand a chance. We found Molly upstairs. Same MO. We think he went equipped with a hammer.'

The question formed on her lips, but she didn't want to acknowledge it. Stealing herself, she asked, 'was she raped?'

'From the way the body was found, I'd say no. He dragged her out of the cupboard she was hiding in while still on the phone to the contact centre and hit her over the head. Her clothes weren't disturbed.'

Lovelace opened the iPad and logged in. The screen was busy with icons and saved files. The background was the Thames Valley Police shield featuring the imposing images of a rearing ox and a stag capped with a swan, representing the three counties. Beneath it, in Latin, the force logo read 'Sit pax in valle tamesis'. *Let there be Peace in the Thames Valley.*

She opened the audio file and listened to the 999 call.

A girl's voice. Hushed. *He's in the house….*

Then the operator spoke. Who? Who's in the house?

I don't know. I think he's killed them.
Lovelace paused the recording and started it again. She
listened carefully to the words the girl spoke. *I think he's
killed them....*

Odd. She placed a mental sticky note there. She'd
come back to that.

Then the operator spoke some more. The girl's voice
came back even softer. Her voice trembled. *I'm hiding.
Upstairs. In a bedroom cupboard.*

It felt like every bad horror movie played out for real
in suburban England.

What's your name, sweetheart?

She didn't reply to that. She stuck a sticky note there,
too.

Please hurry. I think they're dead. I think he killed them....

There it was again. Them. They're. Them. It was a
peculiar choice of words. Not mum and dad, just 'them.'

*Please.... I can hear him. He's moving about downstairs. Then,
Please... He's coming... he's coming up the stairs....*

Lovelace frowned. She heard the operator's voice catch
as she tried to reassure the girl.

He's in the room!

Lovelace's heart raced as she pictured the killing play
out. First, the bedroom cupboard door flying open -
then a scream. A primordial scream followed by a noise
that sounded like a hollow thump. She guessed that was
the kill point. Then the operator spoke, sending a
warning to the killer that she knew wasn't true. Then the
line went dead. There was already enough there to keep
her occupied. Little details that stuck in her head. Why
so impersonal when referring to her parents? Why didn't
she give her name? No, that wasn't the right question,
but she couldn't phrase it in a way that made any sense.

She closed the file down and opened a video file
marked PCPHELPS1019WMV. The video started inside

a squad car as it pulled up outside a house. The street lights were still on, but they were dull. The houses in the street were mostly darkened. A few had lights on inside, the occupants blissfully unaware of the tragedy on their doorstep.

The wearer of the body cam was sitting in the car's passenger seat. The door was opening before the vehicle came to a complete stop. Lovelace watched as PC Phelps approached the house and began knocking on the door. It was a loud knock, a typically authoritative policeman's knock intended to alarm those inside. No reply came. He turned as his colleague arrived at the door.

'Have you tried the door?' PC Harmer asked.

He reached out and pulled the handle down. It was locked. His colleague turned and spoke into his radio. Lovelace could hear more sirens approaching in the distance. 'Six four to control. We're at the house. No lights on. No one answering. Can we get authorisation to enter, please?'

Static silence. Then, 'Six-four. Authorisation granted. Knock the door down. Get in there.'
PC Phelps turned as another squad car pulled into the cul-de-sac, its lights flashing frantically and its sirens wailing. The noise had already lured a few neighbours onto the street, watching.

A young PC rushed up. She was pulling on a high vis over her stab vest. 'No answer?' She asked.

'Nothing.' PC Harmer said. 'You got a ram?'

PC Willis turned and shouted at the driver of the car she had just got out of. 'Sarge. Bring the hammer!'

Sarge was a big man bordering on seven feet tall. He pulled the battering ram from the car's boot and walked to the house. He made it in three steps and lunged the ram straight at the door. He knew what to expect and braced himself for the impact. The PVC door embraced most of the hit and resisted the attack. Sarge stepped back, swung the ram back as far as he could, and slammed it back into the door. He kept this up for a full minute until the door frame finally let go, and they entered the house.

'Police!'

They entered at speed. PC Phelps was second through the door, just behind PC Harmer. The house was in darkness. The torches they carried threw up some detail. The hallway went left and right from the front door. It was a tiled floor. To the left, Lovelace briefly saw what looked like a living room before PC Phelps swung his torch ahead of him and at the stairs. They were carpeted. Lovelace frowned again. That brought up another question and another mental sticky note. With a tiled floor, it was clear that the girl hiding upstairs could hear someone moving downstairs, but how would she hear him coming up the stairs if they were carpeted? It would probably be irrelevant, but she didn't like loose ends. She was always like that, always had been. She must have answers.

PC Phelps turned his torch to the right. He followed his colleague into the kitchen. Again, Lovelace watched the footage with interest as PC Hamer moved around the room, his torch in front of him. This time Lovelace saw something she had missed initially. PC Harmer carried a bright orange taser at full port just above his torch.

He called out, 'Police! I'm armed with a Taser. Show yourself!'

PC Hamer moved around a large oak kitchen table and stumbled over something lying on the floor. He shone his torch down. 'Fuck. Turn the fucking light on!'

PC Phelps found the switch and lit up the room. He turned and looked at his partner. He'd gone as white as a sheet. He stood stock still.

PC Phelps walked slowly around the table. PC Harmer was standing over the body of an adult female. She was lying face up, although it was hard to tell. Most of her face had been caved in. Next to her lay the body of an adult male. His head had been caved in, too. His head lay in a pool of blood and brains.

'Jesus.' PC Phelps turned and called, 'Sarge, you need to see this!'

Sarge came in and strode over to PC Phelps. He looked down at the bodies and then at PC Hamer.

'Right. You,' he pointed at Hamer, 'don't fucking move. You're standing in a crime scene.'

He was about to go on when his partner called from upstairs.

'Sarge!'

'Don't move. Keep your taser up. He may still be about. You, with me.'

The footage stopped there.

Lovelace closed the file and opened the second one. PCWILLIS1267WMV. This body cam footage came from the first woman on the scene, PC Willis. She had leapt out of the car and quickly approached her colleagues at the front of the house.

Sarge. Bring the hammer.

Another minute of her sergeant battering the door down. From this perspective, Lovelace watched PC Hamer draw his taser from his holster and switch it on. As soon as the door went in, so did he, his weapon drawn. PC Phelps was second, Sarge third and PC Willis fourth.

Lovelace watched as the first two policemen went right towards the kitchen. Sarge drew out his baton, and the young PC followed suit. Sarge looked around at his partner. 'Upstairs. Carefully. Challenge anyone you find. You don't like anyone, put them on the floor.' Then, as an afterthought, he said, 'Bec, if he fights back, aim for the head.'

PC Willis took the stairs three at a time and was at the top in a heartbeat. She shone her torch around the landing. Nothing. Just pictures on walls. She opened the first door on her right and shone her torch inside. That's when she heard one of her colleagues call out, 'Sarge! You need to see this.'

She moved into the room, her baton poised to strike down on the first thing that moved. She saw the body as she swept her torch around the room. She was laid out on her front, and the back of her head was a tangled mess of blood and bone.

'Sarge!' PC Willis screamed as loudly as she could. A few seconds later, the light in the room came on, and she turned to meet Sarge as he stood behind her, filling the doorway in its entirety. PC Willis turned, and Lovelace got a good look at the bedroom. It was nicely decorated in salmon pink. The bed was queen-sized with a salmon-pink headrest. The bed was made. On either side were two bedside tables and two lamps. There was a black powerpoint for a cordless phone on the left-hand side. The telephone was lying next to the dead girl. Just behind the dead girl was the cupboard she had taken to for sanctuary. The door was open. PC Willis moved carefully around the girl's body and looked inside the cupboard. There was no one inside.

'Right. Let's sweep upstairs. Be careful of what you touch. Let's just make sure this fucker's not still here.'

PC Willis followed her Sergeant out onto the landing. There were three other doors behind. Two bedrooms and a bathroom. One bedroom was clearly the girl's, given the pictures on the wall and the general mess that went with teenagers. The other room looked like a spare. Both rooms had been turned upside down in a frantic search for something. Had this been a robbery gone wrong? It certainly had that feel about it. The odd thing, Lovelace thought, was that the master bedroom, which the girl had hidden in, hadn't been ransacked. It was untouched, save for the dead girl on the floor.

Lovelace closed the file. Perhaps the killer had been disturbed before he had time to turn over the parents' bedroom. She couldn't entirely escape the feeling that that didn't make sense. If there were going to be anything of value in the house, it probably wouldn't be in the room of a fourteen-year-old girl. Wouldn't you start in the main bedroom?

On top of that, it was the first room you reached at the top of the stairs. Why didn't the killer start there if he was a burglar? More questions that demanded answers.

Lovelace took a sip of her coffee. She had been almost entirely unaware of her surroundings until then. She looked up from her iPad and out at the road ahead. They were on a dual carriageway. A glance at the car's instrument panel told her that Luton was holding the powerful vehicle at a steady eighty miles an hour. He looked across at her. 'We're nearly there.'

She nodded. Outside, the night was slowly replaced by the first hues of a new day. It was almost blue on the horizon, shaded in vibrant reds and yellows. It was going to be another hot day.

She turned her attention back to her iPad. She opened up the web browser. It was logged into several different social media profiles.

'Those are my accounts,' Luton said, 'don't go posting silly shit on there!'

Lovelace smiled. 'I won't.'

She scrolled slowly through Sara Parkes' social media profiles across several platforms. They were all visible to anyone who wanted to look.

She scrolled through dozens of posts. They were primarily family-oriented posts, showing off her home and young family. There were recent posts of Sara and Molly enjoying the heatwave, frolicking in bikinis in their garden. Molly was a sweet-looking little thing with long blonde hair and a sweet smile. To a Detective like Lovelace, it was hard not to feel that Sara Parkes had posted too much information. It was easy to gather where she lived and when she would be out. She posted so many pictures of her home that a professional observer, or potential killer, could easily find a way in.

Dinner at Sam and Mike's at 6 pm - Off to the gym! - Girly day by the pool! - Recommendations for a plumber.. - Sign my petition - Spotted in Cherwell - Drayton Manor Park tomorrow! Early start! - Molly's green out! And then a dozen posts charting their day at the theme park.

Lovelace scrolled through the photographs of the Parkes family's last day. It was a bittersweet process. She couldn't help but meet every happy photograph with the thought that it was to be their last day alive.

'Who's this?'

Lovelace expanded a photograph with two girls in it. One of the girls was Molly Parkes. She was recognisable from all the other pictures her mother had taken. The other girl is featured in many photographs from their day at the theme park. She was of a similar age with the same colour hair and of about the same build.

'Bethany Wright. She's been tagged in a few posts— her profile's private, like Molly's. As far as we can tell, they're school friends. Probably met at the theme park. By the look of it, they spent the day together.'

'Have we contacted her yet?

'Give us a chance! We've not even gone through the crime scene yet! Besides, it's early yet. So let's not break the bad news to a teenage girl before she's had her breakfast.'

Luton had pulled off the dual carriageway, and now they were motoring down a country lane. They came to the edge of a small town, and Luton pulled into a cul-de-sac. Lovelace recognised the house from the body cam footage. Now, however, the front of the house was covered in a white gazebo-type shelter. Men and women could be seen coming and going through the entrance dressed in white body suits and blue overshoes. A uniformed officer stood guard at the door to the gazebo and logged all the comings and goings. On the road outside the house were a dozen marked and unmarked police cars. A mobile police station had been set up nearby. Neighbours huddled together in small cliques, some still wearing their nightwear. There was a buzz in the air. Lovelace felt it the instant she got out of the car.

She felt something else, too—a sense of dread.

Three

Luton pulled the car to a stop near the mobile police station and got out. Lovelace followed. She felt the heat at once, the air con in the car had chilled her skin so much that she had goosebumps down her arms, and now she was outside, the temperature change was marked.

Luton walked up to a suit leaning on the side of the station. He was smoking a cigarette.

'Lucy, meet DS Stanton.'

Stanton stood upright and sucked on his cigarette. He was just short of six foot tall, with a widow's peak hairline slowly receding off the back of his head. He had a friendly smile, though, Lovelace thought, and bright blue eyes that shone out of a heavily sun-darkened face. She held out her hand.

He took it and shook it gently. She hated the way some men squeezed her hand so hard that it hurt and was grateful for his more gentle squeeze.

'Call me Jim. Nice to meet you at last, Lucy. I've heard a lot about you.'

She was sure he had. Most of it was probably bullshit. It usually was.

'Welcome to the madhouse,' he added. 'We're not actually mad, but it helps if you're slightly twisted!'

He laughed at his own joke.

'How's it going in there?' Luton asked.

'The guv'nor's itching to get started. SOCO have finished their preliminary walkthrough. Charlie's inside, getting ready to go in. You coming?'

He flicked his cigarette into the gutter and approached the station door.

'Come on,' Luton said. 'Come and meet the team.'

Lovelace recognised DCI Graham instantly. They had spoken a few times, and on the last occasion, he had offered her a position on his team. It was the most respected team in the Thames Valley area, if not the country. Posts within it were hard to come by, if not impossible. Those who made it onto the team lasted a few years before flying off to bigger and better things. Graham had a habit of collecting the best officers from within the area, sometimes even poaching officers from other forces. To be on his team was one of the greatest compliments you could get as a copper. After serving on Graham's team, your career path was most likely orbital. Lovelace felt a great sense of expectation and a fair amount of doubt. Why had he chosen her? She had asked that question a thousand times, and she had come back empty a thousand times. She was qualified, and she knew that. She had an outstanding arrest and prosecution record. She had passed every exam she had ever taken in the top one per cent. She was a model copper. She knew her stuff, and what she didn't know, she learnt. But there was doubt. Uncle Mike had sat with her shortly after she had graduated.

'The police?' He was shocked. 'They won't like it, especially as you changed your surname back. You should have kept mine. They won't fucking like it at all. They have long memories.'

'It was hardly my fault.' She had argued. 'Why shouldn't I join up?'

'Because they'll remember. They're a close lot, coppers. They'll not trust you. Not trust your reasons.'

'I just want to help. And I want to understand. That's what it's always been about. I need to understand.'

Uncle Mike had lost the argument, as he knew he would. He'd been right, too. They never did trust her. Maybe one or two did, the ones she had worked closely with. Those that had looked past her surname and got to know the Lucy behind it. Most were just ghoulishly curious. That's Lefty Lovelace? She hated the nickname, but she knew better than to challenge it. It made them more determined to use it. Her career felt like it had stalled. And then DCI Graham came along. And again, the question. Why her?

She stepped into the mobile station. Graham smiled at her.

'Good. You're here. We're almost ready to go in. Charlie, this is Lucy Lovelace.'

Detective Sergeant Charlie White was about the same height as Lovelace, but she was far more imposing. Her hair was blonde and wound tightly to the side of her head. She was older than Lovelace but younger than the others. Late twenties, early thirties, she guessed. She wasn't strikingly pretty either, although there was something attractive about her. She had a soft face and small ears that looked like they were pinned to the side of her head. She held out a soft, pale hand. Her face was also colour free. She was almost as natural as the men, with little makeup. Lovelace liked it. She knew how to play the game. She was here on merit and telling them all exactly that.

'Nice to meet you, Lucy.'

Lovelace took the hand. 'You too.'

'Good.' Graham interrupted the meeting. He looked at Lovelace. 'You're up to speed?'

'I think so.'

'Questions?'

'Hundreds!'

'Good. Hold fire on them for a minute.'

Outside, Lovelace saw an older-looking man in an all-white coverall approach the mobile station.

'I think this is our preliminary report.'

Graham opened the door to let him in.

'Morning Professor. Can we get you a coffee?'

Professor Harris stepped into the station and looked around. Including himself, there were now five people crammed into the small space.

'Yes. That would be very nice.'

He sat at one of the tables that lined the small station. There were a host of laptops and other tech littered about. Lovelace and Charlie sat at another table while Luton and Stanton leant nearby. Graham took it upon himself to make the coffee. He placed the cup in front of the Professor and sat opposite him.

Lovelace thought he looked tired and remembered that it was still early. Even though it was hot and the sun was up, most people weren't even thinking about going to work yet, and this man had spent the whole night making his way through a crime scene.

He took a handkerchief from within his suit and wiped his brow.

'Time of death sits comfortably with what you already know.' He began. 'Sarah Parkes went first. I would say she disturbed her killer shortly after they got home last night. There's evidence to suggest he was hiding in the pantry in the kitchen. No DNA to speak of, although we've collected hundreds of fibres for analysis. You never know. She was hit on the top of the head with a blunt instrument, probably a hammer. We haven't found the weapon. He probably couldn't get a swing to hit her side on. Hence the blow came from above her head. She didn't die instantly. I'd say he moved quickly to take down Tom Parkes. He was standing close by. A burn on his neck suggests some kind of electric stun gun or taser immobilised him. He then took a blow to the side of the head, which would have rendered him unconscious almost instantly. Had it ended there, neither would have likely survived their injuries. Only it didn't stop there. Tom Parkes took at least four other hits to the skull. He probably died after the second hit. Sarah Parkes took another two hits, at least. She also probably died after the second blow. It was ferocious and over very quickly. You know from the 999 call that the girl reported that he moved upstairs. He entered the first bedroom on the right and found the girl, Molly Parkes, hiding in the closet. He pulled her out and killed her with a single blow to the head. There is no evidence of a sexual assault.'

Stanton said, 'He was probably spooked. The call centre lady probably saved her from that.'

'Yes. Very probably. After that, he moved from room to room, turning the place upside down.'

'After?' Lovelace asked. 'He did that *after* he killed the girl? You're sure?'

'Yes. Very sure. He would have been covered in blood. He'd just hit three people over the heads with a hammer. We found blood and brain matter in the rooms. He ransacked the rooms after he killed them.'

'But that doesn't make sense..'

'Why not?' Stanton asked. 'It's a burglary gone wrong. He's turned the place over looking for something to take or to make it look like a burglary.'

Lovelace shook her head. 'No. If he's turned the place over to make it look like a burglary, then it wasn't a burglary. He went there for something else.'

'The girl.' Luton said. 'You think this is sexually motivated. So he went there for the girl?'

'Yes. But that doesn't make sense either.'

'Why not?' Luton asked.

'Because if he had time to turn the place over before the police arrived, he had time to rape the girl. Why did he kill her? Why didn't he rape her? And why did he then ransack the other rooms?'

'Perhaps he freaked out,' Stanton said, 'He knows the police are coming, and he panicked.'

Lovelace shook her head. It didn't feel like the killer panicked. To her, it felt like he was in control. She was missing something; she couldn't quite grasp what it was.

Professor Harris took a sip of his coffee. He grimaced as the foul-tasting substance assailed his taste buds. 'Well, all that's up to you lot. We've got as much forensics out of the crime scene as I think we'll get. I'll leave a couple of my people behind to tidy up and try and capture any remaining evidence. The scene's all yours. Let me know when you're done with the bodies, and I'll have a couple of ambulances sent over to collect them.' He glanced at his watch. 'Probably do the autopsies tomorrow, if that's all right. It's been a long night.'

He stood up. Graham took his hand and shook it firmly.

'Remind me never to say yes to your coffee again,' Professor Harris said. 'It's disgusting.'

He smiled at the other detectives and left the cramped little station.

'Okay.' Graham turned to face his team. 'Let's get in there.'

A short time later, five detectives dressed in all-white coveralls and blue overshoes gave their names to the uniformed officer guarding the entrance to the house and stepped inside, one by one. Lovelace was last in.

She stepped through the white tent that covered the entrance to the house and over the broken remains of what was left of the Parkes' front door. She turned left and looked into the room the Sergeant had entered when the police entered the home. Aside from the usual furniture items typical of a suburban home and a large flat-screen television, there was nothing much of interest to her. There was certainly nowhere a fully grown adult could hide. She turned back into the front hallway and the small corridor that led to the kitchen. The stairs were fully carpeted to the point at which they met the hallway floor, which itself was covered in what was now a heavily soiled laminate floor. She guessed that the Parkes family were mobile and that the hallway had become a high-traffic area. From where she had entered the house, she could see where the kitchen was, but the layout prevented anyone from directly seeing into the kitchen. Charlie, Luton and Stanton had already followed DCI Graham into the kitchen to where the bodies of Sarah and Tom Parkes lay. From where Lovelace stood, she couldn't see any of them. It was a curious point, but it wasn't lost on her. Anyone who wanted to hide in the Parkes' home could do so most effectively inside the kitchen. No one coming into the house would know they were there. Her curiosity didn't end there, however. Surely hiding upstairs would have been easier? Perhaps she was wrong… Maybe it was a burglary gone wrong, and the killer had simply been caught in the wrong place at the wrong time. She let out a gentle sigh. She could feel her senses tingling.

Lovelace stepped into the kitchen. Stanton and Luton were stooped over the bodies. Charlie stood behind them, and Graham looked out the window into the rear garden. Beyond the garden fence were fields which swept out into the Oxfordshire countryside and some thick woodland in the distance. It was a beautiful view, marred by the circumstances that had brought them there.

Charlie moved closer to the bodies and began taking photographs on her mobile phone. 'They didn't stand a chance, did they.' She said, more to herself than to anyone else.

Lovelace moved into the kitchen. It was a vast place, clearly the focal point of the family. A massive oak table took centre stage, surrounded by comfortable-looking chairs. It was covered in the day-to-day life of the Parkes' household - utility bills, homework, prescriptions, and shopping lists, all vying for attention. There were unwashed tea cups on the table and the remains of yesterday's breakfast. It looked like the Parkes' had gone out for the day before anyone had the time to clear up. They never got the chance to do it on their return.

Sarah Parkes was lying face down in a pool of blood just in front of the dishwasher. Tom Parkes was lying next to her. Brain matter and pieces of skull were visible through matted strands of bloodied hair. The cabinets and cupboards that edged the kitchen nearest the bodies were covered in blood spatter. The assault had been so violent that Lovelace could see blood patterns on the ceiling.

'The attacker must have come from here…' Luton moved over to a cupboard door and opened it. It was disguised as two doors, but on pulling it open, the entire door opened into a huge pantry. Luton stepped inside and closed the door behind him. A few seconds later, he came out again. 'Fuck me, it's huge. There's even a washing machine and tumble drier in here. It leads into what looks like a bit of a utility room. You could hide there and not be discovered, even if someone else came in looking for something.'

One by one, they all stepped inside the pantry and took a good look around.

'It's odd,' Lovelace said as she stepped back into the kitchen.

'What is?' Graham asked.

'This doesn't feel like a burglary gone wrong.'

Luton gave out a noise that sounded like a snort.

'I mean. The burglary angle doesn't fit.' Lovelace carried on, ignoring the noise. 'Let's say he was disturbed during the burglary. Why was everything ransacked after he was discovered? If he was halfway through gutting this house of its valuables, why did he start doing so after he was discovered?'

'Perhaps he hadn't started yet,' Charlie said. 'For burglary, it was still quite early and light outside. Perhaps he'd just arrived when the Parkes returned and took to the pantry to hide.'

'Maybe. But then, why did he get caught? If there's plenty of places to hide back there, which we've all seen that there is, there's no reason why he couldn't lay low for an hour or so until the Parkes had gone to bed and made off over the fields.'

'He was watching them.' Luton said. 'He was getting off on watching them. It gave him power.'

'I think so,' Lovelace agreed. 'This is not a burglary gone wrong. This is the work of a predator. That he came armed with a hammer would suggest he's been caught doing this before. Perhaps the first time he got caught, he didn't have a weapon and had to rely on brute force. Having a weapon gives him an advantage. Shock was his other weapon. When Sarah and Tom opened this door and revealed the killer, they were probably stunned into momentary disbelief and fatal inaction. He caught Sarah first on the top of her head and reached Tom before he knew what was happening. It was a blitz killing.'

Stanton shook his head. 'If the killer got off on hiding in the house, there'd be evidence, right? He couldn't help getting himself off. He'd have been giving himself a tug behind the door. They'd be semen, at the very least. Or pubic hairs.'

'Not if he's escalated,' Lovelace said.

Graham towered over them. 'Explain?'

Lovelace suddenly felt very vulnerable. These were experienced detectives she was lecturing to.

'Maybe originally that's what he did. When he started. Break into someone's house and get off on the power. Then yes, I would expect to find semen. But predators like this learn and grow. They don't just reach this level overnight. It takes years to get to this stage. They learn and adapt. The fact that there's no semen at this crime scene now suggests the killer came for something else. A higher thrill.'

'The girl.' Charlie said. 'You think he's a pedo?'

Lovelace shook her head. 'Not necessarily. Not exclusively. But in this case, yes. I think he came for the girl.'

'Which doesn't explain why he didn't rape the girl!' Stanton said. 'Or why he ransacked the rooms upstairs after he'd killed them all.'

'No, it doesn't. I can't explain that yet. But I hope I'm wrong..'

Graham caught the inflexion in her voice but didn't challenge her. This was why he'd recruited her. Despite his reservations, this was precisely what he was after. 'So we have two motives for the killings. Either he's an exceptionally violent burglar who tidied up any witnesses to his crimes, or he's a sexual predator whose crimes are escalating. I'm not sure I'm keen on either.'

'Neither are common crimes,' Charlie said. 'The only thing in our favour is that he's likely to be a repeat offender. He's done this before, or something near it, and left a trail. So all we have to do is sniff it out.'

'Okay. So what do we know so far?' Graham asked. He walked over to the back door, which led out into the garden. 'There's every indication that the killer entered and left through this door. He's good at breaking into houses. He's left almost no damage to speak of. It was warm last night and still bright when the Parkes got home. He would never have risked entering from the front; this is the only back door. The blood stains outside say he left this way and made off over the fields. Any observations?'

They were all quiet. Stanton broke the silence. He said, 'If he's a burglar and got here just before the Parkes got home, he would have broken in just before ten last night. We should canvass the neighbours and see if anyone has cameras at the back of their houses. They may have picked something up.'

'If he is a predator,' Charlie said, picking up Lovelace's lead, 'he could have broken in at any time during the day. Best to check the whole day's worth of footage.'

'Good. Have uniform go house to house. Seize any camera equipment that they may have, front or back. Let's not just assume he came in from the back. Cover every angle.'

Graham moved to the kitchen door. 'Once he dealt with the Parkes, all that was left was the girl. If the girl wasn't his intended victim, he must have seen her come in through the door before he hid in the pantry. He killed the parents, so there's no going back. The only witness was in the house. He needed to kill her too. He exited the kitchen into the hallway and turned up the stairs.'

Graham followed his words and the killer's steps, moved out of the kitchen, and stood looking up at the stairs.

Lovelace stood next to him. By her side, on the right of the front door as you entered, stood a small table with a cordless telephone pod and a notepad and pencil.

'He would have known she had called someone,' she said, picking up the telephone from its cradle. 'He would have seen the 'in-use' button lit up.'

'So he doesn't have much time.' Graham sighed. 'Actually, he did, but he didn't know that. He needed to move fast. He needed to find the girl.'

One by one, they climbed the stairs. The fifth step from the top squeaked as Graham stepped onto it and again when Luton, Stanton and Charlie stepped on it. Lucy smiled.

'Well, that explains that.' She said.

Graham turned just as he was about to enter the bedroom on his right.

'Explains what?'

'It was something I couldn't explain earlier. On the phone with the call handler, the girl said she could hear the killer moving about downstairs, and then she mentioned that she could hear him coming up the stairs. Well, the floor is fully hard downstairs, so that's why she could hear him, but I noticed that the stairs were carpeted. I couldn't understand how she knew he was climbing the stairs.'

She walked on to the fifth step, and it squeaked. 'But now I know how.'

Graham nodded at her. It was a small detail, probably irrelevant, but the nod showed it was appreciated. Lovelace glowed.

They entered the bedroom in a sombre mood. The killing of a child was always brutal. Somehow the loss of a future seemed harder to accept in a younger person than in an adult. None of them found it easy to step into the room and gather about the dead body of Molly Parkes.

She was still dressed. There was no sign that the killer had tried to assault her sexually. She still lay where she fell, the back of her head a matted mess of blood and skull. Behind her, the cupboard was still open. The telephone she had used to call the police still lay next to the body, waiting for the forensics team to bag it up. It had already been dusted for fingerprints.

Charlie took some more photographs on her phone. 'Poor girl. I suppose we should be grateful she didn't suffer..'

'Grateful?' Graham spat the word out as though it had deeply wounded him.

'You know what I mean. Not grateful to the killer. Just grateful he didn't make her suffer.'

'I don't think grateful's the right word, but I know what you mean.'

They all stood for a few seconds at the body before Graham said, 'Right. The killer comes in. He sees the empty charging pod for a cordless telephone and knows the girl has called someone. He doesn't have much time. He opens the first cupboard door he comes to, and she's behind it.'

'I don't rate her hide-and-seek skills.' Stanton joked.

It wasn't funny, but everyone could see his point. Lovelace wondered why she had chosen such a bad place to hide. Some part of her knew why, but she didn't know how to phrase it. She was about to proffer her theory when Stanton interrupted her.

'So he drags the child out of the cupboard and whack! She goes down with a single blow to the back of the head. The call handler hears this and suspects the killer is on the phone, so she warns him. The police are right around the corner. He needs to hurry. In a few minutes, the street will be littered with police. He panics. He needs to finish what he started. He needs to burgle the place. He can't have gone this far and leave empty-handed. Did the Parkes' have anything remarkable in terms of valuables? Something specific he was looking for? A Rolex watch or a painting or diamonds. Something valuable?'

'They don't seem the valuables type to me,' Luton said. 'Nice house, sure. Two good cars, both probably on credit. They both have okay jobs but nothing spectacular. I don't see either buying a hundred-grand Rolex or shiny diamonds.'

'Still. It's worth checking out.' Graham agreed. 'He was certainly looking for something.'

Lovelace took a deep breath. Then, calmly she said, 'Not something. Someone.'

They all looked at her blankly.

With a voice verging on frustration, Stanton said, 'Yeah, we get it. He's a predator. He's a sexual monster. We get that that's your line. You've got history. But if he came here for the girl, he found her. But he doesn't get off on her. He kills her. She's done. He moves on. He didn't come here for this girl.'

'No, you're right. He didn't come here for this girl. He came here for Molly Parkes.'

Stanton looked across at Graham.

'Are we even at the same crime scene? This is Molly Parkes. Here. On the floor. Dead. She's the one with half her head caved in.'

'That's not Molly Parkes,' Lovelace said, 'I think that's Bethany Wright.'

Graham's ears pricked up.

'What?'

'It hasn't made sense from the beginning. It all seemed a bit off. I like details. I pick up on them. Not always the right ones, like the stairs, but I always search for the right answers to all the questions. Point one: she never once gave her name to the call handler. Point two: she continually referred to her parents as 'them' or ' they' and never once as 'mum and dad.' Point three: she didn't know where to hide. This isn't her house. Point four: she's the same height and build as Molly Parkes, with the same hair colour and style.'

'You're not seriously entertaining this, are you?' Stanton said, appealing to Graham.

'What I am entertaining,' Graham said, 'is that if this is the body of Bethany Wright, where the fuck is Molly Parkes?'

'Wait a minute!' Charlie said, wheeling around to face Lovelace. That's a hell of a guess. You got anything to back it up?'

Lovelace shook her head. 'Just a theory. But it can be tested.'

'So give us your theory. We'll peer review it.'

'Okay. As you probably already know, despite being a rookie, I have some experience here. I know a little about predators. How they work, and what makes them tick. I'm sure that's why I'm here.' She paused and stole a look at Graham. They all knew who she was. They all knew why she was there. 'I think our perpetrator has set his sights on Molly Parkes. He wants her. He wants her badly. He probably follows Sarah Parkes on any one or all of her many social media profiles. This way, he can get close to Molly. He doesn't even need to expose himself online. Sarah Parkes' online security was woefully poor. I think he probably knew that they had gone out for the day and broke into the house while they were out and waited for them to come home. He probably spent a few hours here, walking around, planning his attack, finding somewhere to hide. His plan is probably to wait until they've all gone to bed before striking. Only it goes wrong. Sarah Parkes discovered him, and she had to die. He doesn't hesitate. And then he kills Tom Parkes. He moves quickly, violently and without mercy. And that's how we know he's done something like this before. He doesn't make a mistake. He's made a mistake before, and he's learnt from it. I said before that I think he's escalating, but I'm not sure that's true. I think he's at his peak and probably only going to get better at it. And he'll get harder to catch.

'Once the parents are dead, he moves upstairs quickly. By now, his fever is at its zenith. He goes into the first room and finds the girl. Only to his surprise, it's not Molly. He's made the same mistake as us. He's seen the girl enter the front door and turn to hide in the pantry. But it's not Molly. They're teenage girls: same height, build, and hair colour. At a glance, they almost look the same. But it's not Molly. So the girl dies violently and quickly. He picks up the telephone and discovers that the police are on their way. But he can't hear sirens. He won't hear sirens for at least another eighteen minutes.'

'So he has time,' Charlie said.

'Plenty of time,' Lovelace continued. 'Plenty of time to track her down. He goes from room to room, pulling the place upside down. Because she lives here, she found a better hiding place than her friend. But he finds her. In normal circumstances, I think he'd probably rape and kill her here, but he doesn't have time. He can probably hear sirens by now, but even if he can't, he knows they're coming. He has a tiny window of opportunity, and it's closing quickly. He grabs the girl and subdues her. It won't be hard. By the look of the photographs, she's a slight girl. It wouldn't take much to overpower her. Once he's done that, he takes off the way he came, out through the back door and across the fields.'

Stanton gave a derisory snort. 'That's some leap! There's no evidence to back it up.'

Graham was more considered. 'It is a leap. But still, I don't like it. Whichever way you look at it, the evidence suits Lucy's theory better than any other. Why does the killer murder them all and then search the house?' He looked at Luton, 'Make enquiries. Find this Bethany Wright girl. Now.'

'Excuse me, sir….'

Everyone turned as a uniformed constable stood on the squeaky stair. No one had heard him until then.

'What is it?'

The constable cleared his throat. 'There's a couple downstairs that would like to speak to you. The lady… she's quite distraught… They're saying that their daughter was staying here for the night. They've come to pick her up.'

'Mr and Mrs Wright?' Graham asked.

The constable nodded.

'Yes.' He said, slightly bewildered. 'How did you know?'

Four

NPAS, the National Police Air Service, had a chopper in the air twelve minutes after the call came through. Lovelace heard the throb of its engines and the faint thud of its rotors as it came into view on the eastern skyline. It came down under a thousand feet from an azure blue sky and banked right as it flew over the mobile station. Lovelace stared out the window and watched as the bird began a detailed grid search of the countryside that swept in all directions as far as the eye could see.

The team had gathered back in the cramped mobile police station parked in the street. Professor Harris sat back at the table with a takeaway coffee mug in front of him. The atmosphere had changed markedly.

Charlie leant in at Lovelace's ear. 'Nice call. That was some good detective work.'

'Thank you. It doesn't help much, though. Now we've got a missing girl on our hands.'

'So, what can you tell us, Professor?' DCI Graham asked.

'It's a bloody terrible business, that's what I can tell you.' He said, blowing into his mug and raising it to his lips. 'The dead girl has a birthmark on her right inner thigh, about an inch long and shaped like a crescent moon. Mr Wright confirms that his daughter, Bethany Wright has the same birthmark on her right inner thigh. It's not an official identification, but I didn't want poor Mr Wright to have to identify his girl while her head's in such a state. We'll take the body back to the lab and tidy her up. We'll get a positive confirmation for you later.'

'And if you were a gambling man?' Graham asked, 'who would you say is lying on the floor up there?'

Professor Harris blew into his cup. 'Having taken a much closer look at the dead girl and comparing it to pictures of Molly Parkes, I can tell you it's not Molly Parkes. I'll confirm it later, but the dead girl's almost certainly Bethany Wright. I'm afraid we all made a bit of a cock up.'

Graham looked at his watch. It was touching 8 a.m. The 999 call had come in at ten o'clock the previous evening. When a child goes missing, every hour that passes makes it less likely that they'll be found alive. Molly Parkes had now been missing for ten hours. Her odds were beginning to drop off the scale. It was a colossal cock up.

'Thank you, Professor. I'd be grateful if you would get back to me as soon as possible. Sorry for calling you back so soon.'

'Not a problem.'

Professor Harris got up and, for the second time that day, nodded a solemn goodbye to the team. He stepped out of the station with a heavy heart. He enjoyed his work but didn't like it much when it involved children. He had a horrible feeling that before the week was out, two young girls would be lying on his mortuary slab. It was a thought that saddened him immensely.

Graham closed the door after the Professor and turned back around. 'Right. Chief Super's going fucking mental.' He waved his hand dismissively. 'No fault, but we need to be better than this. We are better than this and need to get a grip on this situation right now. Steve,' he turned to look directly at DI Luton. 'I want you to take the lead on finding Molly. She's our number one priority. Right now, we've got a hundred officers being drafted in across the county to help with the search.' Graham paused as the noise of the police helicopter rattled the windows.

'NPAS are beginning a grid search from the house and fanning out across the fields at the back of the house. There are twenty square miles of fields, hills, rivers and woodland between here and the next town. For a small, heavily populated island, there's much ground to cover and little time. RAF Brize Norton has volunteered one of their search and rescue helicopters to help us. It's got some fancy spy shit on board. Good for finding people who are trying not to be found. They'll be overhead in half an hour. Just waiting for the MOD to give them the green light. Jim, you're Steve's right hand. Don't leave his side. You two work well together - get this thing done for me. Charlie…' he paused and smiled. 'I'm sorry….'

'Peados and weirdos?' She smiled back. For some reason, women were better at dealing with that end of the criminal spectrum.

'Yes, please. I want the names and addresses of every registered sex offender within thirty miles of this place —particular emphasis on child predators. Go over VISOR. Cross-reference. Get me some names. This guy has to have been on our radar before. Let's find him.'

Lovelace had searched the Violent Sex Offenders' Register before. It was a particularly nasty list of men who took sexual assault to a new low. She didn't fancy Charlie's job much.

'Lucy..' Graham turned and faced her. She was a rookie. He didn't know her skill set yet but knew in which direction it lay. But how to best utilise it? He would need to play his cards carefully here. 'Do a quick door-to-door for me. Nothing detailed; we'll get uniform to do that later. Have a quick scout around, and see if anything pings your interest. Then head back to Kidlington with Charlie and help her run through the sex offenders' register. Go through their profiles. Pick the ones you think will fit our man's MO. I want a short list and a profile of the sort of man we're looking for.'

Lovelace nodded. 'Sure.'

'Sorry, Steve, Jim.' Graham said, turning back to his numbers two and three. 'This is going to be home for the foreseeable. I'll see if I can get some air-con units sent over and chill this place out a bit. From now on, we'll have a morning briefing at HQ at 7 am and an evening debrief at 6 pm. Compulsory attendance. Are we all clear?'

There was an affirmative buzz in the station.

'Good. Find Molly Parkes. Find our scum bag.'

Charlie caught Lovelace on the road outside the station. 'You need a second pair of eyes?'

Lovelace shook her head. 'I think I'm good, thanks.'

'Cool. My car's over there.' Charlie pointed toward several cars parked in a slightly slap-hazard way around the cul-de-sac. 'Mine's the green Mini Cooper. I've got a few calls to make. When you're ready, I'll be in my office with the air conditioning on. Then, I'll drive us back to the station.'

'Thank you. I won't be long.'

Lovelace watched as Charlie walked back to her car. She wasn't sure what she made of her yet. She never rushed to judgement but had a good feeling about Charlie. She had a positive vibe. She was sure she was going to like her.

Chatsworth Drive was a small cul-de-sac that formed the final run of houses along the street that curved in a large semi-circle at the end. It was a large turning arc littered with police cars and the small, mobile police station that housed Luton and Stanton. The first house on the cul-de-sac had a "Sold" sign punched into the front lawn and no noticeable signs of habitation. So Lovelace turned to the next place along, number

Twenty-Two, the Parkes' home, and then to number Twenty-Three, which sat next door. The houses were detached, and between the Parkes' house and number Twenty-Three were two single-story garages separated by two gateways leading to their respective gardens.

Lovelace strolled to the Parkes' neighbours' front door and pressed the doorbell. She heard a bell sound in the distance, followed by footsteps.

The door was opened by a young woman of Lovelace's age with long dark hair that fell neatly over her shoulders. She stooped slightly, owing to her height, and deep blue eyes stared out behind round glasses.

Lovelace held out her warrant card. 'DC Lovelace. May I have a moment of your time?'

Emma Jenkins opened the door wide to allow Lovelace through, and she led her into a clean and well-presented, modern kitchen.

'I've just made tea, would you like a cup?' Emma asked.

They sat across from one another at a tall, round table flanked by bar-stool-type chairs.

'Has something terrible happened next door?' Emma asked.

'I'm afraid so,' Lovelace began, and without much colour, she described the events that had taken place at number Twenty-Two.

Emma Jenkins looked horrified. 'My god, that's terrible. I can't quite believe it.... I spoke to Sarah just the other day, and poor Molly!'

'Did you know them very well?' Lovelace asked.

'I knew Sarah to chat with and have a glass of wine. Molly too. She was such a lovely girl.'

Lovelace picked up the past tense. She thought Molly might not be dead, but it certainly didn't look too good.

'I didn't know him,' Emma continued. 'I saw him often but never really spoke to him.'

'What about yesterday?' Lovelace asked. 'Did you see anything unusual? Anything out of place?'

Emma shook her head. 'No. Nothing. I left home early for work. I saw Sarah to say hello to. She was loading their car up for a day trip. I came home at about three o'clock and left again at about six. I was home just before ten o'clock, just a few minutes before your lot arrived, and started knocking down doors.'

'When you got home at three,' Lovelace asked, 'did you see or notice anything out of the ordinary then?'

Emma shook her head. 'I'm afraid not, sorry. I'm not being very helpful, am I?'

Lovelace smiled. 'That's okay. It's early days yet, and we've got much to work on,' she lied.

Lovelace reached into her pocket and pulled out a business card which she handed to Emma. 'Sometimes you don't realise you've seen something, or perhaps you've seen something and not realised its importance until much later. So if you do think of anything, however trivial you think it may be, would you call me?'

Emma took the card and stood up. From Lovelace's perspective, she appeared even taller than before. Emma turned and slipped the card under a fridge magnet stuck to a tall American-style fridge freezer. She stood looking at the freezer door for some moments.

'Must have broken another one,' she said cryptically.

She turned and saw the bewildered look on Lovelace's face.

'Fridge magnets.' She said. 'I collect them on my travels. I've got hundreds, as you can see.'

Lovelace saw that the front of the fridge freezer was littered with fridge magnets.

'The one from Cuba is missing.' Emma said. 'They fall off a lot. I can't even remember breaking that one, but I suppose I must have done. Unless it's under the fridge.'

Lovelace stood up. 'If you remember anything....?'

'Of course.'

Emma showed Lovelace back to the front door. Lovelace glanced out the window as they passed Emma Jenkins's front room. The street was a hive of activity, and from Emma's front room, she could see almost the entirety of the cul-de-sac. If there were anything to see, Emma would have seen it. Lovelace didn't hold out much hope for a call.

A pilot for British Airways lived at number Twenty-Four. He had only just returned from a long-haul flight to China and had returned home around three am when the street was already buzzing with activity. His wife was away with her parents and had been away for the last week and wasn't due back until later that day. He hadn't seen or heard anything suspicious or odd in the last few weeks.

Miss Williams, a rotund grey-haired woman of advancing years, lived at Twenty-Five. She was distraught by the news that Lovelace delivered and took some consoling. She was a primary school teacher, she explained, and dear Molly had been one of her charges just a few short years ago. She cried and blubbered for some time before finally pulling herself together.

'No, my dear. I'm afraid I didn't see or hear anything. I was in my garden all day yesterday until quite late. No, I wouldn't have seen anything; our gardens are quite secluded from each other; I wouldn't have seen a thing.'

The doctor at Twenty-Six said the same thing. She wore a pair of grey joggers and a dirty white T-shirt. She had been on nights all week and didn't return home until seven in the morning. She had been out most of the day and saw and heard nothing unusual when she had been home.

Number Twenty-Seven was quiet when she rang the doorbell, and as she stood back from the door and looked around, she noticed the curtains twitch at number Twenty-Eight. She rang the buzzer to Twenty Seven again and waited. She heard the latch unlock from the garden of number Twenty-Eight and turned to meet a petite white-haired old lady holding a pair of gardening gloves in her hands. She had a speck of dirt on her cheeks and dirt on the knees of her trousers.

'They're on holiday.' the old lady said breezily. 'I think they'll be back on Monday.'

Lovelace held her warrant card before her and crossed over to where the old lady stood.

'I thought you were the police.' The old lady said, popping a pair of spectacles onto the bridge of her nose and inspecting the card. 'You'd better come through.'

Lovelace was shown around the well-tended garden of number Twenty-Eight. Like all the other houses in the cul-de-sac, the gardens edged onto fields that rolled away behind them but were primarily obscured by high fences and trees.

'This is my husband, Lionel. Lionel Chambers.' Mrs Chambers said as they approached a large patio upon which some ageing rattan furniture sat shaded by a giant parasol. Lionel Chambers was seated in the shade, wearing a pair of old corduroy trousers and a white shirt. An old Panama hat was perched oddly on his head.

'I'm afraid he had a stroke a few years ago and suffers from dementia.' Mrs Chambers said. 'He has good and bad days, but today's not looking too good. It's the noise, you see. It bothers him and has been quite noisy these last few hours.'

As she spoke, the force helicopter made a low pass overhead. Mr Chambers mumbled something incoherent before relaxing in his chair and closing his eyes.

'Has something very terrible happened at the Parkes'?' Mrs Chambers asked as the steady thump of the helicopter's rotors faded into the distance. 'Such a lovely family. He was something to do with the internet, I think. Sarah was a nurse. Molly is such a lovely young girl. So polite and thoughtful. Brought up with manners, unlike so many these days.'

Lovelace noticed the mix of past and present tenses and sensed that Mrs Chambers was enjoying some juicy news from across the street but was equally unable to process the possibility that it somehow involved a child.

'Have you lived here long, Mrs Chambers?' Lovelace changed the subject.

'Edith, please. We've been here almost thirty years now. We bought the house when it was just a plan in an architect's office. Such a beautiful location.'

'Do you know your neighbours well?'

'Oh, yes.' Edith exclaimed. 'We're a very close nit community. Everybody knows everybody else's business!'

Lovelace wondered if that was more the case that Edith Chambers knew everybody's business, given her tendency to twitch at her net curtains.

'Number Twenty-One is empty. I think it's been bought as one of those modern Air CND things. You know, where you rent a house on the Internet for a short time.'

'Air BNB?'

That's it.' Edith said. 'One of them. A shame. Communities need people. Then there's the Parkes at Twenty-Two, dear Emma at Twenty-Three, Mr Layton at Twenty Four. He's a Captain, you know. For BA. Mrs

Layton is very nice, although we don't see much of her these days. Then there's Mrs Williams. She's a Primary school teacher. Then there's Doctor West at Twenty-Six and Debbie and Helena at Twenty-Seven.' Proudly she added, 'they're married, you know....'

'And how long have you known the Parkes?' Lovelace asked.

Edith thought about it for a moment. 'I'm certain Sarah was pregnant when they moved in. They bought it cheap from Mr Pendleton's son. Dear old Mr Pendleton took a tumble down the stairs. As they loaded him into the ambulance, I said I didn't think he'd ever come home again. He died three weeks later, poor man. I'm sure Sarah had Molly about a month after they moved in. Has something terrible happened?'

'I'm afraid so,' Lovelace began sensitively. 'Last night, we found the bodies of Mr and Mrs Parkes in their kitchen and the body of a teenage girl in an upstairs bedroom.'

Edith Chambers gasped. She drew her hand across her mouth. 'Was it an accident?' She asked. 'I know our boilers are quite old. We should get a carbon monoxide alarm for the house....'

'I can't go into the details of the case, but we are treating it as a murder investigation.' Lovelace said.

Edith gasped again.

'Were you here yesterday?' Lovelace asked. 'The Parkes were out for the day, and we believe the killer let himself in while they were out. Could you have seen anything? Anything suspicious or unusual?'

Edith shook her head. 'We were in all day. Lionel has a carer who comes in every other day to give me some time to myself. Yesterday was her day off, so we were here the whole time. I didn't see anything. Not until the sirens about ten o'clock. I'd just retired to bed myself....'

'Did you see anything yesterday? Anything at all? You may not even think it is relevant. A delivery, perhaps? A window cleaner? Cold callers or Jehovah's Witnesses? Anything? Anything at all?'

'Well….'

Mrs Chambers got up and ducked inside her patio windows. She returned a few minutes later carrying a small notebook. Its edges looked well-thumbed. She dropped it onto the table in front of Lovelace.

'I'm part of the Neighbourhood Watch committee.' She said by way of explanation. 'I record things. Things that occur on our street. I have quite a vantage point from my front window. I can see everything that comes into the cul-de-sac. So I record everything that happens, from the time of the window cleaners to the times of certain deliveries. Very little comes up here that I don't see.'

Lovelace opened the notebook and scanned the pages. They were handwritten in neat, cursive writing and were in chronological order. She turned to yesterday and read the contents. Beginning reasonably early in the day, Edith had recorded the event next to the time it had occurred. At 09:15, a delivery van made a drop at number Twenty-Five. She had even recorded the number plate. She had also underlined it in green pen.

'What's this?' Lovelace asked.

'If I have recorded the number plate before and know where it comes from, I underline it in green. Green means safe. That particular driver is from Amazon, I think. He's here almost every day.'

Lovelace read the rest of the day's events. It was mundane, typical average suburban street-level activity. Nothing stood out.

'What made you keep this level of detail on the comings and goings in the street?' Lovelace asked.

'There was a string of burglaries a few years ago in the town. Quite a few homes were targeted over the course of a few days. It worried people. We're all very used to the quiet life here. That sort of thing is quite unusual for us, so we started a Neighbourhood Watch programme, and I started to watch.'

'Has there been anything like that recently?' Lovelace asked hopefully.

Edith shook her head. 'No. Nothing like that.' She said.

Lovelace caught the slight inflexion in her voice.

'Like *that*?' She asked.

'Well…'

'Go on,' Lovelace prompted.

Edith composed her thoughts. 'I'm not sure it's even the same thing,' she said finally. 'It certainly seemed like nothing at the time, and she couldn't be entirely sure, but it did bother her, which is why she came to see me. I record things, you see, as the Neighbourhood Watch co-ordinator, and I think she just wanted me to put her mind at rest.'

'Who did? Who wanted you to put her mind at rest?'

'Sarah.' Edith said, 'Sarah Parkes. She was worried that someone was breaking into her house, moving things around, and taking little things. Things you couldn't be sure you hadn't just lost or moved. She would lose things, you see, and never give them another thought, and then she would find them again where she was certain she would never put them. It annoyed her, to begin with, and then it started to worry her. She came round, and we went through my notes. It put her mind at rest, I think. There was nothing there, and I started to keep a closer eye on her house when they were out, but I never saw anything. I think she put it down to forgetfulness and absent-mindedness in the end. It comes to us all eventually.'

'How long ago was this?' Lovelace asked.

'A month or two ago.' Edith said. 'After a few weeks, I asked her about it, and she said it hadn't happened recently, so I think she tried to forget all about it. I kept a close eye on her house, though.'

Lovelace scanned through the notes in the notebook. Several months of data were recorded there. Deliveries, number plates, window cleaners, canvassers, and unknown callers to several properties were efficiently recorded in Edith's neat handwriting and marked here and there with a green or red pen. She flipped the notebook back a few more pages.

On several dates throughout the previous months, Edith had recorded the partial number plate of a dirty white van that had come into the cul-de-sac before driving off again. From the way the numbers and letters were arranged, it didn't look like a British plate. Lovelace held the notebook in front of Edith.

'Do you remember this van?'

Edith slipped her glasses onto her nose and read the entry. 'Yes.' She said. 'We get a lot of foreign vans in the area, looking for farm work mostly. Fewer since we left the EU, but they still come.'

'It was a European van?'

'It had the Blue flag, and it was left-hand drive,' Edith said. 'But I find them very difficult to read. They're not like ours, are they?'

'I don't suppose you remember the letters beneath the flag?' Lovelace asked.

Edith shook her head. 'No, I'm sorry, I don't. Is it important, do you think?'

'I don't know,' Lovelace admitted. 'But it might be useful information. Do you mind if I take this book? I'll make a copy and return it to you as quickly as possible.'

'Take it.' Edith said firmly. 'I hope it's useful to you. I hope it helps you find the man responsible.'

Lovelace thanked Mrs Chambers, said an unacknowledged goodbye to Lionel, and returned to where DCI Graham ended a call on his mobile phone.

'Anything?' He asked.

Lovelace gave a brief report of her door-to-door and handed Graham the notebook. He opened it and flicked through the pages.

'Fuck me; she's a nosey old sod.' He said.

Lovelace retold Graham what she had learned about Sarah Parkes' fears, and then she pointed out the dirty white foreign van and the partial number plate.

'It could be interesting.' She said.

'It could be. But there's not enough of that plate to get a positive ID. Try it, though, and see what you get. And run every other number plate through the computer and see if anything pops up. You never know.' Graham reached into his jacket pocket and drew out a wallet filled with business cards. He found the one he wanted and handed it to Lovelace. 'When you get back to Kidlington, look this man up. He's the burglary coordinator for the Thames Valley. His name's DS Phil Spencer and there's nothing he doesn't know about burglary and burglars.'

Lovelace took the card and turned to walk away.

'Oh, and Lucy…' She turned back around. Graham smiled. 'Good work today. Keep it up.'

Five

It was a short walk from St Aldates Police Station to the crime scene at Bundles Street. Detective Inspector Alison French picked up an iced coffee from a nearby coffee house and slipped a cake into her handbag for later. She was still drinking her coffee when she turned into Bundles Street.

The previous evening, between 10:30 and 1 a.m., twenty-eight-year-old Mark Pitts had been lured into the side street and stabbed over thirty times. His throat had been slashed, and his trousers had been pulled down, leaving his dead body grotesquely exposed. In a final act of cruelty, Pitts's killer cut off his genitals and laid them on the floor by his body. DI French had seen the crime scene photographs. Whoever had killed Mark Pitts had left his body in such a way as to maximise his humiliation.

French stood in the street and imagined the scene as it might have been last night. It was a small, quiet street with several alleys leading in various directions. There was a street lamp at either end, where the street started and ended, but no sign of apparent light along its length. The alleys that struck out on either side had no lighting at all. They led to the backyards and doorways of the various residential buildings and businesses surrounding the street. Mark Pitts had come to the street for a purpose, but it was unclear what that purpose may have been. It was a street where illicit deals were made and settled. Drugs could be bought and sold with impunity, and working girls could complete their business with almost no chance of discovery. Mark Pitts had previous convictions for dealing in illegal drugs, including a stretch in a Dutch prison for smuggling them. French thought it was undoubtedly why he might have found himself in this quiet, isolated street. She pulled her iPad from her handbag and scrolled through Mark Pitts's colourful criminal history. He was not a nice man. His convictions went back to his childhood and included shoplifting, burglary, assault, drug offences and rape. The latter concerned French. How Pitts's body had been found suggested a sex angle to his killing, as though someone had sought revenge and humiliation.

His first conviction for rape had been when he was just sixteen. The court had gone easy on him then, given his age and previous good behaviour. Some suggested that the girl had initially been a willing and receptive partner but had changed her mind when Pitts's immature mind and body could not control his passion. He received a suspended sentence and a stiff warning from the judge.

His second conviction for rape landed him a three-year stretch. He came out of prison even more violent than before. Prison had become something of a networking opportunity for him. He started to work for one of the prominent crime families that called Oxford their home. They weren't big fish, but they had ambitions in that area. Pitts was useful with his fists and was an imposing figure at 6 feet tall. He slowly became a valuable enforcer for them. When he raped a fifteen-year-old girl six months ago, the family closed ranks and protected him. They intimidated the girl's family and witnesses and hired an expensive lawyer to throw spanners into the legal mechanism that sought to put Pitts behind bars. It worked, too. The case collapsed, and Mark Pitts walked away a free man. But, according to an informant within the crime family's network, Mark Pitts was now on a warning. Rape again, and he'd be dealt with privately. It would not be a pleasant experience for

Mark Pitts. This only begged another question, French thought. Was this Mark Pitts's punishment? Had he raped again? Did the family fulfil its promise, deal with Mark Pitts, and leave his body to leave a clear message to others about the consequences of stepping out of line?

What concerned French more was the possibility that someone from the raped girl's family had taken it upon themselves to meter out justice to Pitts. There was no suggestion that Pitts had raped again and no reason for the crime family to punish one of their own. Particularly one they had spent much money to protect. For French, that theory didn't sit well. Her bet was on the extended family of the raped girl.

French turned to the report gathered from the uniformed officers that had attended the scene when the body had been discovered. Pitts had spent the evening in the company of friends in various pubs and clubs across the city. He had last been seen in a nearby public house chatting up an attractive girl at the bar. No one knew who the girl was or if Pitts had left with her. No one had seen Pitts go or could give a credible reason why he would leave without telling anyone. Reading between the lines, French guessed that Pitts would often do a disappearing act to sell or buy drugs. No one among his friends found it odd that he had just left. No one would say it explicitly, but French guessed that's how Pitts made his money.

French scrolled through the report looking for a description of the girl seen with Pitts shortly before he left the pub. There wasn't one. It was always possible that Pitts had been on a promise when he left the pub. Had Pitts taken his trousers down in anticipation of sex, only to find himself stabbed when he was at his most vulnerable? There were bound to be female relatives of the raped girl. All she needed to do was find out how old they were and whether they fitted the description of the girl seen at the bar with Pitts. If only she had a description!

French looked up at the buildings that lined Bundles Street. There were no CCTV cameras or security devices on any residential or commercial buildings. However, she knew there would be some at the pub, and she also knew that the street on which the pub sat had two cameras directly linked to the contact centre in Kidlington. She had already put in a request for the previous evening's footage. She glanced at her watch. According to DI Williams, the first detective on scene, the pub would be open for breakfast at nine o'clock. It had just gone nine.

French read the rest of the report. She had already read it three times back at the station, but she always liked to do so again whilst she was at the crime scene to give it all a bit of perspective. She found it easier to imagine how a crime occurred if you had a clear picture of the surroundings.

At one thirty in the morning, Pitts's body had been found slumped up against a wall with his genitals exposed. Crime scene analysis suggested that Pitts had met his end in one of the alleys, and his body was dragged to where it was found. Pitts was a big lad, French thought. The crime scene photographs showed a heavy-set young man with broad shoulders and thick-set arms. It would have taken considerable effort for a young woman to drag his body down the length of a narrow alley and display him in the way she had. Had there been an accomplice? It was worth a thought.

SOCO had done an excellent job on the crime scene. The cause of death was yet to be officially determined, but it was pretty clear that either the stabbings or the throat-cutting would be found to be the cause. They had ordered a broad panel of blood tests to see if anything nasty was floating around in his blood, but French was pretty sure she knew what they'd find. Cocaine and alcohol, in high concentrations. They had also picked up several fibres on Pitts's clothing which were being DNA tested. It was a long shot but worth trying. The problem was that Pitts had spent much time the previous evening in close company with many other people. So the fibres could realistically belong to anyone, so it wouldn't help much in identifying a potential suspect.

French closed her iPad and dropped it back into her handbag. The scene had already been cleared up. There was almost nothing to suggest that a young man had lost his life on this narrow, soulless street. Nothing, except a single red rose that had been carefully placed where Pitts's body had been found. Even scumbags had family, she mused.

A few minutes later, she stepped into the Rose and Crown. A young woman with neatly tied-back hair and far too much makeup on her face smiled at her from behind the bar.

'Morning.' She said cheerily.

French looked around the bar. It was a big venue with tables and chairs spread out and away from the bar. There was a collection of fruit machines along one wall and a jukebox that sat in the corner and flashed enthusiastically. It was pleasantly furnished with old photographs of Oxford pinned to the walls. Even at that early hour, several customers were sitting at tables enjoying breakfast, some with a cool beer, others with a more suitable pot of tea.

French showed the barmaid her warrant card. 'DI French.'

'You must be here about the murder.' The barmaid said. 'The boss said someone would collect our CCTV footage.'

She dipped her head below the countertop and popped back up with a CD.

French took it from her. 'Thank you.'

'Do you mind..' The barmaid paused. She picked up a receipt book and scribbled something in it. 'Would you mind signing for it? The boss can be a bit funny.'

'Not at all.' French signed the docket and returned it to the girl. 'Were you working last night?'

'Six til close.' She said.

French took her iPad from her handbag and opened it up to a photograph of Mark Pitts. 'Do you recognise this man?'

The girl nodded. 'I gave a statement last night,' she said, 'I saw him enter the bar around nine-thirty. He was with a group of friends. They sat over there.' She pointed to a nook with comfortable chairs arranged around a circular table. 'They drank a lot. I think he came and went a bit. You know, popping outside now and then. Probably a smoker.'

'Do you have a smoking area?' French asked.

'Yes. Out the back. A bit of a cover for when it rains and a heater for the winter. Not that we need it at the moment!'

'No. No, we don't. And Mark Pitts… he came and went out the back? Or out the front?'

'The front,' The barmaid replied. 'We don't let them take their drinks onto the street. They're not allowed. But some of them prefer to smoke out the front.'

'You say you gave a statement last night? What's your name?'

'Kelly,' the barmaid said. 'Kelly White.'

French scrolled through the list of names that gave statements last night. Finally, she found Kelly White and opened a copy of her statement.

'It says here you saw Mark Pitts for the last time around ten-fifteen. Before that, you noticed he was sitting at the bar talking to a girl.'

'That's right,' Kelly said. 'I went for a break at a quarter past ten and never saw him again. Then, when I returned to the bar, he was gone.'

'And the girl? Was she still here?'

'I can't say I noticed her much.'

'But you noticed Mark Pitts? You paid him a lot of attention.'

Kelly smiled. 'He was pretty fit,' she said shyly. 'Tall, dark and mysterious looking. He was hard not to notice!'

Despite knowing Pitts's dark history, even she had to admit he was an attractive young man. She asked the girl, 'can you remember anything about the young woman who sat with Mark Pitts before he left? How old she was? The colour of her hair? What she drank? Anything at all?'

'Well, now I think about it a bit more, when I came back and saw that Mark had gone, I assumed he'd gone off with her. So I suppose she couldn't have still been here, not if I thought that, right?'

'No. I suppose not.'

'She was pretty,' Kelly said. 'You know, not model pretty but cute girl next door pretty. She had scruffy auburn hair, quite long. I can't remember much more than that. Maybe late twenties or early thirties. I think Mark bought her a G&T.'

'Have you ever seen her before?'

'I don't think so. A lot of people come through our doors, I don't remember them all, so I suppose she may have been here before.'

French held up the CD. 'Let's hope she's on your cameras!'

Kelly didn't look hopeful. 'Probably not. She sat with her back to the one camera in this room the whole time she was there. The other cameras are focussed on the tills, you know, to stop nicking, and there's one in the garden and one at the front door for the doormen.'

'And she never went out the back?' French asked.

'No. She sat at the bar the whole time.'

An alarm bell went off in French's head. If the girl deliberately avoided the cameras, she knew what she was doing. She had come to the bar with the express intention of meeting Mark Pitts and then killing him. She made a mental note to check the relatives of Mark Pitts's teenage rape victim. It was looking more and more likely that Pitts had been the victim of a revenge attack.

French thanked the barmaid and turned to leave. As she did so, she noticed a large television on the wall behind her. It was tuned to the BBC news channel. She stood for a moment, reading the scrolling bar at the bottom. The BBC had picked up on the triple murder at the edge of town, but what alarmed her more was the full-size picture of a young girl with the caption 'MISSING' written in large letters beneath. French had heard about the murders when she had got to work that morning. The police station had been buzzing with the news. Gossip was rife. No one had mentioned a missing girl. That was new.

'It's horrible, isn't it?' Kelly said. 'Makes you feel unsafe in your own home.'

French nodded. It certainly did.

Six

Charlie edged her little car out of the cul-de-sac and drove out of town. The air con blew waves of chilled air at them, and Lovelace caught the faint smell of Charlie's perfume. It was sweet but not overpowering, fragrant but not pungent. It hung in the air briefly before being lost, but the smell stayed with Lovelace for some time. It was a pleasant smell and suited Charlie to a tee. Sweet but not overpowering.

'Did you get anything?' Charlie asked.

'Something and nothing, possibly. Do you know a DS Spencer?'

'Yeah. Nice bloke. Salt of the earth type. I did a stint a while back in Burglary, back when the budgets allowed. Not the sharpest copper you'll meet, but likeable enough. Why do you ask?'

'Graham gave me his number and told me to look him up.'

Briefly, Lovelace outlined what she had discovered during her door-to-door. Then, she held up Mrs Chambers' notebook.

'What are you thinking? That our Unsub may have broken into the Parkes' as some kind of dry run?'

Lovelace smiled at the term 'Unsub'. It was a term used by American law enforcement for an Unknown Subject. People used the term to make it sound like they knew what they were talking about. It felt odd coming from Charlie, but she let it pass. She was growing to like Charlie.

'Maybe. Or maybe it's just a coincidence.' Lovelace said.

'I don't like coincidences.' Charlie said. 'They're all very well in fiction, but they don't work for me in real life.'

Lovelace smiled. 'And yet they happen often enough in real life that we gave it a name.'

'Fair point. Well, Spencer may not be the sharpest copper that ever wore a badge, and he'll never make Inspector, but there's nothing that man doesn't know about burglary. Give him the MO of a job, and he'll give you a likely name.'

Lovelace held the card that Graham had given her. 'I'll look him up when we get back.'

***

Lunchtime found Charlie and Lovelace sat side by side, poring over the names of a thousand men that made up the Sex Offenders' register for the Thames Valley Area. The list of those on the Violent Sex Offenders' register was smaller but more disturbing.

'How the hell do we narrow this down?' Charlie asked as she picked up a massive bundle of papers and held them in front of her despairingly.

'We could probably drop eighty per cent in a heartbeat,' Lovelace said.

Charlie frowned. 'How?'

'Let's think about our man. Who is he? Who is he to Molly Parkes?'

Charlie shrugged. 'Nobody. He's nobody to her.'

'I agree. I don't think he knows her. Not personally. She probably doesn't even know he exists, even though he knows all about her. Most sex crimes are committed by people who know their victims. In fact, I think you'll find that figure to be about eighty per cent.'

Charlie smiled. 'You really are a smart arse, aren't you.'

'It's my thing.' Lovelace agreed. 'So we drop all the men who have committed crimes against women and girls they know. We're after the type of character that preys on people unknown to him. They're two very different types of crimes, featuring the profiles of two very different types of men.'

It took them an hour to eliminate the eighty per cent. In actuality, it was more like eighty-five per cent. The remaining men numbered one hundred and thirty. The pile of papers certainly felt smaller, but the task ahead was not lost on Lovelace. They needed to narrow the field down even further.

Charlie looked across at Lovelace. 'You're supposed to be the profiler. Build me a profile.'

'I'm not a profiler,' Lovelace said. She understood why she thought that, but she was wrong. She wasn't a profiler in the American sense of the term. She didn't profile murderers; she profiled the victims. 'The killers interest me. You know my story. It's hardly a secret. But I don't look at the killers; I look at the victims. Why them? In a crowd of a hundred women, why do some become victims of rapists and murderers and others don't? If I'm interested in the killers, it's in how they pick their victims. What do they look for? Is it opportunity? Yes, in some cases, opportunity knocks, and our man seizes his chance. So, in the case of Molly Parkes, we could probably eliminate opportunists. Our man's a planner. A thinker. This isn't a crime of opportunity; our man has created this opportunity specifically for this girl. If opportunity knocked at this man's door, he probably wouldn't answer it.'

'She's young,' Charlie said. 'Perhaps we can narrow it down that way?'

'Maybe. Our problem is that we only have one victim,' Lovelace raised her hand in apology. 'I know, I know.

One's enough, but it doesn't enable us to properly profile the sort of victim our man is targeting. Yes, Molly is young, but is he targeting her youth? If we had more victims of the same age, we could count that as a profile, but right now, we can't. All I know for sure is that there will have been other victims in the past, and if we don't stop him, there will be more. Our problem then becomes slightly contradictory. The more victims we have then the better our knowledge of our man and his victims become. The problem is that the more victims we have, the better he gets. He's learning his trade, and he's getting better and better at it, and the better he gets, the harder it becomes for us to catch him.'

Charlie raised an eyebrow. She dropped her hand on the list of a hundred and thirty men. 'He's in here somewhere.'

Lovelace shook her head. 'I wouldn't count on that, either,' she said. 'However our killer has got to this stage, he's got here slowly. He's not rushed. This thing inside him has grown and grown over years and years. He's bound to have started small. Little things that never raised a red flag to anyone. Slowly it grows. He expands and learns. He gets older, and he changes. The world changes around him. He may not have killed until recently. That might be a new thing. That might be an escalation. But he's not afraid. The way he left the crime scene suggests we don't have his DNA or fingerprints on file. If that's true, then we've never arrested him, or at least we've never made a conviction. The more he's committed these acts, and the more he's gotten away with it has played into his picture of himself. He probably thinks he's uncatchable.'

'It sounds like he might be!' Charlie said.

Lovelace shook her head. 'We'll catch him. It doesn't matter how good he gets; he'll make a mistake. No, that's wrong. He may not make a mistake now or in the future, but he has made a mistake in the past. We need to learn as much as we can about him and Molly and why he chose her so, we can look backwards. Go back into the past and find a victim then. In the early days, he'll have made a mistake. If we can build a profile of his victims, we could build up a list of possible prior victims. That's where we'll catch him. In the past.'

'So, you think this list of scumbags is a waste of time?' Charlie asked.

'Potentially. But it can't hurt to go and rattle their cages. And I could be wrong. His name may well be on that list. I just don't think it will be.'

'So we need two profiles.' Charlie declared. 'One of our Unsub and one of our victims. Where do you want to start?'

'There's not a great deal to go on with the victim. She's young; she's pretty. Why did he choose her? Why Molly Parkes? How has he come across her if he isn't known to her? How did his path cross hers?'

'A delivery driver, perhaps? A worker at the house? Some visitor at the house?'

Lovelace agreed. 'That's a good place to start. We should look into who has been at the house in the last three months. And workers at her school. People who don't normally work there. This is not someone who she would meet regularly. How does she get to school?'

'No idea. Most kids get driven to school by their parents these days. Molly's school is a good ten miles from her home.'

'There was a bus stop near her home.' Lovelace said. 'I wonder if she took the bus?'

'You thinking the driver looks good for this?'

'Not the driver, no. He'd be too familiar to Molly. Also, he'd get to deal with young girls all the time. I don't think he'd notice one pretty young girl from all the others. No, not the driver. But perhaps someone who drives past the bus stop every morning.'

'I like that,' Charlie agreed. 'He drives past one day and sees something that appeals to his baser nature.'

'But he's not an opportunist. He's a planner. He probably thinks about her from time to time. Then one day, he sees her again and then starts to drive past the bus stop at the same time every day, hoping to catch a glimpse of her.'

'And every day,' Charlie said, 'his obsession grows. Until one day….'

Charlie paused.

Lovelace nodded. 'Exactly. Until one day… Until one day, what? What happened to him that set him off? If you read anything about serial offenders, there's nearly always a trigger moment. Something in life happens that sets them off. It will be major, too. Something life-changing. The birth of a child, the breakdown of a relationship, or the death of a loved one. There will be something. Something lit this man's blue touch paper and set him off. He's done this sort of thing before; I'm certain of that. But not this big. This is a huge escalation. There'll have been a huge moment in his life that set him on this trail.'

Charlie said, 'Okay, we're getting somewhere. He's not an opportunistic killer but an obsessive planner— someone more than willing to kill to achieve his aim. Meeting Molly may have been by chance, but he most likely went away and fantasised about her. Seeing her every day developed his obsession. Sooner or later, he would have taken her, but something happens in his life that sets things rolling. He can no longer control himself. He must have Molly Parkes.'

'He must have known they were out for the day yesterday,' Lovelace said. 'That means he must have watched Molly through her mother's social media pages.'

'We should go through her friends' lists. See if anything shows up there.'

'Her profiles are very public. He wouldn't have needed to be a friend to see her posts.'

'Still,' Charlie said, 'it may have fed into his obsession to get closer to Molly. He could have created a fake profile. How many friends does she have on her Facebook page?'

Lovelace pulled up Sara Parkes' profile on the computer screen before her. 'Shit. Over eight hundred!'

'How many actual friends, then? Let's say Sara Parkes was a popular woman. She may have a close circle of maybe ten friends and an outer circle of up to fifty. If we're being generous.'

'So she's incredibly likely to have accepted any old friend request from pretty much anyone?'

Charlie smiled. 'You'd best print off her friends' list. We'll take a closer look at that.' Then, as an afterthought, Charlie asked, 'Did Molly have any social media?'

'All girls do at that age,' Lovelace replied. 'She had a Facebook profile. I tried to look at it this morning, but it was locked tight. Friends only.'

'Interesting. I wouldn't mind taking a look at her profile.'

'All the computers, phones and tablets were retrieved from their home and bagged up for forensics. Could we get them to the tech boys and see what they can do? I doubt there'll be much there. As I said, it was locked tight. Molly was way more sensible than her mother.'

'I'm sure,' Charlie said, 'but stalkers can be very clever. He may well have found a way in. He may not have been able to stop himself.'

Lovelace nodded. 'I'll get digital forensics on it right away.'

She made a few calls and got the Digital Forensics Team to prioritise Molly Parkes' mobile phone data urgently. She needed to get into all her social media profiles quickly. The man she spoke to sucked air through his teeth and made negative sounds. Lovelace cut him short.

'By the end of play today, please.' She said firmly and hung up.

Charlie smiled. 'Gave you their usual spiel, did they?'

Lovelace rolled their eyes. 'It's not like I'm asking them to come and paint my house. It's their job. You'd think they'd be keener about getting on with it. Especially as a girl's life hangs in the balance.'

The comment lingered in the air uncomfortably for a few seconds. Then, finally, the two detectives locked eyes, and Charlie's expression matched Lovelace's gut feeling. She was almost certain that Molly Parkes was already dead.

Lovelace spent the next hour slowly inputting the registration plates of the cars listed in Mrs Chambers' notepad to the Police National Computer. She cross-referenced all the names it threw up alongside those of the men on the sex offenders' register but came up blank. It was a pity, she thought, that Mrs Chambers didn't live closer to the main road. If their suspect drove past Molly while she was waiting at the bus stop, Mrs Chambers was bound to have recorded his number plate. Lovelace shook her head. It had taken an hour to check the plates Mrs Chambers had recorded driving up a quiet cul-de-sac. And there was no guarantee that if she had registered his number plate, he would be on any list. Lovelace's greatest fear was that the killer wasn't on any list. He was off the grid. No one was watching him.

So even if they had his plate, driving licence, and address, she was quietly worried that he wouldn't throw up any red flags and they would pass him by.

Time and again, her mind came back to Molly Parkes. Why her? Why there? And time and again, she drew a blank. At the moment, there was no reason for it. It was entirely random. But Lovelace didn't like random. She liked patterns. There was a pattern somewhere, but she couldn't make it out. There had to be a pattern. There was always a pattern.

She came full circle, back to the idea that somewhere in the past, there was another victim. Maybe more than one. But they were there. Just where to look?

She pulled out the small business card that DCI Graham had given her earlier. Perhaps she should start with DS Philip Spencer?

'Are you okay for a bit while I go and look up this DS Spencer?' Lovelace asked.

Charlie was head-deep in paper, chewing on the end of a pen.

'Sure.' She said, glancing at the clock behind Lovelace's head. 'I may go and get a bite to eat. See you back here in a bit?'

Lovelace found DS Spencer on the third floor of the building in the corner of an open space office. It was a quiet office primarily staffed by civilian staff dealing with the day-to-day operations of Force HQ.

Philip Spencer was in his forties, she guessed. He was clean-shaven with neatly trimmed dark hair and spectacles that balanced on the edge of his nose. He was dressed impressively in a clean, crisp white shirt with double cuffs and gold links. He was nose deep in a pile of papers as she approached. A full mug of coffee in a cup labelled 'Dad's Mug' and a photograph of him printed on it sat next to a half-eaten sandwich. He looked up and smiled.

'DS Spencer?' She asked.

'As I live and breathe,' he said in a smooth voice etched in good humour. He looked her straight in the eyes. 'And who might you be, pray tell?'

'DC Lovelace.' She held out her hand, and he took it. 'Lucy.'

'Very pleased to meet you, Lucy. What may I ask drags you to my corner of the world?'

She thought she noted a hint of Black Country in his vowels when he spoke. It was feint but equally unmistakable.

'I was told you might know a thing or two about burglary.'

'A thing or two, certainly. Anything specific?'

'I'm not sure, really,' she said. She glanced around Spencer's workspace. Beyond his immediate working area, his desk was exceptionally tidy. Fastidiously so. Everything had a place, and in that place, everything had a purpose. There was a bank of three computer screens and a laptop. Each was switched on and displayed a different screen. 'Who's your DI?' She asked.

'I don't have one,' he replied. Then, by way of explanation, he said, 'I'm the burglary data coordinator for Thames Valley Police. I report directly to the Chief Super, who in turn reports to the big man at the top. So I'm almost my own boss.'

Lovelace pulled up a chair that was nearby and sat down. 'What about the others?' She asked.

'Others?'

'Your colleagues?'

Spencer threw his arms out wide and swirled around in his chair. 'I'm it!'

Lovelace looked shocked. 'Just you? You mean you do this on your own?'

Spencer smiled. 'Generally, when you are on your own, you do things alone. It's the nature of the beast, I'm afraid.'

'So, what is it you do exactly?' She asked.

Spencer tilted his head to one side. Lovelace would come to notice that that was a thing he did when his curiosity was sparked.

'Quite simply, I'm a data analyst. I analyse the data from our twelve local policing authorities stretched over two thousand square miles of beautiful Thames Valley Countryside. Each week the Local Police Authorities gather up the data and pass it down the line to me. Then, on a Monday morning, I collate that data and look for offending patterns. Then, using that data, I predict trends and guide local Police into more proactive anti-burglary measures.'

He turned to look at a large map of the Thames Valley Policing area, which hung on a wall behind him. 'It's a bloody large area. It covers three counties and over two million people. And when it comes to winning the hearts and minds of the public little old me and my department are a long way down the line regarding budgeting requirements. But I do my bit.'

Lovelace cast her eyes over the map. It was indeed a large area. It was one of the largest territorial police forces in the country. It was a mixture of wild, sweeping countryside and large municipal cities interspersed with towns of all sizes.

'That must be a lot of data.' She said.

Spencer watched as the pretty young constable swept her eyes over his map. She looked at everything and noticed everything. She didn't miss a thing. His curiosity was sparked.

'It is.' He agreed. 'I certainly couldn't do it alone without these things.' He ran his hands over one of the computer monitors. 'We have some successes.' He admitted glumly. 'But not enough. Local policing budgets have been hit so hard that most of the time, the Road Crime Units do most of the work. They stumble on an uninsured motor, chase it for a few miles until they take off across the fields, and when they find the motor dumped in a lay-by, it's usually linked to a local burglary. The information comes to me, and I try to find a pattern.' He shook his head. 'Usually, though, they're tourist burglars. They come up the M40, nick a motor in Bracknell, drive into Oxfordshire, hit a few houses and make off home again. So we're relying more and more on luck and old-fashioned policing. What about you? What is it you do?'

Lovelace smiled. They had something in common. 'I look for patterns too. They're just a bit different to yours.'

Now Spencer was truly intrigued. 'Tell me more.'

'There's not much more to tell. I'm just a constable. I'm fairly new to all this.'

Spencer prided himself on the fact that he was a good judge of character. He'd only just met this sweet young Lucy Lovelace, but he sensed there was more to her than *just* a constable.

'Which department are you in?'

'The Major Investigation Team. We're working on the triple murder on the edge of town.'

Spencer drew in a deep lungful of air. He should have guessed she was one of Graham's proteges.

'I heard about that. The station's buzzing with it. Shouldn't you be out looking for the girl?'

'Molly. Yes. I suppose I am in my own way.'

Spencer tilted his head to one side. Lovelace noticed it. 'So what's your talent then?' He asked.

'My talent?'

'Yes. Your talent. Graham collects them like a philatelist collects stamps. You must have some talent that sets you apart from the others. Something he can nurture and make his own.'

'You don't like DCI Graham?'

'On the contrary. I'm his greatest fan. He finds bright young things like yourself, mines the best he can from them, polishes them, and sets them on a path to glory. So, what gift do you have that sets you apart from the others?'

Lovelace knew what Graham was collecting in her. What she didn't understand was why.

'As I said, I'm like you. I look for patterns.'

'Yes, you said,' Spencer prodded. 'But patterns in what?'

'Serial killers.' She said bluntly.

Nothing put Spencer off his stride. He was unflappable. This almost made him flap. 'Serial killers? I didn't know we had any.'

Lovelace paused. She didn't want to tell him her theories. They usually found out about them in the end. She'd have that argument another day. For now, she'd settle on drip-feeding him information.

'Not serial killers necessarily. Killers, in general, I suppose. I look for patterns in murder and murderers.'

'I see. You're a profiler.'

'You could call me that,' she agreed. 'But not in the strictest sense. We all know about killers and murderers and what makes them tick. We see patterns in their lives. We can build profiles of them based on what we know about killers that have gone before. There's very little originality there. There's very little left to learn. I'm interested in the victims. What makes them the victim? What makes them stand out to the killer? The vast majority of victims are murdered by people they know. That's dealt with by normal policing. It has its challenges, but it's not my area of expertise. But what about stranger murders?'

'Like your case?'

'Yes. Just like my case. I try and look at it from the predator's point of view. Imagine a lion stalking his prey in the African Savannah. What's he looking for? Weakness? Youth? Age? Sex? Opportunity? The lion is a stalking predator. House cats are ambush predators. They're different, albeit very slightly. But how do they choose their prey? The lion, it could be argued, selects his victim. But based on what criteria? What thought process does he go through that picks a particular victim from all the others? Then there's the house cat. He is not too far removed from the big cats, but he's a different killer. He senses his prey in the long grass, sits down, and waits. Then, when the mouse passes by.. slap. No more mouse. What kind of killer broke into the Parkes' home, murdered three innocent people and kidnapped a child? Why did my killer choose Molly Parkes? How did he choose her? Is he a stalker or an ambush killer? What do we know about Molly Parkes that could tell us more about our killer?'

Spencer sat up in his chair. 'Which somehow brought you to my desk.'

Lovelace leaned forward in her chair. 'A little while ago, a spate of burglaries hit the area where the Parkes lived. Off the back of that, some of the locals began a Neighbourhood Watch scheme. As a result, one of the Parkes' neighbours started recording all the activity on their little cul-de-sac.'

Lovelace took out the notebook and flicked through the pages.

'She was a detailed note-keeper. She recorded everything and everyone she saw, down to times, descriptions and number plates.'

Lovelace handed the notebook to Spencer, who opened it at a random page.

'Bloody Hell,' he exclaimed, 'I wish there were more people like this.'

He skimmed the pages and passed the notebook back to Lovelace. 'Find anything interesting?'

'Not yet,' Lovelace admitted. 'I will run the plates through the PNC later and see if I get any hits. The old lady that kept the notebook said something interesting, however. Sarah Parkes had told her that she feared she had been broken into recently but couldn't be entirely certain.'

Spencer shrugged. 'I think you'd know if you had been burgled.'

'I agree. Mostly. But Sarah had complained of losing items and finding them again in places she was certain she would never have left them. And other things, little things, that she couldn't quite put her finger on. Is this a thing? Does that happen?'

Spencer nodded slowly. 'It does happen. But it's not common; there's a straightforward explanation in most cases. More often than not, it's kids messing about. They break into a home, usually while the occupants are known to be away, and they help themselves to food and drink. Normally alcohol and normally a lot of it. They very rarely steal anything. If they do, it will be small and untraceable.'

'Has anything like this happened recently?' Lovelace asked.

A recollection fired in Spencer's brain, but he couldn't grasp the detail. He shook his head. 'No. Not recently.'

There was something, but he couldn't bring it to the surface.

Lovelace sat back in her chair, deflated. 'It was a long shot, I suppose.'

'What were you hoping for?' Spencer asked.

'A pattern. Some indication that this was a dry run for what's come next.' Lovelace looked at the map behind Spencer. 'Is this the sort of thing you would have picked up on? Is there any pattern to this kind of behaviour?'

'Yes, I would have picked up on it, and no, there's not normally any pattern to it. It's mostly seasonal. It peaks during the summer and winter months when the schools are off. So it's usually written off as unworthy of too much attention. Just kids messing about. This, however, is slightly different.'

Spencer got out of his chair for the first time and approached his map. He wore pinstripe trousers, perfectly creased. He was growing older gracefully, Lovelace thought. There was no beer belly to speak of, and he moved with vigour and vitality. He must exercise, she thought. Otherwise, he'd be sat at his desk eating terrible sandwiches and getting fat.

'Take this, for example,' he said, pointing to a collection of red pins in the Jericho district. 'Nothing much to go on, to be fair, and most local coppers think it's a bit funny, but..'

'But you don't?' Lovelace asked.

'It could be just high jinks. The hot weather does tend to bring out the morons. But in every one of these fifteen different locations, local women have reported the theft of underwear from outside their homes. Nearly always overnight. And these fifteen are just the ones that have been reported. How many have just written it off as petty crime that's not worth reporting?'

'What do you think is happening?' Lovelace asked.

Spencer shook his head. 'I honestly don't know. I want to think it's just a young idiot out for kicks. Drunks on their way home.'

'Potential sex offender?' Lovelace added.

Spencer nodded. 'That would be my fear. I've recommended an increased police presence in the area during the hours of darkness, but unfortunately, it's not a high policing priority. No one's going to get a gong for catching a knicker thief. We'll have to wait until he's taking the underwear off his victims in person.'

Lovelace looked at the expression on Spencer's face. It seemed to be a theory he was genuinely fearful of.

'Just one last thing.' Lovelace said, opening the notebook and leafing through the pages until she found the entry she wanted. 'My nosey neighbour recorded a partial number plate..'

She handed the notebook to Spencer and pointed at the entry.

'It's a dirty, white, Transit-style van with foreign plates. European plates. She only managed to capture some of the numbers. Does this ring any bells with you?'

Spencer read the entry and handed the notebook back to Lovelace.

'I'm afraid not, no. And I don't think you'll get far with that much of the plate. It's not enough.'

'There've been no burglaries reported recently with a van matching this description seen in the vicinity?'

Spencer shook his head again. 'I'm afraid not. We do get a lot of itinerant European workers around here, or at least we did, and by and large, they cause us no trouble. The vast majority of our burglars are homegrown.'

Lovelace glanced at her watch. 'I've taken up too much of your time.' She rose from her seat. 'Thank you.'

They shook hands. Spencer watched as Lovelace glided out of the office. She had left a marked impression on him. And several questions began to gather in his thoughts. He was about to sit down and work them out when one of the civilian staff members came across with an excited look.

'Was that her?'

'Who?' He asked in all innocence.

'Lefty Lovelace?'

The young man could barely hold his excitement in check. Yes, Spencer thought, she had undoubtedly been pretty, but his reaction seemed strange. Almost embarrassing.

'Constable Lovelace?' He asked.

'Yes, that's it. Lucy Lovelace!'

'Yes. That was her.' Spencer looked at the young man with a blank expression.

The man laughed. 'Fuck me, Spence, you really are a shit detective. You'll never make Inspector!'

He walked away, laughing.

Spencer found it all very odd. He was going to let it pass as the folly of moronic civilian staff when he decided to Google Lucy Lovelace. He spent the next two hours reading all about her and her family and feeling rather stupid.

Seven

When Lovelace returned, Charlie was slumped over her desk, tapping away at the keyboard.

'Good lunch?' Lovelace asked.

Charlie didn't look up. She kept tapping away at the keyboard. A printer nearby burst into life and started spewing out reams of paper.

'Good, thanks. Just don't buy the sandwiches from the canteen, they taste like shit.'

Charlie stepped over to the printer, drew one of the sheets from the pile, and handed it to Lovelace. 'Piotr Nowak. Polish national emigrated to the UK twenty years ago.'

Lovelace said, 'Polish?'

The partial number plate of European descent flashed before her eyes.

'Good lead, right?' Charlie agreed. 'He's not the only European on the list, but he's the best fit I can find. Fifteen years ago, he kidnapped two twelve-year-old girls as they walked past his home and held them in his flat for nearly forty-eight hours until one managed to escape and raise the alarm. He got a life sentence and was released on licence two months ago.'

Lovelace didn't need to ask what had happened during those forty-eight hours. She remembered the case. She had been just thirteen herself at the time.

Charlie said, 'He's on VISOR.'

Charlie was reading through more of the sheets of paper that continued to flow from the printer.

'He's not a very nice man.' Charlie said, handing Lovelace another sheet.

'Why'd they let him out?' Lovelace asked.

'Fuck knows.' Charlie said. 'Why do they ever let these people out? Prisons are overcrowded. They're not the right place for rehabilitation. Blah blah blah ad nauseam. Truth is he was up for parole, and someone said yes. So now he's our problem.'

Lovelace read the sheet of paper that Charlie had handed her. 'I remember this case.'

'Me too.' Charlie said. 'My old man wouldn't let me out on my own for months. I could only go out with an older male friend in tow. It played right into my hormonal teenage hands! She laughed. 'It's a wonder I survived my teenage years!'

The irony wasn't lost on Lovelace. It was a wonder she had survived hers. Her dream rushed back to her. Her father standing in the doorway with a kitchen knife. The fear. The smell of burning.

The printer finally stopped, and the air was filled with a deafening silence and the hum of an air-conditioning unit somewhere in the building.

Lovelace continued to read Nowak's profile. He was a big man. He was just short of six foot three and built of stone. He had a scar across his right eyebrow where a fellow inmate had slashed him with a homemade blade. Millimetres lower, and he'd have lost his eye. It gave him an even more disturbing visage.

'He has several warning markers on his file,' Charlie said. 'One for extreme violence and one for carrying weapons.'

Lovelace looked further down his profile. During the police action to rescue the other girl from Nowak's clutches, one of the first officers through the door was stabbed five times. The second officer was slashed across the face. It took eight pissed-off policemen, three cans of pepper spray and a Taser to subdue him. Even then, he kicked and punched his way to the cells. Fortunately, no one was killed.

'They let this animal out?' Lovelace asked, more in disbelief than anything else.

Charlie handed Lovelace a radio and a can of PAVA. She picked up a radio for herself, a can of PAVA and a pair of handcuffs. During training, Lovelace had accidentally been sprayed full in the face with a can of PAVA. It wasn't an experience she relished, but she marvelled at its effectiveness. It was way more potent than CS gas or pepper spray and incapacitated its victim in seconds. As far as Lovelace was concerned, she'd happily go toe to toe with a black bear, provided she had a can of PAVA.

'Well, he's out and among us. There's no point in labouring the point now. We lock them up; the do-gooders let them out. It's always been that way, and it won't change. The best we can do is get them on the detail. This bloke's got a life licence, and the rules are pretty strict. No interaction with anyone under eighteen. He can't go within half a mile of a school, playground, or anywhere children may gather. He can't start a relationship with anyone with children. He needs to inform us of any relationship he may be in, and we have the right to inform his new partner of the crime he was convicted of. He's on a temporary curfew of between nine pm and seven am. He also has an ankle tag which will display his current location via GPS if we need it.' She held up her iPad and waved it. 'I'm good to go. You ready?'

Piotr Nowak had been given a place to stay at a halfway house in Didcot, nearly fifteen miles south of Oxford. Charlie steered her motor onto the A34 and flew down the by-pass as quickly as the traffic allowed. It took almost thirty minutes before they reached Didcot.

The cooling towers from the power station no longer commanded the view from the road, and all Lovelace could see through the window was a clear azure blue sky and beautiful green countryside. The once iconic Oxfordshire skyline was unrecognisable. Despite the ugly nature of the cooling towers, Lovelace couldn't help but feel that the landscape had lost something in its passing.

Charlie pulled up in a housing estate towards the south of the town. It was an old estate, built during the sixties and now looking every one of its sixty-odd years. The houses were faded and unkempt, the gardens mostly set to lawn but filled with weeds and un-loved. The doors and windows were shabby, with faded paint peeling from them. One or two houses bucked the trend with new windows and doors and evidence that some care had been taken over the gardens, but Lovelace found it depressing to see that they were in the minority. Everything here was neglected, Lovelace thought, and it bothered her to think that probably applied to the people too.

They stepped out of the car and into the raging heat. No children were playing out in the street as Lovelace had done as a child when the unpredictable British weather turned up the thermometer. Knowing the kind of man that had been dumped in their midst, she couldn't but feel that was a good thing. She looked around her. It wasn't the sort of place you'd let kids run free. They were safer in their back gardens. She sighed heavily. The paradox wasn't lost on her. Most abusers worked from home. The man they had come to talk to was thankfully a rarity. She wondered, sadly, if anywhere was safe.

Charlie strode ahead with purpose, with Lovelace a few paces behind. They turned a corner into an area of the estate that was primarily flats. They were squat little things, three stories high, with a door entry system in the middle blocking their access. There were five buildings with what Lovelace guessed would be about six flats each. Charlie walked up to the second block and pushed the door. It was locked.

'Damn.'

She pressed the 'Trades' button, and Lovelace heard a slight buzz followed by a click. Charlie pushed the door, and it opened.

Charlie smiled. 'They don't normally work.'

The door opened out into a courtyard beyond which was a communal garden. Like everything else on the estate, it was unloved and uncared for. On either side of the courtyard, staircases led up to a balcony which ran alongside the edge of the communal garden. The blocks were effectively U shaped. At the back of the garden were a hedge and a metal fence about twelve feet high, topped with barbed wire. Beyond that, Lovelace saw what looked like a largely derelict area leading up to some derelict-looking buildings with smashed windows. It looked like an old shunting yard that had yet to find a new purpose.

Charlie climbed the first set of steps to her left, and Lovelace followed closely behind. When they reached the first floor, they stopped, and Lovelace watched as Charlie noted the numbers on the doors. Then, she looked up at the next flight of stairs.

'He must be on the top floor.' She said.

'What's the plan?' Lovelace asked.

'Follow my lead. Stay close. As Police Officers, we have every right to monitor his movements and Internet use. So look out for computers and tablets. He can't deny us access; it's part of his licence. But he might not like it. So if he makes any move, spray him in the face with your PAVA.'

Lovelace slipped her hand into her pocket and gripped her canister.

Charlie walked up the last set of stairs with less confidence than before. Lovelace sensed a change in her body language. Charlie was nervous. Despite this, she walked up to the door she was looking for, drew her breath, and knocked hard.

'Mr Novak.' She said, 'it's the police. Can you open the door, please?'

Lovelace heard movement from inside. It sounded like someone moving a table.

'Mr Novak, can you open the door, please?' Charlie called out again.

'Yeah. I'm coming.'

He didn't sound happy. Lovelace braced herself as a figure appeared behind the frosted glass door. He was tall, she noted, and when the door opened, she could barely see past the massive frame of Piotr Novak, that stood in a dirty t-shirt and a pair of grey shorts.

'What do you want?'

'It's just a routine check.' Charlie said. 'Can we come in?'

Novak stepped aside. 'I can't fucking stop you, can I?'

Charlie stepped inside and carefully walked past Nowak. He dwarfed her. Lovelace followed.

Nowak seemed lethargic. His movements were slow and staccato. His voice, when he spoke, was slow and laboured. He smelled of body odour and dampness. When Lovelace looked him in the eye, she noticed they were bloodshot, and his pupils were tiny. He was as high as a kite. As Lovelace stepped inside, she sensed a change in his manner. It wasn't much, just a tiny change in the direction of his shoulders. She knew what he was about to do, and he'd picked his time to perfection. There was nothing she could do to stop him. She was angry with herself. She had put herself in a stupid position. She would never let that happen again. Lovelace braced herself as Novak reached out and grabbed her by her hair, and launched her into Charlie's back. They both toppled into Novak's front room. By the time they recovered their senses and got to their feet, Novak had launched himself over the bannister and fallen two stories into the garden. Charlie and Lovelace made it to the balcony in time to see him get up and run through the metal fence at the back. There was a hole in the fence that wasn't obvious to the casual observer.

'How the fuck did he not break his legs?' Charlie asked in awe.

'Did you see his legs?' Lovelace said. 'They were like tree stumps. And by the look of his eyes, he's high on something.'

Charlie spoke quickly into her radio. As she did so, Lovelace launched herself over the balcony and gently made her way to the garden with the grace of a ballerina and the skill of a free runner. The speed with which she moved took Charlie's breath away.

Charlie looked over the balcony as Lovelace chased Novak through the hole in the fence. She considered following Lovelace's example, then said, 'fuck that,' out loud and took the stairs. She was almost twenty seconds behind Lovelace through the fence, all the time giving a running commentary into the radio. Local police units were a few minutes away. Secretly Charlie hoped they'd get there quickly. Novak was a big man.

Novak had a good one hundred-yard head start, and he moved quickly for a big man, but his size told against him. Lovelace was quicker and more agile and younger. He could hear her gaining on him. Rather than attempt to outrun her across the yard, he ducked into the buildings and disappeared. Lovelace watched him vanish and made it to the building a few seconds later. She was too slow. She couldn't see him anywhere. She waited by the doorway for Charlie to catch up.

'He went in here.'

'Good. Let's try and keep him in there for as long as possible. Units are on their way.' Charlie stopped for a moment to catch her breath. Then she said, 'go around the back, see if he comes out. I'll go this way. Don't take him on on your own. Run away from him if you have to. If he's high, he will be hard to stop.'

Lovelace nodded. She watched Charlie run off around the building, then turned and went the opposite way. The ground was hard going. In places, the concrete had been ripped up, and small rocks littered the floor. Lovelace walked around the back of the building only to find herself in a maze of other buildings. They were all in an advanced stage of destruction, brought about by age and weather and, here and there, by the hand of man. Barely an inch of standing wall was untouched by graffiti, and littered about the floor were the remnants of drug paraphernalia and used condoms. Lovelace picked her route carefully, avoiding the detritus of humankind until she came to the edge of another building and turned around the corner. She found herself in a small courtyard with a closed door on the other side. She walked over and tried the handle. It was locked. Her radio crackled. She heard Charlie's voice as she guided the local police units to their location. As she turned around, she realised her mistake.

Piotr Novak stood behind her, blocking her route out of the courtyard. She remembered Charlie's advice about running from the man if she had to. The problem was that there was nowhere to run. The massive frame of Piotr Novak stood between her and safety. She shuddered as she noticed a small detail that she had missed before. A detail that reminded her of her dream of her father as he stood in the doorway holding a kitchen knife. It glinted in the sun as Novak slowly twisted it around in his hand. Lovelace took a deep breath and moved slowly away from the locked door. She tried to remember her training. First things first, don't get trapped. Put yourself into a position where you can move freely. Use your weight and size to your advantage. You're small and agile. He isn't. Make the advantage pay.

Lovelace smiled. She remembered the soothing tones of her sensei, a fat, ageing, grey-haired old man that moved like a kitten and bit like a tiger. He didn't speak English and commanded her in his native tongue. 'Never put yourself in a position where your only choice is to fight. You must always have options.'

She'd fucked that up. He would have been disappointed.

Lovelace held one hand by her side and reached forward with her other, her palm outstretched. With her hand to her side, she gingerly pressed the 'Panic' button on her radio, taking extra care not to show Novak what she was doing. The 'Panic' button cancelled all other radios on that frequency and opened up Lovelace's set, so she didn't need to press the 'Call' button. Every Police Officer in the area was automatically tapped into what was happening.

'Okay. Listen to me.' She said loudly. 'You don't have to do this. We can talk about it. Whatever you've done can't be that bad. You use that knife, and there's no going back. They'll lock you up forever. They'll never let you out again.'

He edged slowly towards her, and she stepped backwards, trying to maintain a safe distance. But, unfortunately, there was only so far that she could go before she would be backed into a corner, and he would start to gain on her.

'Watch him.' Her sensei said softly. 'Watch the way he places his feet. They will tell you where he's going. Watch his shoulders and the way he carries his arms. They will tell you what he is about to do. But most of all, watch his eyes. They will tell you his intent.'

'Seriously. Think about it.' She said. 'I can help you. Whatever it is, I can help.'

He kept edging forward, turning the knife around and around in his hand. His feet moved towards her, and she continued to edge backwards, constantly aware of the wall closing in behind her. His body seemed to relax, and his eyes softened. He was wavering. There was time yet.

'That's it.' Lovelace continued. 'Just put the knife down. Walk away. No one needs to get hurt.'

He paused. She watched the turmoil behind his eyes. He was caught in the midst of a difficult problem made much worse by the fogging of his brain. He stopped twisting the knife. His eyes glared at her. It was as though there was nothing behind the eyes to reason with. Whatever turmoil had been going on in his head had ended. She read his intent as clearly as she read the way he pulled his shoulders back and gripped the knife firmly in his hands.

Lovelace moved her feet into a better position. She had already planned her first moves.

'He will expect to take you down in the first attack. He will use his weight and his build to intimidate and subdue you. Watch him. Read his moves. His body will tell you what he will do before he knows himself. Be ahead of him. Be quicker. You are younger and fitter. That is your weapon.'

Lovelace braced herself for the assault. She knew the moment it was going to come and prepared herself.

Charlie stepped into the courtyard at the exact moment he started to move. Lovelace saw the conflict and confusion in Novak's eyes. It didn't last long. He aborted his move on Lovelace and turned to meet Charlie. He raised his arm, and the knife glinted in the sunlight. Charlie stepped into his space and unloaded her can of PAVA into Novak's face. Novak didn't miss a beat. The darkness was in control. He brought the knife down in a sweeping arc and into Charlie's stomach.

Lovelace screamed, 'No!'

She moved forward, but the gap she had left between her and Novak was big. She watched in horror as Novak quickly stabbed Charlie four more times. By the time she reached Novak, Charlie had fallen to the floor, clutching her stomach.

Lovelace launched herself at Novak and aimed a perfectly timed kick to his head. It took him by surprise and knocked him off his feet. Lovelace landed deftly, regained her composure and waited for him to get back up. It was a good kick, but she knew it wasn't enough. She'd need to deliver many more of those before Novak was done.

'Never repeat the same move twice,' she heard her sensei say. 'He will be expecting it.'

Lovelace watched as Novak got to his feet. He clutched the knife in his right hand, waving it menacingly as his anger and fury drove him towards Lovelace. Lovelace read his every move like a prizefighter in a boxing ring. She used his force and momentum against him as she nimbly stepped out of his reach and delivered her elbow into the crook of his nose. She felt it crack as the bone in her arm met his face, and when she turned around, his face had taken on a crimson hue, but the fury in his eyes was unabated. He swung wildly around with his arm outstretched, and the knife curved a perfect arc in the sun. Lovelace saw it coming and ducked under. When he turned back, she was ready. She reached up and grabbed his arm and launched herself up and over until his arm was bent out of shape and then, with all the strength she could muster, drove down hard and fast on his exposed arm. She heard the bone crack, followed by a fearsome growl from Novak. As he stood up, the knife fell from his broken and twisted grip, and his arm hung uselessly by his side. But the darkness was not yet done, and Lovelace could sense that she hadn't long before Charlie would be lost. Novak screamed like a wounded bear and charged at Lovelace. She ducked to one side and quickly kicked one of his legs, bringing it up behind the other. Novak went down heavily, and Lovelace watched as his face pounded the ground. Yet still, he wouldn't stop. He crawled around using his one good arm and pulled himself to his feet. Lovelace looked around the floor and found a rock almost the size of her hand. It was heavy with sharp edges. She wrapped her fingers around it, swung her arm to one side, and threw it at Novak's head with all her strength.

She knew it was good the second it left her hand. It cut a perfect line in the air and caught Novak above his left eye. She heard his skull crack and watched in silent awe as his face erupted in crimson streaks of blood. For a moment, it looked like he was going to power through that before Lovelace saw his eyes roll into his head, and he collapsed on the floor.

Lovelace was by Charlie's side in a heartbeat. She ripped open her blouse and stifled the panic beginning to rise inside her. Charlie's torso was a lake of ruby red. It seemed to pump out with every laboured breath she took. Lovelace started ripping Charlie's blouse into shreds and pushing them tightly into the wounds, but there were too many for her to apply pressure to all at once.

'Fuck. Charlie. Don't close your eyes. Charlie. Stay with me.'

It was to no avail. Charlie's eyes closed.

<h1 style="text-align:center">Eight</h1>

'Constable Lovelace?'

She looked up. Two men bore down on her. One was older, possibly in his fifties, with grey hair stuck neatly to the side of his head, while the other was much younger with a mop of blonde hair that hung untidily about his head.

'Yes.'

The older man held out his warrant card. 'DI Frampton. This is DS Wright.'

Lovelace was sitting in the back of an ambulance, clutching a bottle of water. Everything had happened so quickly that she was still trying to process it all. One minute she had been trying to stem the bleeding from Charlie's wounds, and the next, she was being ushered into an ambulance while a dozen people crowded over her fallen colleague. It all happened in such a blur. Within minutes an air ambulance had landed, and Charlie had been loaded into its belly before it took off again and banked sharply right before flying out of view. Some officers had restrained Novak before he was loaded into the back of an ambulance. Paramedics were dealing with his injuries.

The paramedic guiding her into the back of an ambulance had checked her over before handing her a bottle of ice-cold water. That's when the suits turned up.

'We're sorry about your colleague. How is she?'

'She's in a bad way, I think. He must have stabbed her five times.' She shuddered at the recollection.

'And you? Are you okay?'

The paramedic answered. 'She's good. Not a scratch on her.'

Frampton looked at the young woman in the back of the ambulance in amazement. She was a pretty little thing with an unkempt head of hair and a pleasant face. She was also covered from head to toe in blood.

'Do you mind if we take a quick statement from you?' Frampton asked, 'while it's all fresh in your mind?'

Lovelace nodded. 'Sure.'

Slowly Lovelace described the events that ended with Charlie's stabbing and the fight with Novak. DS Wright carefully scribbled everything down in a small notebook. DI Frampton said nothing. When Lovelace had finished talking, he said, 'That all seems in order.' He looked across at his DS. Lovelace noticed that they seemed to be silently communicating with each other. 'Just a couple of questions….'

Frampton was about to ask them when DCI Graham appeared at his left shoulder and said, 'Perhaps another time DI Frampton? My constable is in shock. When she's had time to recover her senses, I'm sure we'll be happy to oblige you with a written statement of today's events. Perhaps if you'd like to put your questions in writing, we will address them in due course.'

DI Frampton turned to meet Graham. He didn't smile. 'Of course, Detective Chief Inspector Graham.'

The two men stared at one another for a few uncomfortable seconds before Frampton turned back to look at Lovelace. 'A written statement would do just fine, thank you, as soon as you feel up to it. If you wouldn't mind going into more detail about the fight with Novak.' He paused. 'In particular, I would be grateful if you would describe how Mr Novak, high on drugs or alcohol, armed with a knife, seemingly impervious to PAVA, and built like a tank, is the one with a broken arm, a broken nose and a cracked skull, while you, a small slip of a girl, is almost entirely unharmed.' He turned and smiled at Graham. It was a sinister smile edged with insinuation. 'When she's feeling better, of course.'

The two detectives walked away without saying another word.

'He doesn't like you much.' Lovelace observed.

'I don't like him at all.' Graham said. 'He's a nasty, odious little man. I'd rather hoped he'd retired by now.' He looked up at Lovelace. 'Are you all right?'

'I'm fine. Charlie's in a bad way.'

'I know. I just heard from the hospital that the helicopter landed a few minutes ago. She's still alive.'

Graham handed Lovelace a bag. 'One of the girls at the yard thought you might need a change of clothes. My car's over there. I'll drive us back to the station when you're ready.'

'I'd like to go to the hospital if that's okay. For Charlie.'

Graham shook his head. 'I've sent a constable to be with her. He'll keep me posted on her condition. There's nothing we can do for now. We have to wait. And while we wait, we still have a missing girl to find. Get changed. I'll be in the car.'

***

They drove back to the station in silence. Lovelace stared out the window, reviewing the day's events in her mind. She had done so much wrong. They shouldn't have followed Novak into the derelict site. They should have waited. Backup had been just a few minutes behind them. If they had waited, it could have ended so differently. She closed her eyes and saw the blade flash as it cut a terrible ark in the sunlight and curved into Charlie's stomach. She felt a gut-wrenching sense of hopelessness as the blade wrought a terrifying toll on Charlie as Novak launched at her repeatedly.

And then her father stood in the doorway with a blade in his hands. That same look. That cold, dark and soulless face clouded now by the fog of time. Her mother lying dead on the kitchen floor. That same sense of helplessness. If only they had done things differently…

Police HQ felt edgy. A fallen colleague was a pain felt collectively across rank and file. It affected everyone. Graham walked through the building with a sense of purpose. Lovelace followed a few paces behind. She felt the eyes of a hundred people follow her. She kept her head down, not catching anyone directly in the eye. She didn't want to see the look of disappointment in their eyes, their accusations, their blame. She followed Graham into his office. He closed the door behind them.

'Drink?' He asked, reaching behind his desk and pulling out a bottle of whisky.

'I could certainly do with one,' Lovelace said, dropping herself into a chair opposite Graham.

'They don't blame you, you know.' He said, pouring two large glasses and handing one over to Lovelace.

She picked up the glass and took a long swig. The liquid burned her throat, but it was a comforting burn. It was familiar. Uncle Mike had been a whisky drinker. It had taken some time before she had acquired the taste, but now she revelled in its smokiness.

'Of course, they blame me,' she said. 'I blame me. It's my fault.'

Graham sipped at his drink as he sat down in his wide-backed chair. 'Tell me what happened.'

She briefly explained the circumstances that had taken them to Didcot, 'He wasn't happy we were there,' she said, 'but I didn't think he would go off like that. I could tell he was high when we went in. He seemed lethargic. He didn't seem threatening. And then he just pushed us to one side and leapt over the side. I honestly thought he'd break something. It was a long way down. He was already up and making off when we looked over the side. I followed him over; Charlie took the stairs. By the time I caught up with him, he'd darted into one of the buildings. We should have stopped there. I never saw the knife.'

Lovelace carried on with her story, climaxing with her fight with Novak. There was a long pause while Graham pondered the tale.

'You should know,' he said, 'that we've checked into Novak's movements at the time of Molly Parkes' disappearance. He has a perfect alibi. There's no way on earth that he can be our man. His alibi harms him - it will likely send him back to prison to serve out his time. But he couldn't have abducted Molly.'

Lovelace had felt he wasn't their man, but it had been a good lead. She harboured a terrible feeling that the man behind Molly's kidnap wasn't in the system. He was a ghost, and you had to believe in ghosts before you could see them.

'Tell me,' Graham said, swirling his whisky around in his glass before taking a sip. 'How did a small young woman like yourself take down a man like Novak?'

Lovelace smiled. 'Uncle Mike was into his martial arts. I followed him into it. When we lived in Japan, he hired an old Japanese sensei to teach my sister and me the ways of self-defence. I took it a few steps further. I started competing in a few mixed martial arts events and got quite good at it.'

'Cage fighting?' Graham asked.

'Pretty much. By the time I was nineteen, I was competing semi-professionally. I even had sponsorship deals behind me.'

'But you didn't keep it up?'

'No. I got as good as I needed to get. I was East Asian champion for three years, undefeated. Then I went to University in Tokyo and returned to Oxford for my post-grad in criminology. I didn't need the money. My mum's inheritance paid for all that, and Uncle Mike's not short of a few quid.'

'And then you joined the force?'

'Much to my Uncle Mike's annoyance. He doesn't like you lot very much, not after my dad. He tried desperately to talk me out of it. So I changed my name back too.'

'Your Uncle Mike was married to your Mum's sister?'

'Yeah. After my mum died, he and my Aunt Jane adopted me and my sister and took us back to Japan to look after us.'

Graham nodded. Most of that he already knew. He'd lost touch with the Lovelace girls when they left the country shortly after their father's trial. He approved of Uncle Mike's strategy, especially the name change. People remembered Jack Lovelace. The name still haunted many in the police force. Many of those involved in the case all those years ago were still in the force.

And then, one of the girls returned and re-adopted her father's surname. Then she upset everyone by joining the police.

'Tell me,' Graham said, 'why join up? Why the Thames Valley?'

'I wanted to give something back.' Lovelace said. 'Something my father took. And I'm an Oxfordshire girl at heart. It's my home.'

Graham cast his eyes over the young woman in front of him. She was self-assured and confident but not arrogant. She held herself with dignity and poise and spoke in an educated and refined manner. Nothing about how she carried herself hinted at the terror and horror of her childhood. By all accounts, she was a well-rounded and mature young woman with a bright future.

'You could have taken graduate entry.' Graham said. 'You're more than qualified. You could be an Inspector now. But you didn't. You joined as a Constable. Why?'

'It wasn't about the career.' Lovelace said, picking her words carefully. 'I don't need the money. Money has never been a driving force for me. So I guess in that way, I'm fortunate. I don't have to worry about money like most coppers. But I wanted to know the job from the ground up. I wanted to gain experience in the field. I think that's the only way you can be a good copper. You can't learn that in a book.'

Graham nodded. She was a wise girl, too. He liked her more and more. 'Tell me about the rock to Novak's face. You cracked his skull open.'

'Am I in trouble?' Lovelace asked.

'Not for as long as I have breath in my body.' Graham said. 'But coppers like Frampton will look for ways to take you down. So it would be best if you were careful. Coppers have long memories.'

Lovelace drained her glass, and Graham reached over and topped her up. She said, 'Baseball's a popular game in the Far East. At least, it was in my school. There were loads of American ex-pats and children of servicemen, and it was our summer game of choice.' Lovelace smiled at the memory of her school days. 'I have a wicked right arm and a powerful throw. Accurate too.'

'Novak's cracked skull is a testament to that.' Graham downed his glass and topped himself back up. 'You're full of surprises, Lucy. Is there anything else I should know about you?'

She pondered this for a moment. 'Yes. There are lots of things you should know. But that would rather spoil the surprise, don't you think?'

Graham laughed.

'You should know,' Lovelace went on, 'that I am fluent in Japanese, Mandarin, Cantonese and Russian. I'm good at Arabic, and I can make a passing stab at most European languages. I have a private pilot's licence and can drive articulated lorries.'

'Articulated lorries?' Graham asked in bemusement. 'You have a HGV licence?'

'Yes.' Lovelace said. 'One summer during my Post-Grad degree, I wanted to learn to drive one. So I did.'

'You are quite special, Lucy.'

'Not really.' She said. 'I'm quite normal; I've just been lucky enough to be able to do the things I want to do.'

'And of all the things you could have done, you became a lowly police constable.'

'There's nothing lowly about it,' she countered. 'The best people I have ever met have been coppers. Not all of them, I grant you. But most of them. When they see past my name. Which begs the question I would like to ask you.'

Graham sat back in his chair. 'Go on. I can't promise I'll have the answer.'

'You will,' Lovelace said confidently. 'Because when I joined, my first Sergeant told me I'd never be anything. He said no one would let me become anything in the police force. For a while, it seemed like he might be right. It felt like no one in authority was prepared to give me a chance. I almost quit. And then you offered me a slot in your team. A rare opportunity afforded to few people. Why? Why me?'

Graham sat back in his chair. He reached over to his desk and opened a drawer. He pulled out an old photograph and slid it across the table to Lovelace.

Lovelace picked up the photograph. She hadn't expected that. She caught her breath. It was a photograph she had never seen before, but she recognised the scene immediately. She remembered it too. More than anything else, she remembered the smell —the smell of burning flesh.

The picture was at least fifteen years old. There was a house in the background with flames and smoke bellowing from its rafters and pouring from broken windows. There was a fleet of ambulances and police cars in the background. In the foreground, a man was carrying a girl of about twelve years old in his arms, away from the burning building. Behind him was another man carrying another girl.

Lovelace looked up at Graham and back at the photograph. The man in the foreground carrying the young girl was DCI Graham.

'You were there?' Her voice cracked.

'Yes.' Graham said softly. 'I was there. I carried you out of the building.'

'Not me.' Lovelace said. 'That's my sister, Zoe.'

She pushed the photograph back to Graham. He picked it up and held it in his hands for a few seconds.

'I always thought that was you.' He said.

'No. Zoe was a year older than me. She's a bit bigger. We look alike, though. I can see why you might have thought that.'

There was a long pause while Lovelace juggled a dozen or so questions in her head. Graham watched the turmoil within her. He could only imagine the thought process his young constable was struggling with.

'So you were involved in the case?' She asked eventually.

Graham nodded. 'Yes. From the very beginning.' He paused. 'I knew your father. He pulled the wool over all our eyes. He was a very likeable man.'

'People like my father don't always follow a clearly defined pattern.' She said. 'There were elements of him that were typical. He was able to cleverly absorb himself into the same team that was hunting him. By doing that, he could stay one step ahead for so long.'

'There were signs, though,' Graham admitted. 'They're easy to see now, with the benefit of hindsight. We couldn't see them at the time.'

Lovelace finished her drink and placed it down on the table. She raised a hand as Graham proffered another refill.

'That doesn't explain why you took me on your team.'

Graham reached into his desk drawer again and pulled out a book. Lovelace sighed. The book was titled: 'Like Father like Daughter. The Lovelace story.' Lovelace had penned the book while studying for her PhD. It became a UK-wide bestseller and ruffled a few feathers in the corridors of law enforcement.

'You've read it?' She asked, slightly embarrassed.

'I don't think anyone in the force hasn't.' Graham admitted drily. 'You certainly pissed a few people off.'

'But not you?' She asked. 'You were on the investigation team. You didn't come off looking too good.'

'We looked like bloody fools.' He said. 'I could find little in the book that I fundamentally disagreed with. But for me, the book was something else. I read a book about a young girl looking for answers. A young girl looking to make amends for her father's crimes, something she absolutely couldn't be held responsible for.'

Graham finished his drink and poured himself another.

'Fifteen years ago,' he said, 'I ran into a burning building to save the lives of two innocent girls, caught in a horror of someone else's making. I did that so you could have the life you have gone on to live. We may have failed you initially, but we redeemed ourselves in some small part by saving you and your sister that night. Everyone involved in the case that knew your father and your mother took a huge interest in the lives of the two innocent girls pulled from that burning house. We wished and hoped for the best for you. When your aunt and uncle took you abroad, we all felt it was probably the best thing. We lost touch with you. And then you came back.'

'And here I am.'

'And here you are. And mark my words. Many people in the force are waiting for you to make a mistake. They want you to fail; some will try to make that happen. But I wanted to give you a chance. The same chance I gave you all those years ago. I don't fully understand your motives, but I am prepared to stake my life on you again.'

Lovelace considered the words. She had learned something today about her life that she had never known. She felt ashamed that she had never considered the identity of the man that had saved her life. She had never thought about him once. And now she was sat opposite him.

She stood up. She was no longer the same young woman that had been woken early that morning. She wore a pair of oversized trousers and a loose-fitting blouse that had been lent to her, and her hair must have been at its most dishevelled. Anyone comparing the two women would have sworn they were different people. She dare not look in a mirror. With a renewed sense of purpose, she said, 'I won't let you down.'

Graham watched as Lovelace left his office. He took the photograph and placed it back in the drawer. Then, he took out a small box that was also in the drawer and opened it. It was a medal that had been awarded to him for outstanding bravery in rescuing two young girls almost fifteen years ago. The greatest reward had been seeing one of the young girls all grown up, sitting barely three feet away from him. He closed his eyes and prayed that taking her onto his team hadn't been his greatest mistake.

'Sir?'

He opened his eyes. Lovelace was back in the room. She looked different, but his foggy brain couldn't figure out why.

'Did you forget something?' He asked.

'Forget something?' Lovelace looked bemused. 'No..I..' She looked closely around the room. Nothing had changed, except the photograph was no longer on the table, and a small box was. Graham's whisky glass still had some whisky in it. 'Have you been working all night?' She asked. 'Have you not gone home yet?'

'Home?' Graham felt the fogginess even more.

'Coffee?' Lovelace asked. 'The morning briefing starts in twenty minutes. You look like you could do with a coffee.'

'Coffee? Yes. Thank you.'

Graham watched again as the figure of Lucy Lovelace turned and left the room. He now realised what was different about her. She was wearing different clothes, and her hair was almost tidy.

It had happened again. He looked at the clock on the wall. It was 6:41 in the morning. He had just lost another twelve hours of his life.

Nine

Detective Sergeant Spencer entered the Kidlington station much earlier than usual. He picked his way through the ever-growing throng of journalists that had been slowly growing overnight as news of the murder and kidnap made national headlines. Several regional and national TV crews were setting up at the front of the building, ready for the breakfast news.

Spencer went directly to his office, picked up several files he had been working on the previous evening, and poured himself a strong, sweet coffee. The ones from the machines in the canteen tasted mostly of burnt wood dissolved in stagnant rainwater, so he avoided them where possible. Armed with his files and coffee, he made his way to the conference room on the second floor. He found a seat at the back and sat down. The room was already packed. Detectives from all over the county had been drafted in to help with the investigation. They all vied for space on the floor. Spencer watched them all with amusement. They reminded him of a pack of hungry chickens picking at the floor for food scraps. They made as much noise, he chuckled to himself. Then the fox entered, and silence descended. One by one, the chickens took to their seats.

'Good morning, everyone. And thank you all for your prompt attendance.' Graham took the lead, followed by DI Luton and Laurel to his Hardy, DS Stanton. Spencer enjoyed watching people. They amused him.

'If I may start with an update on Detective Sergeant Wilson.' There was a long pause while everyone expected terrible news. 'Last night, Charlie underwent nearly eight hours of surgery to save her life. I'm pleased to report that the Doctors attending her believe the operation was a success and hope she will fully recover. I am sure you would all like to join me in donating to a fund to help Charlie's recovery. I believe the figure is already at five thousand pounds.'

There was a hum of approval in the room.

'DI Luton - if we could have an update on the search for Molly Parkes.'

Graham stood to one side as DI Luton took centre stage. Luton went into some detail about the lengths the force was going to to track Molly Parkes and the perpetrator of the crime that saw three people brutally murdered and a young girl snatched. The search of the countryside surrounding the Parkes' home had been scaled back overnight but was ramping up again as a new day dawned. Uniformed officers from the Thames Valley District and surrounding forces were being organised into search teams operating in a sophisticated grid formation covering almost a hundred miles of open countryside. DI Luton was hopeful that if Molly were out there, he'd find her.

On the front row, Lucy Lovelace sighed. She was sure they'd find her. But she was equally confident that it wouldn't be a happy ending. Every fibre of her being told her she was already dead, and the killer was escalating. She felt frustrated and impotent. She had spent her life working to this moment, and now she was here, she felt suddenly and inexplicably blind to the solution.

'I believe DC Lovelace and Charlie were working on a list of likely candidates from the sex offenders' register….'

Lovelace caught her name amongst the noises coming from DI Luton. She stood up.

'Yes. Based on what little we know about our offender, we were able to narrow the list to around a hundred and thirty men.'

'Good.' DCI Graham stepped back up. 'Let's divide them up between a dozen detectives. DS Stanton, if you could organise that? Two detectives per suspect. No mistakes this time. Keep your wits about you. Rattle some cages; let's see what type of animal barks back.'

The briefing went on for almost an hour. Work was handed out to senior investigating detectives, who organised and prioritised it among their officers. Every aspect of the Parkes' lives was to be examined in minute detail. Every work colleague, friend, associate, delivery driver, utility engineer, window cleaner, milkman or passerby that had a passing connection to the Parkes' was to be investigated and eliminated from the investigation. No stone was to be left unturned, and no potential suspect was to be left un-kicked - metaphorically speaking.

The room emptied quickly and noisily. Spencer filtered out with the crowd, largely unnoticed. He found a corner of the office where he could sit and wait quietly. He watched as Graham gave further instructions to his inner circle and then returned to his office. Luton and Stanton left the building, and Lovelace followed Graham into his office. She didn't look happy. Spencer moved closer to Graham's office. The door wasn't fully closed, and he could follow the conversation whilst remaining out of sight.

'So what am I supposed to do?' Lovelace asked.

'I want you here, where I can see you.'

'I'm needed in the field.'

'I need you here.'

'Why? What use am I here?'

'What use are you in the field?'

Stunned silence.

'I can help find the girl.'

'Why?'

'What do you mean why? Isn't that what we're doing here?'

Graham sighed. Spencer heard the frustration from where he stood. 'You know where the girl is, Lucy. You know.'

'If I knew where she was, I'd get her.'

'And yet you still know where she is. So far in this investigation, you've had your finger on the detail, and you've not been wrong. Tell me about Molly Parkes. Tell me where she is. Our suspect's in the house. His sole purpose is Molly. He waits. He kills two people who stand between him and the girl. Then he kills another girl. It's not the girl he wants, so he kills her. He doesn't think twice. No qualms, no hesitation. Then he finds Molly and leaves the house with her. Then what does he do?'

Lovelace paused for a moment to gather her thoughts.

'He takes her to where he's parked his car - or van.' She said at last. 'He drives away from the area, but probably not too far. He doesn't have to go too far. No one will start searching yet, even if they realise Molly's missing. He takes her somewhere nearby and rapes her. Then he kills her. She's the last witness. She has to die. He'll dump her body in a hedgerow or woodland. He won't bury her; he doesn't need to. It's a waste of effort. He'll have satisfied that darkness that overwhelms him, and she'll be worth nothing to him anymore. He'll dump her and drive away.'

'So why the fuck do you want to go looking for a dead girl?'

'You think I'm right?' Lovelace asked.

'Of course I do. So do Luton and Stanton. They're good coppers, and they're not stupid. They know they're looking for a dead girl, but they have to look for her. It's our duty, and we'll spend our resources on finding her. But I don't need to waste your resources on her. I want you to spend your time on him. I want you to oversee everything that comes through our door. Put it together for me, Lucy. I need your help to find our man.'

'What if he's not on any list anywhere? What if he's never been on our radar?'

'Is that possible?' Graham asked.

'I think so. If I'm right, if he is escalating, we'll find a trail going back months and years. Whenever he commits an act to satisfy his darkness, he gets better at it. It most likely started small and grew. He probably started at something small and not necessarily of great harm. Stealing underwear, stalking young girls, up skirting. Nasty stuff but not the nasty stuff. But as he progresses, he goes a little bit further. And every time, he gets a little bit better. He learns. And then, one day, he killed someone, and still, he didn't get caught. So he kills again and again and again. We probably miss the links because we're not looking for them. His darkness gets darker, and his fallow time gets shorter. The period between one murder and the next gets shorter and shorter, and the fact that he still doesn't get caught feeds his superiority complex. He now believes he's uncatchable. That's the man I think we're looking for. And I've no idea where to start looking for him.'

'And that,' said Graham solemnly, 'fucking terrifies me.'

DS Spencer pushed the door open and stepped inside Graham's office.

'Perhaps I can help?' He said.

Graham looked up. 'You do know that nothing good ever comes of eavesdropping, Sergeant Spencer.'

'Couldn't disagree more,' Spencer said cheerily. 'I always hear the juiciest things when people don't know I'm listening.'

Lovelace laughed. 'And to think I've heard people say you won't make Inspector!'

'I'll let me let you into a little secret,' Spencer said, 'it was me that started that rumour. That way, people don't push you into the job, and they leave you alone. Don't tell anyone!'

Graham smiled. He'd always had a soft spot for Spencer. He was disarmingly pleasant and cheery. But beneath that, somewhere very deep, was a sharp mind. Many a suspect had been ensnared by his seemingly innocuous nature over the years. He was a Venus fly trap disguised as a dandelion.

'So - what have you got for us?' Graham asked.

'Well…' Spencer started. 'Constable Lovelace came to see me yesterday and made me think..'

'No rank, Phil. You know how I work.'

'Yes. Call me Lucy.'

'Very well… Lucy. You said a few things yesterday that got me thinking. So I did a bit of research and came up with this.'

Spencer dropped a file on Graham's desk.

'What is it?' Graham asked.

'Thirty-two addresses in the Thames Valley area that your killer may have visited.'

Lovelace looked at Spencer in disbelief. Graham smiled. Sometimes it just needed the right person to trigger a positive response in another person. Perhaps Lovelace was the Watson to Spencer's Holmes? Or maybe it was the other way around? Whichever way it was didn't matter. He was pleased that Lovelace had finally lit the flame he knew lived deep inside Sergeant Phil Spencer.

'I put you onto that?' Lovelace asked.

'Yes, indeed.' Spencer said cheerily. 'You told me that Sarah Parkes had worried that someone had broken into her home and moved things around or taken small items of no particular value. It sparked a bit of a memory. A few weeks ago, I received a report from A DC, Sam Paton, who reported several similar cases across the Thames Valley Area. It seemed odd then, but I didn't give it much thought. Until that is, Lucy came to see me.'

There was a long pause while all eyes focused on Spencer.

'Now throw in a dirty white van with foreign plates. What do you have?'

'A dead end?' Lovelace joked.

'No.' Spencer said seriously. 'What you have is a burglar.'

Graham sat forward, his interest piqued. 'Go on.'

'You may not be looking for a sex offender or rapist or paedophile, or anyone that has ever been arrested for that crime, so you won't find him on any of those lists, but you may find him with a history of house-breaking.'

'Yes.' Lovelace exclaimed. 'Yes. That works. That actually works.'

'So the cat you're looking for isn't a lion, he's a common or garden pussy!' Spencer said.

Graham looked up, slightly bewildered. 'A what?'

'An ambush predator,' Lovelace explained. 'He smells their scent and waits until they're ripe for the taking. It's about power. It's not about sex, or children, or anything like that. I'd say our man's a very ordinary, unremarkable man with nothing much about him. He's probably meek. A small man. Quiet.'

Lovelace paused to gather the thoughts building up in her mind.

'Go on.' Graham encouraged.

'This is about power and domination. Domination over women. Domination over the women in our suspect's life. I'd say he was the child of a one-parent home. Just the mother and our suspect. And maybe sisters. There'll be little or no male input. He'll have been abused and dominated by women from an early age. Not perhaps sexually, but certainly mentally abused. Possibly physically. Always by the women in his life. He'll be afraid of them. And then he gets older and bigger, but he's still afraid. His mother or sisters will always be more powerful than him, at least in his mind. They'll be untouchable. So he'll get his revenge on them in some other way. He'll get his revenge on other women. Women he doesn't know. Women that can't control him. Women he's not afraid of. He would have started small, probably while he was still at school. He'll hide in the girl's changing rooms or their toilet blocks. He'll watch them when they think they're alone. He'll sneak a look at them while they're changing or on the toilet. It will give him a sense of power, and it will be intoxicating.

'From there, he'll progress. Slowly at first, but he'll ramp it up as he gets older and braver. The longer he goes without being caught will feed into his delusion. He'll begin to think he can't be caught. He'll hold this power over women, and they'll never know. It will bring him some respite from his home life. He'll watch women, stalk them, spy on them. He'll probably start watching them outside their homes through un-curtained windows. Until one day, he starts watching them inside their homes.'

Graham nodded. 'He starts breaking in.'

'Yes.' Lovelace agreed. 'Now, this will feed his delusions of power over women. Being in the same room as a woman who doesn't know you're there. It will be a thrill that he can't contain. It will give him some sexual gratification he can't get in a normal relationship with a woman. I wouldn't be surprised if that's the only way he can get off. There and then, in a room with a woman that doesn't know he's there.'

'Until one day,' Spencer continued, 'one of his victims discovers him. Maybe she finds him or wakes up to find him standing at the edge of her bed, masturbating.'

'And so she has to die…' Lovelace said, 'And so starts his slow ascent into the monster we know today. Every step he makes will be a learning step. That first murder will be riddled with errors and mistakes; each time he kills, he'll learn. Then, finally, he'll stop making mistakes, but the urge to kill will increase exponentially. So there'll be more murders in the last few years than in the first. And there'll be more to come.'

'But why Molly Parkes?' Graham asked.

Lovelace considered this for a second. Then she said, 'Because she reminded him of his mother or sister. Or maybe even his wife.'

'You think he'll be married?' Graham asked.

'I do. And she'll be just like his mother or his sister. She'll dominate him. Abuse him. Physically, emotionally and sexually. And when he goes out, breaking into his victims' homes, he'll be looking for ones that remind him of her. They're the ones that will have to die.'

'And this,' Spencer said, tapping the file on the table, 'is a list of addresses that have reported break-ins across the Thames Valley area similar to the kind of break-ins we'll be looking for. I've narrowed the field down to houses with remote access to the property. Houses that back onto fields or woodland. Our suspect would prefer not to be seen when entering his victims' homes. I've also included properties in built-up areas with concealed access. I've also narrowed the field by picking properties within a mile from a sighting of a dirty white van with foreign plates.'

'I thought that was a non-runner?' Lovelace asked.

'It was. I made a few phone calls. After further scrutiny, it would appear that many burglary victims have been aware of this vehicle but have not considered it worthy of mentioning.'

'That's good work, Phil. What about the other file you're holding?'

Spencer dropped the other file on the table. 'Twenty cold cases going back twenty-five years in the Thames Valley area that involve women being murdered either in their own home or taken from their home and murdered elsewhere.'

'That many?' Lovelace was shocked.

'Why twenty-five years?' Graham asked.

'Assuming our chap started as a young man, say sixteen years old, when he murdered his first victim and is now probably thirty-five to forty-five, I felt twenty-five years would probably catch any victims unattributed to a serial killer.'

Graham winced. He hated that term. It elevated them above the rank and file of ordinary murderers when they should be given no such credit.

'What made you pick that age group?' Lovelace asked.

Spencer smiled. 'I read your book.'

Lovelace looked at Graham and felt the rouge rise in her neck. That was embarrassing.

Graham pondered their evidence, which amounted to five-tenths of fuck all. It was all speculation. Guesswork. It was a good profile, certainly. The question that remained was, how good?

'How can a multiple killer, however accomplished, avoid detection for over twenty years?' Graham asked.

'He probably hasn't,' Lovelace said. 'Not for twenty years at least. I guess he escalated initially when he was young until a life event interrupted him. Maybe he got a good job, joined the army, went to prison, or married. Some life event that dulled his edge and threw some light over his darkness.'

'And now?' Graham asked.

'Another life event.' Lovelace answered. 'Most probably death in the family or divorce. Men with this kind of obsession can't deny it forever. It would have caused trauma within his relationships. It's unlikely he'll have children.' She paused to allow that irony to sink in. 'But he may have. But some major life event will have set him off on this trail of murder. He won't stop this time. We have to stop him.'

Not for the first time, Graham felt the weight of responsibility sit heavily on his shoulders.

'But where to start?' Spencer pondered.

Lovelace leant forward and tapped the file of cold cases. 'Here. In the past. We'll catch him here. This is where he will have made his mistakes. This is where we'll find the signposts to the present. This is where we'll catch him.'

'I disagree,' Graham said softly. 'I think you're right about finding the evidence in the past, but that's not where we'll catch him. Instead, we should look here,' he said, pointing to the file of present-day burglaries. 'This is where he is now and where we should start looking.'

'That's a hell of a task!' Lovelace exclaimed.

'It certainly is,' Spencer admitted. 'I don't envy your task one little bit.'

Graham smiled. 'Not just Lucy's task, Phil. I want you to work with her. Go through the list and poke about a bit. Dig around, and see what you can find. Get out in the field and start asking questions.'

'Me?' Spencer stuttered. 'That's not really my bag. More of a desk jockey, me!'

'Then it's high time you found a new horse to ride. I wouldn't want you getting splinters. I'm seconding you to work in the Major Investigation Team for the duration of this case. You're to work alongside Detective Constable Lovelace. I'll let the Chief Super know.'

'Really… I…'

Graham held up a hand. He dismissed Spencer's protestations. 'It looks like I may have found a corner of our world that you may be quite good at. I'm not letting that pass. You're to work with Lucy. Between you, I feel you may pick up our man's scent in no time.'

Lovelace stood up and picked the files up from the table. 'Shall we?'

Spencer sighed, defeated. 'Well, I suppose we should.'

Ten

'There's something I need to say.'

They sat in Lovelace's car in the car park of police HQ. Spencer had offered to drive, but Lovelace had overruled him on account that his car was a piece of shit. She used similar words and more. Furthermore, she had said, it was a wonder that Spencer dared drive it into police HQ for fear that a diligent police officer may have impounded it for safety reasons. Spencer could hardly find the words to disagree, mainly because it was largely accurate. He cared little for cars. They were a necessary evil which he thought little about beyond filling them with fuel and taxing them once a year. Lovelace's car, on the other hand, he admitted, was a suitable substitute. It was a brand new Mercedes A class in blood red, and what was more, it had air conditioning that worked. They were sat in the front seats revelling in the freshness when Lovelace said, 'There's something I need to say.'

Spencer waited while Lovelace composed her thoughts.

'My name is Lucy Lovelace,' she said at last, 'and my father is Jack Lovelace. Between 1999 and 2005, my father raped and murdered at least eighteen women and girls in a reign of terror that only ended with the murder of my mother when I was twelve years old.'

Spencer sat quietly and listened to the little speech that he suspected Lovelace had rehearsed a dozen times or more. Until yesterday evening, he hadn't linked the pretty, scruffy-haired young constable with Oxfordshire's most notorious serial killer, the Cherwell Valley Strangler.

'Any questions?' She asked.

Spencer nodded. 'Yes. Why do they call you Lefty?'

Lovelace laughed. It was a nervous laugh. 'Seriously? That's your question. I've just told you I'm the daughter of the infamous Jack Lovelace, and that's your question?'

'Well, honestly, I don't know your father.' Spencer explained. 'I was a beat copper in the day. I had absolutely nothing to do with the case. So until it was pointed out to me, I didn't know you were related to Jack Lovelace. And I don't care.'

Lovelace doubted that. 'But you read my book.'

'Yes, I did. Most of it. I downloaded it last night and speed-read most of it—an excellent read. Well written. I understand it was a bit of a bestseller. That explains the car.'

'It did do rather well.' Lovelace admitted. It had also bought her house.

'I found your criticism of the Thames Valley Police a little hard to accept, though I understand your point of view. You must have ruffled a few feathers amongst the powers that be. But, as I understand it, your father was a very clever and personable man. He managed to infiltrate the very murder squad that was investigating him. You can't help but admire his bravado. Imagine sitting in the very incident room in which the murders you had committed were being investigated. It must have given him a sense of enormous power.'

'Murderers are vain.' Lovelace said. 'They can't help getting excited about the discussion of their crimes. It gives them a notion of superiority. They will do anything to get information about the investigation or be part of it. All murderers will follow the news reports of the investigation. Some will even try and get close to the investigation. Some, like my father, become intricately involved with it. It should have been obvious to the real investigators that the murderer was close. There were signs. People's arrogance led them to overlook him for so long.'

'And yet they got him in the end?'

'At what cost?' Lovelace asked. 'More dead women. My mother.' She instinctively reached the back of her arm and felt for the scars. The fire her father had started at the house had wrought a terrible toll on her mentally and physically.

Spencer noticed the action.

'So why do they call you Lefty?' He asked.

This time Lovelace's laugh was less tense. Spencer was good at disarming people. Lovelace looked across at the man next to her. Everything about the man was disarming. His eyes, his smile, the way he spoke. For a man in his forties, he still had a wicked sparkle in his eyes. He was different from every policeman she had ever met, and she couldn't understand why.

'I'll tell you one day,' she said at last. 'Over a glass of wine and a takeaway when all this is long forgotten.'

Spencer said, 'That's a date. I'll hold you to that. So then, Lefty Lovelace,' he said, opening the file on his lap, 'which of these should we do first?'

***

Yan Kowalski loved and hated his job in equal measure. He loved its independence, the freedoms it afforded, and the opportunity it gave him to explore the countryside in his adopted homeland while equally deploring the habit the English had of giving houses names instead of numbers. It made his life difficult. He tapped the screen of his small portable device and read the name and address. Miss Sarah Lipton, The Green House, Eynsham Road. So far, so good. As he saw it, the problem was that the Eynsham Road was five miles long, with houses interspersed at irregular intervals along its length. Not a single one was numbered. Each one had a name. And sometimes you couldn't read the name because someone had planted a bush in front of it, the writing had faded, or it was a small nameplate with tiny writing on it set on a post two hundred yards from the road. Sometimes all that was left was a faded area where a nameplate once proudly stood. It was frustratingly tiresome. He had so far crawled two miles with his hazard lights on, pausing at fifteen different houses and driveways to try and find a single property. He had stepped out of his van five times to read a nameplate, and each time he returned, he slammed the door to his cab a little bit harder. Finally, on the sixth occasion, he stopped and lit a cigarette. His list for the day consisted of almost eighty per cent of named addresses. It was going to be a two-pack day and a one-bottle evening.

He drove along the Eynsham Road until he came to the next house. He could see the roof line of the property set back from the road, and trees almost completely concealed it. A small pull-off led up to a large wooden gate with no view beyond it. Even though his van was left-hand drive and he was as far away from the property as possible, he could see the nameplate proudly present 'The Green House.'

He pulled into the pull-off area and stepped out of his van. He walked around to a small metal box inset into a brick wall that skirted the property. He pressed the 'Intercom' button.

A few seconds later, a female voice said, 'Hello?'

'I have a parcel for Miss Sarah Lipton.'

'Okay. Hang on a sec.'

Yan heard a click and the faint whirring of a motor somewhere, and then the gate started to swing inwards.

He returned to his van and drove through the gates and around to the front of the house. The house, he noticed, lived up to its name. Unlike most houses around this area, which were built of Cotswold stone, this one was constructed of standard brick and rendered over. The render had been painted green, and the window frames curiously painted pink.

Yan exited his cab and opened the side door to retrieve Miss Lipton's parcel. He carried it to the front door and waited. After a minute, he pressed the doorbell.

To the right-hand side of the door, he noticed a plain pane of glass that looked through into the house. At some point, a telecoms engineer brought the telephone cable into the building and terminated the connection inside. Now, a broadband router stood alongside the telephone in its cradle. Yan was pleased to see that the router pointed into the house, leaving the back to look out the window. Working quickly, he pulled out his mobile phone and knelt at the window. He opened the camera app and zoomed in on the printed label on the back of the router. It had all the information he'd need - the wifi password, which the end user rarely changed, and the management software password, which the end user rarely changed, if they ever used it. Most didn't even know what it did. He stepped back from the window just as he heard footsteps approach.

The door opened, and a woman in her thirties appeared. She was wearing tight-fitting sportswear that seemed to reveal more than it covered and was sweating profusely. She was swigging from a sports bottle as the door swung open.

'Do you need a signature?' She asked as Yan handed over her parcel.

'Yes, please.'

He tapped a few boxes on the screen of his handheld device and pointed the screen at Miss Lipton. She took the plastic stick he proffered and hurriedly scribbled her name in the box.

'Thank you,' Yan said as he took his device back. He turned and pointed at the gate. 'Is there a code or anything I need to get out?' He asked.

'No. Just drive up to the gates, and they'll open automatically.'

She smiled a sweet thank you and closed the door.

Yan returned to his van and pressed 'Complete' on his device. The next job flashed up. Another named property. He sighed.

As he pulled up to the gates, he slowed down. As he edged closer, the gates started to swing open. He looked around for the device that was opening the gate automatically. They were usually operated in one of three ways. The first was some kind of motion detector pointed at a particular point in the drive. They weren't common, as cats and foxes could randomly set them off and open the gate. Some of the more modern ones were more sophisticated, but as it was, he couldn't see one anyway. The second was a beam across the drive which also suffered from the same problem as the motion detector. The most common was a metal wire loop in the ground that detected a metal field above it. It could only ever be activated by something metal as it passed over. He looked at the tarmacked drive and saw evidence of something being cut into the drive and filled over. He smiled as a plan started to form.

He pulled out past the gate and waited for it to close. He picked up his laptop from the seat next to him and opened it up. He clicked the 'Network Preferences' icon and searched for nearby Wifi. It found the network ID almost instantly. He clicked 'connect' and typed in the password. It connected instantly. He smiled. People never changed their passwords.

The distance between his laptop and the router inside Miss Lipton's front door was pretty long, and he didn't hold out much hope of being able to watch Netflix very easily. But that was okay, as that wasn't what he wanted to do. He quickly typed in the router's IP address on the label on the back and waited for the window to open. He typed in the management username, factory defaulted to 'admin' and then typed in the password. He did not doubt that this would work. If she hadn't bothered to change her router's password, she almost certainly never changed this one. He was right. Yan sat in his cab and smiled again as he moved inside Miss Lipton's router. First, he changed the management password so only he had access. Then he opened a port on the device to access the router outside the network, enabling him to log on to the router from anywhere in the world. After that, he had a quick look at all the devices that were connected. There were loads. Some of which were obvious, some not so much. He picked up two laptops, one iPad, three Android phones, several Alexa devices, two TVs and what he thought was probably a fridge. A couple of extra devices only introduced themselves as serial numbers, so he couldn't tell what they did. But there was one other device that he took particular interest in. It was 'Guardian', which was also the name he saw written alongside a Security box on the outside of the house and on one of the cameras he spotted while driving out.

Miss Lipton's home security was internet-enabled, and soon he'd be inside that, too.

***

Lovelace and Spencer plotted a route that started with the property furthest away from Police HQ. It was a small village approximately twenty miles south of Banbury. Lovelace drove with a heavy right toe and pushed the car rapidly through the narrow country lanes. After the first few minutes of driving, Spencer started to relax. He was always nervous as a passenger, and cocky young drivers scared him the most. He watched the young constable deftly manoeuvre the car through several tight bends and started to relax. She was an extraordinarily competent and smooth driver. He turned to the file on his lap and reviewed the cases he had isolated the previous evening.

The first one they were heading to was reported to the police four months ago. The complainant, Miss Laura Hampshire, had reported the theft of several small, expensive trinkets from a bureau in her bedroom. At first, she had thought little of it, thinking she must have mislaid them, but when she started to miss several other items and began discovering other things in places where she was sure she would never have put them, she called the police. Detective Constable Sam Paton made a detailed report and issued a crime number so that Miss Hampshire could claim on her home insurance for the value of the missing trinkets. In his report, he noted that there was no obvious sign of a break-in, and the incidents were so vague and random that he wondered whether Miss Hampshire had been mistaken. On a side note, he wrote that she had been extremely distressed and worried about the incident, mainly as she lived alone. As a result, DC Paton advised Miss Hampshire to make a few changes to her security.

Before they drove off, Spencer called Miss Hampshire. He said there was nothing to worry about; it was just a routine follow-up, and would she be in if they came now?

Spencer looked up from his files as Lovelace drove over the crest of a hill and down into a small valley. At the bottom of the valley, they drove into a chocolate box village of quaint, Cotswold stone houses, with a single post office and stores and a public house at the edge of a village green. It was the quintessential English village with well-trimmed hedgerows, expertly manicured lawns, and well-tended herbaceous borders in full bloom. Spencer remembered a Latin phrase he'd read in a recent book—Et in Arcadia Ego. Even in paradise, there was death. Had death stalked this village? Had death come here? Had Miss Hampshire had a lucky escape? Or was it something else?

Lovelace pulled up at a small cottage at the edge of the village.

'This is it.'

The cottage's front door opened as they walked through the gate at the end of a small path.

Laura Hampshire was a handsome woman in her early fifties. Though feathered with grey, her hair was still dark and hung freely about her shoulders. She had piercing blue eyes that still sparkled with youth, though the lines about her eyes told a story of age and experience. She smiled as they approached.

'Sergeant Spencer?'

Spencer held out his warrant card, which Miss Hampshire took and scanned.

'This is Constable Lovelace…'

'Come in. I've made tea.'

They sat in the garden in the lea of a vast umbrella that took the worst out of the sun. The garden was huge and went on in a straight line for at least the length of a football pitch. At the very bottom was a shed and a vegetable patch, as well as several fruit trees. On one side, the garden was overlooked by Miss Hampshire's neighbours and on the other, a tall, recently re-painted wooden fence bordered a field of corn that stretched out for several acres.

Miss Hampshire poured tea and offered biscuits.

'You said you were following up on my little burglary?' She asked.

'That's right,' Spencer said, leading the conversation. 'Purely routine, I assure you. We're trying to build a picture of this type of offence, and the type of person who might be committing it, to see if we can be more proactive in catching the person responsible.'

'Is it a very common thing?' Miss Hampshire asked. 'I got the impression from the young Detective who took my statement that he thought it might have been all in my head.'

'Might it have been?' Lovelace asked.

'It might - yes. Yes, it very much might have been. Except things did go missing. And I've never found them since. Small things, you know. Trinkets and the like. Rings and necklaces. Not the sort of thing I'd notice straight away. It's not like I came home one day and my television was no longer on the wall, or my car was no longer on the drive. These things you'd notice right away. It was things you'd not necessarily look for one week from the next, and then one day, when you did want them, you couldn't find them. It was frustrating, to begin with. I'd assumed that I'd lost them or accidentally thrown them away. So I accepted that it may have been my fault. That I was somehow to blame. One does get more forgetful with age.'

'What changed?' Lovelace asked.

Miss Hampshire took a sip of her tea. 'I came home one evening a few months back and thought I saw something, or rather someone, in my garden. Right at the very back. He just stood there. He was watching the house and watching me. I went next door to my neighbour who came round with his dog, but the man had made off. Over the fields, probably.'

Spencer said, 'You never reported this to the police? It's not in the crime report that you gave DC Paton?'

'It was one of those things, Sergeant. I'd had a few drinks that evening, and when you live alone, you do feel quite vulnerable. Richard, my neighbour, was very kind. He searched all over but found nothing. We laughed about it and put it down to an overactive imagination.'

'Do you still think it was just your imagination?' Lovelace asked. 'I mean. What changed? What made you think you had been burgled? Something scared you enough to call the police.'

'I didn't want to look silly,' Miss Hampshire said. 'It was nothing. Nothing much…'

'But it bothered you?' Lovelace asked.

'Yes. It bothered me very much. And I just wondered, you know, if they were related. And the more I thought about it, the more convinced I became that I had been burgled.'

'And what was it that made you convinced that you had been burgled? That it wasn't your imagination?'

'You'll think me silly.' Miss Hampshire said.

'We won't,' Lovelace said in all honesty. 'I promise you we won't.'

'Well…' Miss Hampshire gathered her words. 'I thought I could smell him.'

'Smell him?' Spencer asked.

'Yes, Sergeant. I could smell him. One night, I woke up thinking I could smell a man's deodorant. I don't have male visitors, and there's no chance I could confuse the smell with something else. It was very much a man's smell.'

'What did you do?' Spencer asked.

'I did what most sensible people do when they wake up at night and think they can hear noises or smell smells. I convinced myself that I was dreaming and went back to bed. In the morning, the smell had gone.'

Lovelace said, 'According to DC Paton's report, you were convinced that someone had been in your house. He said you were distressed and very worried.'

'Yes. That's true. I was. But sometimes, it's tough to explain yourself, particularly when it all seems rather vague. A few times, I have woke up to that same smell. Sometimes I have felt convinced that someone was in my house. I've had poor Richard over here several times searching my house. The poor man must think I'm quite off my head.'

So much for not having male visitors, Lovelace mused.

'And when things started to go missing or appear in places where I knew I would never have put them, I called the police.'

'According to DC Paton's report,' Spencer added, 'he advised that you make a few changes to your security. May I ask, have you done any of that?'

'Yes. In that, at least, he was very helpful. He advised putting some anti-climb paint on my fencing and some privet hedges on my side of the fence. They do have some very nasty thorns. I've had security lights fitted front and back, and I got a local security company to install some cameras, though I can't for the life of me work them out. Apparently, you can view the footage on an App. I'm afraid I'm not very tech savvy.'

'What was the name of this company?' Spencer asked.

'Guardian, I think. Something like that. They're based in Oxford.'

'Just a few more questions, Miss Hampshire,' Lovelace said. 'Are you aware of any other incidents like this locally? Any other residents complaining of anything similar?'

She shook her head. 'No. I can't say that I do. It's fairly quiet around here. People know each other's business.'

'And no burglaries?'

Again she shook her head. 'No. Not for a long time.'

Lovelace asked, 'And you've noticed no one suspicious? No one hanging around without any particular purpose?'

'No. Again, we're a small community. Things like that get noticed.'

'And have you ever seen a dirty white van with European plates in the area?'

'Several of those,' Miss Hampshire admitted. 'They're very common around here. Migrant workers from Eastern Europe mostly looking for work on the farms. Some of the delivery drivers use foreign vans. I can't say that one, in particular, stands out.'

Lovelace and Spencer got up to leave.

'Just one more thing,' Lovelace said as Miss Hampshire opened the front door to let them out. 'I wonder if you'd mind if we spoke to your neighbour, Richard? Just to get another view on your incidents.'

'I should think that would be okay,' Miss Hampshire said without hesitation. 'He works from home most of the week. And Buster's out in the garden, so I think he's in today. It's Richard Wilkins.' She added in anticipation of Lovelace's next question.

Lovelace and Spencer opened the gate to Richard Wilkins's house and walked up the path.

'Suspect or witness?' Spencer asked.

'Or unsuspecting participant in the sexual frustrations of a middle-aged woman?' Lovelace said.

'You think she made it all up for the attention?'

'I think it's a distinct possibility.' Lovelace said.

Richard Wilkins showed them through into a well-laid-out open-plan kitchen with a stunning view of the countryside beyond. His garden was as long as Miss Hampshire's but laid almost entirely to lawn with an uninterrupted view across the Oxfordshire countryside.

'How can I help?' He asked.

Richard Wilkins was early forties, Lovelace guessed. He had a pretty face with dark eyebrows atop even darker eyes. They were friendly eyes, Lovelace thought, and she could see why Miss Hampshire may have become besotted by her handsome neighbour. He was tall, with broad, athletic shoulders and a t-shirt that hung flat across his stomach.

'It's purely routine,' Spencer said, as if by rote. 'We're following up on Miss Hampshire's burglary.'

'Oh, that.' He said, surprised. 'Didn't think anything had come of that,' he went on. 'Bit of something and nothing, if you ask me.'

'What makes you say that?' Lovelace asked.

'Well, I think she's a bit lonely in that big old house all by herself.' He said by way of explanation.

'You think she made it all up?' Spencer asked.

'Not made up, exactly,' Wilkins said. 'Over exaggerated, perhaps. I think she wanted the attention.'

'Your attention?' Lovelace asked.

'Yes. That's exactly what I mean. I think she's always had a bit of a thing for me; she doesn't know how to get my attention. I've been around her house a few times in the middle of the night searching for some mystery man she thinks is there. And she's always wearing something provocative. You know, loose-fitting silky underwear and the like.'

'The sort of thing someone might wear to bed?' Spencer asked.

'Yes. Exactly,' Wilkins said, missing the very thinly veiled sarcasm from Spencer. 'You'd think she'd put on some kind of robe or something.'

'Perhaps if she's scared, fearing for her life, thinking that there's a man in her house, the last thing she contemplated before running to her neighbour for help would be her state of undress?' Lovelace didn't veil her sarcasm in the slightest.

'Oh, well, I suppose, when you put it like that. She did seem quite terrified at the time.'

'I believe there was a time when Miss Hampshire thought she saw a man at the bottom of her garden?'

'That's right. Buster and I gave chase. He took off across the fields.'

'You saw him?' Lovelace asked.

'A shadow, nothing more. Couldn't tell you any more than that.'

'But you reassured Miss Hampshire that it was nothing?'

'Of course. I didn't want to alarm her over something and nothing. Probably just a vagrant looking for food. They sometimes camp out in the woods just over the hill. I didn't want to worry her.'

'You never equated the stranger in Miss Hampshire's garden to her missing trinkets or her genuine fear that someone was in her house?' Lovelace asked.

Wilkins looked genuinely shocked. 'Good lord, no. Do you think they are? I honestly thought she was just being a bit absent-minded. At best, I thought she had a thing for me. I never thought for a moment...'

'Thank you, Mr Wilkins,' Lovelace cut him short. 'You've been accommodating. We'll show ourselves out.'

'You didn't like him very much, did you?' Spencer asked as Lovelace drove out of the village.

'Self-interested muppet.' Lovelace said. 'I think he loved the attention Miss Hampshire gave him as much as she craved his attention. And in the middle of all that, there's a possibility that a very dangerous animal got very close to Miss Hampshire. So close she could smell him.'

'Why do you think he didn't kill her?' Spencer asked.

Lovelace shook her head. 'I've no idea. Maybe she wasn't the right one. Maybe she had the security installed before he could make his move. But I'm certain she's had an unwelcome visitor quite recently.'

Spencer pondered that thought—*Et in Arcadia Ego.*

The following two stops bore no fruit. The telephone number Spencer dialled for the first one was no longer in use, and the occupants of the property were not the ones who had made the original complaint. They had no forwarding address for the previous tenants and knew of no burglaries in the area in recent months. The second property they visited had a 'For Sale' sign in the garden. Mrs Shaw, an elderly woman prone to gossiping, who lived next door, explained that the poor woman who owned the house had recently driven her car into a tree off the A34. Whilst the tree still stood, Mrs Ellington, a widow, did not. She died instantly, reunited once more with her husband. Lovelace suspected Mrs Shaw had much more to say, but they quickly made their excuses and moved on.

Slowly but surely, they made their way through the list, curving a haphazard line through the Oxfordshire countryside. Laura West lived in a small cottage on the edge of the Cotswold Hills. She was at least sixty years old, Lovelace thought, and proudly declared that she had

never been married. She had come home one evening
and suspected she had been the victim of a break-in.
Several items had been casually thrown about the place,
and she was sure that one or two items were missing,
although she wasn't entirely sure, as she was apt to
mislay things and find them again a few months later. A
smell? Yes, there may have been a smell, and it may well
have been a man's smell, although it wasn't a smell she
was familiar with.

In the next two hours, they followed up on a dozen
properties on the list. They could eliminate five of them
as they shared very little in common with the other cases
they were investigating. In particular, they were looking
for women who lived alone in a house with secluded or
protected access, had reported burglaries where little was
taken if anything, and where the complainant had
reported an unusual or unfamiliar smell. In some cases
they revisited, the complainants had been convinced that
someone had been in their house, although they couldn't
quite express why they felt that way. When Spencer
brought up the smell, they all agreed that there had been
an unusual smell. Musty. A man's scent. It had made
them feel vulnerable, but at the time, they couldn't
understand why. In all cases, the break-ins had been a
one-off affair or had ceased once the police had been
called. None had reported any further instances in the
last month.

By early afternoon they drove into a small town not far
from Oxford. It was a quaint riverside town with an 18th
Century stone bridge that joined the two halves. They
went over the bridge to the west side and pulled into a
car park.

The town had a bustling town centre which was
thronged with day-trippers. Bars and restaurants sat
along the riverside and down squat little alleys that

meandered off the main street. Down one of those squat little alleys, they entered a barber's shop called 'Snip Snip'.

It was blisteringly hot inside. All the windows that could be opened had been opened, and a door at the back had been opened to create some draft through the building. Five pedestal fans did their best to cool the air down but to little effect. In one corner of the building, a young man was having his hair shaved almost to the nap of his head.

A bright little thing at the reception desk greeted Lovelace and Spencer as they walked through the door. She was around eighteen, Lovelace thought. Probably the apprentice.

'Just a cut, is it?' She asked cheerfully, directing her question at Spencer. She barely glanced at Lovelace. They were almost entirely a male-centric enterprise, though they never refused a customer, whatever their gender, but the girl had seen Lovelace's hair as she walked in and doubted whether there was anything that could be done.

Spencer held out his warrant card. 'To see Sarah Finch.'

The girl turned on her stall and yelled through a door behind her. 'Sair! There's a copper here to see you.' Then, turning back to face Spencer, she said politely, 'She'll be with you in a moment, sir. If you'd like to take a seat.'

They stood for a minute before Sarah Finch appeared through the door. She was wiping crumbs from her tunic and chewing wildly.

'I'm just having my lunch break,' she said, waving them through the door. 'Come out the back; it's cooler.'

They followed Sarah through the door and down a narrow corridor which led out to a courtyard beyond. It was surrounded by buildings and cast in shadow on all sides. Lovelace was pleased to find that it was a good ten degrees cooler. There were several plastic picnic chairs in the courtyard, and Sarah took one and sat down. She pulled a packet of cigarettes from her tunic pocket and lit one. She offered the packet to Spencer and Lovelace, who declined the offer. Smokers were literally a dying breed, Lovelace thought.

'So, what's this about?' Sarah asked.

She sucked hard on the end of her cigarette and let the toxic fumes fall lightly from her nostrils. Lovelace watched her as she quickly took drag after drag before allowing the smoke to almost entirely encompass her. Despite the smoking, Lovelace thought she wasn't an unattractive young woman. She had dark eyes delicately enhanced by the make-up she wore and several earrings grouped in one ear. Her hair was long, tied into a ponytail, and streaked in vibrant blues and purples. Her skin was pale and untouched by the sun, which gave it an almost translucent look and her fingernails were tipped in deep blue.

'You said something about the burglary?' She asked.

Spencer pulled up one of the other plastic chairs and sat down. Lovelace remained standing.

'Yes, that's right,' Spencer said. 'We're currently reviewing some of our outstanding cases to see if we can't put some of them to bed. So we were wondering if you could tell us a little more about the report you made.'

'Is this an insurance thing?' Sarah asked.

'Why do you say that?' Lovelace asked.

'Because I cancelled the claim. There was no need in the end. They started ringing me up, all suspicious-like. Thinking I'd made it up for the insurance and then bottled it. The bastards put up my premiums.'

'Why don't you start at the beginning.' Spencer suggested. 'Tell us what happened.'

Sarah sucked the cigarette to the point that the flame touched the filter before flicking it into the courtyard. She took another out and lit it.

'Not much to tell, really.' She said. 'Me and this fella were knocking about for about a year before we split up. Then I noticed some stuff was going missing, and other stuff was being moved about. One day, I'd get up and find my toothbrush in the kitchen. Silly stuff, mostly. Stuff I couldn't be sure I hadn't done by accident. You know, like taking the milk out of the fridge and pouring it into your cup but then putting the cup back into the fridge and then standing there like an idiot trying to pour boiling water onto a pint of milk. You don't remember doing it, but you must have done. I once lost my fags. I spent a full hour looking for them. I could've sworn I had a new pack, but I couldn't find them. So I gave up and made myself a cup of tea and opened the fridge for the milk, and there they were, right by the ketchup.'

'You say things went missing?' Spencer asked.

'I thought so,' Sarah said. 'Sometimes, I'd just find them somewhere else. But then I lost my father's watch.'

'Your father's watch?' Spencer prompted.

'Yeah. It's all I have to remember him by. It was the most expensive thing he ever bought himself. He always said that wherever he went in the world, if he found himself hard up and in trouble, he'd always have a couple of grand on his wrist to help him out. So I was furious when it went missing.'

'You thought it was your ex?' Lovelace asked.

Sarah nodded. 'Seemed logical. He was a bit of a twat. He had a spare key to my house and refused to return it. I was certain it was him, so I reported it to the police and had the locks changed.'

Spencer said, 'None of that's in the crime report. Nothing about your ex?'

'I didn't want to get him into trouble,' Sarah said. 'I still love him.'

'Love?' Lovelace caught the present tense immediately.

'Yeah. We got back together.'

'And your father's watch?'

'I found it.' Sarah said. 'I'd never lost it at all. It was never stolen. That's why I cancelled the claim. I apologised to my old fella, and we just got back together.'

'You don't think he stole it to hurt you and then put it back?' Lovelace asked.

'I'd already changed the locks before I found the watch. So if he did steal it, he'd have never got it back in the house.'

'Do you live with your boyfriend?' Lovelace asked.

'Not yet. Hopefully, next year.'

'And do you still miss-lay things?' Lovelace asked.

Sarah shook her head. 'Not for a while. Not since I got back together with my boyfriend.'

Not since after you changed the locks, Lovelace thought.

'So there's been nothing for a while?'

'No.'

'And have you ever wondered if someone was in your house while you were there? Without you knowing, I mean?'

Sarah shook her head. 'No. No, I don't think so.' She stubbed her cigarette out on the floor. 'Look, I've got to go back to work. Is there anything else you need to know?'

'No, that's all I think.' Lovelace said. 'Except...' She paused. 'Would you mind if we spoke to your boyfriend?'

Sarah looked doubtful. 'I'm not sure that's a good idea,' she said.

'We're not looking to make trouble, I assure you.' Lovelace said reassuringly.

'If you did, I wouldn't press charges anyway.' Sarah said.

'Why would you?' Lovelace agreed. 'After all, technically, nothing's been stolen.'

'That's true.'

Reluctantly Sarah gave the address of a garage a ten-minute walk away. Her boyfriend was called Paul Harris.

Spencer bought them both an ice cream from a street vendor, and they followed Sarah's directions to her boyfriend's garage. It was a busy little place off the town's main road.

The boyfriend was a twenty-something young man with a mop of blonde hair and an angular, albeit greasy, face. They were shown into an office by the garage manager, who found Paul and showed him through. He wrung his hands nervously on an old rag as he entered.

'What's this about?' He asked.

Spencer explained the purpose of their visit.

'She's not brought that up again, has she?' He asked.

'It's just a routine enquiry.' Spencer added.

'I never stole anything from her. Never. Not once.'

'Have you seen the watch?' Lovelace asked.

Paul nodded. 'I've tried it on. It's a nice watch. I never stole it.'

'Not even to put it back later?'

'Why the fuck would I do that?' He asked

'Because, and I quote, you were being a "bit of a twat."'

There was a brief pause, at which point Paul smiled and said, 'Yeah, fair point. I was a bit of a twat. But I never stole that fucking watch. It means way too much to Sarah. Her father's death broke her heart. I'd never do that.'

'But you admit to being a bit of a twat?' Spencer asked.

'Yeah, I was.'

'In what way?' Lovelace asked. 'What did you do?'

'Look,' Paul said, picking his words carefully. 'I'll be honest with you. I thought she was seeing another man behind my back. It's what broke us up, to begin with. Of course, she denied it, but you know, don't you? Sometimes you know. It's like you can smell him on them. It's like he lingers.'

'His smell?' Lovelace asked.

'Yeah. Like, I suppose how women sense their men are cheating. Their perfume lingers. In this case, it was his aftershave.'

'And you smelt this on Sarah?'

'Yeah. On her clothes. After we split up, I let myself back into her house to collect my things, and I could smell him everywhere. She fucking denied it, but I could smell him. So I went a bit crazy. I started saying lots of crazy shit and sending stupid messages. I regret it now, but I was angry at the time.'

'Then what happened?' Lovelace asked.

'She accused me of stealing her watch. And I didn't fucking steal her watch. I bet he did, though.'

'And then she found it?'

'Yeah, that's right. She changed the locks, and then she found the watch. She came grovelling back to me, apologising and everything.'

'And you took her back?'

'Yeah. I love her. That's what you do when you love someone.'

'And this strange man,' Lovelace asked. 'Have you smelt him since?'

Paul shook his head. 'Nope. I reckon he's long gone.'

'And it doesn't bother you that she may have had another man?' Lovelace asked.

'Nah. No harm done. Not exactly squeaky clean myself! Had a free pass, if you know what I mean!' He added with a chuckle.

Lovelace and Spencer excused themselves and strolled back to the car.

'A pattern's certainly beginning to form,' Spencer said.

'There is,' Lovelace agreed, 'but not the right one.'

'What do you mean?' Spencer asked.

'So far, we could fairly assume that someone's letting themselves into people's homes across the district. But to what end? What's he achieving? He's not taking anything particularly big or expensive, and there doesn't seem to be any sexual motivation to it.'

'That we know of..' Spencer interjected. 'Perhaps he gets off on being so close to women without them knowing. Perhaps that's his thrill.'

'Perhaps..' Lovelace said doubtfully. 'But these are all fairly recent cases. With Molly, we see an escalation——a sharp rise in his offending. If the two were related in any way, I'd expect to see these burglaries happen last year, not this year. There'd be a curve in his pattern of offending. I'd expect to see one or two of these burglaries escalate into a sexual assault. Even murder. Only then would I expect to see a case like Molly's. I can't seem to tie in Molly's case with these cases. I mean, think about it. All the burglaries we've investigated today have been single females living alone. Molly lived with her parents. It's not the same MO.'

'It's also not entirely different.' Spencer said. 'And these cases we're looking at today are just a snapshot of all the reported burglaries in the region in the last twelve months. What if he's on some cycle of offending? He starts small, breaking into houses while the occupants are away, sometimes hidden in the property when they return, all for some power trip or sexual thrill. Until one day, he meets his perfect target, and she dies. Then he's sated. He goes back to being average Joe living an average life until he has to start all over again. And so the cycle continues.'

'I suppose..' Lovelace agreed reluctantly.

'So what we'd need to do is cover more of the past. Look for patterns of burglaries followed by a rape or a murder, a lull, and a continuation. The MO of the Parkes' murder is different but feels the same. The signature's the same. My money's on them being linked. We need to sew them together.'

'How many more are on the list for today?' Lovelace asked as they reached her car. She opened the doors, and they climbed inside. She started the engine and fired up the air conditioning. The day wasn't getting any cooler.

'Five more,' Spencer said, pulling out his file and running down the list of names. 'The next one's a Jane Wilson. Reported a break-in at her home a couple of months ago.'

Spencer dialled the mobile number on the crime report and left a message on Miss Wilson's answer phone. Ten minutes later, they pulled up outside her house.

It was a small semi-detached house of faded Cotswold stone at the edge of a small town bordering the northernmost point of Oxford. As they pulled up in front of the house, Lovelace saw a figure in the neighbouring house stand up and watch them through netted curtains.

'We're being watched,' she said as she joined Spencer on the path leading up to the house.

'This is rural England,' Spencer said. 'Of course we're being watched!'

They knocked hard on the front door and waited. Then, a moment or two later, they knocked again.

'She's on holiday.' A voice said behind them.

They turned to face an old woman looking at them behind thick-rimmed glasses.

'Do you know when she'll be back?' Lovelace asked.

'It's been a couple of weeks,' the old woman said, scrunching up her wizened face trying to remember. 'Actually, it seems more than that. She should be back any day now.'

'Do you know where she went?' Lovelace asked.

The old woman stared at Lovelace with piercing green eyes that looked bigger behind the thick-rimmed glasses. 'Who's asking?'

Lovelace held out her warrant card.

'The police? Why? What's happened?'

'Nothing's happened,' Lovelace reassured her. 'We're following up on a report Miss Wilson made to us a few months ago.'

'About her burglary?' The old woman asked.

'Yes. That's right. Did she speak to you about it at all?'

'She was quite terrified, poor child, although there didn't seem to be much substance to it. I don't think anything was taken, but she was certain someone had been in her house.'

'Did she give any reason why she thought that?' Lovelace asked.

'She didn't say anything to me,' the old woman said. 'But I suppose she must have had her reasons, don't you think?'

'Yes, I suppose she must.'

Lovelace turned away and faced Miss Wilson's home. She could see the letters and newspapers piling up through the frosted glass of her front door. There were many letters. And something else. Something that struck her as odd. She stepped up to the door and watched as something moved. It was black and solid and covered the edge of the glass where it met the door. Only it wasn't solid, she noticed. Instead, it was made up of hundreds and hundreds of smaller bits, all of which were moving. She dropped to her knees in front of the letterbox and gently pushed it open. The smell caught her at the back of her throat, and she felt the bile rise into her mouth. She'd met that smell before. She knew exactly what it was. She closed the letterbox and stood up. Spencer saw the look on her face.

'We need to get in.' She said calmly.

'I have a key,' the old woman announced. 'For emergencies only.'

Lovelace took the key from the old woman and slowly inserted it into the lock. She looked across at Spencer as she pushed the door open and pushed back the pile of letters. He had a fateful, resigned look on his face. They both knew what was coming.

The smell sat heavily on the stagnant warm air, gushing past them through the open door. A thousand humming blue bottles erupted from the floor and mingled in the air. They stepped inside the corridor, and Spencer closed the door behind them. As repugnant as the smell was, the flies were potential witnesses. Forensics would not be happy if he let them all out.

Lovelace shielded her nose with her hand, but it was futile. The smell was all-encompassing and powerful. They moved slowly through the house, carefully pushing doors open. She knew she'd found the place when she pushed open the last door on the ground floor. The noise was horrific. Flies. Millions of them. They both stepped inside the room and swept the flies from around their faces.

The sight that greeted them was almost as offensive as the smell that assailed them. The decomposing body of Miss Jane Wilson was lying on the floor, naked and bloodied.

Eleven

Dan Hodges watched as his wife got out of bed and walked naked to the bathroom. She had a good figure still, he admitted, clothed and unclothed. It had been the nurse's uniform that she had recently put on that had led to them spending the early afternoon in bed. Despite the raging heat of the day that beat a relentless drum on the windows of their house, they had spent an enjoyable, if somewhat sticky, half an hour making good on his promise that he would always want to have sex with her. Anywhere and anytime and in any manner that either of them desired. This had kept their marriage fresh and honest for so long. Even with the advent of two kids that had robbed them of their youth and their sanity at times, they still desired no one other than each other.

Rachel returned to the bedroom, retrieving her underwear from the floor. She sat at the foot of the bed and began to dress.

'I'm going to be late for work.' She said truthfully but with no real hint of concern. She picked her uniform from the floor and tried to shake out an annoyingly formed crease.

Dan flew back the covers of the bed and revealed his naked body. 'Sure you don't want to hop on for another go?' He asked.

Rachel slapped him playfully on his bare leg. 'You're not a teenager anymore, Dan. I'm not sure I could breathe life back into that again so soon.' She cast a lustful eye over his body.

He looked down and sighed. 'You're probably right. I might enjoy it if you tried, though.' He added hopefully.

Rachel climbed onto the bed and straddled him. She kissed him and said, 'The kids will be back from school in a minute, and I'm going to be late for work.'

She slipped off the bed and slipped her tunic over her shoulders. 'What are you doing tonight?' She asked.

'Yan's coming around in a bit. May have some work for me in Bracknell.'

Rachel held her tongue. She didn't like Yan. There was no particular reason for it, and he'd never done anything to warrant her dislike, but she had never really taken to him. He gave her the creeps. But ever since Dan had lost his job, he had been her husband's constant friend and supporter. He had somehow managed to put enough work Dan's way that they had managed to keep their heads above water. But still, there was something about him she didn't like.

'He's all right, you know,' Dan said as if reading his wife's mind. 'He's a good bloke. Hard-working. He sends most of his earnings back to Poland for his wife and kids.'

'I know. I never said he wasn't. Why doesn't he bring his wife here?' She asked.

Dan slipped out from beneath the covers and pulled on his shorts. 'She doesn't want to leave. With the money Yan earns here, she has a pretty good life over there.'

Rachel finished buttoning up her tunic, walked over to the windows, and drew back the curtains. The street below was filled with teenagers making their way home from school. She picked one from a group of small boys jostling each other across the road. He was small with an oversized rucksack and a head of curly blonde hair. She would know that head anywhere, the twelve-year-old head of her little boy. She watched as he crossed the road and walked up their garden path. She heard the lock turn and the door open, followed by an oversized rucksack being casually discarded at the foot of the stairs and the unmistakable sound of shoes being launched from sweaty feet into the hallway. Boys never learned. Moments later, she heard the TV being switched on and a games console firing into life. Even on such a hot day, the lure of his games console was too much.

Across the street, she watched as a group of teenage girls made their way down. They had discarded their school blazers and twisted their shirts so their mid-riffs were on full show. Those that wore skirts had raised them as far as they dared go. She was pleased to see that her daughter had resisted this urge and was still dressed much as she had been when she had left the house earlier that day. They crossed the street and gathered at the foot of the path to her home. As they did so, a dirty white van pulled into the road and stopped beside them. She felt her heart sink a little. Yan.

Despite her misgivings, she had to admit Yan was good-looking. He had a chiselled face with well-defined features and an engaging smile. He spoke excellent English and used his unusual accent to his advantage. The girls were used to Yan, and they all said hello as he got out of his van. They were flirty with him, as only teenage girls can be, and he played up to it and rubbed their immature egos. They jostled with him, and they laughed and giggled nervously. It was essentially harmless; she knew that. At least, it was from the girls' point of view. That kind of attention from a fully grown man made them feel older and more mature. But she couldn't help but worry about Yan, how he looked at them, and how he casually laid an arm across their shoulders. She watched as Issy broke away from the group amid a flurry of goodbyes and walked up the path to the house. Yan followed.

'I don't like the way he looks at her.' She said, giving air to her thoughts.

'What?' Dan said, dropping a clean t-shirt over his head.

'I don't like the way he is with Issy. He looks at her weirdly.'

'She's fifteen, for fuck's sake.' Dan said.

Rachel looked at Dan despairingly. 'She's not a child, Dan. She's a young woman.'

'She's a child. Yan would never be like that with her. That's sick.'

'I'm just saying that he looks at her funny. Creepy.'

'You just don't like him.'

She heard the key in the front door and the door open. Issy and Yan must have entered at the same time.

'I don't think we should leave them alone together.' Rachel said pointedly.

'You're serious?'

'Yes.' She said.

Dan knew his wife intimately. They argued occasionally and didn't always see eye to eye about everything, but that's what made life interesting. Their differences were often what bound them together. But on their children, they were always united.

'Okay,' Dan said. 'I'll make sure he knows he's not to come here unless he knows one of us are in. I'll talk to him. I'm sure he's just being friendly and means nothing by it, but I'll tell him we're uncomfortable with it.'

Rachel smiled. She noted the 'we're' and appreciated the solidarity. Then, she walked over to Dan and slipped her hands into his shorts. 'If you're awake when I get home, maybe I'll try and breathe some life into him?'

Dan felt his body respond, which was a pleasant surprise given that it hadn't long gone into recovery. He was about to find a witty retort when he heard footsteps on the stairs and Issy cry out, 'Dad! Yan's here!'

'I have to go to work.' Rachel recovered her hand and slipped into the bathroom.

Dan found Yan in the lounge setting up a game with Connor. He was friendly with his boy, too, but Dan had to admit that it wasn't quite in the same way as with Issy. Perhaps there was something in what Rachel had said? Or maybe they were just used to seeing the bogeyman in everyone these days?

'Have you got any homework to do, Connor?'

'Nah,' he said, not taking his eyes off the screen for a second. 'They didn't give us none.'

'They didn't give you any,' Dan corrected. He hadn't had much education, but his lack of care about English riled him.

'Well, if you already knew, why did you ask?' Connor replied, smirking.

Yan held up his hand, and the two high-fived each other.

'He got you there, man!' Yan said, laughing.

Neither of them looked up from the screen. They were as bad as each other.

'Right, I'm off to work.' Rachel had come down the stairs quietly and retrieved her car keys from the table. She kissed Dan and laid a kiss on Connor's head. 'Dad will make your tea. Be good.'

He nodded. Sometimes it was as much as they could get when his console was on. Rachel gave Dan a knowing look and left. Moments later, Issy bounded down the stairs in a pink bikini and a silk throw about her waist. She reminded Dan of her mother when she was that age. The thought threw him a little. He suddenly remembered what he and Rachel had gotten up to about his daughter's age, which terrified him.

'I'm going to catch some rays before it's too late.' She said as she glided gracefully through the lounge and towards the French windows.

Dan noticed as Yan turned his head and watched Issy open the French windows. He watched as Yan's eyes traced a line over Issy's figure.

'You want me to rub oil on your back?' Yan asked jokingly.

Issy ignored the comment, but Dan didn't. He'll have a word with him later.

Yan looked up and caught his friend watching him carefully. He said, 'You up for some work later?'

Dan nodded. 'Sure. I'll just put the kid's tea on, and we can head out.'

***

Sarah Lipton felt a cool breeze brush lightly over her forearm, briefly causing the hairs to stand on end. It had been expensive, but the little air-conditioning unit she had installed at her home office had been worth every penny, particularly given the summer they were having. She also had the foresight to install one in the bedroom and a corresponding unit in the basement, where her exercise equipment was located. Her friends had mocked her mercilessly when she had shown them what she had done. English summers were prone to being long and wet and were rarely warm enough or long enough to warrant such an extravagance. She smiled to herself as she recalled how those very same people were now desperately angling for invitations to The Green House so that they may take refuge from the intense British summer that was raging outside.

She typed a few more words into the laptop on her desk, re-read them and then pressed send, satisfied they were grammatically in order. There was a little 'woosh' sound as the e-mail departed. She wouldn't get a response today, but then she hadn't expected to either. She closed the lid of the laptop and picked up her mobile phone. She opened her photo app, held the phone upwards at an angle and took a selfie. She added a few words of commentary and pressed 'Share.'

Another day, another dollar. #workinggirl

Perhaps that had been the wrong hashtag? She nipped back into her post and changed it.

#hardworkinggirl

The responses came thick and fast.

Looking good, girl! Check you out! Are you done for the day? Kelly's crying off. Still up for the Refuge? Table's booked for 8! Gonna be a long night! Don't get a cab; you can stay at mine…

She switched off her phone at 300 likes and laid it on the lid of her laptop.

Even though she mainly worked from home, she had made it a thing to get dressed in the morning as if she was going to work. It added normality and routine to her day and helped her ease into work. Now that she was finished for the day, she relocated to her bedroom and slipped out of her clothes. There was enough time to shake off the day's stresses with a quick workout before she needed to get ready for the evening. She found a clean set of clothing she had bought for her exercise routines and quickly changed into them. She stood before her full-length mirror and admired herself in the reflection.

She wasn't in bad shape, she thought, despite her struggles. Certain parts of her body had failed to respond to healthy eating and exercise, and these she had adjusted with the help of a plastic surgeon. It had been tasteful and carefully done. It was barely possible to tell which parts of her had been crafted in that manner, and she had left her face entirely alone. It was the part of her that she liked the most and had not altered it for fear of making a mess of it.

She walked into her open-plan kitchen and retrieved an ice-cold bottle of water from a huge American fridge that sat in one corner. She returned to her office to grab her mobile phone and found it on the table beside her laptop. From there, it was a small stroll to her exercise room. She performed several warm-up routines and then fired up her internet-enabled exercise bike that stood on a small plinth looking out of a wide window onto the rolling Oxfordshire countryside.

She placed her water bottle on a table nearby and snapped a full-length selfie of her climbing onto her bike. She filtered the image to look more professional, faded the edges and added a small commentary followed by *#workhardplayhard*.

She watched as the 'likes' ticked up to an impressive 410, and the comments started to appear. She read a couple and then set her phone to one side. She'd go for about an hour on the bike before showering and changing. She'd be in town by 7. o'clock.

For Sarah Lipton, life was pretty good.

***

Even though Yan's van looked like it had seen better days, it never failed to impress Dan with how clean and tidy it was inside. Every time he had ridden in it, it had felt showroom clean. It was like that now, with a polished dashboard and pristine footwells. The afternoon sun shone through crystal-clean windows and reflected on almost every possible shiny element in the cab. Even the gear knob glowed. It smelled clean, too. Almost fragrant.

They drove through the outskirts of town with the windows open. It felt odd to Dan to have to sit on the right-hand side as if something was missing. When he sat in Yan's van, it always felt as if he should be driving, not be the passenger. It was an odd sensation he could never entirely reconcile.

They stopped at a set of traffic lights at a large junction. Yan whipped out his phone and opened up a social media app. He found what he was looking for and handed the phone to Dan.

'Look at the tits on that!'

Dan looked. She was pretty, he admitted, and they were a good pair, tightly wrapped in form-hugging lycra, which almost showed more than it hid.

'Friend of yours?' He asked.

'I wish!' Yan laughed. 'Wouldn't mind getting my head stuck into those!'

Dan handed the phone back. As much as he liked women and enjoyed the way they looked and wasn't averse to the odd pornographic movie, he could never quite grasp the pleasure of talking about real people in that way. It seemed impolite. He'd hate for anyone to talk about Rachel like that. Or Issy. So many men did, though, and it often felt like he had to join in. It was a bonding thing. He didn't like it.

'Who is she then?'

'Just some bird. Delivered a parcel to her today. She answered the door like that, with her tits out and everything. Reckon she was up for it!'

It looked to Dan as if she was only up for exercising, as the photograph showed her climbing onto an exercise bike in body-hugging clothes.

Yan scrolled through her pictures and found another. He gave the phone to Dan just as the lights went green, and they moved on.

'Read the comments.' He said.

Dan held the phone in his right hand and scrolled through the comments with his thumb. The picture was of the same woman as before, only this time, she was holding a young cat in her arms. The image had generated nearly 500 likes. The comments were largely banal and sycophantic.

'What am I looking for?' Dan asked.

'There.' Yan pointed. 'About halfway down. What does it say?'

It didn't say much, but what it did say spoke volumes. The girl in the photo would be out of her house around 7 pm that night and wouldn't be back until the early hours of the following morning. It was a girls' night out, and it seemed as though the celebrations would go on for many hours.

Dan finally clocked it. 'Is that where we're going?'

'Too right,' Yan said eagerly. 'You should see the house, man. Fucking huge! And it's about half a mile from her nearest neighbour and will be empty in an hour or so.'

Dan smiled and relaxed a little bit. So Yan wasn't just a perv; there was method to his madness.

'We'll go just as it's getting dark,' Yan said, knowing full well that it didn't really get dark at this time of year. But he was comforted by the fact that the Green House was nice and secluded and ripe for the taking. In the last three months, the two had successfully lifted nearly a hundred grand in small, fence-able items in the Cherwell Valley district.

It had been Yan's method in the first place to keep it small and tidy. In his job as a delivery driver, he was very often in a position to know when households were likely to be out or, as in the case of Sarah Lipton at the Green House, he was able to hack their social media and leave it to the owners themselves to let him know when they were out. Armed with their name and address and, in most cases, knowing what they looked like, Yan could stalk his victims and build up a hugely detailed action plan. Social media was the key that let him into their homes. He knew everything about them when they left for work, where they ate, where they shopped, and, courtesy of the habit people had of photographing everything they owned and ate, he was able to build a detailed layout of their homes and where their most valuable possessions may be. Dan had been a reluctant participant, to begin with, but needs must when the Devil sings, and Dan's needs had been getting progressively worse after he had lost his job. After the third night's work, Dan became a keen and willing participant. It was easy money. To keep Rachel happy, Yan lent Dan the money he claimed he was 'earning' while out at night and every month or so, Yan would drive back to Poland with a van full of supplies and return with a handsome cash payout. Once Yan had recovered his loan and expenses, the money was divided equally between them. Dan was beginning to earn some serious cash.

Yan pulled up at another set of traffic lights. 'Keep watching her posts. She'll let us know when she's left. We'll head over after that.'

Dan nodded. He watched as a small gaggle of schoolgirls crossed in front of the van. He looked over at Yan and watched as his friend followed the group of girls as they passed by. His gaze tracked them as they stepped onto the pavement and began to walk away from them. He was still watching them when the lights changed to green. The honking of a horn behind him woke him up. Yan put the van into gear and accelerated away. He laughed.

'Man, I'm fucking easily distracted!'

Dan had noticed. He was beginning to see all too well how easily distracted he was by schoolgirls. He'd need to have a serious word with Yan.

***

Police HQ at Kidlington was buzzing. Word had already spread that detectives had found another body on the Molly Parkes case. No one was sure yet whether the two murders were related, but when did that ever stop a good gossip? Outside, the press vans had started to multiply, and requests for official statements were flooding in. Alongside the local news, some nationals had arrived and were feeding off the frenzy. Murder was juicy. A missing girl and murder upped the ante by a huge mark, and another murder, related or not, put Oxfordshire at the centre of national news.

Detective Chief Inspector Graham watched the throng of reporters from his office on the second floor. Spencer and Lovelace had stumbled onto the discovery of another crime scene, and whether that was by luck or judgement remained to be seen. As it was, he now had a second live crime scene and a fourth body, all in less than twenty-four hours. The fan was beginning to spin rapidly, and it wouldn't be long before the shit went through it.

'Coffee?' A soft voice broke the silence.

Graham's secretary hovered at the door. She held a cup in one hand and some biscuits in the other. She entered the office and laid them on the desk.

'Thank you, Irene.'

'You're welcome,' she said.

Irene was a good-looking woman in her late forties and had been Graham's silent partner for almost fifteen years. She was not only his secretary and PA but also a friend and confidant. There was little she didn't know about DCI Graham, and what she didn't know probably wasn't worth knowing. She floated next to the desk as Graham stared out the window.

He had aged recently, she thought. He no longer walked with the purpose that had once directed his life. Instead, he seemed lethargic and uninterested. His shoulders slumped, and he walked slowly. His once full head of dark hair, peppered with grey in recent years, hung listlessly about his ears and lacked shine and vibrancy. There was a darkness about him, and it scared her.

'Is there anything else?' Graham asked, turning around to find that Irene was still behind him, watching him.

'Your appointment,' she ventured slowly, 'is in forty minutes. Shall I drive?'

'Cancel it, would you, Irene? Re-book if you can. Maybe next week. When things have calmed down.'

'Do you think that's wise?' She asked. Her voice was soft and melodic. It carried no strength, and it was often hard to determine her meaning when everything she said was said in the same soft non-threatening way. And yet Graham felt the words acutely. She had been the first to notice, long before it had occurred to him that anything may be wrong. She had picked up on the little things one doesn't see in oneself. The slight change in habits and actions and, occasionally, in how one said things. And

Irene had noticed. Of course, Irene had noticed. She was probably the best detective he had ever employed, even though she had no qualification to be so.

'There's been another murder,' Graham said, as if by way of explanation.

'I heard.' Irene said. 'It's all over the station.'

'I'm afraid it's quite urgent.'

'Do you think the victim will recover?' She asked.

'She's dead, Irene.' Graham said, looking at his secretary like she had gone quite mad.

'Good.' She said, not meaning it in the way that it came out. 'Then she'll still be dead tomorrow. But, on the other hand, you are still alive, and I'm rather keen to keep it that way.'

She stood at the foot of the desk and looked Graham square in the eye. There were few people in the world with the sheer strength of will to face him down, and Irene was probably one of the very few that he'd allow to do so without receiving a tirade of fire in return.

Graham smiled. Everyone needed an Irene, even when they were awkward.

'Re-book for tomorrow,' he said at last. 'I have to go to the crime scene. It's important. Make me a new appointment, and I promise I'll go.'

'Very well. Do I have your word?'

Graham's word was the mark of the man he was. Once offered, he never broke it. 'You have my word.'

'Good.' Irene smiled. Another day wouldn't hurt. 'If you don't go, I'll inform the Chief Superintendent and have you placed on indefinite leave.'

Now it was Graham's turn to smile. 'Do you know,' he said, 'I think you would.'

It was another thirty minutes before Graham managed to get to his car. He had made a dozen phone calls before he could leave the station. He had fended off requests for a statement from the BBC and other news organisations. He passed their enquiries onto the press office, who, despite knowing less than the office cat, had a perfect line in obfuscation. They would tie the press up with little snippets of nothing in particular while avoiding straight-out lies. Above all else, Graham had stressed, make no mention of a serial killer. The Chief Super had demanded to know what the hell was going on and why hadn't they found the girl yet, and did they know how much all this was costing. Graham rubbed his ego briefly and assured him he would have all the facts within twenty-four hours. He doubted the truth of that statement, and the only thing he did believe was that Spencer and Lovelace had stumbled on something important, and he was determined to get to the bottom of it.

Deep down, he fretted to himself that there was more to this case than met the eye, and he worried that there was, in fact, a serial predator at large.

He started the engine to his big cat and felt her purr. He slipped her into 'drive' and pulled out of the station. At the crossroads, at the end of the road, he stopped. No cars were coming, but still, he waited.

He looked up and to the right and then to the left. Finally, he pulled out and turned right, and headed home. He felt that there was something or somewhere he needed to be, but he couldn't think what or where that was. It had gone five o'clock, a bit early for going home, but perhaps it had been a quiet day. It had undoubtedly been hot. Maybe he'd have a salad for his tea? He had some prawns in the freezer, which he could defrost under the tap. He could almost taste them.

Without thinking any more about it, DCI Graham drove home.

Twelve

Darkness brought with it little relief from the heat of the day. On the contrary, it contributed to its intensity. The heat radiated from the tarmac in the street and hummed from the walls of the buildings. The night acted as a cloak that wrapped itself around the heat, and everyone gathered in the small house that once belonged to Miss Jane Wilson felt the cloying claustrophobia that went hand in hand with the presence of violent death.

Scenes of Crimes had attended the scene within minutes of Spencer's call to Graham at Police HQ. It was a high-priority call, and they responded quickly. The insects that had fed on the decomposing body of the murdered woman were collected in their thousands and transferred to the lab for forensic analysis. Jane Wilson was photographed in situ, and the forensic scientists tried to gather what evidence they could from her body. When they had completed their work, she had been carefully lifted onto a gurney and removed to the morgue, where an autopsy would be completed in the morning. A small team of forensic experts then went through Jane Wilson's home searching for clues as to her death. Fingerprints were gathered from doors, door handles, and windows at the house's lower part. Cups and glasses were examined in minute detail, and phones and laptops were carefully gathered and bagged. It was a slow procession of police officers and scientists that came and went through the blue tent that had been erected at the front door. A constable stood in a high-viz jacket, recording the visitors' names and rank and the times of the comings and goings. No detail was missed, however small. Nothing went unnoticed or unrecorded.

For several hours now, the street had been the focus of some interest from locals and passers-by. Television crews had caught a whiff of something exciting and pitched up at the end of the street, interviewing residents and recording pieces to camera. The crowd dwindled as the evening wore on, bored by the lack of anything interesting to see or film. The television crews remained. Some were setting up for the ten o'clock news.

The smell of death had largely dissipated inside the house, but no one there could entirely escape its presence. DI Luton and DS Stanton had arrived a couple of hours previously, and Luton had assumed control in the absence of DCI Graham. Luton was now the Senior Investigating Officer, and he dropped into the role effortlessly, much as Graham had intended him to do. Graham's absence was remarked upon but not dwelled upon. There was work to be done, and DI Luton was up to the job.

The senior forensics officer gave his verbal report to Luton and the team in Jane Wilson's kitchen. It was large enough for six people to gather comfortably as the house had been extended at some point, and the kitchen doubled in size. Spencer sat at the kitchen table next to Lovelace, drinking water from a plastic bottle the forensics team had brought. Walking around a crime scene in the blistering heat with extra layers of clothing was thirsty work, and forensics came well-lubricated. DS Stanton leant by the kitchen sink, which looked out onto a small courtyard. DI Luton stood in the centre of the room conducting affairs like a maitre d' in a posh restaurant. Professor Harris sat at the kitchen table opposite Spencer and Lovelace. He'd arrived early in the proceedings and leant a studious eye over the activities of the forensics team, to whom he was ultimately responsible. He had performed an on-scene analysis of the dead woman and waited patiently to give his initial report. He had been expecting another body quite soon but hadn't expected this.

The forensics officer gave his initial report while standing beside the fridge, drinking from a water bottle. There were no apparent signs of a break-in. There were no marks to speak of in or around any of the locks to the house, and all the windows and their attendant locking features were seemingly intact and undamaged. They had lifted half a dozen prints from various locations around the house and recorded those locations. They had taken a preliminary print from the deceased woman and were left with five unaccountable prints. Given time, and access to the dead woman's friends and family, he was sure they could eliminate most of the rest. Any remaining prints may well belong to the murderer. Unfortunately, he could not take any forensics from the dead woman herself due to the advanced state of decomposition. He passed any responsibility for that over to Professor Harris, who agreed that retrieving usable forensics from the victim during the autopsy would be challenging. He feared that any forensics would most likely have decayed.

'What can you tell me about time of death?' Luton asked.

Professor Harris hated that question. Forensics was an exact science, as all science must be, but stating an accurate time of death was fraught with dangers and contraindications. Jane Wilson had lain dead in her front room for some time, and combined with the intense heat of the last few weeks and the fluctuating temperatures inside the house, he was doubtful if he could pinpoint a time accurately.

'I can say she has been dead for a couple of weeks at least,' he said. 'Some of the insects we have collected may well be able to narrow that down for you, but I'm afraid it won't get much better than that.'

Lovelace said, 'She was due to go on holiday a few weeks ago. Her neighbour had assumed that's where she was.'

'That coincides nicely with this,' the forensics officer said, opening a large briefcase and fumbling around its contents. Then, finally, he found what he was looking for, tightly wrapped in a protective sheet, and handed it to Luton. 'It's a plane ticket dated almost three weeks ago. There's also a half-packed suitcase in one of the upstairs bedrooms and the usual gubbins that a woman like Miss Wilson would have packed for her holidays.'

Luton took the plane ticket. 'Any return ticket?' He asked.

The forensics officer handed Luton another ticket, also tightly wrapped in a protective sheet.

Luton read the date. 'The return ticket was almost a week ago. How come no one reported her missing?' He looked at Lovelace for an answer.

Lovelace shook her head. 'No idea. We've discovered that Jane Wilson was a freelance copywriter working for an Oxford advertising company. We've set up a meeting with the CEO first thing. Hopefully, we'll know more then.'

Luton passed the first plane ticket over to Professor Harris. 'This ticket was due to be used three weeks ago. Any chance our body could have been lying here all that time?'

Professor Harris nodded. 'Absolutely. I'd say that fits quite nicely. I'll know a bit more tomorrow when I've had a chance to get a better look at the body. Good witnesses, bodies. They don't lie.'

Luton dismissed the forensics officer with a simple thank you. Then, he held out his hand to Professor Harris. 'What time will you be performing the autopsy?'

'About 9 am.' He said promptly, forestalling the eager detectives' urgency.

'Good. Please let us know what you find as soon as possible.'

'Of course. DNA testing, toxicology, and the like will take a few days, but we shall know more tomorrow.'

Luton nodded. 'We'll need a cause of death as soon as possible.'

Professor Harris stood up. 'Well, I can tell you now that she took quite a beating to the head. Most likely with a small, rounded object, possibly a hammer. There's a burn mark on her neck, too, I think. I'll have a more detailed look at it tomorrow.'

'Like the Parkes'?' Luton asked hesitantly.

'Very much so,' Professor Harris agreed. 'But let's not jump the gun. I'll let you know more tomorrow.' He turned and smiled at the team. 'Good day to you all.'

'Bloody hell,' Stanton said after Professor Harris had left, 'You think they're connected?'

Luton looked across at Lovelace and Spencer. He didn't like Spencer much, and he didn't trust the girl. She was trouble, and he was useless. But Graham had sent them off on an errand, and they had come up with this. It was a damn site further than he had got with the missing Parkes' girl, and it annoyed him. The links with his case threatened to overtake him and overshadow his opportunity to shine. He needed to take charge, especially in Graham's absence. No one free-wheeled at MIT. Only the best could drive.

'Graham told me about your theories. Want to share them with us?' He asked.

'Not really a theory,' Spencer said, recognising in Luton the qualities in a man he despised. 'We just tried to work out what sort of man would break into people's homes and tried to find a pattern in offending over recent months that fitted that pattern.'

'And that led you here?'

'We identified a series of break-ins that followed a similar pattern of offending. We can't be sure if it's the man we're after about the Parkes' murder and kidnap, but we can't be sure it isn't. So we are building a profile of an offender that we need to catch bloody quickly.'

'Go on.' Luton said.

'What we do know,' Lovelace said, 'is that someone in the Cherwell Valley area, possibly the greater Thames Valley area, is breaking into homes while the occupants are out and, more alarmingly, sometimes while they're in the house. Of the several homes we've identified, we're sure the occupants have had an unwelcome visitor recently.'

'How does this compare to Jane Wilson's murder?' Luton asked.

'At the minute, it doesn't,' Lovelace admitted. 'Actually,' she said, correcting herself, 'it does compare to Jane Wilson; it just doesn't compare to the Parkes' murder.'

Stanton shook his head. 'What?'

'Like Jane Wilson,' Lovelace explained, 'all the cases we've uncovered have involved single women who live alone in properties with concealed or protected access. The Parkes are different in that the killer struck a house with more than one occupant. He took a huge risk, which doesn't fit the profile we're developing for the other cases. One speaks of a cowardly man that hides in the presence of women, who may or may not strike out when discovered, and the other of an incredibly violent man who is prepared to risk a fight with another man and woman to reach the object of his desire.'

'The Parkes' girl?'

'Exactly.'

'So you're saying we could be looking for two active predators?' Stanton asked.

Spencer shook his head. 'I don't think so. I think it's the same man. We're just not seeing whatever binds the two cases together.'

Stanton sniffed. What the hell did he know anyway? Spencer had no place at MIT. He wasn't even a good detective. Luton was having similar thoughts, but he held them back. For whatever reason, Graham had seconded him to the team, and he wasn't about to go against his wishes. You didn't always see Graham's master plan, but there usually was one. He said, 'So we just need to wait and see if the injuries to Jane Wilson match those of the Parkes'. If they do, we could have another serial killer on our hands.'

The words fell like a hammer in the stillness of the kitchen. The irony wasn't lost on any of them.

***

Yan pulled his dirty white van into a lay-by a few miles from the Green House. The night began to drop its shadow over the countryside, but the western skies still shone with vibrant reds and purples as the day slipped quietly away. Yan had scouted the area earlier in the day after he had delivered his parcel and before he had moved on to the next delivery. The lay-by was small and secluded and far from prying eyes. He had also kept off the Eynsham Road, hoping that his presence wouldn't be commented on after they had completed their night's work.

'Where is she?' Yan asked.

Dan opened up the phone and scrolled down Sarah Lipton's social media. 'She left a couple of hours ago.' He held up the phone for Yan to see. There was a group photograph of several women in a bar in Oxford. Yan smiled.

'Good.' He looked out of the windscreen and at the coming night. It was beginning to darken nicely. The shadows were starting to soften the edges and hide the detail of his surroundings. It would be dark enough when they reached the Green House. The remaining light in the sky wouldn't hamper them at all, and he was comforted by the fact that their target that night was a long way from its nearest neighbour.

Yan opened the lid of his laptop and connected it to the internet via his phone. He tapped away at the keyboard for a few seconds before smiling. It was all straightforward.

'What's that?' Dan asked.

'She has security at the house—a couple of cameras, one watching the front and one watching the back. There's an alarm, but I don't think it's connected to anything. Miss Lipton probably gets an alert if one of the cameras is triggered.'

'That's not good.' Dan said, slightly alarmed. The advent of small, cheap, internet-enabled security systems had muddied the waters for men like them. The ease with which these things could be installed and operated had made life difficult but not impossible. Yan had proven on more than one occasion to be a bit of a geek where these things were concerned. Dan often wondered if he'd missed his calling. 'Can you get around them?' He asked.

Yan pressed a button and closed the lid. 'Done. All switched off. Ready?'

Now it was Dan's turn to smile. 'Ready!'

Yan drove slowly away from the lay-by and headed into the Oxfordshire countryside. He turned onto Eynsham Road and drove a few miles before pulling onto a small pull-off. Two massive wooden gates blocked their route. Yan climbed out of the cab and opened the side door. He had had the foresight to disable all the interior lights on his van so their presence wouldn't be noticed, and he'd driven the last mile or so with his lights off. Dan was amazed that he had found what he sought in the dark. A few seconds later, Yan reappeared at the door holding a shovel. His face was now covered with a mask. Even though he'd disabled the security at the house, he couldn't guarantee there weren't other systems in place. Experience taught him that it was best to be careful.

'You drive,' he said. 'I'll open the gates.'

Dan slipped off his belt and slid across the seats to the driver's side. He watched Yan's form disappear into a hedge further down the lane. He waited a few seconds with his foot on the clutch and the van in gear. He'd feel safer once they were inside the property and away from the road. Even though the area was quiet, it wouldn't be that way forever. Sooner or later, someone would drive by, and he didn't want to be sat there when they did. He didn't have to wait long. Just as his nerves were beginning to fray, the leaves of the gates started to sweep open. He waited until the gap was wide enough before driving through. Yan was the other side, still holding the shovel in one hand and waving Dan over to a corner of the drive near the house. A few seconds later, the gates began to close again, and Dan switched off the van and got out.

'You never fail to surprise me,' Dan said quietly.

'It's easy when you know how,' Yan replied in hushed tones. 'A loop in the ground detects a metal field, so the gate opens when you drive up to them. They also respond to shovels!'

'Simple when you know how,' Dan agreed.

'Come on,' Yan said, eager to get going. 'I've seen a way in.'

Dan pulled a mask down over his face and followed Yan as he made his way down the side of the house. Dan noticed the place was reasonably modern as they edged their way to a side window. Even though it was dark, he could make out the green hues of the render, and curiously, here and there, the owner had trimmed the building in pink. He wondered how they managed to get it past the local council's planning department but then cynically remembered that money buys influence.

Yan stopped near a window that looked out onto a small yard. Dan noticed that the top window was slightly open. Yan paused for a moment before waving Dan over.

'Lift me up,' he said quietly.

Dan interlocked his fingers and held them down to retrieve Yan's foot. As he stepped onto his hands, Dan raised his friend towards the open window.

'Hold it there!'

Yan wasn't exactly a small man, and the muscles in Dan's arms flexed as Yan shifted his weight. A few seconds later, he relaxed as Yan suddenly pulled up his foot and vanished into the house. Somehow Yan had managed to push his arm into the top window and reach inside to open the larger window. As Dan climbed inside, he noticed that the handle to the window had a lock, and the owner had left the key in the lock. Sometimes people make it too easy.

Once inside, the two thieves took stock of their situation. They dared not switch on any lights, so they waited a few minutes while their eyes became accustomed to the dark. Now, almost instinctively, they began to work as a team, each man following his own method but complimenting the other as he did so. Yan stole out of the room they were in and headed upstairs while Dan took care of the ground floor. Even though they knew that the owner was out for the evening, possibly even the whole night, they had made a plan to cater for all eventualities. It wasn't unheard of for the owner to return unexpectedly, so now they expected it. Sarah Lipton's last social media post had been posted a few minutes ago from a club in the centre of Oxford.

Given that it would take at least thirty minutes for Sarah to run into a problem, change her plans and return home, the two thieves set their smartwatches to give them a nudge within that time frame. Once that had happened, the two would meet up at the same place they had gained entry and leave together. They now had twenty-eight minutes.

Yan moved swiftly from room to room, carefully opening doors and drawers to search for valuables. By the time his watch began to buzz, he had managed to spirit away nearly two hundred pounds in cash, a host of what looked to be high-value jewellery and three expensive-looking watches. He estimated the yield was worth a couple of grand in their pockets once other expenses had been taken care of. He returned to where they had broken in and found a shadow standing by the window.

'Did you get much?' He asked.

The shadow moved closer, and in the darkness, Yan could just about make out Dan's eyes through the mask.

'Not much,' he admitted. 'A bit of loose change and a couple of tablets. I did find this, though.' Dan held up a rusty-looking tin. He popped open the lid and held out its contents.'

'Fuck me,' Yan exclaimed, momentarily forgetting to be quiet. 'How much is there?'

Dan ran a thumb over the end of a large wad of banknotes. 'Dunno. A few grand, I reckon.'

Yan fought off the urge to do a celebratory jig. Time was up, and they needed to be gone.

'Come on, let's go.' He said, climbing through the still-open window and jumping onto the hard floor below. Dan followed, and the two of them closed the window behind them in the same manner as they had got in.

Yan climbed into the driver's seat and fired up the engine. The noise of the diesel engine starting always sounded much louder when they tried to be quiet. It always felt like the sound rumbled into the night, waking everyone up. But it was getting late, and Yan knew no one was nearby to hear. He waited until Dan had climbed in and drove towards the gate. The gates opened for them and let them out. Yan drove onto Eynsham Road, switched on his lights and headed back towards the city. No one paid any heed to the dirty white van with foreign plates as it mingled into the late evening traffic.

***

Detective Inspector French finished copying her notes from the day and leaned back in her chair. Had she forgotten anything?

On the desk in front of her were a dozen or more
photographs retrieved from the CCTV control centre in
Kidlington and blown up to capture a good image of
those she was tracking. Even though the cameras across
the city were state of the art, once a still copy had been
gathered and the image expanded, the resulting
photograph was grainy. If they had been tracking the girl
on the night, they could have used the cameras'
technology to zoom in on her face and pull up a decent
photograph. They could even have put it through their
facial recognition software to hunt for a possible match.
As it was, she was left with little more than a long-
distance shot in poor light. To make matters more
complex, none of the force's cameras had managed to
catch the girl from the front. She had been careful to
hide her face as she had walked around the city. French
had been lucky enough to stumble on footage from a
nearby off-licence which the girl had seemingly been
unaware of. The resulting photograph was still
unsuitable for facial recognition, but French was sure
she'd recognise her if she met the girl in person.

She successfully tracked Mark Pitts' movements on the
night of his murder. He had visited three local pubs and
a nightclub. The Rose and Crown had been his last stop.
All of his friends had given statements to the police, but
French doubted if any of them were entirely
trustworthy. Mark Pitts had led a criminal life, and some
of those he associated with that night were known to
the police. They were well versed in giving statements,
but French doubted if any of them had ever been a
witness before. Nevertheless, all of the accounts agreed
on one thing: the mysterious girl who had made his
acquaintance shortly before his murder.

She was about five-eight in height and of slight build.
She had shoulder-length auburn hair tied back in a

ponytail. She was late twenties, most guessed, although she had a youthful, fresh face, barely touched with make-up. She was pretty, too, and some of the girls in Pitts' circle of friends had been jealous of her and the attention Pitts was lavishing on her. No one was entirely certain when she appeared or even if Pitts had known her before the night of his murder. The consensus was that she had appeared by his side about an hour before arriving at the Rose and Crown.

French had spent several hours combing through their CCTV footage, trying to trace Pitts' movements. Finally, approximately one hour before arriving at the Rose and Crown, the girl appeared by Pitts' side. But something alarmed French about the footage. Before Pitts and the girl joined, the mystery girl had tracked Pitts and his friends across the city. She had followed him and bided her time. She had been stalking Pitts, monitoring his movements and activities. French watched as the girl tracked her prey across the city, watching and learning. She had carefully picked her moment and lured the fly ever so closely to her web. Pitts was out of his depth and just an hour from his death.

Try as she might, French couldn't find a possible accomplice among the hordes of revellers that night. As unlikely as it seemed, the pretty, slight young woman had taken on the powerful Mark Pitts by herself, cut his throat, dragged him into the open, and displayed him like an obscene shop mannequin.

French had gone through the female relatives of Pitts' most recent rape victim. There were loads but not one that closely matched the description of the mystery girl. Of the few that were similar, French ran into perfect, unbreakable alibis.

So French cast her net wider, pulling up previous victims' relatives and then the known associates of the crime family that Pitts had worked for. The former revealed no leads, and the latter was more complicated than it appeared. Although they were generally small fry, the crime family operated a professional outfit and had a tight, fearsome hold on their activities. As hard as she looked, French could find nothing about the mystery girl. She remained elusive.

But there was something about the girl and how she operated that worried French. There was something professional about her and the way she had tracked Pitts while managing to keep her identity hidden and obscured.

French closed her eyes and rubbed her temples. Had Pitt's murder been a professional hit? But why display his body in the way she had? Was it a warning to others? To the crime family? Or was it something else, something ultimately more worrying?

'Still at it?' A voice came from behind, jolting her back into the moment.

DI Frampton was the source of the voice, and he stood in the half-light of French's computer screen. Frampton had been French's first partner when she had moved into the Criminal Investigation Department. He had been a good mentor, and she had learned much from their time together. Although Frampton was a largely unlikeable character with a disposition for upsetting his colleagues with his abrupt and aggressive manner, French had a soft spot for him.

Age, French noted, had recently been unkind to her old friend. He had grown rounder and fatter through inactivity, and his face was beginning to show signs of heavy drinking. But he still had a wicked glint in his eye, and a swift and sharp tongue and French had no doubt the old Frampton was still there, underneath all that padding.

'I think I'm done,' French said, switching off her monitor. 'Fancy a drink?'

'You must have read my mind,' Frampton said. 'I could wash this bloody day away with a cold pint or two.'

'Tough day?'

'Not especially. Too bloody hot. Can't seem to get away from it.' Frampton approached the desk as French stood up, dropping her handbag over her shoulders. 'What's this?' He asked, picking up some photographs of French's mystery girl. 'Is this the Pitts' case?'

'It is. Lots of leads but no dogs to pull to heal.'

Frampton dropped the photographs on the table. Unfortunately, they were too grainy to get a good idea of who the mystery girl was. 'Witness or suspect?'

'Suspect, I think. She's the last person to have been with Pitts on the night of his murder. Pitts leaves the Rose and Crown and disappears down an alley, where we find him dead a little later. Mystery girl vanishes into thin air. I've got no CCTV of her after she leaves the Rose and Crown, and nobody can quite remember if she left with Pitts or not. I don't like her. I don't like her, and apart from this image from a local off-licence's CCTV, I've got no decent picture of her.' French reached down and held out the photograph. 'She conveniently hides her face from all the official CCTV cameras in the city centre. I got this one by chance.'

Frampton took the photograph and studied it in detail.

French said, 'And I've no fucking idea who she is.'

Frampton felt his spirits surge. 'I do.' He said. 'The girl in this photograph is Detective Constable Lucy Lovelace.'

Thirteen

The offices of Pendleton Banks, the advertising company for which Jane Wilson freelanced, were set deep in the heart of central Oxford. The building glowed a deep orange in the early morning sunlight as Lovelace and Spencer walked through the automated doors into a large, freshly air-conditioned reception. It was fully carpeted and laid out like an informal lounge with comfy chairs and a small sofa set next to a bureau upon which sat a drinks machine and a neatly typed sign welcoming visitors to make full use of its facilities. Across the floor, at the opposite end of the room, an older woman, fully attired in a close-fitting business suit with neat hair and well-manicured fingers, looked up and smiled as they approached.

'Good morning,' she said, glancing from one to the other but focussing on Spencer as she spoke. 'Welcome to Pendleton Banks. Do you have an appointment?'

'We do.' Spencer held out his warrant card. 'DS Spencer. DC Lovelace to see Richard Banks.'

Lovelace admired how the receptionist showed no interest in them, carefully concealing her interest behind uninterested eyes. She'd make a good poker player, Lovelace thought.

'Yes, of course. Mr Banks is expecting you. Take the lift behind you to the fourth floor. Mr Banks has made the boardroom available to you. I'll let him know you have arrived.'

Richard Banks came as a surprise to Lovelace. He was much younger than she had expected, with youthful looks set around piercing blue eyes cropped with a head of neatly brushed blonde hair. He wore a pin-stripe suit that looked as though it was brand new, and it perfectly complimented the athletic build of the man that wore it. When he spoke, it was with well-clipped tones and perfectly enunciated words. Lovelace little doubted that just a few years previously, Richard Banks had been schooled in one of the nearby universities and poured out into the world as a fully formed and well-educated adult. He gripped their hands firmly but not aggressively and showed them to the boardroom.

'Do come through. I'm afraid this has all come as a shock to us all. I could hardly believe it when I heard. Such terrible news. Poor Jane.'

He spoke humbly, and genuinely, Lovelace thought. It was easy for Lovelace and Spencer to take sudden death and the brutality of mankind in their stride as neither of them were strangers to the darker side of life, particularly Lovelace. Lovelace often wondered what it would be like to be ignorant of the world around her.

'Can I get you something to drink?' Banks asked.

They waited as coffee was brought in and laid on the large oak table. Lovelace and Spencer sat beside one another while Richard Banks took a chair opposite.

'I've asked all our staff to make themselves available to you this morning,' Banks said. 'I've cancelled all our meetings for the day so that we may be at your disposal.'

'Thank you,' Spencer said, 'tell me, Mr Banks, what is it you do here, exactly?'

'We're an advertising company.' Banks said. 'Except we eschew the traditional world and exist almost entirely in the virtual world.'

'The internet?' Spencer asked.

'Mostly.' Banks nodded. 'But anywhere that technology exists, so do we. We manage the technological advertising of several multi-million-pound companies across the world.'

'That sounds very impressive,' Lovelace said. 'May I ask who the Pendleton in Pendleton Banks is?'

'My business partner. We have an office in Los Angeles. He manages our US clients and East Asia; I manage Europe and the Middle East.'

'Can you tell me how long you employed Jane Wilson?'

'She was never employed by us directly. We employ several freelance writers and copywriters. Jane had freelanced for us for about six years, I think. I'd have to check with HR to confirm that.'

'What was she like?'

'A very talented young woman. She was well-liked by everyone.'

'And how often did she come to the office?'

'We meet every Monday morning, and most freelancers attend Friday afternoon. It's become a tradition to go out for a drink on Friday evening. I think colleagues who socialise together very often work better together.'

'Do you go to these yourself?'

'Of course. I'm as much a part of the team as everyone else.'

'Did Jane have any issues with any members of your team?'

'Not that I'm aware of. HR would know if there was an official issue. It would have been recorded. I'm afraid I didn't know her well enough to know of any personal issues she may have had.'

'You weren't that close?'

'No. Our relationship was entirely professional, beyond sharing a bottle of wine on Friday evenings with everyone else.'

'Can you tell me,' Lovelace asked, 'why no one in this office noticed that Jane had been missing for over three weeks?'

'I've been wondering that myself,' Banks said solemnly. 'We pride ourselves on being a bit of a family. Close-nit. I'm ashamed to accept that we should have noticed she wasn't here. Freelancers can come and go as they please, within reason. Jane informed us of her holiday plans and when she would be away, and she was pencilled in for this week's Monday morning meeting. I'm afraid we all assumed she'd taken another week off.'

'And no one commented on that?' Lovelace asked.

Banks shook his head. 'No. No-one. At least not to me.'

They thanked Richard Banks for his time and boardroom use and asked to speak to HR.

The HR Director was a small, mousey-looking woman in her late forties with grey hair and a lived-in face. She confirmed that Jane Wilson had been on their books for nearly six years. She didn't know her very well, personally, and had no reason to know Jane beyond her professional capacity. As far as that went, there were no issues on her file from or about Jane Wilson. To the HR Director, she was little more than a name on a contract somewhere. No one had raised any concerns to her that Jane had not returned to work that week and despite having one or two work commitments, as a freelancer, she was free to come and go as she pleased.

'How many people work for this company?' Spencer asked.

'In this country?'

'Yes. From this office.'

'Twenty in total. We have eight freelancers; the rest are directly involved and work out of this office. They are all here today.'

She handed Spencer a typed sheet of paper with Pendleton Banks' letter heading.

'That's a list of their names in alphabetical order. When you wish to speak to one of them, dial three from the telephone.'

On the table in front of them sat a squat-looking electronic device with a handset that looked like a telephone receiver. Spencer looked blankly at the device and then at the woman from HR.

'On this?' He asked sceptically.

'Yes. Just pick up the handset, and the screen will light up. Just press three. Is there anything else I can do for you?'

They said no, and the small, mousey-looking woman left the room.

Spencer picked up the list of names. Lovelace watched as he read the list of names in front of him.

'Where the bloody hell do we start?'

'At the beginning. Let's do it alphabetically.' Lovelace said, taking the sheet of paper and scrolling her eyes down the list. 'Let's start with Will Anderson.'

They came and went over the course of the next few hours. Every Pendleton Banks team member was professional, well-spoken, and dressed for the boardroom.

Jane Wilson had been universally liked. No one had any issues with her, and she was unaware of any problems that Jane had had with anyone else. Yes, they had all known that Jane was away on holiday, and they were all surprised that she had not returned to work that week. No one thought to raise her lack of attendance as out of character or were particularly concerned that she had not come back to work. Yes, in hindsight, it did seem odd, but although Jane was well-liked and a popular member of the team, not one person claimed that they were more than work colleagues. The term 'friends' was bandied about with little thought to what that meant. It seemed to Lovelace and Spencer that Jane Wilson counted no one within Pendleton Banks as her friend.

That was until they interviewed Stacey Wainwright.

Stacey was an attractive young woman of about Lovelace's age. She was graced with ebony black hair that hung thickly about her head in small, well-tended curls. She had the darkest eyes that shone from a sweet, innocent-looking face, and her skin was a deep Mediterranean brown. She had a sultry, dark aura that Lovelace found deeply attractive, and when she spoke, there was an inference there that spoke of a brilliant young woman.

She answered Lovelace and Spencer's questions fluidly and without hesitation. Her voice was silky smooth and tinted with the slightest accent that Lovelace couldn't quite place. She told the same story as everyone else in Pendleton Banks, but Lovelace saw something else. She saw pain. Genuine pain that couldn't be hidden from Lovelace's scrutiny.

'Jane wasn't anyone's friend, was she?' Lovelace asked.

'Everyone liked her.' Stacey said.

'But no one knew her, did they? Beyond the office?'

'Not really. Jane was a very private person. She socialised with everyone, but I don't think she liked many of them.'

'Did she like you?' Lovelace asked.

Stacey suddenly reached up to her eyes and burst into tears. It was the first genuine emotion they'd seen in Pendleton Banks since they had arrived that morning.

Lovelace stood up, walked around the table, and put her arm around the young woman.

To Spencer, she said, 'Get some coffee, would you?'

Spencer returned a few minutes later with a tray of coffee and several biscuits on a small plate. He was pleased that the young woman had recovered her composure and softened under Lovelace's kindness. He didn't like to see young women cry. It was one of the few things about human nature that got under his skin. It upset him to see other people upset.

'You must think I'm being silly.' Stacey said.

Lovelace squeezed her hand. 'Not at all. Jane liked you, didn't she?'

'I've not been here long,' Stacey explained. 'I came straight from university. Jane was kind. She took me under her wing and looked after me. We became friends. She tended to keep her professional life separate from her work life. I think I was the only exception.'

'Why was that, do you think?' Lovelace asked.

'I think I reminded her of herself. I'm freelance too. It isn't easy. There's a bit of them and us thing in the office. Jane protected me from most of it and showed me how to get along. We worked together a lot.'

'Did you ever go to her home?' Lovelace asked.

'Yes. All the time. My flat's very small and difficult to work from. We very often worked on projects together.'

'Did you not find it odd that Jane went so quiet for the last few weeks?'

'I did. She normally posted a few pictures on her Instagram page, but she didn't post once. So I said as much to Mr Banks, and I went around to the house a few times, but the neighbours kept telling me she was away. I feel so bad, knowing she was lying there all the time.'

'You shouldn't blame yourself,' Spencer said reassuringly. 'There was nothing you could have done. It's no one's fault that she wasn't missed. And actually, you did miss her. I'm sure that would have meant a lot to her.'

Stacey dabbed at the corner of her eye with a handkerchief. 'Do you think so?'

'I'm sure of it,' Lovelace said. 'Do you know if Jane had any friends outside of work? Any family? Boyfriends?'

Stacey shook her head. 'There's no family. Her parents were old when they had her. They died years ago. She has no siblings. I don't know about other friends. She must have had some from school and university, but I never met them. They probably only got together occasionally. Jane was always busy with work.'

'What about boyfriends?' Lovelace asked.

'There was one last year,' Stacey said. 'They split up around the time I met Jane, and she took me under her wing. I never met him, but she spoke of him occasionally.'

'In a good way or a bad way?' Spencer asked.

'Not a good way,' Stacey admitted. 'I suspected he'd hit her once after they had split up. She wouldn't admit it, but I was convinced of it. There were bruises she couldn't account for.'

'Do you remember his name?' Spencer asked.

'No. But I think he commented on one of her Instagram posts.' Stacey opened her mobile phone and began scrolling through the app. 'Here. This was Jane's profile.' She handed the phone to Lovelace, who began scrolling through Jane Wilson's posts.

There weren't many posts. Jane Wilson was very limited as to what she posted. She only had a handful of followers, and most of them only posted occasionally. She scrolled through a dozen photographs before finding what she was looking for. It was a post from almost two years ago. It was a selfie of Jane and a man around her age. They looked fresh-faced and happy. There were several comments below and one which mentioned the man in the photograph by name. Oliver Bowden. Lovelace passed the phone over to Spencer.

'That's been helpful, Stacey. Thank you.' Lovelace said. 'Just one last thing. Did Jane complain of anything in the last few weeks or months? Anything that might seem a bit silly or unusual? Stuff around her house, that sort of thing?'

Stacey shook her head. 'No, I don't think so. Although…'

'Go on,' Lovelace prompted. 'I said it might be silly.'

'It's not so much silly as not very important. I'm not sure it's what you mean, but about two months ago Jane asked me if I'd borrowed her perfume. She had an expensive bottle of the stuff that she kept for special occasions in her medicine cabinet in the bathroom. One day she went to look for it, and it had gone.'

'Did she get angry with you?' Spencer asked.

'No, not at all. She couldn't remember the last time she had used it, and it was almost empty, so she thought perhaps she'd thrown it out. She asked me in passing.'

'What made you remember that?' Spencer asked.

'I don't know. Except I'm sure I left some jewellery at Jane's house once. I stayed over sometimes, and I'm sure that's where I left it. I just thought that Jane had thought it was hers and put it away.'

'Did you mention this to her?' Lovelace asked.

'Yes. We looked through her stuff, but we couldn't find it. I thought maybe I'd left it somewhere else. So Jane bought me some new jewellery for my birthday.'

'I think that's all we need. Thank you, Stacey.' Lovelace said. 'If you remember anything else, could you call me?' Lovelace handed Stacey her business card.

'Of course.' Stacey folded the paper and slipped it into a pocket. She dabbed her eyes with her hanky and left the room.

An hour later, they had completed their interviews with the employees of Pendleton Banks, and Lovelace was back in the driving seat of her ruby-red Mercedes, weaving it slowly through the streets of Oxford. Spencer opened Lovelace's iPad and searched the Police National Computer for Oliver Bowden. The results were not entirely unexpected.

'I think we need to chat with Mr Bowden,' Spencer said, scrolling through his list of convictions.

'What have you found?' Lovelace asked as she slowed to let an Oxford Tube bus pull out.

'Our Mr Bowden's a bit of a bully. Three restraining orders from ex-girlfriends and two convictions for assault. One suspended and has expired, and one prison term for six months four years ago. Nothing recent.'

'Sounds like the sort of man I'd like to meet,' Lovelace said, and the statement didn't go entirely unnoticed by Spencer. 'Anything about Jane Wilson there?'

Spencer shook his head. 'Nothing.'

'So if he was beating her, she did nothing about it.' Lovelace said.

'Or she did what she should have done and left him.' Spencer corrected.

'And then he returned anyway and took his anger out on her?' Lovelace wondered. 'He certainly fits our profile of the sort of man we're looking for.'

Spencer nodded. 'He's certainly a person of interest.'

'Let's go rattle his cage, shall we?' Lovelace said. 'Have you got an address for him?'

Spencer pulled Oliver Bowden's driving licence details from the Driver and Vehicle Licensing Agency's database. 'It's an address in Witney.' He typed the postcode into the Mercedes' sat-nav. 'It's not far.'

Lovelace gunned the Mercedes' powerful engine past the Oxford Tube bus as it pulled into a bus lane. Within ten minutes, they had reached the Wolvercote roundabout in Summertown and the city's outskirts. She turned onto the A40 and headed west towards Witney.

Lovelace hesitated as she pulled up outside Bowden's home. The incident with Charlie was still raw, and with Bowden's record of violence against women, she didn't want to get into another confrontation with an aggressive man. She had no worries about her abilities to defend herself, but Graham's words still rang in her ears. *There are many people in the force are waiting for you to make a mistake.*

She was about to leave the car when Spencer laid a hand on her arm.

'Wait. Look.'

Lovelace looked up at the target house. A man in his late thirties dressed in shorts and a white t-shirt had left the house and locked the door behind him. He was carrying a large hold-all slung about his neck and a second, smaller bag in his left hand.

'Does that look like a man about to do a runner?' Spencer asked.

'It certainly does,' Lovelace agreed as she opened the car door and stepped onto the street.

Lovelace had her warrant card in her hand as she approached Oliver Bowden. She thrust it into his face as he closed the boot of his car, having just placed his bags inside. There was a momentary look of shock on his face, followed by resolution. Lovelace stepped back to make things easier for him and watched as an athletic-looking Bowden took to his heels and bolted down the street.

Spencer reached Lovelace just as their man took off. He looked at her, bemused.

'Are you going to run after him?' He asked.

'No.' She said. 'Are you?'

Spencer smiled. 'I haven't run for so much as a bus in damn near thirty years, and I'm buggered if I'm going to start today.'

'Me neither. The last bloke I chased got a broken face, and I'd rather this one had the ability to speak to us.' Lovelace turned and smiled at Spencer. 'Men think they can fight you because you're small and female, and then when they start losing their ego, insists that a girl can't possibly beat them, so start being even more aggressive, and that's when I have to hurt them. And then I get into trouble. So we'll call this one in and let uniform round him up.'

Spencer started to admire the young constable in whose company he had been so recently thrust. He had never enjoyed partnering with other coppers, preferring his own company to dealing with the egos and pissing contests of other men within his profession. Sometimes the woman were worse, constantly pushing to be better than the men. It was tiresome, and he never played their games. It had almost worn him out to the point of quitting. Graham had seen that and found a better use for his talents. It had meant working alone, but that had been no hardship. And now, here he was, enjoying active policing all over again in the company of a pretty young constable who was a brilliant detective, even if she did look like she'd just got out of bed and stumbled through a bush. Life was beginning to take a strange turn, and he was fascinated to see where it might go.

He had no idea how twisted it would become.

***

Sarah Lipton sensed something was wrong the moment she stepped through her front door.

It was nothing tangible. There was nothing she could immediately put her finger on and say, *this, this is what's wrong*, but she felt it nonetheless. Perhaps it had been the drink, she wondered, as she stepped into the house and threw her keys onto the small table by her front door. Maybe she shouldn't have driven so early after her night out in Oxford. She had gone carefully down the A40, taking extra care not to draw attention to herself, just in case. The country lanes had felt tighter and twistier than usual.

She felt a sense of relief as she clicked her buzzer, and the large oak gates to the Green House swung open and quietly closed behind her. Safety.

Perhaps that was all it had been. Anxiety coupled with a sense of foolishness and stupidity. She had felt okay to drive and couldn't have stayed longer at Claire's. Listening to her making love to her latest squeeze had bordered on embarrassing, and when he had suggested Sarah join in as they ate breakfast and drank coffee, she had taken her cue to leave.

Her house was quiet, and she liked it that way. The only noise she heard as she climbed the stairs to the first floor was the sound of the cat flap as Banjo came and went. She'd feed him in a bit. But, right now, all she wanted was a long soak in the bath and to climb into clean clothes.

She stepped into her bathroom and began to fill her large bath. It was a free-standing, Victorian-design enamel bath with chrome taps. She poured a large glug of bubble bath into it and watched as the foams began to form.

She removed the clothes she had worn the night before and donned a full-length white robe. It felt nice and comforting against her skin. She carried her dirty clothes downstairs and dropped them into a basket in the utility room.

Banjo was suitably happy to see her. He purred as he meandered through her legs as she made herself a cup of strong, sweet tea. She then opened a pouch of food for the cat and squeezed it into his bowl.

Once she had returned to the bathroom and turned off the taps, she let her robe drop from her shoulders and fall to the floor. She stepped into the hot water and slowly lowered herself into the bubbles. Within a few minutes, the heat had sufficiently relaxed her and she began to doze. She roused herself to drink her tea, then lowered herself back into the hot water. She was starting to nod off again when her sense of unease began to grow. She couldn't place the source of her anxiety, but it made her feel extremely uncomfortable.

She heard the door to the bathroom open. Banjo enjoyed bath time and often balanced on the edge of the bath and tried to eat the bubbles. She dropped one arm over the side of the bathtub and waited for Banjo to rub his nose over her fingers. But Banjo never came.

Instead, she felt something else. A hand. A man's hand. She felt his presence as he loomed over the bath, and everything she had felt since she had got home suddenly made sense.

But it was too late. The dark form lunged at her, and she tried to fight him off, but she couldn't get a purchase on him. She fought him desperately and with every ounce of her soul, but he was too strong. She tried to get out of the bath, but his hands clawed at her naked body, and then the blows started to rain down on her and slowly but surely, she felt the darkness come. And then she felt a pain surge through her body, and her neck burned. She resisted the lure of unconsciousness, but it was too much. She felt the futility of it, and she clawed the air, desperate to make her escape, and then the final blow came, and everything went dark, and she toppled out of the bath.

***

'I'll drive you.' Irene, DCI Graham's secretary, said as he dropped his jacket over his shoulders. It was too hot to wear a coat, but he always felt undressed without it.

'I'm perfectly capable of driving myself,' Graham responded, slightly irritated.

'I know,' Irene said, 'Like yesterday when you drove yourself to a crime scene and drove home instead.'

'I had things on my mind. I got confused.' It pained him to admit weakness, but it didn't matter with Irene. She knew everything anyway.

'And that's why I'm driving you.' She said with an air of finality he knew was foolish to challenge. 'Your appointment's at 5:30. If we leave now, you can buy me a coffee at their nice little coffee shop.'

Yes, he thought, that nice little coffee shop at the hospital where people wait to get bad news. I'm afraid your wife has four weeks to live. Would you like a cookie with your caramel latte? Graham hated hospitals. Perhaps it was better if Irene did drive. He wasn't entirely convinced that if he drove himself, he wouldn't just go to Scotland instead. Much nicer scenery. Much less stress.

It was probably stress, anyway. Stress did that. And he did have a stressful job.

'Fine.' He said, handing over his keys. 'You drive.'

They were at the front doors to Police HQ. Irene could just about see Graham's big car in the car park.

'Guv'!'

Irene sighed. It sounded urgent. She could hear the inflexion in the voice. Graham could only be manipulated so far. When it came to work, everything else came second. She knew instinctively that there would be no point in arguing.

They turned to see Stanton standing behind them. There was a look of urgency on his face.

'Guv'. They've found a body.'

Graham looked at Irene, who sighed again. 'I'll re-book for tomorrow.' She handed the car keys to Stanton. 'Don't let him drive.'

Fourteen

Several questions bothered DI Alison French. The first of which, and the one that had kept her up half the night, was whether or not the girl in the photograph was Constable Lucy Lovelace. Frampton had been convinced. He had met her and seen what she could do when fired up. Novak had been high on drugs and was built like a weightlifter, and Lovelace had taken him down with ease. There was no doubt in DI French's mind that she was undoubtedly a capable young woman and a woman capable of a high level of violence, but with Novak, she had been fighting for her and her colleague's life. Was Lucy Lovelace capable of cold-blooded murder against a defenceless man?

French shook her head. She didn't know. But the question remained. Was the woman in the photograph that they had captured from an off-licence CCTV Detective Constable Lucy Lovelace?

French had taken the image to the tech guys and tried to improve it, but she was still left with a grainy, black-and-white image. They had taken the image and tried to run it through facial recognition, but it had come to nothing. French took a photograph of Lovelace and ran that through the same facial recognition software, but the CCTV image was too poor to make a positive match. Frampton's identification of Lovelace was good, dependable, and based on an experienced officer's professional eye. Frampton had made a career out of never forgetting a face and being able to spot a suspect in a crowd of thousands, but even he had urged caution.

'Don't go in all guns blazing. You'll need more than just my ID. Go to DCI Graham with anything less than a closed case, and he'll destroy you. You need more. You need to go digging.'

So French had done precisely that. She started digging.

The Lovelaces' history was a matter of record. Fifteen years ago, Jack Lovelace, known as the 'Cherwell Valley Strangler', had been given a whole life term at The Old Bailey for the rape and murder of fifteen women. He had been further convicted of the murder of his wife and attempted murder of his daughters, Zoe and Lucy. After the trial, Jack Lovelace's sister and her husband formally adopted the two girls and flew them to Japan, where they completed their school education. Both girls were educated at a university in Tokyo before Lucy returned to the UK, changed her name back to Lovelace, attended Oxford University to study a PhD in criminal psychology, wrote a bestselling book and joined the Thames Valley Police. Nothing in Lovelace's history suggested a woman capable of such a senseless murder.

Late the previous evening, French had downloaded Lovelace's book to her Kindle and retired to bed with it and a bottle of wine. She didn't know what she hoped to find. Some insight into Lovelace? A motive for why she might want to kill a man she had never met before?

On her way to work that morning, she called in at a bookshop and bought a physical copy of the book. It sat on the table in front of French with several dozen Post-it notes placed at important intervals. Digital was okay, but you couldn't write notes in the margin.

The book itself was well-written and well-researched. It tracked the life of Jack Lovelace from a professional man and father of two to a twisted and desperate serial killer who went on to murder his wife and attempted to kill his children. Lucy Lovelace treated the subject with great compassion and understanding and tried to find a deeper understanding of men like her father. She spoke of his victims with an almost tangible sense of regret and remorse, as though she, Lucy Lovelace, was somehow responsible or linked to their deaths. She sought to find the answer to his murderous spree for herself and her father's victims. In that, it felt as though she had failed. She couldn't find the answer. Perhaps there wasn't one.

However, an overriding theme throughout the book had been Lovelace's contempt and anger at the police for their failure to catch her father early on in his reign of terror. If anyone had been at fault, it had been the Thames Valley Police and bit by bit, she dismantled the way they handled the investigation and held up their failures for the world to see.

And then Lucy Lovelace joined the force.

A great deal didn't make any sense to DI French. Lovelace had no reason to join the force she despised, so why had she? What drove a young woman whose father had raped and murdered women like herself, some of whom were not much older than Lucy had been when her father had been arrested, to return to the UK, revert her name to Lovelace, and join the Thames Valley Police?

Was it revenge? Was Lovelace somehow seeking to make amends for the sins of her father by learning to catch other men like him? Or did it go deeper than that? If the law couldn't touch men like Mark Pitts, could Lucy Lovelace? Did she murder him to avenge his victims, to make amends for her father's crimes?

French sighed. It was getting far-fetched. It was all very 'Dexter-esque.' But she couldn't entirely escape the feeling that Lovelace's motives for studying criminology and criminal psychology and joining the police were part of a greater purpose.

But what was that greater purpose?

'By the look of the body and the advanced state of decomposition, I'd say she probably died within an hour of being kidnapped.' Professor Harris gave his determination in a sombre monotone voice edged with genuine sadness. He had been expecting this, but the discovery of the girl's body earlier that afternoon brought little solace. Two dog walkers who had strayed from a nearby public footpath found her lying face down in a shallow ditch with a small brook that trickled beneath her. She was completely naked save for a single sock, and a hammer-like instrument had severely battered her head. There was the suspicion of a burn on her neck. There was evidence that she had been raped, but Professor Harris couldn't confirm this. Any DNA evidence would most likely have been washed away by the water that trickled underneath her.

Across the fields that stretched out in every direction, a hundred police officers and forensics officers were spreading out, looking for evidence. A helicopter buzzed in the sky above them.

DI Luton had taken charge of the crime scene the moment he arrived. DS Stanton had arrived shortly after him with DCI Graham, and Lovelace and Spencer had found the crime scene shortly after that.

A country lane meandered near where the girl's body had been found, but not close enough for anyone who used it to see the poor girl. There was a bridleway that crossed the road approximately two hundred yards away. It left the road and sloped gently away and down the hill within a few metres of the crime scene. The bridleway was large enough for a vehicle to drive down unnoticed. At the bottom of the hill, where they were all now gathered, there was no possibility of being seen from the road as it turned away and disappeared behind the brow of another hill. It was the perfect location for the killer to have chosen, and that local knowledge didn't go unnoticed by Lovelace. As the crow flew, the crime scene was little more than a mile from where Molly Parkes had been taken.

Professor Harris dabbed his brow with a small hanky.

DI Luton gave voice to the question on everyone's lips. 'Are we sure this is her this time? Are we sure this is Molly Parkes?'

Professor Harris nodded solemnly. 'I am one hundred per cent certain that this is Molly Parkes. We'll need to do a formal identification, of course. I've had hair samples taken for DNA analysis, and we'll compare them with the DNA from her parents. But even without that, I'm positive this girl is Molly Parkes.'

'Very well,' Graham said. 'Then let's start showing this poor girl some of the respect that her killer couldn't afford her while she was alive.'

He waved over two waiting men with a body bag and a stretcher. They carefully picked the small girl up and tenderly wrapped her in a large white sheet before laying her into the body bag. Then, they lifted her onto the stretcher and walked the few meters to the bridleway, where an unmarked private ambulance waited to whisk the dead girl to the morgue. The team of detectives and Professor Harris walked respectfully behind and watched as the ambulance pulled away and drove slowly back up the bridleway to the road.

'He picked a good spot.' Lovelace remarked as the ambulance reached the road and disappeared from view.

'He had all the time in the world here. No one would have seen him.'

'You would never have found this spot by luck. Not in the dark.' Spencer added.

'He has local knowledge, that's for sure.' Graham agreed. 'Whoever we are after knows his territory well. He's an Oxfordshire man. I'm certain of that.'

'Well, that narrows the field somewhat,' Luton remarked dryly.

DCI Graham ignored the comment. He was fully aware of how complex the case was becoming and was even more profoundly aware of the difficulty in narrowing down their field of suspects. What bothered him even more, was that there weren't any suspects. They now had five bodies - Mr and Mrs Parkes, their daughter Molly, Molly's friend Bethany Wright and Jane Wilson. And to cap it all off, he wasn't entirely convinced they were all by the same hand, which compounded his difficulties even more. When you added to the mix an infuriated Chief Superintendent complaining of spiralling costs and no results and a national media that was beginning to pick up the scent of a serial killer story, it was hard not to believe that the shit was about to hit the fan.

Graham looked across at DC Lovelace. She would either be the thing that destroyed his career or made him a legend in the force. The jury was still out on which way that may go. The serial killer angle was beginning to bother him. If the press found out that the daughter of Jack Lovelace, Oxfordshire's most prolific serial killer, was working on the case, they would tear him apart. So he somehow needed to get a grip on the case and fast.

'Where are we with the Wilson investigation?' He asked.

'We've named Oliver Bowden as a person of interest in her murder.' Spencer said. 'We haven't overtly accused him or named him a suspect, but we're hoping that if someone is hiding him, it might scare them into giving him up.'

'How are you getting on with the burglary aspect? Any new leads?'

'Nothing new.' Lovelace admitted. 'Nothing tangible, but I think we're onto something. There's something there, but the threads are so bare it's hard to tie them together.'

'You reckon there's something in this perv that's breaking into people's homes? You don't think it's just some kid fucking around for shits and giggles?' Stanton asked.

'I do think there's something in it, and no, I don't think it's a kid doing it for kicks.' Lovelace said. 'This man breaks in when people are at home or before they are home and waits for them to return. That takes a special kind of nerve. I don't think a kid is going to get off on that. And he takes things, little things. Keepsakes and mementoes. And then, now and then, for reasons we don't yet understand, he strikes out and rapes and kills his target.'

Luton said, 'But how does that tie in with the Parkes'? The MO is different. It's not a single female living alone.'

'I think they're connected.' Spencer said. 'I think it's the same offender.'

'That's easy to say,' Luton said, 'but can you back it up with a fact?'

'No. Not yet.' Lovelace said. 'But I agree with Phil. It's the same signature. I think the killer has escalated. He's grown and adapted. He's changed, and his methods are changing. He's getting better at his work, and his confidence is growing. If anything, he's becoming more dangerous.'

'So no one's safe?' Luton asked.

'No. Females, in particular, are at increased risk, but any man that stands in his way will get the same treatment. He's targeted single females so far, but if the Parkes' case is connected, he'll target anyone.'

'Do I have any good news to go to the Chief Super with?' Graham asked.

He was hit with a wall of silence and four blank expressions.

'Anyone else want to give him the good news?' Graham asked.

Stanton said, 'That's what you get the big bucks for, guv'.'

Graham laughed. If only that were the case. 'Okay. There's nothing more we can do for today. You two…' He looked at Spencer and Lovelace. 'I need someone to parade before the press, show them that we're doing something, that we've at least got a grip on the case. Find Oliver Bowden. Guilty or not, he'll make a good smokescreen. So find him and arrest him. And get me some more names. Get me some fucking suspects.'

'Yes, guv'.'

'You two,' This time, he turned on Luton and Stanton. 'I need you two back at the station. There's a press conference tomorrow at one o'clock. We will announce the identity of the body we found today and launch a drive for information regarding the killer. Someone out there must have their suspicions. We're going to make a big push for information, and recent experience would tell us that that will be a huge pool of data for us to collate. So we're going to be busy.'

Graham looked back at Lovelace. 'I need to know if the Parkes' case is related or if we're after two killers. Find me a connection.'

Lovelace nodded. She was beginning to form an idea.

'Somehow,' Graham said, 'I need to find a way of telling the people of Oxfordshire that they are in extreme danger from this man and that they need to ensure that they lock their doors securely.'

'That may not be enough.' Lovelace said. 'They'll probably just be locking themselves in with him.'

Graham looked at Lovelace in horror. She was right. People weren't even safe in their own homes. The thought terrified him.

***

Lovelace gunned her ruby-red Mercedes through the narrow country lanes with incredible skill. Spencer no longer gave her driving another thought. Instead, he sat and relished the cool air washing over him.

'Where are we going?' He asked.

'Back to the Parkes' home. I've got an idea.'

'You think you've found a connection?'

'Maybe. We'll soon find out.'

Molly Parkes' naked body had been found a mile from her home in a straight line, but the lanes that took her to her death snaked through the Oxfordshire countryside more haphazardly. Lovelace pulled into the quiet cul-de-sac, having driven nearly two miles. It hadn't taken long. A few minutes was all it took. Molly's last drive had been a short one. Mercifully so, Lovelace thought.

It was early evening, the western skies were still ablaze with the day's fiery sun, and the heat resonated in the air.

Lovelace pulled her car into the Parkes' drive and killed the engine. The front of the house was awash with flowers and cards from neighbours and friends of the dead family. News of the discovery of a body in a nearby field had led to hundreds more visitors to the house, each paying their respects in their own way. Across the lawn in front of the house lay hundreds of wreaths and flowers and, here and there, teddy bears and toys for the two girls. A television crew was setting up on the road for the late evening news, no doubt speculating on the discovery nearby. Nothing grabbed a headline more than a dead girl and the potential for a serial killer. The identity of the body discovered in a ditch across the fields had not yet been released, and this only served to fuel people's interest. People were buzzing. Lovelace stepped out of the car and sensed it in the air.

A young girl of barely thirteen walked up the road clutching a small teddy bear. She placed it neatly on the lawn near a photograph of the two girls taped to a small wooden post in the centre. Next, she took a candle from her pocket and stuck it into the soil. Then, taking a lighter from her pocket, she carefully lit the taper until it took and grew into a tall flame. There were hundreds of other candles just like that one scattered across the lawn, each one flickering in the still air.

'It's beautiful.' Lovelace said, almost under her breath.

'It is.' Spencer agreed. 'There's much love for those girls.'

'Those poor girls....'

Lovelace walked around the lawn and read some of the cards left with the wreaths. So many of them were from strangers from all over the country. People who had never met the girls and knew nothing about them but who had felt their pain from a hundred miles away.

Life could be cruel, Lovelace thought, but she was still amazed by the love and kindness that another person could offer.

A woman who had walked with the teenage girl stepped over to Lovelace. She handed her a small flier.

'It's this weekend if you want to come. If you wanted to pay your respects.'

Lovelace read the flier. It was hastily assembled on a home computer and printed in black and white. There was a picture of the two girls and a date and time. It was a candlelight vigil to be held this coming Saturday at 9 pm.

'Thank you.' Lovelace said. 'I will.'

'Bring your best singing voice.' The woman said. 'There'll be some hymns, but I think the school are organising a small band to play the girls' favourite songs.'

She turned, took the girl's hand, and walked away, handing out fliers. Lovelace handed the flier to Spencer.

'The modern curse.' He said. 'Collective grief.'

'If it helps the children, I can't see that it can do any harm.' Lovelace said.

'I suppose not.' Spencer said. 'So, what did you want to look at in the Parkes' home?'

'Nothing.' Lovelace said. 'I want to go and speak to the neighbour.'

Lovelace and Spencer walked up the small path to the neighbour's house and pressed the buzzer. They heard a sound go off in the distance, followed by light footsteps. The door opened, and a young woman of Lovelace's age stepped up. She was tall with long legs and a slim frame, and she seemed to compensate for her height by slouching down ever so slightly, which made her look hump-backed. She had long, dark hair held back in a ponytail and wore thick, round glasses that framed deep blue eyes.

'Yes?' She said irritably.

Lovelace held up her warrant card. 'DC Lovelace, this is my colleague DS Spencer. We spoke a couple of days ago if you remember. May we come in?'

They sat in a modern front room with a large flat-screen television perched on the wall in the corner. It was a woman's house through and through. It was neatly decorated in subtle pinks and greens, and the occasional painting tastefully enhanced the walls. Across the fireplace sat a large oak beam topped with pictures of the owner with friends and family.

'I'm sorry if I was a little tetchy,' she said, laying three cups of tea onto a large oak coffee table. 'Those bloody reporters keep knocking on the door asking for interviews. If it's not them, it's bloody grief tourists walking all over my lawn. It's bloody constant. Day and bloody night. It's bad enough living next door to… you know… that. The "House of Death", they're calling it. I've not had a decent night's sleep since it happened. I mean, it could so easily have been me, couldn't it? What if he'd broken in here instead of next door? I've had all the locks changed and extra ones fitted to the windows. I'm too scared to open the bloody windows, even in this heat! I mean, is nowhere safe anymore?'

'Actually…' Lovelace stumbled over the words forming in her head. She shifted her tone slightly. 'How long have you lived here?' She asked.

Emma Jenkins took a sip of her tea and sat back into the arms of a huge armchair. 'Five years this Christmas. Cost a bloody fortune then, too. I probably won't be able to sell the bloody thing now, will I? I mean, who's going to want to live next door to that? I mean, what will happen to the house? No one's ever going to want to live there, are they?'

'You'd be surprised.' Spencer said. 'You may even find your house goes up in value. As for next door, I can't say what will happen. In many cases, the local authority buys the place and knock it down, planting a memorial tree in its place.'

'What is it you do for a living, Miss Jenkins?' Lovelace asked.

'Please, call me Emma.' She said. 'I'm a travel agent. I design bespoke trips for professional people.'

Rich people, Lovelace thought.

'What's this about?' Emma asked. 'I think I told you everything I knew when you were here last. And I gave a formal statement to a young copper who came round later.'

'I know,' Lovelace said. 'But we've learnt a few things since then. A few things that are challenging the way we are looking at the case. What we're trying to do is work out why the killer targeted Molly Parkes. At the moment, we believe someone is targeting women who live alone, so why did he target a household that contained a fully grown man? It does seem to run counter to his MO.'

Emma shrugged. 'I don't know. But he wanted poor Molly.'

'But why?' Lovelace asked. 'How did he pick her when all the others have lived alone?'

Emma looked even more confused. She shook her head. 'I'm not sure I can help.'

'I think you can, actually,' Lovelace went on slowly. 'I want to ask you about something that may have happened a few weeks ago.'

Emma looked even more confused. 'A few weeks ago? Like what?'

Lovelace shook her head. 'I don't know. I want you to tell me.'

Emma looked across at Spencer for clarification. It was only beginning to dawn on him what Lovelace was driving at, and his face wore an expression of someone rapidly putting the pieces in place.

'I'm sorry. I don't know what you mean.' Emma declared.

'I want you to think.' Lovelace said calmly. 'I want you to think carefully about the last few weeks, maybe even months. I want you to think about how you live here and what you do. Please try and remember all the things you have lost and never found. Or lost and found in an unusual place. Somewhere you wouldn't normally have put them. I want you to think about the silly little things you can't quite explain, no matter how stupid you think they are, and I want you to tell us about them. Like the fridge magnets.'

Emma sat up and perched on the end of her seat. The fridge magnets had poked her interest. It was odd… 'There's nothing. Not really.'

Lovelace smiled. 'Okay. Tell us about the "Not really."'

'I'm not sure it's any use to you. It is quite silly.' She took a moment to digest her thoughts. Silly little things. 'I have lost a few things. Small things. Pieces of jewellery. Nothing major. Things I've probably just put down somewhere and thrown out accidentally or lost on a night out.'

'Go on.' Lovelace encouraged. 'There are other things, aren't there?'

'Well, yes. There is. I have a lock of hair from when I was a small girl. I keep it in a small box as a keepsake. My mother gave it to me before she died with a lock of her own hair. I can't find it anywhere. I've searched high and low for it. I can't find it. And do you know, I'm not even sure I can remember if I ever had it in this house.

My last memory of it is in my last home, and I can't remember what I've done with it.'

'Do you find that you're losing more things lately?' Lovelace asked.

'It does seem more common. Or it did.'

Lovelace smiled again. Despite having a happy face, Spencer noticed that she didn't often smile and only smiled when she was getting things right.

'It stopped a few weeks ago. That feeling went away too, didn't it?'

'Oh, my god! How did you know?'

Silly little things.

'I don't mean to alarm you,' Lovelace said gently. 'But I have a responsibility to you. To keep you safe. I think the man who killed the Parkes next door didn't set out to target them. I think he came here first. I think he targeted you. I think he broke into your home while you were out and stole little things, like the fridge magnets and your lock of hair. I even think on several occasions you may well have been in the house together, at the same time, without you realising. You may have suspected, however. You may have sensed or felt his presence without fully understanding it.'

'Oh my god! Am I safe?'

'I think you're safe.' Lovelace said. 'At least I think you're safe now. He won't return here, and you've already tightened your home security.'

'But why?' Emma asked. 'Why me? And then why did he change his mind?'

'We think the man we're after targets single women living alone. He breaks in, steals things, and moves items around. It gives him a sense of power. Then, as he grows in confidence, he hides away in your home and remains there while you go about your life. In most cases, the victim never knows he's been there.

Sometimes, and for reasons we don't yet understand, he strikes out and kills.'

'But why the Parkes? What made him change his mind?'

Lovelace shook her head. 'We don't yet fully understand how he chooses his victims, but I think having chosen you, he came here and broke in. I think he was probably here one day when Molly Parkes walked up her driveway after school, and he saw her and chose her. For whatever reason, he suddenly and very desperately wanted her. From that moment on, you were safe, and poor Molly wasn't.'

Emma gasped. 'My god, I think I feel sick. I can't stay here. Not tonight. I don't think I can ever stay here again.'

Emma stood up. 'Do you mind? I need to call my dad.'

Spencer and Lovelace reassured Emma that she was safe, that the focus on the street was too great for the killer to chance a return, but she had made her mind up.

'I'll be okay.' She said. 'I'll call my dad. I can go and stay with him for a while. I need to pack a bag.'

She paused as she went to go out of the room. 'You wouldn't mind coming with me while I pack, would you? Just in case?'

Lovelace nodded. 'Of course.' To Spencer, she said, 'Call Graham, let him know what we've discovered. It links the cases perfectly.'

Twenty minutes later, Lovelace and Spencer were on the road back to Oxford.

'She was properly freaked out,' Lovelace said as she guided her car along the narrow lanes.

'I don't blame her.' Spencer said.

'What did Graham say?'

'He said well done. It's enough for him to connect the cases. We're officially after a serial killer, but we're not allowed to use those words. There is one other thing, though.'

'Go on.' Lovelace prompted.

'Our chap Oliver Bowden has been to see a solicitor. He's going to attend Banbury police station at ten o'clock tomorrow morning voluntarily, and would we like to go and rattle his cage for a bit? Graham says we'll hold him for the full twenty-four hours so he can at least take some of the pressure off the press conference.'

Lovelace smiled again. Spencer was beginning to like it when she smiled.

Fifteen

Irene watched as her charge paced his office like an impatient child, constantly wringing his hands and mouthing the words of his speech as he recited it in his head. DCI Graham had aged in the last few weeks like she had never seen before. His skin was pallid, his hair listless and grey, and he moved like a man of greater years. But there was still that fire in his eyes, and while it lasted, she knew he would go on, denying whatever it was that was killing him from within.

She had her suspicions. She had an uncle once who had gone to bed with a glass of whiskey and a cigarette but who never got to taste either. He had lain on his bed and died instantly. An aneurysm had fired in his brain, killing him before he knew what had happened. Was that what was going on in Graham's head? Would he suddenly drop dead, unaware of his fate? She didn't know, but it scared her. On the diary in front of her, she had circled Friday's date. She had cleared his schedule and was determined he would make his appointment. She was mulling over a strategy to ensure this would happen when her thoughts were interrupted by the arrival of a young woman who hovered hesitantly over her desk.

She looked up to see a professionally dressed young woman in her thirties who carried a simple black handbag over her shoulder and wore a lanyard around her neck, declaring that she was Detective Inspector Alison French.

Irene smiled sweetly and said, 'Good morning.'

'DI French to see DCI Graham. I have an appointment.'

Irene knew she had an appointment as she had been the one to arrange it. 'Yes, of course. Please take a seat; I'll let the Chief Inspector know you're here.'

Irene tapped lightly on Graham's door and walked in. 'Your nine o'clock is here.'

Graham stopped pacing and looked out of his office at the young woman sitting there. He glanced at his watch. It was all very inconvenient. He was a busy man. There was a great deal to think of and an even greater deal to do.

'Very well.' He said at last. 'Show her in.'

DI French sat opposite Graham. She declined the coffee that was offered and waited patiently while Graham's dutiful secretary poured him one from a nearby machine. She placed it on the table before him and quietly left the office.

'So what can I do for you, DI French?'

What indeed. DI Frampton had suggested that she speak to Graham in person and share her theories with him. It was a simple courtesy and one which Graham would appreciate.

'Tread carefully,' Frampton had urged. 'He's a waspy fucker. Wind him up, and he'll sting you. You're there purely as a courtesy to him. Rub his ego a bit. We all love that from time to time. Then lay out the facts and your theories. Give it to him straight. Don't colour it in fancy words. Just say what you've got and see what he says.'

Now she sat before the infamous DCI Graham and felt slightly intimidated. No, that wouldn't do, she thought to herself. She was a respected DI in her own right and had worked bloody hard to get there. So she steeled herself against the feeling and said, 'I'm investigating a case of murder that occurred in central Oxford a few nights ago. Mark Pitts.'

Graham nodded. "I heard about that. Seems like justice caught up with the man in the end.'

'Perhaps,' French said gently, choosing her words carefully. 'He wasn't a nice man, and he had many enemies, and he's not an innocent fifteen-year-old girl, but murder is murder, regardless of who the victim is.'

Graham watched as the fire burned behind French's eyes. He saw passion there, and he liked it. 'Very well put.' Graham said. 'And how can I be of help to you?'

French paused. She reached into her handbag and pulled out a manila envelope. 'As part of my investigation, I have tracked and traced all of Pitts' contacts on the evening of his murder. I've identified everyone he was in contact with that evening and taken statements from them all. All that is apart from one young woman.' She held up the manilla envelope. 'This young woman shadowed Pitts that evening before making his acquaintance. They were together for most of the evening right up until his death. As far as I can tell, she was probably the last person to see him alive. No one saw them leave together or remembers when she left the pub.'

French laid out some photographs from the CCTV footage they had captured of the young woman.

'Is this all you've got?' Graham asked. 'You can't see her face in any of them.'

'She was cautious,' French admitted. 'She knew the location of every CCTV camera in the town centre. Even some of the lesser known ones.'

She let the implication of that linger in the air. French took another photograph and laid it on the desk before Graham. She watched his expression carefully. There was nothing. Not a flicker of recognition. Not even an eyebrow moved. If he recognised Lucy Lovelace in the photograph, he didn't show it.

'She wasn't aware of a camera in a local Off-Licence. I've had the image blown up. A colleague of mine has identified the woman in the photograph as Detective Constable Lucy Lovelace.'

She gave it straight. Graham's face showed no emotion. He was as cold as ice, French thought. It was no wonder barristers feared meeting him in the courtroom. Many a rising ego had been burned down in the face of Graham's evidence.

Graham picked up the photograph and gave it his full attention. French waited.

'There's certainly a likeness.' Graham agreed at last.

'Would you say the woman in the photograph was Lucy Lovelace?' French asked.

'I would not say that, no.' Graham replied. There was no hint of animosity or bitterness. It was very matter-of-fact.

French took the photograph back and placed it back in the envelope. Then, she began gathering up the other pictures.

'May I ask if we have Lucy Lovelace's DNA on file?' French asked.

'You may,' Graham said. 'And no, we don't.'

'Isn't that unusual?' French asked. 'As part of a Major Investigation Team, wouldn't it be customary to have attending detectives' DNA on file as a precaution?'

'That's right, it is. But it's not compulsory. In any case, Constable Lovelace is due to give a sample of her DNA as soon as it becomes possible. I'm afraid we rather threw her in at the deep end with this case. We've just not yet had the time.'

'That's okay.' French said. 'We've pulled very few pieces of evidence from the victim. And we do have Jack Lovelace's DNA on record. So we'll run that against anything we find and see if we can find a familial match.'

French placed the last few photographs in the envelope and slipped them into her handbag.

'I came here purely as a courtesy to you,' French said. 'I believe the woman in the photograph to be Lucy Lovelace, and I intend to find the evidence that ties her to the murder of Mark Pitts. I wouldn't want your association with Constable Lovelace to be a source of embarrassment.'

'I appreciate your candour, Inspector French, and your courtesy is noted.'

Graham stood and held out his hand. French took it.

'I believe you are mistaken,' Graham said, 'but I wish you all the best in your investigation.'

'Thank you, sir. Of course, if we move to make an arrest in this case, we will do so with great care. I will keep you informed of any major advances.'

'I would appreciate that, Inspector. Thank you.'

Graham sat back in his chair and watched DI French leave his office. She had impressed him greatly. She was undoubtedly one to watch.

He pondered the photograph French had just shown him and began wondering. It was curious, of that much he was sure. It was very curious indeed.

DI French sat in her car in the car park of police HQ at Kidlington and sighed deeply.

'Well?' Frampton asked.

They had driven together to Kidlington that morning, but Frampton had refused to go into the meeting with Graham.

'He fucking hates me. You'd be better off on your own.'

French had reluctantly agreed. She left the car running with the air conditioning on and was grateful for the icy air that washed over her on her return.

She shook her head. 'Nothing doing. He categorically denies that the woman in the photograph is Lucy Lovelace. He did admit that there was a likeness, though.'

'He could hardly deny that, could he? That would look suspicious. The woman in the photograph is Lucy Lovelace. I'm fucking sure of it. Anyone can see that.'

French was more circumspect. 'It's not certain though, is it?' She said. 'And even if the woman in the photograph is Lovelace, it's not evidence of murder. There's no proof she killed Pitts.'

'Maybe not,' Frampton agreed. 'But it makes her worth investigating. We should watch her closely. Get her under surveillance.'

'There's no way the boss will go for that. There's no money for overtime.'

'Leave that with me.' Frampton said. 'Not everyone's a fan of DCI Graham. Even fewer are fans of the Lovelace name.'

French pulled on her seatbelt and was about to pull out of her space when a familiar figure approached a ruby-red car in front of them and opened the driver's door. A smartly dressed man in his forties opened the passenger door and climbed in.

French studied the driver carefully. It was the first time she had seen her in the flesh, and she looked just like the image taken from the Off-Licence's CCTV camera. She was about five-eight with wispy auburn hair that hung untidily about her head. She was pretty, too, with deep brown eyes beneath well-maintained brows. French took a photograph from the manila envelope and compared the two faces.

'You were right, Bill. The woman in this photograph is definitely Lucy Lovelace.'

* * *

Lovelace and Spencer paid little attention to the couple in the car in front of them. As was usual for Lovelace, she was aware they were there and had even recognised the man who sat in the passenger seat, but beyond the briefest of recognitions, she gave neither of them any more thought. Instead, she slipped her car into gear and manoeuvred out of her space. The barrier opened automatically as she approached it, and she powered out into the street.

'Surely the M40 would be quicker?' Spencer said as he noticed they were going the wrong way.

'It is. Normally. But this way's more fun to drive.' Lovelace said as she pointed the nose of her ruby red Mercedes towards Woodstock.

Once they had escaped the confines and restrictions of the city, Lovelace toed the accelerator, and they flew down the A44, past the erroneously named London Oxford airport and on towards Woodstock. Once the dual carriageway ended, Lovelace revelled in the pleasure of driving, letting her small car power into the corners effortlessly whilst pulling powerfully out the other side, falling and rising with the contours of the road.

Spencer watched as Lovelace took a right at the roundabout for Chipping Norton and powered up to ninety miles an hour along the straights. The road here was narrower and the bends tighter, but Lovelace took each in her stride, and the miles fell away in short order. Before long, the outer estates of Banbury slowed their progress, and they fell in with the remnants of rush hour.

They signed in at the front desk of the police station and were shown through to the back office.

Sergeant Wilkins, a colossal figure of a man with broad shoulders and hands like saucers, showed them to an interview room near the custody suite.

'We thought you'd want to set up in here.' He said in a soft Irish brogue as he pushed open the door to a room named "Interview Room One."

'This will be perfect.' Spencer said as they walked in.

'There's CCTV recording. It's on all the time. If you need it switched off, let me know.'

'No. That will be fine.'

'There's a CD recorder. Do you need discs?'

'No, thank you, we've brought our own.' Lovelace said as she sat at one of the chairs facing the door.

'Tea? Coffee? It all tastes like shit if I'm honest. We don't even give it to the prisoners.'

Lovelace and Spencer knew the quality of station drinks and avoided them where possible.

'I can send out for a decent drink if you like. There's a place just across the way which do a pretty good latte.'

Spencer looked up at the beast of a man that spoke in soft tones and spoke of "pretty good lattes." The world was a strange place, and men like Sergeant Wilkins were the pastel shades of its oddity.

'Perhaps when our guests have arrived.' Spencer said. 'If you could show them through to us when they arrive.'

'They're already here. Been here twenty minutes. We've got them up in one of the family rooms. Want me to bring them down?'

'Yes, please.'

The fleet of foot Oliver Bowden was more circumspect on their second meeting. He avoided eye contact when he was shown to his seat opposite

Lovelace and Spencer, and he looked to his solicitor for direction once they had settled.

Lovelace pressed "record" on the machine beside her and said, 'Interview with Oliver Bowden at 09:45 hours on Thursday the 9th of August. Present are Detective Constable Lovelace…'

Spencer said, 'Detective Sergeant Spencer.'

They both looked at Bowden's solicitor, who said, 'Edward Frankly, Mr Bowden's solicitor.'

All three looked at Oliver Bowden, who stared vacantly at his solicitor.

'Am I under arrest?' He asked.

'If you could just say your name for the benefit of the recording, Mr Bowden.' Lovelace asked firmly.

'Oliver Bowden.' He said, not looking away from his solicitor. 'Am I under arrest?' He asked again.

'I must caution you, Mr Bowden,' Lovelace said, 'that anything you say here today is being recorded and may be used as evidence. You are not under arrest and free to leave at any time.'

Bowden held his solicitor's eyes and said, 'So we can just leave?'

'I would advise against it, Mr Bowden.' Spencer said. 'If you choose to say nothing, which is your right, or if you decide to leave, we will arrest you, allowing us to hold you for at least twenty-four hours.'

'That won't be necessary,' Frankly said, 'I have advised Mr Bowden to co-operate in your investigation fully. However, I must add that Mr Bowden is here voluntarily and of his own free will.'

'Noted.' Lovelace said shortly. 'So why did you run away from us, Mr Bowden?'

'I didn't know who you were.' Bowden said, finally taking his eyes off his solicitor and addressing Lovelace directly.

'I believe I addressed you by your name, showed you my identification and identified myself as a police officer. Which bit confused you?'

'I panicked.' Bowden said. 'I just heard about Jane. That she had been murdered. I knew you lot would come knocking.'

'Why would you think that?'

'Because I knew Jane. We'd been in a relationship recently. It hadn't lasted long, but I knew you'd come asking questions.'

'That's what we do when someone is murdered, Mr Bowden.' Lovelace said. 'We ask questions. It's our duty to the murdered. We talk to everyone who knew the victim and ask many questions. Very few people we question pack a bag and try to run away, so the question remains. Why did you run away?'

Oliver Bowden looked across at his solicitor for guidance. Mr Frankly nodded.

'Because I have form.' He said, finally.

'For domestic violence?' Lovelace asked.

'Yes.'

'Do you enjoy beating up women?' Lovelace asked.

'Constable Lovelace, really! That's beneath you.' Frankly said.

'But there have been quite a few, haven't there, Mr Bowden? You have several convictions and cautions for domestic violence against former partners, and several Court Injunctions prevent you from contacting or being near some of your former girlfriends?'

'Look,' Bowden said, 'all of that's true. I don't deny it. I can't deny it. It's all there in black and white, but I got help. Look… see… I got help.'

Bowden handed over a piece of paper that his solicitor handed to him. It was a type-written letter emailed to

Frankly and Carson, Solicitors, late the previous afternoon. Lovelace read it and gave it to Spencer.

'For the record,' Lovelace said, 'Mr Bowden has handed us confirmation from an official source that he is receiving ongoing treatment for anger management.'

'It's more than that,' Bowden said, his voice almost pleading. 'They help. They really do. I've got it under control. I've not hit anyone since…..'

He paused and looked across at his solicitor.

'Since you hit Jane Wilson?' Lovelace asked.

'Do you have any evidence of that, Constable?' Frankly asked.

'Did you ever attack Miss Jane Wilson?' Lovelace asked.

Bowden looked trapped. His solicitor shook his head.

'No comment.' Bowden said.

'Did you know, Mr Bowden, that most women who suffer domestic violence and are later found murdered are killed by their violent partners?'

'Really, Constable Lovelace, that is not proof.' Frankly exclaimed.

'It isn't.' Lovelace agreed. She looked at Bowden. 'But you can see why we would want to talk to you, can't you?'

'Do not answer that, Oliver.' Frankly said, recognising the danger.

'I do need some kind of answer to the question.' Lovelace said. 'Do you understand why we would want to talk to you?'

Exasperated, Bowden said, 'Yes, of course I bloody-well understand. I'm not stupid.'

'Oliver, I strongly advise you to limit any further answers to questions with a polite "no comment."' Frankly said.

It was too late. Lovelace pounced.

'So you admit that you did hit Jane Wilson?'

'I...I...' Bowden realised his error. Then, dejected, he said, 'No comment.'

'It makes sense,' Lovelace continued. 'You have a habit of committing violent offences against your partners. So it was only a matter of time before you killed one of them.'

Frankly opened his mouth to warn his client, but he was too slow. The fury rose in Bowden's face. His lips began to tremble, and his face began to turn a shade of red. He clenched his hands into a fist, and for a moment, Lovelace and Spencer braced themselves for an attack. But none came. Instead, Bowden closed his eyes and took in a huge lungful of air. They watched as the tension in his shoulders dissipated, and as he released the air from his lungs, his whole body relaxed.

Bowden opened his eyes and said calmly, 'I hit her once. I didn't mean to. It was an accident. It was a genuine accident, and I know I am in no position to be believed. I accept that. Jane and I had a good relationship. She knew about my past, and she knew I was going for counselling. She really helped. Then one day, I made a mistake, and she called it off. I didn't blame her. I still don't. Not one bit. I begged forgiveness and promised it wouldn't happen again, but the words sounded cliched, even to me. She did the right thing and ended it, and we went our separate ways. I haven't seen Jane since then. When I heard she was killed, I knew you'd come for me. I knew it, and I was scared. That's why I ran away. I didn't want to be fitted up for something I didn't do.'

Lovelace stole a glance at Spencer. He was smiling.

'We try not to fit people up these days, Mr Bowden.' Lovelace said. 'We do prefer getting the right people.'

'Yeah, but you make mistakes. You hear about it all the time. First, you find someone you like for a crime, and then you find the evidence to fit.'

Lovelace couldn't argue with the truth of that. Sometimes they were guilty of looking for evidence once they had a suspect in mind. So many cases had gotten lost because of that tunnel vision. It wasn't the case here.

She said, 'Oliver Bowden, I am arresting you on suspicion of the murder of Jane Wilson. You do not have to say anything, but it may harm your defence if you do not mention when questioned, something you later rely on in court. Do you understand?'

Bowden nodded. 'Yes. But you've got the wrong man. I didn't kill her.'

She didn't say it, but she didn't think for one second Oliver Bowden was a killer. She remembered Graham's plea to them to take the pressure off the investigation before the press conference later that day. They would use Oliver Bowden as a red herring to dangle in front of the press while secretly concentrating on the real killer.

Lovelace pressed "stop" on the recorder. Then, to Bowden, she said, 'We'll just take you to the Custody Suite and process you. We can hold you for twenty-four hours while we investigate Jane's murder. After twenty-four hours, we'll either charge you or let you go. If you didn't kill Jane Wilson, I promise you you have nothing to fear from us.'

'He didn't do it.' Spencer said sometime later. They had taken Bowden to be processed and left him in the care of the custody officers while they retired to the station's refectory to talk.

'I agree.' Lovelace said as she bit into a muffin.

'Did you see what he did when he started to get angry? He practically meditated in front of us. That's some serious control he's exercising there.'

'That took some effort.' Lovelace agreed. 'I can't help but respect the man for that. He's identified a problem, and he's sought help for it. That's not the sort of man we're after. And the way he spoke. He's admitted he has a problem and has taken responsibility for it. No blame, no recriminations. No attempt at mitigation. He's the opposite of the man we're after.'

'Which doesn't get us very far…' Spencer grumbled.

They looked up as a uniform approached their table.

'Are you Lovelace and Spencer?' He asked.

'We are.' Spencer admitted.

'Sergeant Beauchamp. I wonder if I could have a moment of your time.'

He hovered anxiously, and Lovelace noted that people did this when they knew who she was. Some came to talk out of curiosity and some out of duty, but the anxiousness was always the same.

'Please,' Spencer waved his arm casually. 'Take a seat.'

Sergeant Beauchamp sat opposite and cleared his throat. He was an older man with thinning black hair slicked back over his head. His face was brown and well lived-in, and his teeth showed signs of yellowing. The fingers of his right hand were identically stained, and there was the faint aroma of tobacco as he spoke.

'It's a small thing, really.' He began. He held a folder in his left hand and laid it carefully on the table in front of him. 'Probably just wasting your time.'

Lovelace liked it when people started a conversation in that way. When they suspected they might be wasting your time, it nearly always turned out they weren't. She was intrigued.

'Got a fella whose wife went missing about a year ago. He's a nice bloke, a bit sad though if you know what I mean. They'd been married a few years, no kids and his mum had died fairly recently, and then his missus upped and left him. Well, we went and had a nose around, made some enquiries, and couldn't find anything important. He was convinced that something bad had happened to her. He still is convinced. But…'

'But you don't think so?' Spencer asked.

'We dug quite deep. It turned out she was a bit nasty. Aggressive type, dominant and loud. She pretty much bullied him, according to her friends. Nothing physical, like mental stuff, mostly. She was quite controlling. When we started looking even deeper, we found half a dozen men in the background. She'd been having affairs behind his back for years. Pretty much since the day they got married.'

'You think she ran off with one of them?' Lovelace asked.

'Convinced of it. There was a man in the background fairly recent to her doing a bunk. We couldn't find out much about him but discovered he vanished around the same time.'

'You think they left together?'

'All the evidence points that way.'

'And there's no chance the husband's done them in?'

Sergeant Beauchamp dismissed the idea out of hand. 'Not a chance. Like I said, he's a sad one. Wouldn't say boo to a goose. He's weak. Pretty pathetic, really. But still… I quite like the fella. He's nice, you know?'

Lovelace nodded. She knew.

'Thing is…' Sergeant Beauchamp continued, 'the poor fella comes in like every other month or so, you know, to check how the investigation's going. I haven't the heart to tell him there isn't an investigation to speak of. When he comes in, I do a quick check on the PNC and stuff, but she doesn't appear anywhere. She's probably living the life of Reilly in Spain or something, far away from our eyes. She's still on the Misspers' list, but beyond that, there's not a lot more we can do. He goes away and then comes back in another couple of months.'

'So why do you think this might interest us?' Spencer asked.

'Because of the killings. The Parkes family and that poor young girl. Then there's the latest one found in her home, all dead-like, and then there's that body that's been found. I assume it's the Parkes girl? The one that was missing? Anyway, he's called the station a few times and turned up today wanting to know if his missing wife's case is related?'

'Any reason you can think of why it should be?' Spencer asked.

Sergeant Beauchamp shook his head. 'Nope. No reason at all. But that doesn't stop him from thinking they are. He's all alone, see. He gets an idea in his head and can't escape it. He turned up a little while ago wondering if the body you've found is his wife. I've told him it's probably that little girl, but he doesn't want to leave until he knows. I knew you two were here today, and I was just wondering if you'd have a word with him. See if you can put his mind at ease.'

'Is that the details of his wife's disappearance?' Lovelace asked, indicating the folder on the table.

'Yes. There's not much. A statement from him when the wife vanished and a couple from her friends. Like I say, there's not much.'

Lovelace pulled the folder to her and opened it. Sergeant Beauchamp had not been wrong when he said it wasn't much. From the gist of it, none of the missing wife's friends were entirely surprised when she left, and

all of them thought she'd turn up one day. She turned to
the husband's statement. It was all very matter-of-fact.
He'd gone to work one morning and returned later that
day to find his wife was not home. This was not unusual,
and it was nearly forty-eight hours before he reported
her missing. She had a reputation for staying out
drinking, sometimes not returning home until the
following day. Overall, there was nothing to tie in her
disappearance with the case they were working on now.
But still, it was better to be safe than sorry.

'Okay.' Lovelace said. 'Show us to him.'

Sergeant Beauchamp showed them to one of the
family rooms, where he introduced them to Adam
Sinclair.

'Adam, this is Detective Sergeant Spencer and
Detective Constable Lovelace. They're part of the
investigation team looking into the recent murders.'

Adam Sinclair stood up and shook their hands. He was
a meek-looking man of thirty years with thin blonde hair
that parted down the middle. He was Lovelace's height,
and his handshake was soft and effeminate. His eyes
were the purest blue, shining from a friendly, demure
face.

'Is it.. is it my wife?' He asked. His voice was stronger
and more guttural than Lovelace expected, and it seemed
out of place with the appearance of the man she saw
before her.

'Please, take a seat, Mr Sinclair.'

The three of them sat down together across a glass
coffee table. Sinclair sat at the edge of a comfy sofa
while Lovelace and Spencer took an armchair each.
Sergeant Beauchamp took his leave and closed the door
behind him.

'What makes you think your wife has been murdered?'
Lovelace asked gently.

There was no notable change in Sinclair's body language. He remained very matter-of-fact. Almost aloof, as if he had risen above his involvement and was looking at the case from a third person's objective.

'My wife has gone missing.' He said plainly. 'No one has seen or heard from her in over a year. People don't just vanish.'

'Actually, they do.' Spencer said, painfully aware of the statistics that said exactly that. 'Sometimes people go away and don't come back. It's painful for those they leave behind. You're unable to get any closure. There's no finality to it. We do understand how difficult it is.'

'Do you?' Sinclair said. 'I wonder… when someone goes missing, there's very often a small police enquiry followed either by a full-blown missing person's search or murder enquiry. What I often wonder is why some cases get the full attention of the authorities when other cases are left unanswered?'

'I'm not sure I understand.' Spencer said.

'I see it all the time.' Sinclair said. 'You tend not to notice the small details until it happens to you. You read on Twitter or Facebook that so and so has gone missing, and can anyone help and then you never hear about it again. Then one day, someone goes missing, and it's all over the national news. So why do some people count and not others?'

'Usually, when someone goes missing,' Lovelace explained, 'we dig into that person's life. We dig up their past and learn everything we can about their story. When we've done that, we can see if their going missing is out of character or if something in their life would indicate why they might want to vanish. Then, once we've created a full picture, we can see if further investigation is needed.'

'And you've decided that my wife's disappearance doesn't warrant further investigation?'

'On the whole, I'd have to say no, it doesn't.' Lovelace said frankly. 'Given your wife's history, it would seem reasonable to assume she has gone away of her own volition.'

'Because of the affairs?'

'Yes. Did you know about the affairs?'

'Some of them,' Sinclair admitted. 'We had an open relationship. You see, we couldn't have kids, and she took it hard. She started playing around a bit. She'd come home from work and go straight out on the lash. Sometimes she wouldn't come back for a day or two. But she always came back in the end. Always.'

'Is that why you think she has come to harm?' Lovelace asked.

'Yes. She always came home.'

'Is there anything else you can tell us?' Lovelace probed. 'Anything about your life together that you haven't told us before? Anything that might make us want to take another look at your wife's case?'

'I can't think of anything,' Sinclair said. 'I've been over that day in my mind a dozen times. I can't think of anything.'

'Did you often get home after your wife?'

'Yes. Usually. Only she took that day off. I got home about six that evening, and she wasn't there.'

'Did you talk to her at all that day?'

'No. I left home at seven-thirty, and I never saw her again.'

'Was there any indication of a break-in?'

'Nothing at all. The house was locked up. I work for a security company that deals with security for commercial properties. I'm sure I'd have noticed if someone had broken in.'

'Why did your wife take that day off? Was it pre-planned?'

'No. She felt unwell in the morning, so she stayed at home.'

'Had you any cause to think you may have been burgled in the weeks and months before your wife's disappearance?'

For the first time, Lovelace saw Sinclair's eyes sparkle with interest. He was bored with the mundanity of police investigations and had undoubtedly heard all of those questions before. But he hadn't heard that one. That one was new.

He pondered the question for some time before shaking his head and saying, 'No. I can't think of anything like that. Why? Is it important, do you think?'

'It might have been. We may have been able to link it with our investigations.'

Lovelace watched as Sinclair's shoulders dropped in defeat. He could not accept that his wife would leave on a whim, but try as he might, he couldn't see another answer.

'What about the body you've found?' He said, at last, desperately clutching at something to hold on to. At least a body would be closure.

Lovelace shook her head. 'We haven't released the information to the public yet, but I can assure you the body is not your wife's.'

Sinclair looked entirely deflated.

'I'm sorry.' Lovelace said genuinely.

'That's okay,' Sinclair said sadly.

Lovelace took out her business card and handed it to Sinclair. 'Perhaps if you remember anything else or think of something you hadn't thought of before, you could telephone me?'

Sinclair took the card. 'Yes. of course. Thank you for your time. I'm sorry it's been wasted.'

'Not at all.' Spencer said. 'We're here to help when we can.'

They escorted Sinclair from the family room and out into the main reception. They watched as Sinclair stepped out of the building and onto the street. Lovelace thought he looked sad and doleful from a distance as he walked along the street and disappeared from sight.

'What a depressing man.' Spencer said.

'I feel sorry for him.'

'By the sound of it, he's had a lucky escape.'

'Still. He seemed lonely.'

'He should buy himself a puppy.' Spencer joked. 'At least it wouldn't bully him!'

They laughed and walked back inside the station.

***

'Sarah, it's Alice again. Can you give me a call when you pick up my messages?' Alice dropped the call and sat back in her chair, slightly worried.

'Still no answer?'

'No.' She replied.

'How many messages is that now?'

Alice thought about it briefly and said, 'Six or seven. It's not like her, Max; she always returns my calls. And there's nothing on her social media feeds. No Facebook, no Twitter, no Instagram. At the very least, I'd have expected her to post on Instagram.'

Max was finger deep in a bag of crisps. He took out a few and popped them into his mouth. Then, between crunches, he said, 'Do you want to drive over? See if she's in?'

'Do you mind?' Alice said. 'It would put my mind at ease. What if she's hurt herself and can't call for help?'

'Sure. We'll take my car. She doesn't live far away, does she?'

'Twenty minutes at most….'

Fifteen minutes later and Max slowed his car to a crawl as Alice tried to remember how far down Eynsham Road Sarah lived. It was very rural, with isolated houses scattered here and there in seemingly random order.

'I think it's the next one. I'll know it when I see it. She's got some big oak gates across the entrance.'

Max drove slowly down the lane until a pair of enormous oak gates appeared. They were set back from the road and blocked their way. Alice stepped out of the passenger seat and walked to the intercom set back on a post. She pressed the "call" button and waited. Max pulled down the window, and the two waited patiently while the intercom made the call. Finally, after a minute, it hung up.

Alice looked across at Max. She looked even more worried than before they had set out earlier.

'Do you know the code?' Max asked.

Alice looked at the intercom. A small panel was beneath the "call" button with numbers written on it above the corresponding buttons.

'I did.' Alice said. 'But she's probably changed it since then.'

'Give it a try.' Max said.

Alice typed in the four-number code that she dug out from her memory and was amazed to hear the panel buzz and the gates begin to swing open. Alice hopped back in the car, and Max drove through the gates and turned around to the front of the house. He was amazed to see that it was primarily painted green and the window frames had been coloured pink. Money didn't buy you taste, he thought to himself as he marvelled at the beautiful house hidden behind the colour.

'Her car's here,' Alice said with a notable hint of concern etched onto her voice.

They exited the car, and Alice walked over to the front door and pressed the buzzer. She cupped her hands around her face, pushed her eyes to the glass door, and looked inside. She couldn't see anything apart from Sarah's cat, who looked back at her through the window. Alice pressed the buzzer again. The sound echoed behind the door, but no one came.

'Anything?' Max asked.

'Nothing.' Alice said quietly.

'There's a window that's slightly open around here,' Max said, beckoning Alice around the side of the house. 'I could probably get my arm in and pull the window latch.'

'Do you think we should?' Alice asked, torn between her worries and the realisation that she may be making a mountain out of a molehill.

'What's the worst that could happen?' Max asked.

'We get arrested for breaking and entering?'

'Sarah's your friend. I'm sure she'd understand. And besides, I'm not breaking anything, and we're not going to steal anything..'

'I suppose.'

'And what if she is inside and hurt and can't ring for help?'

Reluctantly Alice agreed, and between them, they managed to push Max into a position where he could reach inside the small open window and unlatch the larger one. Together they both climbed inside the house.

Nervously they began a search of the house. Alice called Sarah's name at the top of her voice, but no reply came. Instead, she found herself dancing with Buster the cat, who had taken that opportunity to wrap himself around her legs. She knelt and gave him some fuss.

'Where's mummy, hey?' She said as Buster nudged her with his head. 'She wouldn't go anywhere without caring for you, now would she?'

Max came out of the kitchen. 'There's nothing down here. The cat's bowl's empty. Not much water left either.'

'Max, I'm really worried. Sarah would never leave Buster like this, never!'

'Perhaps we should ring the police?'

'Maybe. Let's search upstairs first. I'll just feed Buster.'

As Alice and Buster entered the kitchen, Max took the stairs two at a time and quickly searched the bedrooms. Then, a few minutes later, he stepped into the bathroom.

Alice met Max as she began to climb the stairs. He was coming back down them, and he was as pale as a sheet.

'Max? Are you okay? What is it?'

Max took Alice by the hand and led her back down the stairs.

'We need to leave.' He said, his voice tinged with fear.

'Max? Max, what is it? What did you find?'

He struggled with the words. They came at him in no particular order.

'Sarah. It's Sarah. I'm sorry Alice but Sarah's dead. She's been killed.'

Sixteen

The conference room at Thames Valley Police HQ at Kidlington was filled almost to capacity. Cameramen from ITV, the BBC and Sky News were setting up directly in front of a plain wooden plinth set upon a small stage backdropped by a large flag with the logo of the Thames Valley Police printed on it. A crew from CNN had caught the whiff of a big story, and one of their microphones rested on the plinth, surrounded by others. There was a big story coming, and the sense of excitement in the large crowd was tangible.

The hum of voices eased as Detective Chief Inspector Graham walked out onto the stage and adjusted one of the microphones. Stanton and Luton stood on either side of him with their arms crossed behind them. Graham looked across at one of his press officers and said, 'We good to go?'

The press officer looked down at his laptop's screen and then back at Graham. He held a thumb up in acknowledgement. The press conference was being live-streamed across the internet with simultaneous broadcasts across the panacea of social media feeds that belonged to the force. Several million people across the globe had already joined the live stream. No one had to wait for the ten o'clock news any more. That gave Graham a short window of opportunity to dictate the narrative.

'Good afternoon, ladies and gentlemen; my name is Detective Chief Inspector Graham of the Major Investigation Team at Thames Valley Police. I have a short statement which I would like to read out to you. I would be grateful if you could hold back any questions until the end. Is everyone ready?'

Graham looked around the room at the hoard of press that arrived to hear his statement. He recognised one or two familiar faces, but most were unknown. He had never spoken to as many people at a single press conference before. It unnerved him a little. The gravity of what he was about to say was not lost on him. The Chief Super had wanted to hold off on the serial killer angle, but Graham had insisted it was included in his speech. The Chief Constable had the final say. 'We can't hide this from them. We should be upfront with them, or they'll never forgive us. Not after last time. If there's a desperate killer out there, they must be told. They need to be able to protect themselves, and they can't do that blind.'

Graham steeled himself.

'Very well. Then I'll start.'

He cleared his throat.

'Four days ago, Tom and Sarah Parkes were brutally murdered in their own home by an unknown assailant who also killed fifteen-year-old Bethany Wright. Since then, every resource available to the Thames Valley Police has been utilised in the search for Molly Parkes, who we believed was kidnapped by the killer. Thousands of officers from Oxfordshire and surrounding counties have been involved in the search for Molly. I want to thank them and the RAF for their help and assistance in supplying us with sophisticated search and rescue equipment. Their help has been invaluable.

'As many of you know, a body was discovered yesterday in fields approximately a mile from the Parkes' home. I am aware of some speculation in the press about the body's identity, but I can only now confirm that the body is that of fifteen-year-old Molly Parkes. She was raped and murdered within an hour of being taken.'

There was a sudden gush of excitement, and a wall of flashes went off in Graham's face. He held up a hand, and the gush deflated.

'I am sure you are all also aware that there was a discovery of another female found brutally murdered in her home. She had sadly lain undiscovered for some time before my officers found her. Jane Wilson had been savagely attacked, raped and murdered in the safety of her own home. I can now confirm that the officers that discovered Miss Wilson were following leads in the Parkes' case. It is my belief and the working assumption of my officers that we are looking for one offender in both cases.'

Another gush. Another wall of flashes.

Graham paused. He waited as the hum died off. 'In the course of our investigation, we have encountered several disturbing and, quite frankly, alarming facts that we now wish to share with the general public. Naturally, we do this with some trepidation. We do not intend to alarm anyone, scare anyone, or cause any unnecessary fear in the community. Still, we believe it is our moral and legal duty to share with you what we know, and fear may be happening.'

The silence in the room was profound. Nobody spoke or dared look away.

Following our investigation, 'We believe that the offender we are tracking targets single females living alone within the Thames Valley Area, particularly around the Cherwell Valley district. We believe he has broken into many homes in the area while the occupant is out and steals or moved items of small value. We believe he may be collecting these items as some sort of memento. We believe he may have struck dozens of times over an indeterminate period. In many cases, the target may not even have been aware that they had been the victim of a break-in. We also fear that, in some cases, the offender remains on the property when the occupant returns home. In two cases, we know that that has ended in tragedy.'

Two dozen hands rose in the throng of press. Graham ignored them.

'We would urge residents to be extra vigilant in their security. While we hunt this man, we strongly recommend not leaving your windows and doors unlocked, even if you are inside your home. If you can take extra precautions, please do so.

'If you believe this man may have visited you at any time in the near or distant past, please ring us as soon as possible. Our dedicated telephone number should be appearing on your screens now. However mundane or insignificant you may think it, please call us. Let us judge the facts. Let us help keep you safe.

'To anyone who thinks they may know this man or have suspicions of a brother, father, uncle or friend, please call us. Give us a name. Someone knows this man. All calls will be in the strictest confidence, and you won't be asked to give your name. Very well, I'll take questions....'

Everyone stood at once. Graham's press officer took his microphone to a man in the front row of seats. There was a hierarchy in play, despite the illusion of chaos. Seniority won.

'Jack Harbour, BBC. You say the killer targets females living alone, but how does that relate to the murder of the Parkes family?'

'At first, we weren't sure that it did. However, on further investigation, we're now confident that the same man is responsible in both cases. We believe he has escalated his offending and no longer solely targets women who live alone.'

'So, no one's safe?'

'No.' Graham said bluntly. 'No one should consider themselves safe.'

'Lacey Winslow, Sky News. DCI Graham, do you expect people to close their doors and windows? Even when they're in their homes? Do you realise it's almost a hundred degrees out there? It's been one of the hottest years on record, we're all suffering in the heat, and you expect people to close their windows?'

'Yes, I do. It's not safe to leave them open. It's a small price to pay, but we think our man is an opportunist. He enters people's homes without making it obvious they've been broken into. So don't make it easy for him.'

Graham's press officer carried the microphone to a small man on the second row.

'Jonathon Price, Central News. You say the killer breaks in while people are out and waits until they return? Is it possible that many people in Oxfordshire have been in this man's presence without knowing?'

'That's possible, yes. In fact, we're sure of it.'

'Why does he do that? Is he getting some sexual gratification from it in some way?'

Graham shook his head. 'I'm afraid I really couldn't say. I'm not a psychologist; I'm not here to speculate on his motivations. I'm here to stop him. I'm sure I can leave the speculation in your good hands..'

There was a faint chuckle of amusement in the crowd.

Four rows back from the front, a young woman in her twenties stood and took the microphone. She was smartly dressed and lightly made up. She had carefully prepared her question and threw it at Graham directly.

'Clare Hampton, Oxford Times. Can you tell me, DCI Graham, if it's true that Lucy Lovelace, daughter of Jack Lovelace, the infamous Cherwell Valley Strangler and herself almost a victim of a serial killer, is working with you on this case?'

The room exploded with excitement. No one had seen that coming. Everyone looked to the young reporter with renewed respect. If it was true, it was an explosive revelation.

'There are hundreds of officers working on the case, Miss Hampton. Each is as important as the other.'

'Is that a yes or a no?'

'I'm not sure it's relevant.'

'You don't think it's relevant that the daughter of Oxfordshire's worst serial murderer and a man who embarrassed and disgraced the force now works for it and is part of the team looking for Oxfordshire's second worst serial killer? I think it's very relevant.'

From the rising hum in the room and the continuous flashing from the cameras at the edge of the room, it was clear to Graham that everyone else thought it was relevant too.

Graham cleared his throat. 'Yes, Miss Hampton. Detective Constable Lovelace reports to me directly as part of the Major Investigation Team.'

To the north of the county, Lucy Lovelace said, 'Fuck,' and all the eyes in the room that had one minute been watching a live stream of the press conference now turned their gaze on her.

'Fuck.'

'That's rather aptly put.' Spencer agreed. He stood and looked about the room filled with uniformed and plain-clothes officers. 'Right. Well, you lot can all fuck off too.'

'It's our station, mate.' A voice said from the other side of the room.

'Right then,' Spencer said, undeterred. 'We'll fuck off then. Come on. Up you get.'

Lovelace got up and followed Spencer out of the room.

'Fuck.' Lovelace said again.

'If you say that again, I will take it as a proposition and get you drunk.' Spencer said.

'No, you wouldn't. You're too much of a gent.'

'I'm an illusion.' Spencer said, smiling at her sweetly. 'But no, you're probably right. So I suppose we'd better go back to Kidlington?'

'Graham's going to fire me.'

'Probably.' Spencer said. 'But it's been fun.'

'Seriously. He's going to fire me.'

'No, he won't,' Spencer disagreed. 'This case is now guaranteed to make international news and plop us all over the front page of every rag this side of Moscow. I wouldn't be surprised if Graham leaked the whole thing himself. This way, he controls the narrative, and 99% of the conversation will no longer be about how we haven't even got a single suspect....'

'Do you think...' Lovelace asked, hopefully.

'Excuse me...'

The familiar figure of Sergeant Beauchamp hovered warily nearby.

'Yes?' Spencer said curtly.

'I thought you might be interested in this...' Sergeant Beauchamp handed Spencer a digital printout that had just fallen across his desk. 'I was watching the press conference. I thought this was right up your street.'

Spencer read the sheet. Now it was his turn to swear.

'Fuck.'

'What is it? Lovelace asked.

Spencer handed Lovelace the sheet. 'There's been another murder.'

***

Forty-five minutes later, Spencer and Lovelace drove through a pair of large wooden gates and up to the front of the Green House. There were a dozen police cars on the drive and a throng of policemen moving around. An incident van had been brought up from Kidlington, and it sat looking squat and out of place to one side of the drive. On the road past the house, camera crews had begun to gather, sniffing the faintest smell of another murder. Traffic police had set up a roadblock a mile apart at either end of the Eynsham Road and diverted what traffic it could around the scene. In the air, a press helicopter hovered a hundred feet up and was banking slowly around the house, taking an aerial shot of the latest scene for the ten o'clock news.

Lovelace and Spencer could hardly hear themselves talk for the noise. They watched as Stanton walked over, clutching a cigarette in one hand and a radio in the other. Under the helicopter's noise, he said, 'DI Luton's taking charge. DCI Graham's been summoned to the headmaster's office. Reckon he's getting the mother of all bollockings!'

Lovelace glanced at Spencer, who ignored the implications of Graham's meeting with the top brass. 'What's with the helicopter?' He asked.

'Steve's on the phone with Air Traffic Control. That's the fourth chopper to fly by in as many minutes. He's getting a No-Fly zone put in place for a mile in either direction on health and safety grounds.'

As he spoke, the helicopter banked sharply right and began to rise into the sky. As it went, so too did the noise until all that could be heard was the faint din of a hundred voices in conversation.

'What's the score?' Lovelace asked. 'Is it one of ours?'

Stanton nodded glumly. He sucked the end of his cigarette. 'Yeah, reckon so. Victim's thirty-two-year-old Sarah Lipton, a financial consultant for a big firm in Oxford. She lives alone. She worked mostly from home, too. Went out on a night out with friends the night before last and returned home yesterday morning. No one had heard from her in the last twenty-four hours, and one of her mates was concerned. So she and her boyfriend came in and let themselves in through an open window at the side of the house.'

'The window was open?' Lovelace asked.

'Not by much,' Stanton said. 'But enough. We reckon it's where the killer gained entry.'

'No other signs of forced entry?'

Stanton said there wasn't.

'Let's see the body.'

They gathered in the bathroom on the first floor. It was a nightmarish scene. The body of Sarah Lipton was still in-situ, sprawled out next to an ornate free-standing bath. Once forensics photographed and examined the body, one took a bathrobe and placed it over the victim.

Lovelace noticed the bath was still full of bath water, although not quite full to the brim. There were signs that Sarah Lipton had been in the bath when her killer struck. She had fought for her life, and much of the bath water had splashed onto the floor and the surrounding walls. What was left of the water in the bath was coloured with her blood, indicating that she had been struck first while still in the bath. On the floor, where Sarah Lipton now lay, blood pooled around her head. The bathrobe that covered her naked body was soaking up much of the blood that no doubt covered her head.

Lovelace looked up at the ceiling and the walls. There was blood spatter all over them. Sarah Lipton had taken a horrific and violent beating.

'We think she was still in the bath when he struck.' Stanton said. 'She put up a bit of a fight. There are skin and blood remnants beneath her fingertips. We're confident we can pull up some decent DNA from them.'

That's all well and good, Lovelace thought, so long as the killer was on file. But, unfortunately, she was pretty sure he wasn't. The man was a ghost.

Stanton moved around to where Sarah Lipton lay. 'He pulled her out of the bath and dragged her here. There are signs of sexual assault, but we'll need to wait for the autopsy to know for sure.'

'If it's our man,' Spencer said glumly, 'I'm afraid she won't have been spared that indignity.'

'No. Quite.' Stanton reached down to the body and pulled back the makeshift cover. 'Once he'd finished, he hit her. He hit her multiple times with a small-headed blunt instrument, probably a hammer.'

'Like the Parkes and the girls and Jane Wilson.' Lovelace said.

'Exactly like that. And he hit her a lot. There's a burn mark, too. Here. Just like the others. I'm pretty sure that's how he incapacitates them.'

Lovelace and Spencer looked down at what was left of Sarah Lipton's head. It was a grim sight, and neither of them could look for long.

'That's a lot of rage.' Lovelace said.

'It is.' Stanton agreed. 'She'd have most likely been unconscious after the first blow and likely dead after the second.'

'And yet still, he kept hitting her.'

'He's certainly got some issues.' Stanton agreed.

'Barely four days after Molly Parkes..' Lovelace said, thinking aloud.

Spencer looked across at his partner and tilted his head to one side. Lovelace recognised the movement. Spencer was intrigued.

'What do you mean?' He asked.

'It's not long. Not long enough.' Lovelace replied. 'Some serial killers kill and then don't kill for a long time. It's their downtime if you like. Their fallow time. Whatever satisfaction they get from the kill sates their appetite. Whether it's the rage or the sexual gratification they get from the kill, most killers don't feel the need to kill again until they lose that gratification. Some will return to the crime scene to re-live it or follow the news reports. They'll get off on the coverage. They'll buy into the collective grief, attend the funeral or services, and even offer their services to the police. Whatever they need to do to keep the feeling alive. In some cases, that could be years, sometimes months.'

'But four days is a bit soon?' Spencer asked.

'Way too soon. He's like a drug addict who needs more and more to reach the same level of gratification and needs it often. So he'll kill again, and it will be soon....'

Stanton and Spencer looked at the young Constable and saw the fear in her eyes.

'And we still haven't a fucking clue who he is.'

***

'No work tonight?' Rachel Hodges asked as she poured herself another glass of wine.

She was sitting on the couch watching the television when Dan came through from the garden, wiping his greasy hands on an old rag.

'Not tonight. Yan thinks he may have some work for me tomorrow if that's okay.'

'Yeah, sure.' She said, although Dan noticed the inflexion in her voice.

'Everything okay?' Dan asked.

She nodded at the television screen. 'It's just these murders,' she said. 'It's got everyone a bit freaked out at work. Some of the girls are having sleepovers, so no one stays at home alone. It's just got me a bit worried, that's all. When you're not here, it's just me and the kids. It's scary.'

'I heard about that on the radio.' Dan said. 'There are some sick fucks about.'

'I don't know what to do with the kids,' Rachel said. 'I'm on nights tomorrow. I might ask Mum if she'll stay over for the night. I don't want to leave the kids on their own.'

'That's a good idea. I'll lock up the gin!'

'Dan! Don't be mean.'

Dan leant over and kissed his wife. She pushed him away. 'You stink! Go and have a shower! Sometimes I think you love that bike more than me!'

'Well, you're both a pretty good ride!' He joked and then dodged the remote control that Rachel threw at him.

He picked the remote control up and put it on the small coffee table, just out of his wife's reach. He was about to go up for a shower when something on the television screen caught his eye. He picked up the controller and turned the volume up.

A female television reporter was standing on a country lane, giving her piece to the camera. Behind her, a bank of police cars littered the road.

She spoke with a presenter's edge.

'After today's explosive press conference - another murder, deep in the heart of the Oxfordshire countryside. Not since Richard Ramirez terrorised the suburban communities of Los Angeles in the early eighties has one community felt under such sustained attack. It's not without good reason that he's been named as England's Night Stalker.'

She said more, but Dan no longer heard the words. He watched in horror as the pictures changed to an aerial shot of the crime scene from about a hundred feet away. It was a familiar house. It was green with oddly painted pink woodwork. His heart missed a beat. He had been in that house just a couple of nights ago.

The pictures changed to a drab-looking press conference.

'To anyone who thinks they may know this man or have suspicions of a brother, father, uncle or friend, please call us. Give us a name.'

Yan.

Then it came to him again. Yan.

I don't like the way he looks at her.

Dan remembered his conversation with Rachel on the same day they had broken into the Green House.

I don't like the way he is with Issy. He looks at her weirdly.

And then, again.

I'm just saying he looks at her weirdly. Creepy.

Yan was weird. And he was creepy; he couldn't deny that. He paid way too much attention to girls and didn't like how he was with women in general, but still. A killer? Yan?

But whichever way he looked at it, he couldn't escape the unease that crept over him.

'Dan?'

He turned and looked at his wife.

'Are you okay?' She asked. He had gone white.

'Yeah.' He said uneasily. 'I've got to go out for ten minutes. I've run out of beers. Just going to pop to the offy. Do you need anything?'

'Chocolate. And lock the door behind you.'

Ten minutes later, Dan stood in the queue at his local supermarket with a six-pack of beers, a large bar of milk chocolate with nuts, and a pay-as-you-go mobile phone. It was the cheapest in the store, and he'd only need it for five minutes. He unboxed it in the street and dropped the packaging in the bin. It took five minutes to register it and another minute to call 111.

'I've got some information. About these murders. I've got a name for you.'

Dan wasn't a snitch, but there were limits to his loyalty. As he made the call, he thought of his wife and daughter, Issy. And then he thought of Connor and the man that sat next to him on the floor of his front room playing video games. There was every chance he could be wrong. There was no proof: just a random coincidence and a bad feeling.

'One moment, please.'

There was a slight pause while Dan's call was transferred. He had a second to change his mind. He held the line.

'Good evening. Thames Valley Police.'

'Yeah. I've got a name for you. About these murders.'

'Would you like to give your name, sir?'

'No.'

'Very good, sir. And the information you want to give is regarding the murders?'

'Yes. You should look at a man called Yan Kowalski.'

'Can you spell the surname, please.'

'K-o-w-a-l-s-k-i.'

'Thank you, sir. And what makes you think this person may have something to do with the recent murders?'

'Just look into him, will you? It's good information.'

Dan Hodges hung up the phone and dropped it into the bin. He walked away with his chocolate and beer. He'd done his bit. It was up to them now.

Across the county, one of the hundreds of volunteers that manned the phones in the incident room at Kidlington typed the name Kowlaski into the report of the telephone conversation he had just had.

Since the press conference that afternoon, the phones had been ringing off the hook. They had received information on almost two thousand names, each carefully logged and filed. Some had been flagged on VISOR, and the sex offenders register and warranted immediate investigation. Their names were forwarded to a task force of nearly three hundred police officers specially tasked with interviewing suspects.

Yan Kowalski raised no red flags. The volunteer clicked 'save' on his file, and the name disappeared among thousands of others.

<h1 style="text-align:center">Seventeen</h1>

The afternoon wore into the evening until the shadows drew long pictures on the ground, and the sun slowly dropped beneath the horizon. The evening sky exploded in vibrant colours as the pale blue of the day gently faded to dark. It was a dusk full of the colours of summer, and it was in sharp contrast to the sombre mood of those investigating the murder at The Green House.

Lovelace and Spencer had remained at the crime scene for the rest of the afternoon, trying to piece together the final moments of Sarah Lipton's life. Luton and Stanton came and went like men on a mission, guiding and directing the team of forensics officers that swarmed over the house like blue ants. There was a sense among all those involved that events were beginning to overtake them.

DS Stanton found Lovelace and Spencer pouring over documents in Miss Lipton's home office.

'Find anything?'

Lovelace shook her head. 'Not a thing,' she said glumly. 'She worked from home three days a week and spent two days at her office in the city.' She turned the page of a document she was reading. 'Clayton Thorpe Ltd. Looks like some sort of hedge fund management company. Very wealthy. Sarah looked to have some major clients with some very deep pockets. All of which gets us nowhere.'

'Boyfriends? Exes? Any hint that she may have had a visitor recently?'

Everyone knew what Stanton meant by "visitor."

Spencer shook his head. 'Not a thing. No recent exes and no current boyfriend. We've spoken to her best friend and a couple of work colleagues, and the victim hadn't mentioned any concerns to them.'

'The boyfriend angle is a dead end anyway.' Lovelace said. 'The reason we're not finding anything in our victim's lives is probably because they are all strangers to our killer. He doesn't know them or come into their lives until the last minute. Even when he does come into their lives, they most likely aren't aware of him.'

'So how the bloody hell are we going to find him?' Stanton asked.

'Well, his victims aren't picked entirely at random. There's a method to it somewhere.' Lovelace explained. 'We're sure he picked Molly because he saw her from the neighbour's house, but we don't understand why he picked the neighbour in the first place. Somewhere along the line, he's had cause to meet his victim and for whatever reason, they've made an impression on him and he's targeted them directly. All the victims must be connected in this way. The question is, how did he meet them? Did he pass them in the street and follow them home? Did he come to their homes as a tradesman or a delivery driver? We just don't know.'

'And every time he kills,' Spencer added, 'rather than leaving more evidence and clues for us to follow, all he does is muddy the waters some more.'

'And the more he kills, the better he gets.' Lovelace said.

'And the harder he is to catch.' Stanton finished. He sighed. 'Well, there's nothing more you two can do here; you might as well go home.' He paused. 'Graham's been on the phone.'

Lovelace stole a glance at Spencer, who pretended not to notice. They waited.

Stanton said, 'He wants to see you first thing.'

Lovelace nodded. She felt the firing squad lining up for duty.

She drove Spencer home and pulled up outside his house. Neither spoke, but Spencer could feel the tension and see the anxiety writ large across Lovelace's face.

'Do you want to come in for a coffee?'

'I'd prefer something stronger.' Lovelace replied, her voice faintly dulled by worry.

'I have wine, gin and whiskey.' Spencer said cheerily.

'I should probably go home..'

'Bollocks.' Spencer said bluntly. 'Let's have a drink.' He looked at the clock on the car's dash. It had just gone eight o'clock. 'I don't know about you, but I'm starving too. I'll buy us a takeaway. What do you fancy? Indian?'

'I could murder a curry.' Lovelace agreed.

'Good. That's settled, then. You can meet Sophie.'

'Who's Sophie? Your wife?'

'Good god, no. Not that miserable harridan. Sophie's my daughter. She spends half her time at her mother's and the other half at mine. She picks and chooses as she pleases, and by the look of all the lights in my house, it looks like tonight's my lucky night.'

'She picks and chooses?' Lovelace queried. 'That's some relaxed parenting!'

'She's sixteen going on twenty-six.' Spencer explained. 'Come on. I'll open a bottle of wine. You look like a red kinda girl?'

Spencer was mildly alarmed to find that the front door was unlocked. That wasn't unusual as most people left their doors unlocked when they were home, particularly in the small village they called home, but with an opportunistic killer on the loose, he would have to have a word with Sophie.

Spencer's home was a modest modern house on the fringes of a quiet village at the edge of Cherwell Valley.

There were good views from the front of the house as it looked out over darkened fields. In the distance, Lovelace could make out the silhouette of a forest, back-lit by the sunset.

'Come on through.'

Lovelace followed Spencer into a small, well-lit hallway, past an antique coat rack and a small mahogany table. An old telephone sat on the table, reminiscent of a bygone era. She followed Spencer along the hallway and into a large, modern kitchen. Black marble worktops ran along the wall's far side, beneath which a 1930s-looking black flue topped a substantial six-ring cooker. In the middle of the room was a rectangular island that ran almost the entire length of the kitchen. A sink with chrome taps sat at one end, and at the other were four bar-type chairs placed on either side.

Lovelace was impressed. The smart, well-dressed Detective Sergeant had good taste in home decor, too, she noticed. Spencer was full of little surprises.

Spencer opened one of the cupboard doors and reached up for two fat-bottomed wine glasses. He picked a bottle from a rack that sat, fully stocked, on the floor next to a large, black refrigerator. He took one of the stools and sat down, pouring two glasses of wine. Lovelace sat opposite him.

'Did you get a glass for me?'

Sophie Spencer came through the door with a flurry. She was dressed in a pair of grey joggers and a blue hoodie. She was pretty, Lovelace thought, with a mature face that lied about her age. She didn't look a day under eighteen. Her hair was the darkest black that was currently tied back in a ponytail. As she entered, Lovelace noticed that she tilted her head to one side, like she had seen Spencer do on several occasions. Sophie Spencer was intrigued.

'Sorry,' Sophie said, slightly embarrassed. 'I didn't realise we had company.' She looked sternly at her father. 'If I'd have known, I'd have worn something better….'

'Sophie, this is Lucy. Lucy, this is my daughter Sophie.' Spencer said, skilfully ignoring the rebuke.

Sophie held out a small hand that was soft to the touch.

'Pleased to meet you,' she said in well-clipped, accent-free tones. 'Dad rarely brings friends home.'

'Lucy is a colleague.' Spencer said by way of explanation.

'Really?' Sophie's eyes lit up. 'How very interesting. Dad never brings colleagues home!'

Sophie pulled up a chair next to Lovelace and sat down.

'Can I have a glass?' She asked.

Spencer reached up for another glass and poured a small one for Sophie.

'That's very mean.' She said. To Lovelace, she said, 'He's very tight with his wine.'

'You're very young.' Spencer said.

'To drink in a pub? Yes, I am,' Sophie said. 'To drink in my own home, I only have to be over five. Which I am.' She pushed her glass back at her dad. 'So don't be mean.'

Spencer relented and filled her glass up.

They ate takeaway food whilst sitting at the island. Lovelace turned down a second glass which was fervently ignored by Sophie, who re-filled their glasses.

'You can take the spare room.' Sophie said. Lovelace had started to argue, but Sophie refused to enter into a discussion about it. As far as she was concerned, the matter was settled.

They talked for hours about nothing in particular. Lovelace learned a great deal about Sophie and her father and the strained relationship the two of them had with Sophie's mother. They discussed Sophie's schooling and what she wanted to do for a career. They talked about boys or lack thereof and spoke about Lovelace, who carefully and skilfully avoided dealing with any facts about her life, continually bringing the conversation back to Sophie, who never noticed the deflection. Lovelace was using her skills as an interrogator to butter Sophie up and kept her talking. Spencer watched the display with an increasing sense of appreciation. He made a mental note never to underestimate her.

They opened a second bottle of wine, much to Spencer's annoyance, but he soon felt his mood soften. It was nice to see Lovelace and Sophie get on so well. Sophie was apt to be a little too social and friendly, and he detected in Lovelace a kindred spirit who preferred her own company and the sound of silence to the innate chatter of a teenage girl. However, Spencer was no fool, and he was well aware that the two girls were closer in age to each other than Lovelace was to him. Nevertheless, it was nice to watch them open up and relax.

As the night drew on, Sophie retired to bed, not before topping her glass up and kissing her father affectionately on the cheek.

She came to Lovelace and kissed her on the cheek too. 'It was lovely to meet you,' she said, her words slightly less well-clipped than they were a couple of hours ago. The wine was beginning to take its toll, and Lovelace saw the shadow behind Sophie's brown eyes.

Lovelace turned to Spencer when she had gone and said, 'She's nice. She's a credit to you.'

'I can't take all the credit,' Spencer joked. 'Her mother gave birth to her!'

'The thing I can't understand,' Lovelace went on, 'is why you don't want to be Inspector. You're good. You're clever. You have a lovely house, a beautiful daughter, and probably the most boring job in the Thames Valley Police. It's like you're sitting behind a desk, slowly waiting to retire and die. You're so much better than what you've settled for.'

'I don't think I've settled.' Spencer countered. 'But I can see why you might think that. And to begin with, I did want all that. I took all the courses, passed all the exams, and made the right noises to the powers that be. All my pins were lining up nicely.'

'So what happened?'

'I realised I didn't want all that. First, it was my wife that wanted it. Before that, it was my father that wanted it. Everybody wanted what they thought was best for me. One day I suddenly realised that that wasn't what I wanted. I didn't want the stress or the responsibility. I just wanted to go to work, do what needed to be done, and come home.'

'You must have a purpose?' Lovelace asked.

'Must I?' Spencer countered. 'Why?'

'Because everyone has a purpose. Something to live for, something that gets them out of bed in the morning and drives them on.'

'What drives you?' Spencer asked.

'Nice deflection.' Lovelace said. 'But I asked first. So go on. Tell me. What drives Detective Sergeant Phil Spencer enough to keep him sane at work?'

Spencer smiled. 'For one thing,' he said, draining his glass of wine and pouring another, 'I don't think I have the most boring job in the Thames Valley Police. I find it rather interesting. But I never wanted to be a copper. That was all my father. He was a policeman, as was his father before him. It was something of a family tradition. Normal police work bored me. I like puzzles and mysteries; as you know, police work is nothing like you see on the telly. It's all very structured and linear. There's no individuality anymore. Everything's a process. There are rules and procedures. There's no romance in it. I like what I do because it allows me to think for myself and draw conclusions without following a flow chart. And also, I don't get to mix with people very much, which suits me to the ground.'

He laughed as if he had made some sort of joke, but Lovelace couldn't help but see the honesty in what he said. Spencer preferred to be alone, but he most certainly wasn't lonely.

'So, what did you want to do?' Lovelace asked.

Spencer grabbed his wine and stood up. 'Come on then; I'll show you.'

Lovelace followed Spencer to a small door at the far side of the kitchen. He unlocked the door and stepped inside, reaching the wall behind him and switching on the light. Lovelace followed.

They had stepped inside what Lovelace guessed was once a very basic garage. But now, it was anything but basic. Three motorbikes were lined up side by side at the far end, and Lovelace recognised their shape. On two walls was hanging every piece of engineering equipment any self-respecting mechanic would have been proud to own. Lovelace looked around in awe. There were some pieces of equipment that even she didn't recognise, and they all hung from the walls in a scene of visual harmony. There were lathes, drills, and welding equipment lodged into every spare corner of the room, and Lovelace's eye was drawn to a worktop upon which sat an old-looking motorcycle in the early stages of renovation.

Lovelace walked over and ran her hand over the frame. 'She's beautiful.'

'It's a 1930s Brough Superior.'

'I know.' Lovelace said. 'It's the same model T E Lawrence was riding when he died.'

Spencer didn't look surprised. The fact that he wasn't surprised about Lovelace didn't surprise him anymore. She was something special.

'You know your history?' Spencer asked.

'I know bikes.' Lovelace replied.

'I've been working on her for a couple of years. I reckon I've got a couple to go before she's good to ride. I found her rotting in the garden of an old man who had been burgled. He let me have her for a song.'

'So you wanted to be a mechanic?' Lovelace asked.

'An engineer. I started stripping motors and engines almost before I could walk, to see how they worked. Engines fascinate me. Any parts I can't get, I machine myself. I love it. It's honest.'

Lovelace stepped over to the other three motorbikes lined up at the front of the garage. There was a sports tourer in gunmetal, a Harley Davidson painted in British racing green, and a Suzuki Hayabusa in blue and white with Japanese writing on its tail. Lovelace walked over to the 'Busa, draped her leg over the seat, and picked up the bike so she was in the riding position.

'You look like you've done that before.' Spencer said.

'Once or twice,' Lovelace said cryptically. 'I have a second generation new model ', Busa.'

'Really? I didn't think the new model was out yet. Didn't they stop making them?'

'They did.' Lovelace said, smiling. 'My Uncle Mike is the European Project manager for Suzuki Motorcycles in Japan. I grew up riding Suzukis. The ride height of this beast was altered in pre-production so that I could ride it. She's a big bird, but she's delicate. Sensitive. Uncle Mike had a prototype of the new model shipped over for me to ride.'

Spencer stared at Lovelace with his mouth wide open. 'You're kidding me? I'd love to see it.'

'I'm not allowed to ride in the day in case bike spotters see it. But, if you don't mind riding in the dark, I may even let you have a go….'

'That,' Spencer said, 'is a date.'

***

It had been an exciting day. He sat in front of his computer screen and watched the clip repeatedly. It was a news bulletin from earlier in the day. He had missed it the first time as he had been away from the house, but he soon caught the thread on his social media feeds. He played the clip again and again and again. He was absorbed by it. Fascinated. It drew him in and excited him.

Can you tell me, DCI Graham, if it's true that Lucy Lovelace, daughter of Jack Lovelace, the infamous Cherwell Valley Strangler and herself, almost a victim of a serial killer, is working with you on this case?

And again and again and again.

Lucy Lovelace. Jack Lovelace. The Cherwell Valley Strangler. Serial killers and murderers. Fear.

It aroused him.

He paused the clip on a still photograph of Lucy Lovelace alongside a photo of her father. *The Cherwell Valley Strangler.*

And they had given him a name too. Oxfordshire's Night Stalker. The Night Prowler. He liked that. It appealed to him. He was somebody. Somebody to be reckoned with.

And they had no idea. She had no idea. Lucy Lovelace, daughter of a serial killer, so close, and she didn't know it. It was intense. He could feel the excitement rise in his veins. He was a master of the game.

He trawled the internet for news. He searched Lucy Lovelace and absorbed every nugget of information he could find. He searched for her on social media, but she was nowhere to be found. She was elusive. Unknown. Then there was the man in the suit. The older man who smelled so sweetly of cologne that it made him feel sick. Detective Sergeant Phil Spencer.

He was elusive too, but he hadn't expected to find much. Men of that age weren't into social media as much as women of Lovelace's age. But still, he looked. He craved knowledge as much as fear. Knowledge was power. And knowledge gave him fear, which was his most incredible power. Power over them all. Absolute power.

And then he found it.

He almost missed it. It was a small detail, but he revelled in those. It was an online post from the Thames Valley Police nearly four years ago. Detective Sergeant Spencer receiving an award for something or other. He didn't care about that. It was the girl that caught his eye. The caption that went with the post named her as Spencer's proud young daughter, Sophie.

Sophie.

He clicked on the picture and expanded it. He narrowed in on the girl. She was pretty, with dark hair. She was wearing her school uniform. She wore a blazer over a crisp white shirt and a pleated skirt. He expanded the picture and manoeuvred the image until he could see the badge on the blazer. It said simply, "Cherwell Valley High School."

Interesting. Within seconds he had pulled up the social media feeds for Cherwell Valley High School. He poured over them all, looking for the pretty little girl with dark hair. It took him an hour, but he found her. It was a hockey tour in 2018. She was fourteen then, but she looked the same.

He sat back in his chair. Then he scrolled through his social media feeds, looking for Sophie Spencer.

This Account is Private. Send a friend request to see this user's posts.

Facebook, Twitter and Instagram. Locked solid. He trawled the less common social media sites, but the result was always the same. Sophie Spencer's accounts were shut tight. And if she was sensible enough to keep her accounts private, he knew very well that she wouldn't accept a friend request from a stranger. But there were other ways.

He went back over Cherwell Valley High's posts and looked again at the hockey tour from 2018. In the photograph, Sophie was joined by the team, proudly waving their hockey sticks. He copied all their names and wrote them down. He then went back over other posts and wrote down the names of two dozen of Sophie's school peers, boys and girls, of around her age group. He then went back online and found a photograph of an unknown boy of about sixteen. Using simple software, he manipulated the image until he had a picture of a boy in Cherwell Valley High's uniform standing with the school as a backdrop.

Familiarity was a dangerous tool.

He created several fake social media profiles using this boy's image and began inviting Sophie's peers and friends to join him. Not everyone at Cherwell Valley High shared Sophie's sense of security and privacy. At the very least, most of the boys had open accounts for anyone to see. As the evening drew on, he had acquired a dozen friends. Some were quite chatty. He indulged them as much as they bored him, giving him an opening into Sophie Spencer's life. And that was where he wanted to be.

He would need to be patient now. It was getting late. He opened Sophie's Facebook feed and sent a friend request. He would start there. Facebook was the easiest site to farm the information he wanted.

He sat back in his chair and closed his eyes. He could feel the sensation beginning to rise. The game was on.

Eighteen

Spencer made them both a hot breakfast of bacon and eggs and brewed a fresh pot
 of black coffee. They sat in his garden under the shade of an awning as the morning sun made its fiery ascent of the eastern sky. Lovelace felt dulled by the previous evening's drinks, and she shielded her eyes from the brightness while she drank her coffee. She never felt the pain of a hangover, but it always made her feel lethargic. She had showered quickly, tied her hair back as best she could, and was drawn to the patio by the smell of bacon.

Spencer looked immaculate in a crisp white shirt with gold cuff links and precisely pressed trousers.

'I trust you slept well?'

She had. She had slept the sleep of the dead, and only her alarm, set for six in the morning, had roused her.

'Very well, thank you. I want to pop home before we go to the office and put on some fresh clothes.'

They chatted about nothing in particular until the coffee reached their senses and lifted them.

Sophie entered the garden wearing a long white robe with her initials stitched onto them. She sat down and poured herself a coffee. She declined the bacon and eggs Spencer offered and opened her phone.

'Aren't you going to be late for school?' He asked.

'Free morning.' She said bluntly.

Spencer looked at Lovelace and said, 'Sometimes she manages as many as three words before lunch.'

Sophie sighed and opened her social media profiles. A dozen notifications were waiting for her, all of which had occurred through the night. She clicked on them individually, liking or "hearting" each one as if by rote. One or two she commented on, adding certain emojis as she saw fit. There were also two friend requests. She declined the first one without paying much attention. She did not recognise the person in the photo and had no friends in common, so it was most likely a bot or some random weirdo. The second picture was also unfamiliar, but the boy wore a Cherwell Valley High School Uniform, and they had at least twelve friends in common. She clicked "Accept" and thought no more about it.

'I'm going for a shower. I feel yuk.' She stood up to leave. 'It was nice to meet you, Lucy. You should come again.'

'Do you need a lift anywhere before we leave?' Spencer asked.

'No. I'll get the bus.'

'Oh, and Sophie,' Spencer said, 'next time you're in the house alone, lock the door behind you. And close all the windows.'

Sophie gave her father a curious look. 'You're serious?'

'Deadly. Promise me you'll lock the doors and windows behind you. And when you're at your mother's, even if your mother's at home. Promise me you'll lock the doors. At least until we catch this man.'

Sophie nodded, smiled a sweet goodbye to Lovelace and skipped inside the house.

'You ready to go?'

Lovelace drove them back to her house, and Spencer waited in the car while she ran inside and got changed. She returned smelling fresh and wearing clean clothes, but her hair remained scruffily unchanged.

Twenty minutes later, they walked into police HQ and up to Graham's office.

'There you are. You're late.'

DCI Graham looked old, Lovelace thought. He looked untidy, too, and that was unusual for him. He was nearly always well-presented, but today he looked markedly dishevelled. Lovelace put it down to the case and the stress he was under.

'We need to talk.' he said, looking directly at Lovelace. Then, to Spencer, he said, 'Wait out here, would you? I'll need to talk to you too, in a moment.'

Lovelace stole a glance at Spencer, who merely smiled at her. She entered Graham's office, and he closed the door behind her.

Before Graham could say anything, Lovelace said, 'I want you to know it wasn't me. I never told the press I was on the case. I never told anyone.'

'I know you didn't,' Graham said as he walked slowly around his desk.

'You can't know that, but I wanted you to know it wasn't me.'

'I do know that,' Graham said, 'because I leaked the information.'

Lovelace looked at him, slightly confused. 'Why?'

'It would have come out eventually,' Graham said as he sat in his chair. 'It was better that we controlled the flow of information. And besides, we had fuck all else to tell them.'

Spencer had been right. Graham had used her to deflect attention to the lack of progress in the case. She wasn't sure who was smarter. Graham for doing it, or Spencer for seeing the play as it unfolded.

'But that's not why I wanted to see you.'

'It isn't? I'm not fired?'

'Of course not. The chief's a bit apoplectic, but he always is. He'll get over it. I need you by my side. Where I can see you.'

'So what was it you wanted to see me about?'

'Firstly, you should know that Charlie regained consciousness through the night. She's still very poorly, but I think she could do with some friendly faces around her.'

Lovelace breathed a sigh of relief. Although she hadn't recognised it until now, the anxiety of Charlie's condition had worn heavily on her.

'Oh, thank god. We'll go and see her later. Secondly?'

Graham paused, and the anxiety flooded back to Lovelace. She had a horrible sense that she wouldn't enjoy whatever Graham was about to say. The longer Graham paused, the greater her anxiety became.

'Guv'?' Lovelace asked.

Graham reached down onto his desk, selected a piece of paper from the vast quantities there, and handed it to Lovelace.

'It's come from above. From the very top. I'll support you whatever you decide to do.'

Lovelace read the sheet of paper. It was an email from the prison governor at Her Majesty's Prison, Long Lartin, a Super Max facility hidden in plain view in the Worcestershire countryside. It was a prison for Category A prisoners. Only the very nasty and very dangerous were held within its unassuming walls. One among their number was her father, Jack Lovelace.

'What does he want?' She asked.

'No one knows. But he's asked to see you. He says he has information that pertains to the case you are on. I can only assume that your involvement has reached his ears.'

Lovelace looked down at the email. It was an official pass for her to attend the prison that day to speak to her father. It wasn't the first time he had asked to see her. He had sent her a visitor's pass every month since his incarceration. Every month for fifteen years, she had thrown it away.

'Send someone else.' She said plainly.

'I would,' Graham said softly. 'But he refuses to speak to anyone but you.'

He paused to let the information settle in Lovelace's brain.

'And if I refuse to go?' She asked.

'Then you have my full backing. Whatever information he has dies with him in that shit hole. We can crack this case without him.'

'I think it's BS.' Lovelace said. 'He doesn't know anything. He's playing us. It's what killers like him do. They want to get involved and be a part of the game. He'll want something. Nuggets of information to get off on. Or it will be something else. A play for concessions. He'll want something.'

'I agree.' Graham said. 'He can't possibly know anything that can help us. But..'

'But?'

'But the top brass are getting nervous. They think, at the very least, he may have some insight into the murders. This is coming from them, not me. If you decide not to go, I'll back you up.'

Lovelace folded the pass and slipped it into her trouser pocket.

'Okay,' She said at last. 'I'll go. But for you, not for them. And if I feel uncomfortable, I'll leave. With absolutely no hesitation.'

'I would expect no less.' Graham said, and then at the top of his voice, he shouted, 'Spencer!'

Spencer opened the door and walked in.

'You two are off on a road trip to HMP Long Lartin to visit Lucy's father. She's not to be left alone with him at any time. Do I make myself understood? I'll ring the Governor. That's the deal. Both of you in the room or neither of you in the room. If he doesn't like it, he can fuck off.'

Spencer looked at Graham and then at Lovelace. 'Okay. Let's go, then. I'll buy the ice creams.'

Ten minutes later, Lovelace's ruby-red Mercedes was motoring through the Cotswold Hills towards the peaceful Vale of Evesham.

*****

The proximity alarm at the front entrance to HMP Long Lartin shot out an angry and loud message declaring that anyone trying to bring a mobile phone into the facility would face the full consequences of the law. It said something about drugs and other illegal substances, but Lovelace and Spencer had made it through the door by then.

The reception area was more like the security gate at an airport. On three sides, the walls were reinforced glass which allowed those behind a good view of those entering the prison. To one side, a young prison officer had thrown open a hatch and looked out enquiringly.

'Can I help?' She asked.

Lovelace and Spencer dropped their warrant cards onto the desk and waited while the young officer checked their names alongside the official register of guests.

'Wait here.' She said, picking the warrant cards up and closing the hatch behind her.

Lovelace and Spencer watched as she went over to the desks behind her, which were crewed by nearly a dozen other prison officers. As the main gate for the prison, security was very tight, and each of the dozen sets of eyes closely monitored the screens in front of them. The young prison officer handed the warrant cards to what looked like a supervisor, who glanced at them before speaking into a radio. He walked out of the office and around to the glass wall separating Lovelace and Spencer from the rest of the prison. The supervisor looked across at the main desk, where the young officer had returned and nodded. There was a short buzz, and one of the reinforced glass panels swung inwards.

'DS Spencer. DC Lovelace. Please come through.'

They stepped into the main reception area.

'I'm afraid we will need to search you. May I ask if you have a mobile phone on your person? Any drugs of any description? Any needles or anything that may be used as a weapon?'

They both said they hadn't. The supervisor led them through a metal detector before they were body searched by more security. Lovelace was patted down extremely efficiently by a middle-aged woman with calloused hands. When they were done, they were led through a series of locked doors and into the main prison. Some security was very high-tech, while some was slightly more basic. Even in a supermax facility like this, Lovelace noticed, some of the best security was a simple lock and key. Many prison officers walked around with a huge ring of keys about their waists.

The supervisor led them through the building into a vast open space divided by fenced squares. Within some of the squares, several prisoners played games and exercised while some took advantage of the sun that bore down upon them. They walked the length of the open space until they came to a building that Lovelace guessed was the main office block. They were led through another series of locked doors until they were shown into the waiting area.

'The machine's on a free vend if you want a drink.' The supervisor said, indicating an old vending machine in the corner. 'The Governor knows you're here; he'll be with you shortly.'

'I was expecting to see my father.' Lovelace said.

'You will. The Governor wants a word first.'

The supervisor smiled and left the room. Lovelace heard a door being unlocked further down the corridor.

'I hate this place.' She said quietly.

'It is a miserable place,' Spencer agreed. 'Have you been here before?'

'Once.' Lovelace said. 'When I came back to the UK, I came to visit my father, but I changed my mind. I decided then that I would never see him. Never.'

'Just say the word,' Spencer said, 'and we'll leave.'

Lovelace smiled. 'No way. My curiosity has been piqued. Besides, I promised Graham.'

The door swung open, and a young man dressed in a well-fitting suit entered. He held a soft hand to each of them and said, 'Mark Seymour. I'm the governor here at Long Lartin.'

To Lovelace, he looked more like an over-dressed bank clerk than a prison governor. His hair was well-cropped and gelled back stylishly behind his ears. He was clean-shaven, and his eyes sparkled a vibrant green. His voice was soft and powerless when he spoke, but Lovelace detected a sharp mind behind the eyes. You had to be a specific type of character to manage the kind of people who made it to HMP. Long Lartin, Lovelace thought, and Mark Seymour didn't look the type. He barely looked capable of managing an under ten's football team.

'I'm sorry to divert you like this; I just wanted to catch you before you went in to see Jack.'

'Is there a problem?' Lovelace asked.

'No, no problem.' Seymour said. 'I just wanted to bring you up to speed on Jack Lovelace. Before you go in and see him.'

'I don't think you can tell me much about my father.' Lovelace said curtly.

'Perhaps not,' Seymour said. 'But the father you knew is not the man you will meet today. He's changed. He's an entirely different character.'

'Leopards don't change their spots.' Spencer said.

'We don't peddle cliched soundbites here, Detective Sergeant. We deal in rehabilitation and second chances. No one that comes here is beyond help. We firmly believe that leopards can change their spots if they want to. He speaks of you often,' Seymour said, focusing on Lovelace. 'He was overjoyed to hear that you had agreed to see him. He's talked of nothing else for years. Meeting his daughters again. He sent you and your sister a visitor's pass every month since he came here.'

'Has my sister ever been here?' Lovelace asked.

'No. Jack receives no visitors. Only his lawyers'

'Why would he want lawyers?' Lovelace asked. 'Is he appealing his sentence?'

'Good Lord, no. Nothing like that.' Seymour said. 'Jack has come to terms with the fact that he will never leave prison.' Seymour paused. 'I suppose you've heard about HMP BlackRock?'

Lovelace had heard of it. There were few in the country who hadn't. But, unlike many political exercises that effectively polarised public opinion, the project known as HMP BlackRock had received almost universal approval. Ethan Mackay, a Scottish billionaire and social philanthropist, had designed and built a prison on an island three miles off the coast of North West Scotland to hold only those who had received a whole-life tariff for their crimes. It was a modern, state-of-the-art prison built on a rocky outcrop in the heart of the Atlantic Ocean, designed to be the last place these prisoners ever went. As well as the prison, Mackay had built a small village on the island to host those who would work there. He had built a cinema and a pub, and a supermarket. Prison Officers would work three months on and three months off and would be paid handsomely for it. It was due to open in the autumn.

'Your father has received notification that he will be one of the first prisoners to be transferred to HMP BlackRock. He's appealing the decision. Hence his lawyers.'

'That would explain why I am here.' Lovelace remarked.

'I don't think so,' Seymour disagreed. 'Not entirely, anyway. I genuinely believe he loves you. He's wanted to see you for so long. If there is anything we can do to help your father, then I think we have a moral duty to do so, don't you think?'

Lovelace shook her head. 'No, I don't. I think we have a moral duty to his victims. To my mother. We have a duty to respect their memory, not my father's. He can go to BlackRock and rot there. They all can.'

'Oh, dear. I was rather hoping we'd be on the same page on this. Singing from the same hymn sheet, as it were.' Seymour sighed. 'If only you could see the improvements your father has made. If only you could take a moment to understand him, to see the guilt and regret.'

'Do you know what I'd like you to see?' Lovelace asked. 'I'd like you to see the beaten head of a fifteen-year-old girl that we found in a field after she had been raped and murdered. We found her wearing a single sock. I'd like you to see the face of a decomposing young woman beaten to death in her kitchen, and the beaten face of another young woman attacked while taking a bath. We found her lying naked in her own blood. She had been raped and beaten so hard that her skull had been crushed. Men like my father are sociopaths. They don't feel guilt or remorse or regret. They have no feelings beyond those that spur them to greater evil. They live solely for their own ends. It's all a game to them, and they play people like you like you were strings on a guitar, and the music they play is dead, and you dance to their tune like it was some heartfelt bloody melody.'

Seymour stood up. 'Well, we shall have to agree to disagree.' He walked across to the door and opened it. He turned and said, 'I'll have one of my men take you to the visitor's suite. Good day to you.'

Spencer waited until the door had closed. 'I think you upset him.'

'The man's an idiot.'

'I think that's the impression you gave him!' Spencer chuckled. 'I rather enjoy it when people piss you off. Very entertaining.'

Lovelace smiled. Spencer never seemed to get annoyed about anything. He was calm and reserved, and his manner was contagious. She felt herself relax. All she had to do now was face her father.

***

A prison guard showed them out of the building and across to another several hundred yards away. It was a new building with sparkling glass windows and heavy, reinforced doors. Security around this particular building was tight. Every corner had a bank of cameras looking in all directions. Even inside the building, the security continued. Everywhere was intensely monitored. As they walked in through the door, Lovelace wondered who it was, exactly, they were watching. They waited as the guard locked the door behind them.

'Follow me.' He said cheerily, bounding like an expectant dog at the end of a lead. He strolled off down a corridor before stopping at a grey door. He slipped a key from the chain around his waist, slipped it into the lock and opened the door.

Lovelace and Spencer walked in and looked around. It was a small room, not dissimilar to the interview rooms at Kidlington, and was equipped with similar electronic equipment. A recording device sat on a metal table in the centre of the room, and four uncomfortable-looking metal chairs sat around it. Everything was screwed to the floor. Not even the recording device could be lifted and used as a weapon. In the corner of the room, a security camera blinked at them.

'Is that on?' Lovelace asked, knowing full well that it was.

The security guard said that it was.

'I want it turned off.' Lovelace said. Her voice indicated that it wasn't open to negotiation.

'I'm afraid that won't be possible...' The guard said hesitantly.

'Either it's off, or I am.' Lovelace said. 'So speak to whoever you need to but get it switched off now.'

'I'll talk to the governor.' The guard said. He closed the door behind him, and Lovelace could just about make out the guard speaking into his radio.

Spencer sat on one of the metal chairs. Lovelace took the one next to him. A few minutes later, the blinking light of the security camera went off.

Spencer's head dropped to one side. 'Do you think it's off?' He asked.

'Probably not.' Lovelace replied. 'And if it is, they probably have some sound recording. You notice they haven't given us access to a lawyer's room?'

'Client confidentiality.' Spencer said. 'They can't record anything in there.'

'But they can in here.' Lovelace agreed. 'I wonder why they want to listen to our conversation?'

'Human curiosity.' Spencer said. 'This place is a zoo, with all manner of nasty creatures to gawp at.'

A door closed along the corridor, and Lovelace and Spencer looked at the door expecting it to fly open at any second. But, instead, it was almost another ten minutes before the door opened, and a prison guard walked in.

This time it was a young woman barely out of her teens. She was immaculately presented with tidy dark hair tied back in a bun and flawless skin. Her uniform was crisp and recently pressed, and the buttons and buckles sparkled in the light. She barely glanced at Lovelace and Spencer as she walked in and stood over the back of one of the chairs beyond them.

'In you come then, Jack.' She spoke with a sense of familiarity and kindness. Lovelace and Spencer watched the door as Jack Lovelace came in and took one of the opposite seats.

Lovelace felt her heart miss a beat. Her father had barely changed in the last fifteen years. She still remembered the eyes. The eyes of the man that had brutally stabbed her mother to death in front of her. The eyes of the man that shed not a single tear as the fire raged about them. They were the devil's eyes and still shone with the same evil that had shone so long ago. Lovelace felt an almost irresistible urge to get up and leave, but she held on. She fought the rise of panic that she felt stir in her chest and subdued it, pushing it back down as far as it could go.

But her father was different, she noticed. The hair was grey and receding. His eyebrows were bushier, and his face was bearded lightly, tinged here and there with the colours of age.

But the eyes. The eyes were the same. She felt compelled to watch them as though captivated by them. It was the same Jack Lovelace that she saw behind them, the same evil, sociopathic son of a bitch she had declared she would never lay eyes on again.

Jack Lovelace hadn't changed. He'd just got older and fatter.

The young prison guard smiled sweetly at Jack and said, 'We'll be outside, Jack, if you need us. Just shout.'

She looked at Lovelace, but she didn't smile. Friendship was reserved for her prisoner. Lovelace wanted to grab her by the hair, drag her out into the corridor, and explain that she was the type of girl her father liked to brutally rape and murder before cutting off a lock of her hair as a keepsake. The fact that she was assigned to Jack Lovelace was probably down to his manipulation of the people around him. Even now, he could make things happen for his own benefit. The young officer was just another piece of the game he was playing. But what part was she playing, Lovelace wondered.

The door closed, and the silence roared.

'Hello, Lucy.' Jack said at last. 'My beautiful girl. I've missed you so much.'

'What do you want, Jack?' Lovelace asked. It was a firm question, delivered matter-of-factly, but Spencer heard the turmoil in her voice.

'I wanted to see you.'

'Bullshit.'

'I sent you a visitor's pass. Every month.'

'I know. I got it. I put it in the bin. Every single month. That should have told you something, Jack.'

'It did. It told me you were angry with me. I understand that. Zoe won't come and see me either.'

'And yet here I am.' Lovelace said. There was no emotion in her voice. She was firmly under control. 'So, I'll ask you again. What do you want?'

Jack Lovelace sat back in his uncomfortable metal chair and smiled. The edges of his mouth curled up. Lovelace could see a complex series of thoughts cross his eyes.

'What do you want, Jack?' She asked again.

'I can help you. I know who you are looking for.'

Spencer sat forward. He said, 'Do you know who's committing these murders we are investigating?'

Jack Lovelace looked across at Spencer for the first time since he had walked into the room.

'I don't know who you are.' And then, before Spencer could introduce himself formally, he said, 'Actually, I don't care who you are. I don't want you here. I never asked to see you, but apparently, you two come as a package, so I'll tolerate you. But don't talk to me. I don't want to hear another word come out of your mouth. I want to talk to my daughter.'

Spencer looked across at Lovelace, who held her father's eyes.

'That's not how this works, Jack.' She said confidently. 'If you want to talk to me, you have to talk to my colleague. If you don't want to talk to him, then we'll go. Both of us and you'll never see me again.'

Jack smiled again, but this time the corners of his mouth turned into a snarl.

Lovelace said. 'Detective Sergeant Spencer asked you a question. Do you know the identity of the man we are investigating?'

The snarl snarled.

'I said I know who you are looking for.' He threw a look at Lovelace.

'And the price of that information is what?' Lovelace asked. 'What do you want, Jack?'

'I know you, Lucy. My beautiful daughter. All grown up. I know you. I know who you are. I know many things. I know who you are looking for.'

'You don't know shit.' Lovelace said. 'You're stuck in this prison and never getting out. You don't know a thing that could help me.'

'You'd be surprised what I know.' He said as the snarl eased back into a smile.

Lovelace shook her head. 'I don't think I would. You couldn't possibly surprise me anymore. We've heard about HMP BlackRock. All this is about is you trying to get concessions from us. But I've got to tell you, that won't happen. Nothing you can tell us can help us, and there are no rewards on the table. This isn't the Silence of the fucking Lambs, and I'm not Clarice fucking Starling, and you are certainly no Hannibal Lecter.' Lovelace leant closer to her father and held his eyes. 'There will not be a nice glass of Chianti, and you are certainly not having friends around for dinner. If you have anything to say to me, spit it out. I'm a busy woman, and I have a scumbag to catch and being here is not helping.'

Jack Lovelace crossed his legs and folded his arms. It was a movement that took Lovelace back to her youth. It made her feel uneasy.

'I know you, Lucy. I know what it is you're searching for in life. I can help you if you let me. Come and see me again.' He looked at Spencer. 'Come alone next time. I'll tell you what you want to know. And I don't want anything from you. Nothing at all. But I can help you find who you are looking for.'

Lovelace stood up. 'This is a waste of time,' she said. She looked at Spencer. 'I'm done here.'

Lovelace opened the door and turned to look at her father. 'There's nothing you could tell me I would want to hear, and you certainly don't know me.'

She closed the door behind her.

Jack Lovelace held his pose on his metal chair. Not a single emotion crossed his face. Then, to Spencer, he said, 'I'm not going to talk to you. Don't waste your breath.'

Spencer grinned. 'There's nothing I want to ask you. But I will tell you this for nothing. That young woman is a credit to her mother, uncle, and aunt. Everything she has become, she has become despite you, not because of you. Every ounce of that girl is good and kind, and the fact that she has dedicated her life to stopping people like you should tell you everything you need to know about who she is. I doubt for a second that you have any clue who she is. She is diametrically opposite to you in every way.'

Spencer got up and opened the door.

Jack said, 'You only know about people from what they show you and tell you. People have secrets. Things you don't know about them. Do you know Lucy's secrets?'

Spencer looked back at the killer in the room behind him. Don't get drawn in, he told himself. Don't let him play you.

'Goodbye, Jack. Have a nice life.'

Spencer caught up with Lovelace in the car park. He walked up to her and draped an arm over her shoulders.

'I'm proud of you.' He said. 'You handled that very well.'

'Do you think?' She asked. 'What if I've made a mistake? What if he does know something about our killer?'

Spencer looked her in the eyes. 'Well,' he said, 'If I may use the words of a brilliant young woman that I know, ahem, "He doesn't know shit!"'

Nineteen

Lovelace and Spencer were just north of the city when their phones rang in tandem. DCI Graham's name flashed up on the car's display. Spencer looked at his phone and saw that it was DI Luton.

'Here we go,' Lovelace said as she hit the green phone icon on the display. 'Guv?'

'Where are you?' The voice was crisp and matter-of-fact.

'We're about half an hour away, tops. If it's about my father....'

Graham interrupted her. 'No. It's not about him. Steve's trying to ring Spencer. Get him to answer.'

Spencer looked quizzically at Lovelace. She shrugged her shoulders, and Spencer answered his phone.

'Listen carefully,' Graham said. 'Steve's giving Phil an address. I want you there ten minutes ago. Don't spare the horses. Whatever it takes.'

'Guv? What is it?'

'The contact centre's just taken several 999 calls from people concerned about an alarm going off.'

'Alarms go off all the time.' Lovelace said sceptically.

'They do.' Graham agreed. 'But it's a rape alarm. And one of the witnesses claimed she saw the figure of a man move about in the upstairs window of the house moments before the alarm was activated. Uniform are racing to the scene. They should be there in five. Armed response is also attending, and we've got the chopper airborne. I want you there now.'

Spencer had already taken the address from Luton and was typing the postcode into the car's sat-nav. The display said twenty minutes.

'We'll be there in ten.' Lovelace said, and she nailed her toe to the floor. The tiny ruby red's engine fired instantly into life, and Lovelace steered the little rocket south towards their destination.

They reached the address in ten minutes. The force helicopter was in the air, over the house, sweeping an arc around the area. Five police cars were scattered along the street, and an ambulance had just arrived. The paramedics were grabbing their kit from the side of the van, and Lovelace and Spencer watched as they were rushed inside a plain-looking house by two heavily armed police officers. A crowd was beginning to gather, their interest spiked by the arrival of so many officers and the noise of the helicopter in the sky.

A heavily set man in his thirties wearing a cap that said "Police" across its peak stopped Lovelace and Spencer as they made their way to the scene. He held a Heckler and Koch semi-automatic machine gun across his chest. A handgun sat in its cradle at his hip.

'Step back, please. You need to step back.'

Spencer held aloft his warrant card.

'Sorry, Sarge.' The man said.

'What's going on?' Lovelace asked.

'We had several reports of a suspect on scene. Witnesses reported seeing the homeowner enter the house about thirty minutes ago, and after about five minutes, they heard a rape alarm go off. One witness claimed that just before the alarm went off, she could see a figure move about in an upstairs window. A few of the men folk decided to try and break in and set about kicking the front door down. Reckon that probably saved her life.'

'She's alive?' Spencer asked.

'Yeah. She's in a bad way. She's taken quite a beating. Paramedics are with her now.'

'What about the suspect?' Lovelace asked.

'He took off across the fields at the back of the house. A couple of men gave chase and tracked him as far as the woods. They lost sight of him there. We're drawing in resources from all over the county, trying to swamp the area with as many troops as possible. There's a good chance we'll get him.'

Lovelace doubted that, but she admired his optimism. He would have been prepared for this. He would have had some kind of escape plan.

'Where are the witnesses that called it in?' Lovelace asked.

The man with the gun nodded to a group of people talking to a young Police Constable outside a house opposite the scene. Lovelace and Spencer crossed the street and introduced themselves.

'DS Spencer, DC Lovelace. Can I ask who made the 999 call?' Spencer asked.

A large woman in her fifties said, 'I did. I saw him in the window upstairs, and when I heard the alarm, I knew it was him. I've seen it on the news.'

'Which room did you see him in?' Lovelace asked.

She pointed up to a room at the left of the building. 'Thought nothing of it at the time. I mean, you don't, do you? You think things are normal until you realise they aren't. Then when I heard the alarm, it got me thinking. Got me worried, you know? I wondered what with everything on the news about this madman. So I called 999.'

'You did the right thing,' Lovelace said. 'We'll take an official statement from you later, Mrs…?'

'Hogarth.' The woman said.

'Mrs Hogarth. I don't suppose you could describe the man?' Lovelace asked.

'Didn't see him. More of a glimpse, if you like. I wasn't sure I saw anything. You start to doubt yourself, but then when I heard the alarm….' She left the words to linger.

'I phoned 999 too,' a man in a flowery shirt and tight shorts said.

'Mr…?'

'Will Collins. I'm her neighbour. I work nights. She was lucky I was home. I thought it was odd when I saw her come home, and then when the alarm went off….'

'She's not normally at home at this time of day?' Lovelace asked.

'Not normally. She's a hairdresser. She works in a small salon in town. Her normal days off are Monday and Tuesday. Always works on a Friday.'

'Does she have a boyfriend or husband?' Spencer asked.

'She has a regular squeeze.' Will said. 'Split up a while ago, but I think they got back together. They don't live together.'

'And who was it that knocked her front door in?' Spencer asked.

Will Collins looked sheepish and avoided Spencer's eyes. A man next to Mrs Hogarth said, 'Tom Hogarth. Me and the lad put the door in. It's what you do, right? You can't just stand by and let these things happen. Not if there's something you can do about it. You lot were taking a bloody age to get here, and we had to do something.'

'By all accounts, you probably saved the young woman's life.' Spencer said. 'I understand you gave chase?'

Tom Hogarth grunted. 'Once the door came off, we rushed in. I heard the back door go, and by the time I got there, I saw this figure make off over the fence and across the fields. We lost sight of him when he got to the woods.'

'Could you describe him?' Lovelace asked.

The two men shook their heads.

'Anything at all?' Lovelace asked. 'Height, weight, build? Anything at all?'

'I reckon he was a small fella,' Tom Hogarth said. 'Five five, or six. No weight to him to speak of. Not stocky or anything. Quite a slim bloke, I should say. He was wearing all black. Had a black hoodie, too.'

'Okay. Thank you.' Lovelace said. 'If you wouldn't mind making yourselves available to give a statement, that would be greatly appreciated.'

Lovelace and Spencer went over to the house, where a stream of police officers was going back and forth. Paramedics were clearing their way out of the house with the body of a young woman on a stretcher. One held a saline drip above her head as they carefully edged their way to the ambulance. She was covered in blood, and they could barely make out the features of her face beneath it. Lovelace caught her breath as she recognised the oddly coloured hair and the piercings in the girl's ears.

'Shit.' She said loudly. 'We know this girl.'

'Who? Who is it?' Spencer asked. Nothing about the girl was familiar to him, and her face was a bloodied mess.

'It's the girl we interviewed from the salon. The boyfriend works in a garage. The girl with the missing watch. Sarah Finch.'

Spencer looked at the young woman on the stretcher and admired Lovelace's powers of observation. He could barely remember the girl and couldn't link the bloodied mess in front of him to anyone he'd recently met.

'How is she?' Lovelace asked one of the paramedics.

'She's got quite a head wound, but she's conscious. Just. Excuse me, but we need to get her to the hospital.'

Lovelace stepped aside as the stretcher was lifted into the ambulance, and the doors closed. Minutes later, the ambulance pulled off, sirens wailing, and screamed out of the street.

A black Jag pulled up in the space the ambulance had just vacated, and Luton, Stanton and Graham poured out of its stomach.

'Well?' Graham asked.

'She's conscious, but in a bad way.' Lovelace said. 'She's someone we interviewed a couple of days ago. She's one of the people we think may have had a visitor recently. But, unfortunately, it appears he may have come back.'

'And the suspect?' Graham asked.

Spencer shook his head. 'Nothing there. Three witnesses but not one of them got a good look at him. Small bloke. Thin. Wears black.'

They were interrupted as the force helicopter flew overhead. In answer to Graham's look, Lovelace said, 'They won't find him. He'll be long gone.'

'So,' Graham said, his voice etched with growing despair. 'He strikes again, and we are no closer to discovering who he is.'

'But we do have a first-hand witness.' Lovelace said. 'We've not had that before. So that might make a difference.'

'It might.' Graham pondered. 'You two get over to the hospital. Get a statement as soon as you can. Just in case, I'll get some armed guards posted at the hospital. But, for fuck's sake, get me a lead on this before we're all back on traffic duty.'

***

The Accident and Emergency Department heaved with people. Lovelace and Spencer made their way through the throng of injured and sick people and pushed to the head of a queue waiting patiently at an understaffed desk. They ignored the comments directed at them, and Lovelace flashed her warrant card at a nurse behind the desk.

'You had an injured young woman rushed in here about half an hour ago. An assault victim. Sarah Finch.'

The nurse nodded. 'That's right. She's in resus' at the mo. The doctors are looking at her.' The nurse leant over the desk conspiratorially and said, 'They say she's one of the Night Prowler's victims. Is that right? He attacks during the day as well?'

Lovelace gave no response. 'We need to see her. Where do we go?'

The nurse pointed at a set of doors to her right. 'Through there. You'll need to get past the guards, however. Once you're through, you should see a nurses' station right ahead of you. Someone there will help you.'

They reached the uniformed policeman at the door, who blocked their way with a sinister-looking gun held at high port across his chest. He examined their warrant cards and pushed the door open with his foot.

Spencer turned to him as he passed through the door and asked, 'Are you the only guard?'

'No, guv'.' The police officer said. 'There's four of us in all. All entrances and exits covered.'

'Good. Well done. Carry on.'

Lovelace turned to Spencer as they reached the nurses' station. 'Carry on?' She asked, bemused.

'Men with guns scare me.' Spencer said with no hint of embarrassment. 'I couldn't think of what to say.'

Lovelace smiled.

They caught a nurse as she flew by and were directed to a young man in a different coloured shirt conversing on a telephone. They waited patiently while he finished the call.

'Dr Aziz?' Lovelace asked.

'That's right.' He replied with a faint West Country accent. Lovelace and Spencer showed their warrant cards, and he nodded knowingly. 'Ah, yes. Miss Finch. Bloody hell, you're quick. We've barely had a chance to triage her.'

'She's our only witness.'

'I see. Are the rumours correct, then? She's one of the Night Prowler's victims?'

'We think so,' Lovelace said. 'That's why we need to speak to her quite urgently.'

Dr Aziz sucked the air through his teeth as only doctors and mechanics could. He shook his head. 'She's taken quite a blow to the head. We're sending her for a CT scan right away.'

'It won't take long,' Spencer said in his sweetest voice. 'Just a couple of questions. Is she conscious?'

'Oh, yes.' Dr Aziz said. 'She's awake and talking. She's groggy, mostly because she's a bit punch drunk. She took a couple of severe blows to the head. Not enough to kill, but she will have quite a headache.'

'There was much blood.' Lovelace said.

'Always is with head wounds. Mostly superficial. She has a bit of a gash, and we suspect she may have a fractured skull, but we'll know more after the scan.'

'So, can we see her?' Lovelace asked.

'I suppose it can't do any harm.'

Dr Aziz led them down a short corridor and pulled aside a curtain that concealed a bed and a bank of medical computers that blinked and bleeped in unison. A nurse leaned over the patient, gently wiping blood from her face.

'Miss Finch. There are some detectives here who wish to speak to you. Is that okay? Do you feel up to it?'

Sarah Finch recognised Lovelace as she walked in. When she spoke, she spoke slowly, her voice crackled with pain. 'Yes.'

Lovelace walked over and took Sarah's hand in hers. 'Hi, Sarah, do you remember us? We came and spoke to you a couple of days ago.'

Sarah nodded. With her spare hand, she wiped a tear from her eyes.

'I remember you.'

'We'd like to ask you some questions while everything's still fresh in your mind. Is that okay?'

Sarah nodded again.

'Were you at work today, Sarah?'

Sarah nodded. 'Yes. I left the house for work at about eight this morning. I locked the door. I'm sure of it. Everyone's talking about....' She grappled with the emotions welling up inside. 'About him...'

'Is it usual for you to go home in the afternoon?' Lovelace asked.

'No. I was supposed to be in till five but didn't feel well, so I went home early.'

'So you returned home unexpectedly?'

Sarah nodded. Lovelace glanced at Spencer, standing at the foot of the bed.

'What happened when you got home?'

'I felt ill, so I went straight up to bed. I opened the door to my bedroom, and he was standing there.' She shuddered with the recollection. 'I froze. I couldn't quite work out what was going on. I tried to find sense in it. Like, had he wandered into the wrong house, or had I? I've done that before, you see. Mind you, I was a bit drunk then. Before I could react, he came at me. He was so cold. So quick.'

'You set off some sort of alarm?'

'Yes. All the girls at work bought one, so I got one too. I took it out of my pocket as I walked into my bedroom. I don't even remember setting it off.'

Lovelace stroked the back of Sarah's hand. She had dry hands and was quite rough to the touch. 'Did you recognise the man that attacked you, Sarah?'

'No.' She sniffed.

'Have you ever seen him before?'

'No.'

'Could you describe him?'

She shook her head. 'It was all very quick. He was dressed all in black, and he wore a hoodie. His face was in shadow. His eyes, though. I saw his eyes. He had horrible eyes.'

'How big was he? Do you remember?'

'Not very big. Quite a small build, I'd say. A small man.'

A small man.

A tear welled up in one of Sarah's eyes. Lovelace brushed it away. 'You're safe now, Sarah. These people are going to look after you.'

'What if he comes back? What if he tries to finish the job?' Sarah cried.

'He won't.' Lovelace said, not genuinely trusting the truth in the statement. 'But just in case, we're going to keep an armed guard at your door until we catch this man.'

Sarah looked up and searched for the honesty in Lovelace's eyes. She found it, but still she asked, 'What if you don't catch him?'

Lovelace had never considered it to be a possibility. It never occurred to her that they would never catch him. She squeezed Sarah's hand. 'We will catch him. I promise.'

***

'I owe you my life.'

Lovelace stroked back a waft of Charlie's hair that had fallen across her face.

After finishing their interview with Sarah Finch, Lovelace sought out Charlie. Spencer made his excuses and went off to source coffee and make some phone calls. Charlie had burst into tears when she saw Lovelace walk through the door. For the second time today, Lovelace brushed back the tears that flowed down a cheek.

'I hear you gave him a bit of a kicking!' Charlie said once she had gathered her composure.

'I might have slapped him about a bit.' Lovelace joked.

'Who would have thought a little thing like you could do that!'

'I'm full of surprises.' Lovelace said. She looked about the room. Hundreds of Get Well Soon cards were jostling for space on every available flat surface. Flowers of every conceivable variety bloomed from a dozen vases. 'You are certainly a popular girl!'

'It's funny how almost getting stabbed to death was all it needed to get some attention. I mean, if I'd known, I'd have got stabbed sooner!'

'Please don't joke about that,' Lovelace said. 'I thought you were dead for sure.'

'We Scots are made of sterner stuff!' She joked. 'And besides, he was pretty crap as a wannabe killer. He missed every vital organ by at least a millimetre.'

'Do you know how long you'll be in here?' Lovelace asked.

'At least a month. They want me to lie still while I heal. I'm fucking bored of daytime telly already.'

'I can bring some stuff next time I visit. What do you need?'

Together they compiled a rescue list. It was mostly books.

'Visiting hours are pretty relaxed, although some older nurses snort like dragons. Come and sit with me when you can?' Charlie asked.

Lovelace leaned over and lightly kissed her cheek. 'Try and stop me.' She got up to leave. 'I'll stay longer next time; I just wanted to see you.'

'Got a killer to catch?'

Lovelace nodded. 'Yes, I do.'

Charlie said, 'Lucy when you catch him, don't kill him. Don't make him a legend.'

Lovelace held the door open for a second.

'I'll try not to.' She lied.

***

The sun had long since set, but the heat remained. From Graham's office on the first floor at force HQ in Kidlington, five police officers gathered around a large oak conference table, drinking and eating takeaway food.

It was a very informal gathering. Graham had hit pause on the investigation and gathered his team together. He ordered Chinese food from a local fast-food restaurant and bought two dozen bottles of ice-cold beer.

Stanton took a long swig from a bottle and said, 'Forensics have been all over the Finch house. No obvious sign of a break-in, and fuck all evidence to gather. No fingerprints and no DNA. It's like he was never there.'

Luton agreed. 'He's a ghost. We dropped a tight net over the area within minutes of the call. We had police swarming the area in all directions. Nothing. He just vanished.'

'He's good.' Lovelace admitted. 'He knows his stuff. He knows the area well, too. He's a local man for sure.'

'And given that no DNA that we find leads us back to anyone on our sex offenders register probably means he's never been caught. For any crime. Ever.' Spencer scooped some noodles from a tin-foil container and skilfully manoeuvred it into his mouth.

'Which all leads us where?' Graham asked.

Everyone looked at each other across the table. They were no further along in the investigation than when the Parkes family was brutally murdered, and Molly Parkes was kidnapped. It was a point that the Chief Superintendent had made to Graham during a conference call he'd held a couple of hours ago. There had already been mutterings of discontent as far up the line as it was possible to go. The local member of Parliament was threatening to ask questions of the Home Secretary as to the suitability of the local police force to deal with such a high-profile serial killer case. Graham had until Monday to get a grip on the situation before it was taken out of his hands. It was a career-defining moment for all of them.

'I need a new strategy.' Graham said. 'The contact centres are choking under the weight of calls they're getting. The rate of triple nine calls has increased markedly in the last two days. We've increased the uniform presence out on the streets, but most of them are getting tied up dealing with frightened calls from members of the public thinking they're next on the Night Prowler's list. Half our officers are checking under people's beds and behind sofas while the other half are chasing shadows down dark alleys. And I have nothing to reassure them with.'

'Surely he'll have had enough by now?' Stanton asked. 'He can't keep this up, can he?'

'That may be the worst thing for us right now.' Lovelace said, and everyone looked at her as if she'd lost her mind. Then, by way of clarification, she said, 'It looks like he's peaking. His attacks are becoming way more frequent. His desire to kill is moving faster than his capabilities. If he carries on, he may well make a mistake. But, on the other hand, if he stops… he may come back later down the line a lot better than he already is.'

'So you're hoping he strikes again? On the off chance he might make a mistake?' Luton asked in disbelief.

'Not necessarily. But he left a witness today. He may leave more tomorrow.'

Graham shook his head. 'We can't afford that to happen. We need to get a hook into this thing.'

'Then we need to draw him out.' Spencer said.

'How?' Graham asked.

'Actually,' Lovelace said. 'That's not a bad idea. He's a narcissist. He'll be loving all the attention this is getting on the news. All this focus on him. There may be a way there to play up to his fantasies. To get under his skin. I guarantee he'll be following this investigation.'

'So what do you suggest?' Luton asked. 'Appeal to him directly? Make up some bullshit about getting a breakthrough on the case and see what he does? Something like that?'

'Something like that…' Lovelace said. She got up suddenly and left the office. She came back moments later with a piece of paper in her hands. 'Or maybe something like this,' she said, handing the paper to Graham.

Graham carefully considered the paper and then laid it down in front of Luton. They read the piece of paper one by one and passed it around the table until it reached Spencer.

'Interesting.' Spencer said. 'What's your idea? The killer returns to the scene of the crime?'

'In a manner of speaking.' Lovelace said. 'Killers take keepsakes because it reminds them of their actions and helps them re-live the experience. Sometimes they'll go back over the routes they have taken to try and re-live the moment. It gives them a thrill. Some will turn up at reconstructions to marvel at their superiority or give interviews to the press, like the Soham murderer. Some will attend funerals, and some will visit grave sites. Some,' Lovelace went on, picking up the piece of paper from the table, 'will attend memorials to the victims.'

She held the flyer the young girl gave her when they visited Molly Parkes' neighbour. The memorial for the two murdered young girls was set for tomorrow night.

'My gut tells me he'll be there.' Lovelace said. 'He'll want to be a part of it. It will give him a thrill. It will appeal to his sense of superiority.'

Graham smiled. 'Good.' He said quietly. He looked up at Lovelace and then at his team. 'Make me a plan. Let's catch this son of a bitch.'

Twenty

As the senior of the two, Spencer held the briefing. He wasn't keen on it, but Graham had insisted, and Lovelace, who hated speaking in front of a crowd, had agreed it was the most suitable suggestion. They had spent most of a hot Saturday morning at Spencer's desk drawing up a plan of action. It wasn't much of a plan, but it was their only one. They delivered it to Graham, who signed off on it.

'Spencer, you take the briefing. This one's down to you two. There's a conference at three o'clock for you to deliver the plan to the troop commanders. That'll only give you a few hours before the memorial service for the girls. Can you be ready?'

'We'll be ready.' Lovelace said. She handed Graham a sheet of paper. 'Can we have this?'

Graham perused the shortlist. 'Consider it done.'

At three o'clock, Spencer stood before a room of over a hundred senior police officers and cleared his throat. Behind him was a heavily congested crime wall upon which the photographs of every identified victim, along with crime scene photos, maps, documents, and scribblings of the Major Investigation Team, had been stapled. It was a busy wall, but it lacked anything of substance. It was a timeline, nothing more.

'Good afternoon, ladies and gentlemen.' Spencer said, and the room fell quiet. Lovelace stood beside Spencer, wearing a crisp white shirt and long, dark trousers. She had just finished fighting her hair into submission, and it was begrudgingly holding on to a sense of style. Spencer, Lovelace noticed, was once again immaculately dressed, wearing a well-fitted pin-stripe suit and polished brogues. When he spoke, his voice boomed across the room. No one was in any doubt as to who was leading the briefing. Luton and Stanton had been sidelined slightly, and neither enjoyed the sensation. It further aggravated them that the daughter of a serial killer and dead-end copper had done it to them. Their egos smarted from it.

'At seven-thirty this evening, a memorial service for Molly Parkes and her friend Bethany Wright will be held outside the Parkes' home at Chatsworth Drive in Cherwell. The girls' school has organised the event, which will likely be attended by upwards of a thousand people, maybe more. We expect a heavy press presence in the area and have already placed a no-fly zone over the town. It is also likely that many mourners from all over the county, if not the country, will head to the service to pay their respects. Such has been the interest shown in this case that we also expect hundreds of grief tourists and dark tourists to attend.

'We also believe that this man…' Spencer pointed to the photograph of a man's face that had been blacked out, which took centre place on the crime wall, 'to also be in attendance.'

Beneath the photograph were the words, 'Unknown Subject.'

'Everyone in this room has been handed a folder with the names and photographs of one hundred of our most notorious sex offenders that live within a hundred miles of Cherwell. We want to know if any of them come within ten miles of the event. To that end, we have installed Number Plate Recognition cameras at strategic locations on all routes leading to Cherwell. We have also installed Facial recognition cameras at these locations to aid us in identifying our suspects.

'To keep a low profile at the Memorial service, we have asked some households if we can install facial recognition cameras within their homes. I'm pleased to say that we now have a large area of the cul-de-sac covered by these cameras.

'Our presence at the service is going to be low-key. We'll have uniformed traffic officers dealing with traffic issues away from the area and a token squad car at the service with two young PCs at hand as a token of our respect. They will not be there as part of the investigation team. We do not want our killer to think we are using the service to identify him. We want him to think he's smarter than us.

'We will be here,' Spencer went on, pointing to an industrial area on the map behind him, 'at a warehouse five miles away, keeping a low profile and watching events from a bank of monitors currently being set up. Thames Valley has twenty trained spotters who will be among the officers watching these monitors. In addition, the Metropolitan Police have kindly seconded a dozen of their trained spotters, who we will install among the mourners at the service.'

Spencer paused for breath. 'It's not just the faces on the sex offenders list we are looking for. The case is a little bit more complex than that. We believe our unknown subject has most likely never been in trouble before and has avoided coming to our attention.'

'Jesus.' A voice said from the front. 'How are we supposed to know him when we see him.'

'Because you're all good coppers.' Spencer replied swiftly. 'Because you've all got a copper's nose and an instinct for when things aren't right. So if you see a man in his thirties who looks a little out of place, who's come on his own and doesn't look like he's in the right place, call him out. We'll track and watch him, and when he leaves the service, we'll wait till he's gone a respectful distance and traffic can pull him over for a routine stop.

That way, we can gather as much data on potential suspects as possible. So we need you to keep your eyes peeled. Let's gather as much information as we can. This is the best chance we have.'

'So there are no suspects?' The voice asked.

'We have three persons of interest.' Spencer said, pointing to the photographs of three men further along the wall. 'They are not suspects, but we would certainly be interested to know if any of them attend the service. The first one is Richard Wilkins. He's the neighbour of a woman we believe may have been visited by our unknown subject in the last few months. Before yesterday he was the only witness who had seen our man. The second is Paul Harris, the on-off boyfriend of Sarah Finch, currently the only survivor of the so-called Night Prowler.'

At the back of the room, DCI Graham flinched. It was force policy to avoid the use of nicknames for the killer.

Spencer went on. 'Sarah did not identify Paul Harris as her attacker, and given her description, it is unlikely to be him; however, if he makes an appearance, we'd sure like to know.

'Our third suspect is Oliver Bowden, who we arrested after discovering Jane Wilson's body. He was released after twenty-four hours on police bail. Again, we think it's unlikely to be him or, in fact, any of the three men we've mentioned, but we're cautious about them. If you see them, let us know.'

The briefing continued for another half an hour. Then, slowly but surely, the room began to diminish in numbers as various orders were handed out, and the senior officers left to relay the information to their troops.

'Well done,' Graham said as Spencer finished briefing the last officer. He glanced at his watch. 'It's a couple of hours before the memorial service. Take a break. Get something to eat. It could be a long night.'

***

Connor ran in through the front door, dumped his football boots in the hall, and bounded up the stairs two at a time. Dan Hodges followed his son through the door, retrieved the boots, and carried them into the kitchen.

'How'd they get on?' Rachel asked. She stood beside the cooker stirring something in a large iron pot.

'They lost.' Dan said. 'Ten nil.'

'Oh.' Rachel said. 'How did he take it?'

'Badly.' Dan said. He walked out the back door and threw the boots onto the yard. Issy was lying on the lawn, sunbathing. He came back in and kissed his wife. 'Smells nice.' He placed his hands on her hips and let them drift.

'Stop it, Dan; I have to go to work.'

'I know. It's the uniform that does it to me.' He joked.

'I've nearly finished your dinner,' Rachel said, deftly changing the subject. 'I'll leave it in the oven dish. You'll need to heat it up for thirty minutes.'

They were interrupted by Issy, who walked into the kitchen with a large towel wrapped around her, her hair tied up in a bun while wearing a trendy pair of sunglasses. Her skin glowed from the sun.

'Can I go to Lauren's tonight? She's having a sleepover. Her mum says it's okay.'

'Sorry love, I'm working tonight,' Dan said, 'And your mum's on nights all week, you know that.'

'Connor will be all right,' Issy pleaded. 'He's nearly thirteen.'

'He's too young to be left alone all night.' Rachel argued.

'You can go out.' Dan said. 'I'm not getting picked up until gone ten. So long as you're back by then.'

'Why don't you invite Lauren here?' Rachel said. 'I'll bring us back some breakfast after my shift.'

Issy bounced. 'Can I? Okay. Thanks.' In the following moments, she took off outside, slipped out of her robe and launched herself back onto the towel draped over the lawn.

'Why so late?' Rachel asked, turning to look at her husband.

Dan shrugged. 'No idea. Yan said he had something to do beforehand.'

He'd wondered himself. He'd been wondering about Yan since he dropped his name to Crimestoppers. For a day or so, he'd heard nothing from Yan. His mind had leapt to conclusions. Had the police picked him up? Was there something in Yan's past? Was Yan the Night Prowler?

And then he had called entirely out of the blue like nothing had happened. But, of course, Yan wasn't aware that anything *had* happened. He didn't know about the phone call he had made. He was entirely oblivious.

'I've got a job Saturday night. You up for it?'

Dan had debated saying no, but their little jobs were pulling in some serious money. He was beginning to live the lifestyle he had always wanted for himself and his family. Reluctantly he agreed. And if the police hadn't arrested Yan, he couldn't be the one they were after, surely? And when he thought about it, could Yan be the Night Prowler? It did seem ridiculous. So he said yes.

'Good.' Yan said. 'I've got something to do first. Pick you up around ten, okay?'

***

DI Frampton sat down next to DI French and smiled. 'The boss has okayed the surveillance on DC Lovelace.' He placed a carrier bag by his feet and pulled out a bottle of chilled white wine. 'Fancy a glass?'

'What took so long on the surveillance?' French asked as Frampton poured them both a large glass of wine.

'Fucking office politics.' He said. 'The boss was reluctant to go face-on with Graham. You know what he can be like. The boss is a bit soft, and Graham's a bit spiky. And when you start investigating one of your own, the old grapevine starts buzzing. So the boss went to his boss, who dipped his fingers into the pot and paid for a team from West Mercia to do the surveilling. That should keep the gossips at bay. Budget's taken a bit of battering, and the boss will probably want a body part or two if you're wrong about this.'

'Me?' French exclaimed. 'If I'm wrong about this? You put me on to her in the first place!'

Frampton nodded sagely. 'And I'm right, which is how I know you've nothing to worry about.'

French thought otherwise. The photograph of the mystery woman seen with Pitts on the night of his murder haunted her day and night. She had a copy pinned to her computer at work and one stuck to the fridge door at home. It looked like Lovelace, and the woman she saw in the car park at Kidlington was a contender. But still, the doubt lingered. What if she was wrong? She looked at the photograph again and then at a copy of a photo of Lovelace in her Thames Valley Uniform. It had to be the same woman.

'I've been over her past.' French said dejectedly. 'Apart from the fact that she's the daughter of a convicted serial killer and psychopath, nothing in her history even hints at the possibility that she's capable of murder and brutal mutilation. She's clean. She's so clean she fucking shines.'

'Perhaps she's inherited her father's sociopathic tendencies?' Frampton suggested. 'You can inherit everything else.'

'I looked into that.' French said. She scrabbled around her table for a piece of paper. 'Here it is. They call it the "Serial Killer Gene." It's known as Cadherin-13 or CDH13. People with this gene are more prone to phycological disorders like depression and bipolar disorder. It's been found in a lot of serial killers.'

'See. She's inherited her evil.'

'And yet,' French said, 'It's mostly bullshit. Famous scientists don't have clever children. Brilliant doctors don't create brilliant doctors. Dickens' children didn't become famous authors, and neither did Shakespeare's. No great artists created fabulously artistic children, and neither did the world's greatest musicians. Serial killers don't breed serial killer children.'

'Nature balances.' Frampton said. He took a large gulp of his chilled wine and swallowed it down. 'Tall parents don't have children that are as tall as them. They come out shorter, although generally taller than the average. Small people have slightly taller children, though shorter than the average. Thick parents have slightly more intelligent kids who are probably thicker than their friends, while intelligent parents probably have less intelligent kids who are probably more intelligent than their friends. Nature's levelling out. Balancing. Serial killer parents probably have fewer serial killery kids who are less of a serial killer than their parents but more so than the rest of us.'

French raised an eyebrow. She wasn't aware that Frampton was capable of that depth of thought.

'And yet,' She said, 'There's never been a run of murderers in a family before.'

'You'd be surprised.' Frampton said. 'I bet there are loads. And anyway, isn't it unusual for serial killers to have children?'

'It is unusual,' French agreed.

'So it would be hard to examine whether or not serial killers breed little serial killers?'

French sighed.

'Look. Frampton went on. 'Let's see what the surveillance picks up. We've got seven days. You never know; it might prove fruitful.'

French drained her glass and refilled it. She didn't know it then, but she wouldn't have to wait that long for a result.

Things were about to come to a head.

***

Lovelace drove into Chatsworth Drive and pulled onto a long driveway adjacent to the Parkes' home. Emma Jenkins had gone to stay with her father somewhere in Wales and was more than happy to let Lovelace and the team set up an observation post in her house.

'There's probably milk in the fridge.' She had told Lovelace over the telephone. 'And some food. Don't let it go to waste. I'm not coming back anytime soon.'

Emma had guided Lovelace to where she had hidden a spare key, and it bothered Lovelace to think that people still left keys to their homes under plant pots in the garden.

About an hour before the service, half a dozen police officers and technicians arrived and carried expensive-looking equipment into the house. They set up the cameras and surveillance equipment in the front room, which looked out onto the street, and in the front bedroom, which gave a bird's eye view of the whole area. A bank of radios and monitors was installed in the front room, and by the time the first mourners started to arrive, they were set to go.

The monitors were switched on one by one, and the radios began to crackle. Lovelace carried a radio on her, which was linked directly to the warehouse a few miles away where Graham oversaw the operation.

A police technician opened his laptop and tapped at the keys for a few seconds. Then, he smiled as a screen popped up, and faces appeared within it.

'We're up.' He declared proudly, showing Lovelace and Spencer the fruits of his labour.

'Facial recognition.' He explained. 'As our cameras pick up a face, it trawls our files for any matches. We've got several cameras on the street and one or two on the approaches. This way, we should be able to record the images of everyone who attends tonight.'

Lovelace watched a monitor nearby as it stored the photographs of the attendees. 'Is this even legal?' She asked.

'Graham secured a warrant from a judge to allow us to record images of people attending. It's a public street, so it's technically not illegal.' The technician explained. 'We have to destroy the images of people unrelated to the investigation within seven days.'

Lovelace walked over to where Spencer stood. He watched a monitor in front of him, which showed an ever-growing procession of people into the cul-de-sac.

'Do you think he'll come?' He asked.

Lovelace suppressed the anxiety that rose inside her. 'I hope so. The question is will we notice him if he does?'

***

He was hot. Sweat formed on his brow, and he wiped it clear. He took a drink from a can on his desk, but it didn't quench his thirst. Nothing seemed to quench his thirst anymore. The more he drank, the more he needed to drink, and the more he needed to drink, the darker his thoughts became.

He steeled himself and trawled the internet. But even that wasn't enough anymore. The pictures were unreal. The people were unreal. Nothing was real anymore.

His phone lit up as a notification came through. It was a Facebook 'Like.' He opened the app and went to his notification list. *Sophie Spencer liked your post.*

He felt the urge grow. He opened Sophie's profile and scrolled through it. She was rare among teenage girls because she only posted occasionally. There was little to find in her photographs and posts that led him any closer to her. And yet…

He opened a photograph that Sophie had taken several weeks ago that he had missed at first glance. Now he took a more profound interest in it. She was standing in the garden of her house somewhere in Oxfordshire. It was the "where" that he had been focussed on. Until just then, he had been coming up empty. He expanded the photograph until the detail in

the background was all he could see. He wasn't
interested in Sophie right then. Instead, he was
interested in the large house in the background. It was a
house he recognised. A house he had been to recently.

He knew where that house was.

Now he knew where Sophie Spencer lived.

Suddenly the urge compelled him. He glanced at a
clock on the wall in front of him. It was seven o'clock.

There were things he had to do first.

Twenty-One

Camera two. Male, late thirties, receding hair.'

'Roger that. Stand by.'

Camera two found its target and zoomed in. The image was swiftly uploaded to the Facial Recognition Software. No match.

'That's a negative. Male is not alone. He's with a woman and two small kids.'

'Copy that.'

The control centre five miles from the Memorial Service was buzzing with activity. No one was without a task. Over a hundred pairs of eyes followed a hundred faces on a bank of television monitors. At the centre of it all stood DCI Graham flanked on either side by Luton and Stanton. Between them, they guided and directed proceedings. It was a huge task made less simple by technology.

'White male, camera eight. Small build. He's wearing a dark hoodie.'

Camera eight found its target.

'Negative control. He's one of ours.'

And so it continued. Officers on the ground directed the control staff to people who tweaked their senses. They looked for men in their thirties and forties of slight build who looked out of place in the environment.

'Don't ignore the men that come with families.' Lovelace had urged. 'He may well have children.'

The Memorial Service for the two girls had begun at around seven thirty and had been led by Bethany Wright's parents, who laid a wreath at the door of the Parkes' home. They read prayers and sang hymns. Children from the girls' school read poems, and the school band played the girls' favourite songs. By eight-thirty, the crowd had swelled almost to capacity. Spotting faces in the crowd of mourners began to get harder and harder, but the undercover officers kept directing the camera operators as best they could.

From the Jenkins' house next door to the Parkes', Lovelace felt the weight of responsibility fall heavily on her shoulders. It had been her call, and a significant amount of the force's budget had been spent putting the surveillance into operation. But, even though Graham had downplayed the night's operation's significance, Lovelace knew their time was running out. He had to come. He had to be in the crowd somewhere. But no matter how hard she scrutinised the screens before her, she couldn't see him.

By nine-thirty, Lovelace noticed a marked reduction in the number of mourners packed into the cul-de-sac. Slowly but surely, they were beginning to ebb away and, with it, their hope of identifying their suspect. The spotters in the crowd continued to call out potential suspects, and their photographs were stored in the force's database, but so far, no one was giving them any cause for hope. Not even one of the faces on the sex offender's register appeared. Lovelace felt disheartened. It was turning out to be a disaster.

At ten thirty, Graham called the operation off. He spoke on the radio to the various field commanders directing their staff. 'Okay. That's it. Pack up, people. De-brief at 8 am sharp tomorrow morning.'

He rang Lovelace directly. She answered the phone in the garden of the Jenkins' house. She had gone outside to watch the darkness chase the sun over the horizon. She was watching the stars when her phone rang.

'Don't be disheartened.' Graham said, and Lovelace noticed an odd slur in his voice. It sounded like he had been drinking. 'We've gathered hundreds of images for us to look at. If he came tonight, we'd have taken his photograph. So it will only be a matter of time before we make the link.'

'He came. I'm sure of it. He wouldn't have been able to resist.'

'I agree.' Graham said. 'So tomorrow, we start going through the photographs and linking them to potential suspects. Until then, go home. Get some rest.'

***

They sat in Lovelace's car outside Spencer's house.

'Do you want to come in?' Spencer asked. 'I think Sophie's in. I could order takeaway?'

Lovelace declined. She didn't feel much like socialising. She had pinned all her hopes on the killer appearing at the girls' memorial service and was finding it difficult to hide her disappointment that he hadn't.

'Perhaps next time.' She said, and Spencer noted the negative way in which she said it.

'If he was there, we have him on camera.' Spencer said reassuringly.

'What if he wasn't?' She asked.

'He was there.' Spencer said. 'We just didn't recognise him. But we will. Sooner or later, we'll pick up his thread.'

'I hope you're right.' Then, more enthusiastically, 'I'm sure you are. He was there. I guess we'll spend Sunday blowing up pictures of all the men who turned up!'

Spencer grinned. 'I'll look forward to it!'

Lovelace drove home along the small country lanes and backstreets of the city. She drove idly, not paying much attention to where she was going but submerging herself in the process rather than her destination. It was cathartic but not cathartic enough. By the time she pulled onto her drive, her mind was buzzing with more questions than she had answers to. She needed to clear her mind of the noise and free herself to think; there was only one way she knew how to do that.

She quickly changed into black motorcycle trousers, boots and a reflective Goretex jacket with "Suzuki" written along the arms and opened the door to her small garage. Her motorcycle glinted in the harsh neon strip light that crossed the ceiling. She slipped the key into the ignition and turned it until the bike's huge power plant rumbled to life. The bike was perfectly tuned, and she sat in the close environment of the garage, purring quietly to herself. Lovelace pressed the small button on her key fob, and the folding garage doors slowly opened.

Lovelace thought the night was breathtakingly warm, possibly the warmest it had been so far, and she began to sweat beneath her protective clothing.

'Dress for the slide,' her Uncle Mike had told her, 'not the ride.'

Lovelace picked up her helmet from the side and carefully pulled it over her ears. She tucked her untidy hair up and away from her eyes and donned a pair of leather gloves. She climbed onto the 'Busa, dropped it into first gear and pulled out into the street. She pressed the button on her key fob and waited while the garage doors closed behind her. Then she edged her motorbike out onto the road and negotiated the quiet streets of Oxford until the open road beckoned her. She powered the bike away from the city until the street lights no longer lit the way, and the only light was the powerful beam of the bike's LED headlamp, which twisted and turned as she lay the machine one way and then the other, carefully following the contours of the road.

She noticed the car as she made her way from the city. It had joined her three streets from her house. It was probably a coincidence, but she didn't like coincidences. As she took a left, so did the car. When she took a right, the car did too, and it fairly matched her for speed as she drove onto the faster stretches. It could have been an unmarked police car, as she knew they operated across the city at all hours of the day and night. However, she had held fast to the speed limit and had given it no cause to stop her, but still it followed. Uncle Mike had warned her not to ride the bike in the daytime as it was a concept model and not yet available to buy. She knew that bike lovers would recognise its form as it rumbled past them and knew very well that it would stir a lot of interest. She waited until she had dropped down onto the A40, and the car was a couple of bike lengths behind her before she dropped the 'Busa into a lower gear and twisted the throttle.

Lovelace felt the adrenalin surge as every element of the bike's 1300cc engine worked in harmony to propel her to over one hundred and fifty miles an hour in the time it took the car's occupants to realise she had gone. She strained every muscle in her arms to grip the motorcycle and hold herself steady. Her eyes scanned everything in front of her, and she concentrated on the spot she would be at in a few seconds, constantly adapting and reassessing as she went. Finally, after five minutes, she slowed to a safer speed and pulled off the road and onto tighter, darker lanes.

She was alone. The dark lanes twisted and turned ahead of her, and she rode the bike as if she and the machine were one being. She drove like that for nearly an hour and gave no more thought to the car that had followed her. Then, as she crested a hill before her, the sky ahead suddenly lit up as lightning streaked across it.

The countryside before her became day and then back to night in the blink of an eye.

She rode on as the storm gathered.

***

Dan Hodges had been careful to ensure that his daughter and her friend were out of the way when Yan turned up on his doorstep. He had packed them off to Issy's bedroom when he heard his dirty white van pull up outside. Issy hadn't needed any persuading. Yan was beginning to give her the creeps, and she wasn't shy about expressing her feelings.

'He's a perv.' Issy said to her friend as they climbed the stairs. 'I think he fancies me,' she added, and the two girls giggled.

As Dan opened the door to Yan, he called up the stairs, 'Make sure the doors are all locked. And don't go outside. Not until I'm back. Keep the windows closed.'

Yan was stood on the pavement as he stepped outside. He looked flushed in the face, and his breathing was fast.

'Everything okay?' Dan asked.

'Couldn't be better.' Yan grinned. 'Come on; we've got work to do.'

They drove for thirty minutes to a small village on the edge of the Cotswold Hills. Yan parked his van in a small lay-by just outside the village under a dark canopy of overhanging oak trees. He switched off the engine, and they sat silently in the darkness. Dan sensed emotion in his friend, but he didn't question it. He seemed fired up and excited. Even as he wondered about his friend's state of mind, he began to feel the first dose of adrenaline seep into his veins. He always felt this before a job. He felt a rush of nerves and excitement. He felt anxious and exhilarated at the same time. His heart raced, and his senses tightened.

Yan opened his laptop and logged in to one of his social media sites.

'Okay. She's out.' He declared at last, and he reached out for the handle of his van. 'Come on, let's go.'

Dan followed his friend as he crossed the road and climbed over a small Cotswold stone wall into a small wood. They walked in darkness through the trees until they came to a fence overlooking a small hill that folded into a lightly lit village. Dan pointed out the object of that night's visit. It was a large cottage that sat on its own at the edge of the village. A light was on in one of the upstairs rooms, and a small antique light glowed above the back door.

Dan stayed close to his friend as he scaled the fence and walked quickly across the field. He stopped suddenly as they neared the halfway point as the door to a neighbour's house flew open, and a bright security light came on, casting everything nearby in a harsh light. Dan felt his stomach rise into his mouth. The light was so bright that he was convinced they were both lit up by it. The neighbour moved about in his garden for a second and emptied some glass bottles into his recycling bin. Then, he disappeared back into his house, and thirty seconds later, the security light went out. Yan stayed stock still while his eyes were re-accustomed to the darkness. Dan felt his heart rate return to normal, although the adrenalin was pumping hard.

They reached the garden to the target house and scaled the small fence that blocked their way. The antique light threw out an orange glow, but nothing Yan was too concerned about. No other neighbours overlooked this garden, so they were unlikely to be seen. Despite that, he carefully watched the door as he crept closer to the house. He didn't want to be surprised by a drunk neighbour suddenly coming out of the house for a sneaky cigarette. When he reached the house, he hunkered down on his knees, and Dan joined him.

Yan reached up for the back door handle and turned it slowly. It was locked. He felt it might have been, but it was worth checking. People can be careless sometimes. He looked up and saw that the kitchen window was open at the top. Dan held his hands for Yan to climb onto and launched him towards the opening. After a minute of fussing with the latch on the larger window, it sprung open, and the two men climbed in. They pulled the window until it was almost closed, and they sat silently on the kitchen floor. They dared not move for a few minutes, and both men strained their senses, listening for any movement nearby. They heard nothing. It was deathly silent.

Without saying a word, Yan signalled that he was going upstairs. Dan nodded and set about searching the lower part of the house. He rapidly passed through the house, picking some notable items and returning them to the kitchen. He waited there for twenty minutes for Yan to come back.

After thirty minutes, Dan looked at his watch. He didn't like to stay too long. It was dangerous. People were known to come back unexpectedly. So he waited another five minutes and listened carefully to hear his friend moving about upstairs. He was beginning to get concerned when he heard a floorboard creek. Yan was still searching upstairs.

Dan stole quietly out of the kitchen and into the hallway. He stood at the foot of a carpeted staircase and listened. Nothing.

Come on, Yan, he pleaded to himself. It was taking too long. Yan was taking too long. He looked at his watch. They had been on site now for nearly three-quarters of an hour.

Fuck this, Dan thought. He gripped the rail that ran up the wall and climbed the stairs.

'Yan!' He cried out as quietly as he could muster. 'Yan.'

He crept along the landing towards the room where the light was coming from. He knew Yan was too sharp to go into that room as the light would cast his shadow onto the curtains, but he looked just in case. There was nothing there.

He pulled the door closed and heard movement in the room behind him. He gripped the handle and pushed it open.

'For fuck's sake, Yan, we need to go,' he said, louder than he intended. He heard his words echo in the silence.

Something was wrong. Against his better judgement and despite the sound in his head of Yan calling him a fucking moron, he reached out for the light switch and turned it on. He stepped into the room and stood there, stunned.

Yan was lying on the floor in a pool of his blood. His head had been smashed in. Dan's brain tried to process the information, but it worked too slowly. He didn't hear the door close fully behind him or see the figure in black that stood behind it. He didn't hear him as he stepped forward, raised a bloodied hammer, or felt any pain as the Night Prowler slammed it into his head.

Dan Hodges was dead long before he hit the ground.

***

Lovelace couldn't hear the thunder over the engine's hum and the whisper of the wind as it cut across the front of her helmet, but she knew it was there. As she rode the bike through the twisty lanes, the storm gathered pace above her, and the lightning intensified. There was no rain yet, but Lovelace could sense a change in the air. She gave herself another hour before the storm would come and her ride would be cut short. She didn't mind riding in the wet, but it wasn't as much fun, and the 'Busa was less forgiving if you made a mistake. It was a great bike to ride but a difficult one to pick up again if you dropped it, and she didn't fancy explaining to Uncle Mike how she had come about sitting next to it in a hedge.

Lovelace turned the machine onto a small lane and drove along its length until the trees closed in on either side. She noticed the first droplets of the impending storm gather on her visor and was about to turn around and go home when the bike lights came down on a dirty white van with foreign plates parked up in a small lay-by. She pulled up behind it and looked at the plates. It matched the partial number plate they had been given several days ago. Was it a coincidence? Probably, but she didn't like coincidences. After all, they gave it a name for a reason.

She rode on to the end of the lane until it came to a T-junction, and she turned right and dropped down into a small, dark village. There was no street lighting; the only light she had to see by was the headlamp of her bike and the occasional security lamp as she passed a house. She pulled over in the middle of the village and turned off the engine. She removed her helmet, sat quietly in the dark, and listened.

There was no sound save for the hoot of an owl somewhere and the distant rumble of thunder. She looked at each house along the street, drew a mental picture of the village in her mind, and worked out which houses could be approached from the fields leading up to where the dirty white van was parked. She slipped the bike's stand down, climbed off, and slowly walked up the street. She passed each house slowly, looking for any hint that something wasn't quite right.

Without thinking, she retrieved her phone from an inside pocket and dialled Spencer's number. He answered after two rings.

'Lucy?'

'Phil, I think I've found the van.'

There was a pause.

'Where?'

'A small village called Maudsley. The van's parked up in a lay-by outside the village.'

'I know the village. You're only a couple of miles away.'

Until then, Lovelace had no real inkling of where in the world she was. She had ridden aimlessly and was quite surprised that she had come almost full circle.

'Wait a second…'

Lovelace stopped outside the gate of a large cottage. A light had just appeared in a bedroom window and then gone off again. There was the sound of something, but she couldn't make it out. It was odd, though. She couldn't put her finger on it, but something felt off.

'There's a cottage about five houses in as you drive through the village. It's set back from the road but overlooks fields at the back. Phil, I think there's someone inside….'

'Lucy, it's probably the owner….'

'Something's wrong…I have a bad feeling….'

'Lucy, I'm going to hang up and call 999. Do not go in the house. Lucy, did you hear me?'

'I-I heard you. It's Lavender Cottage. Phil, I've got to go in. Someone's life may be in danger.'

'Lucy….'

It was too late. Spencer cursed as the line went dead.

Lovelace carefully pushed the gate open and stepped inside the grounds of Lavender Cottage. She stole quietly up to the house and stood for a minute trying to listen for sounds from inside, but none came. Slowly she edged around the side of the house until she came to a gate. She pulled the handle down, but it held firm. She reached up to the top and felt for a bolt on the other side. She found it, drew it back, and carefully opened the gate. It never surprised her how lax some people were with their home security.

She strolled around the back of the house until she came to a kitchen window. She felt around the edge and found that it was slightly ajar. She opened it and climbed inside. She waited a moment as her eyes acclimatised to her surroundings. There was a door opposite her, and beyond it - darkness.

She crept about the ground floor, constantly listening for any sound. She jumped as the storm gathered nearby, and a flash of lightning lit the house up. The thunder came a few seconds later, rolling and echoing about the hills. Stealthily she climbed the stairs. A glint of light shone from beneath a bedroom door, but this was at the back of the house and couldn't have been the light she saw from the street. Lovelace walked up to it and pushed the door open gently. The room was empty.

She turned and pushed the door open behind her. The room was dark and deathly quiet. This had been the room that she had seen the light come from. She reached up along the wall until she found the light switch and turned it on.

She didn't hesitate for a second. She knew she was in danger, and she reacted instantly. She turned and pelted along the landing until she reached the stairs. She took them in two bounds and hit the floor running. She couldn't see him, but she sensed him. He was there, in the house, watching her. She needed to get out fast, and she made a beeline for the kitchen and her escape.

And then she saw him as he came out of the shadows. He moved with speed and purpose, and she was transfixed by him as each step he took brought him ever closer to her.

And then the darkness came.

Twenty-Two

'I thought you were dead.'

Lovelace winced as the nurse clipped the wound with a surgical staple.

She had seen him coming just in time. As he launched his attack, she stopped abruptly and ducked. It caught him by surprise, and the hammer fell short of its target. It glanced at the back of her head and ripped the skin open. The impact was enough to drop Lovelace to the floor, and for several terrifying moments, she drifted in and out of consciousness. She knew she was powerless to stop him, and in her lucid moments, she felt sure he would launch his final attack, but he didn't. He stood over her for a moment and then quietly walked away.

And then Spencer had come, cradling her bloodied head in his lap while they waited for the paramedics to arrive.

'I'm sorry,' Lovelace said as the nurse drove another staple into her head. 'I didn't mean to scare you.'

'You should have waited.' Spencer scolded. 'He could have killed you.'

'He could have,' Lovelace agreed. 'But he didn't. I wonder why he didn't?'

Spencer shrugged. He didn't care why; he was just glad he didn't. 'Perhaps he heard me coming. Armed response were seconds behind me. He must have heard their sirens too. Perhaps it spooked him.'

'Perhaps…' she agreed, but she wasn't convinced. She felt that he had recognised her and, for whatever reason, had chosen to spare her. 'What about the bodies upstairs?'

'That's a bit of a mystery.' Spencer said. 'The homeowner has no knowledge of them. The working hypothesis is that they were doing the place over.'

'Burglars?'

Spencer nodded. 'Luton and Stanton are working on it as we speak. We should know more in the next few hours. But by all accounts, they stumbled on more than they were expecting.'

The nurse clipped another staple into the back of Lovelace's head. 'There you go. All done.'

'Miss Lovelace?' A young Doctor pulled back the curtain to the booth and stepped inside. She closed the curtain behind her.

'Yes.'

She held up a scan of Lovelace's head. 'Bad news is you're going to have quite a headache. The good news is nothing's broken.'

'I can go home?' Lovelace asked.

'We'll need to keep you in overnight for observation. You can never be too careful with head injuries..'

She was about to add more but was interrupted by Lovelace jumping off the bed.

'I'd like to go home.' Lovelace said.

'I really must insist….' The young Doctor said lamely.

'So must I,' Lovelace said firmly.

'It's okay,' Spencer said, 'I'll look after her.'

'She'll need monitoring. Constantly. At least for a few hours.'

'Then that's what I'll do.' Spencer added.

'Very well.' The young Doctor sighed heavily. 'I'll just go and arrange the discharge papers.'

Lovelace declined the offer of Spencer's bed and reclined on his large sofa instead. Spencer brought out a large duvet and several pillows, and before long,

Lovelace had leant her head back and drifted off to sleep.

When she woke, the world was a different place. Daylight streamed in through open curtains, and the rain fell heavily outside. The once azure blue sky was dark and gloomy, and the air was cooler.

Lovelace sat up and felt the back of her head. She had a huge lump, and the pain streaked across her eyes. On the floor in front of her, Sophie was sat, crossed-legged, eating cornflakes from a bowl. She looked up as Lovelace moved.

'Morning!' She said cheerily, and her sweet, smiley face cheered Lovelace. 'Do you need painkillers?' She asked.

Lovelace said yes, she did, and Sophie disappeared into the kitchen, returning a few minutes later with two paracetamol and a steaming cup of hot tea.

'Breakfast?' Sophie asked, and the thought turned Lovelace's stomach. She declined the offer, knocked back the two tablets and lay back on the pillows.

'Morning.' Spencer said as he entered the room. 'How are you feeling?'

'Like a bear with a sore head.' Lovelace said. Then, suddenly, she said, 'Shit! My bike. Where's my bike?'

'In my garage.' Spencer reassured her. 'When you fell asleep, I went back and retrieved it. She's a beautiful beast. Sophie stayed up and watched you all night. It may have taken me longer to ride the two miles back than you would expect!'

Lovelace smiled. To Sophie, she said, 'You watched me all night? Thank you.'

'That's okay. Dad didn't want you drowning in your sick.' Sophie said, spooning cornflakes into her mouth.

Spencer's large flat-screen television caught Lovelace's attention. The BBC news had just started, and the scrolling banner was bullet-pointing the day's news across the bottom of the screen. Lovelace recognised the scene before her as the news anchor led to the story of the Night Prowler and the discovery of two more unidentified bodies in a village in the Cherwell Valley.

'Do we know who the bodies are yet?' Lovelace asked.

Spencer nodded. 'Yes. I'll bring you up to speed when you feel up to it.'

'I'm up to it now.' Lovelace said, sitting up. She felt her head throb, but she ignored it.

Spencer had seen the look that shot across her face. 'Drink your tea. There's no rush.'

Lovelace took a sip and then looked back at the television. She remembered seeing a news crew at the memorial last night, and now she saw the images they filmed. The journalist was giving a piece to camera, but Lovelace ignored the words. Behind them, the crowd sang a hymn and held candles up to the night sky.

And then she saw him.

He was there, in the background, keeping a low profile and avoiding standing out in the open. Lovelace sat up straight, her pain forgotten.

'Can you pause that?' Lovelace asked.

Sophie took the remote control and pressed "pause." She had been too slow. The image had moved on.

'Can you rewind it?' She asked.

Sophie rewound the image until Lovelace cried, 'Stop!' She climbed off the sofa and kneeled within inches of the television screen. She turned and looked at Spencer, and her eyes shone.

'Can you see him?' She asked Spencer.

Lovelace sat back from the television. Spencer stood before it and looked at the crowd of faces in the image. It took a few minutes before he edged closer to the screen and smiled.

'Fuck me!' Spencer exclaimed. 'I never expected that.'

They gathered in Graham's office at force HQ. Graham sat at the foot of the large oak table, looking older and greyer. His skin had taken on a waxed complexion, and his eyes sat back in darkened sockets. Everyone that walked through the door had noticed the striking change in his appearance, but no one mentioned it. The stress of such a high-profile serial killer case was bound to take its toll, and the lack of movement in the case had deepened Graham's anxiety. The call he had taken from Spencer two hours ago had changed things markedly, but no sign of it showed on Graham's face.

Luton was holding court. He was standing at the side of the table closest to Graham. He was detailing the discoveries he and Stanton had made since discovering two unidentified bodies in a cottage in the village of Maudsley moments before the attack on Lovelace.

Lovelace and Spencer sat at the far end of the table, eager to share their discovery. They had gathered as much information as possible and piled into Graham's office with arms full of paperwork.

'Victim number one is a Polish national named Yan Kowalski.' Luton said, laying a mugshot of the man before them on the table. 'Our colleagues in Warsaw have been kind enough to email us some information about the man. It seems he's had quite a criminal career. He spent five years in prison in Poland for armed robbery before coming to the UK sometime in 2010. As far as we can tell, he's pretty much stayed off our radar regarding his criminal activities. Certainly, nothing that would give us cause for concern. However, his activities and movements have been subject to some oversight by Interpol and our National Crime Agency. It seems Mr Kowalski has been moving a considerable amount of stolen property across Europe: small stuff mostly, but high value. We're talking paintings, jewellery, pottery, antiques, gold, silver, you name it; if it fits into hidden compartments on his van, he'll move it. The traffic goes both ways. A good deal of stolen contraband from the EU makes its way to buyers here in the UK courtesy of Mr Kowalski's van. Our current working hypothesis is that Yan is not only a fence and a stolen goods trafficker but also a burglar. Hence his appearance last night in a cottage in Maudsley.'

'What about the other man?' Graham asked.

'A married man by the name of Dan Hodges. Has two teenage kids. We've nothing on the man, no criminal record, and no markers on his file. According to his wife, Dan lost his job about ten months ago and has struggled to find employment. He and Yan were mates from a few years ago, and, in recent months, Yan has been offering Dan some paid security work in and around Oxford. In reality, Dan climbed on board Yan's little criminal enterprise, aiding in his burglarious activities. Dan's wife has supplied us with dates when her husband and Yan were out on their so-called security work, and we've matched that with several reported burglaries in the district. But here's where it gets interesting..'

'A few nights ago, Crimestoppers took an anonymous phone call from someone alleging that Yan Kowalski was a good fit for the Night Prowler. Unfortunately, Yan's name threw up no red flags, and he was filed along with thousands of others.'

'Any reason why someone would suspect Yan?' Spencer asked.

'None whatsoever,' Luton replied. 'I've spoken to the Polish Police, and there's nothing in Yan's past to suggest that kind of criminal activity. A thief, yes. But no sexual deviance or violence against women.

'So we played a recording of the phone call naming Yan as a potential suspect to Dan's wife, who confirms the voice is that of her husband.'

'A falling out among thieves?' Spencer asked.

'We don't think so. Dan's wife, Rachel Hodges, confirms they were concerned about Yan's behaviour towards their teenage daughter. The night of the phone call to Crimestoppers was the same night that the reports of the murder of Sarah Lipton at the Green House went public. Again, we're just speculating, but Dan may have been with Yan when they burgled the Green House. We can't be certain, as Miss Lipton did not report any burglary. However, Rachel Hodges confirms that on the night before Miss Lipton's murder, her husband and Yan were out on a spurious security job, and we have no reports of any burglaries that night. We've spoken to Miss Lipton's next of kin, who can't be certain but who believe items are missing from Miss Lipton's possessions. Items they feel certain should be there.'

'So,' Lovelace said. 'Our two burglars hit a house on the same night that the Night Prowler also picked? That's a bit stretched.'

'It is.' Luton agreed. 'Until you appreciate that the MO of the burglars and the Night Prowler are the same. They target the same people and the same houses and wait until the owner is out of the house before entering. Of course, the end result is hugely different, but it was only a matter of time before their paths crossed.'

'So why did the Night Prowler not kill them the first time but did kill them on their second meet?' Spencer asked.

'Again, I can only speculate. When we catch this man, we can ask him directly; until then, we are assuming that although they hit the same house on the same night, they hit it at different times, or the Night Prowler was able to remain hidden while they went about their work. Last night, in Maudsley, the two men hit a much smaller property than the Green House, and we think that one of them accidentally stumbled on The Night Prowler, ending with his murder. Once one of the men was killed, it was only a matter of time before he killed the other. The Night Prowler has only left one witness, and that was pure luck on her part.'

'So why didn't he kill me?'

Luton shrugged his shoulders. 'I don't know. He may have heard Spencer and the Armed Response Unit arrive, or maybe he spared you out of professional courtesy.'

The latter bothered Lovelace. She felt sure that he had recognised her. He had looked down on her as she lay on the floor, entirely at his mercy, yet he never finished his work. He had spared her. But why? To what end?

And now she had a name to go with the dark figure the press had named "The Night Prowler."

'Lucy,' Graham said, 'I believe you and Spencer have a suspect in mind?'

Luton sat down, and all eyes were focused on Lovelace. She stood up and felt the blood rush from her head. She held on to the table and steadied herself. She needed to remember that she had taken quite a hit to the back of her head.

'Last night's vigil for the two girls that were murdered may have been more successful than we imagined,' she began, trying to contain her excitement. 'None of the spotters in the crowd or the control room could spot anyone who has since held up to be a useful suspect. Everyone we highlighted and checked has proven to be of no use. It seemed to be that our suspect declined to take the bait. Until that is, I saw this.'

Lovelace threw several copies of a still photograph across the table taken from a BBC recording filmed during the vigil. 'The BBC has very kindly submitted all their footage of last night's vigil for forensic analysis. We're getting better pictures blown up as we speak, but this one will suffice for now.'

They all took a photograph and perused the image.

Stanton asked, 'should we know this fella?'

Lovelace shook her head. 'No. You shouldn't. And that's why he's our number one suspect.'

'He's our only suspect..' Graham added glumly.

'We only need one.' Lovelace said.

'Who is he?' Luton asked.

Lovelace paused. 'His name,' she said, 'is Adam Sinclair. Approximately one year ago, his wife went missing and hasn't been seen since. We think he murdered her and has been on a killing spree ever since.'

Twenty-Three

'It must take such a toll on a man. First, his poor dear mother died so quickly, and then Hannah left soon after. Poor man. It must have taken such a toll.'

Lovelace and Spencer had left the briefing at Kidlington with orders from DCI Graham to take a big shovel and do some deep digging into Adam Sinclair. So they had driven through the storm to where Sinclair lived and knocked on the door of one of his neighbours' houses.

They sat in the front room of the elderly Mrs Pritchard, drinking tea from bone china cups and eating stale biscuits from a tin. Mrs Pritchard had welcomed them into her home with an eagerness bordering on excitement.

'How long have you been neighbours?' Lovelace asked.

'I've lived here most of my life. God rest his soul; my husband has been gone for almost thirty years. The Sinclairs moved in the moment they were married. Now then, when was that?'

Mrs Pritchard pondered the question for a full minute before saying, 'yes, it must have been about twelve years ago - I remember poor Mr Sampson being wheeled down the path by the ambulance people. I said then, "Doris, that's the last you'll see of Mr Sampson." And how right I was. He was in hospital for nearly a month before he finally passed. He had a fall, you see. Pushing on ninety-five, he was. And when you get to our age, it's not quite easy to come out of hospital again. And I think the Sinclairs bought it soon after. Quite young they were. He was a bit younger than her by a couple of years, but they made such a lovely couple. If I remember rightly, they moved in straight away, stripped the place back to plaster and started again. Brought the place into the present. She had a good job, and he was quite a handy young man.'

'What were they like?' Spencer asked.

'He is very quiet,' Mrs Pritchard said, 'and reserved. He doesn't like to talk very much. He always seems to be inside his head, with his thoughts, but he couldn't be a nicer young man. I can't tell you the number of times he has helped me with bits around the house. Never a murmur of complaint, and never once has he taken a penny from me for all the little jobs he's done.'

'And Hannah?' Spencer asked.

Mrs Pritchard gathered her thoughts. 'Well, I wouldn't want to speak out of turn. Don't get me wrong; she wasn't a horrible young woman; she just wasn't very nice. Well, now you see, that's not entirely true, either. She was nice. She was very nice to me, always happy to stop and have a chat over the fence or pop to the shops for me when I ran out of milk or sugar and such. It's just….'

'Yes?' Lovelace prodded.

Mrs Pritchard leant closer to them, her head tilted slightly, and her voice dropped to a level above a whisper. 'She wasn't very nice to him. I used to hear them from time to time. Late at night, usually after she had come home from the pub, she liked to drink, I'm afraid, and it did get a grip on her. My dear late husband was a drinker, and they can be cruel when it gets a hold of them. Not always physical, you know. My husband never laid a finger on me, not once in thirty years of marriage. But he could be very nasty. Some of the things he would say to me. And I heard them come from her mouth too. She could be very cruel to him. And, do you know something,' Mrs Pritchard went on, 'I never once heard a raised voice from him. Not once. He seemed to take it all in his stride.'

'Was she ever physical to him?' Spencer asked.

'I think so.' Mrs Pritchard said. 'I saw a few bruises on him from time to time. Of course, he shrugged them off, but that's what people do.'

'Do you think he was afraid of her?' Lovelace asked.

'No.' Mrs Pritchard replied firmly. 'No. I think he was desperately in love with her. I think that's why he never left her. I certainly don't think it was fear that kept him there.'

'You said earlier that his mother had died quite quickly? What do you know about that?'

'Cancer.' Mrs Pritchard said. 'It seemed that she was diagnosed one day and died the next. I never knew her that well. She came around from time to time. She was married for a while to Hannah's father. That's how the two kids met. Adam was fourteen or so, I think. Hannah must have been around sixteen or seventeen. They were thrown together when their parents met. Until then, I don't think Adam had a very nice childhood. His mother drank, too, you see. And she had many partners, and I don't think they were very nice to Adam and his sister. I think the sister left when she was seventeen.'

'Do you know where the sister lives?' Lovelace asked.

'Not a clue, I'm afraid. Never met her.'

'Earlier, you said that Hannah left Adam. What makes you say that she left him? Isn't it possible that she may have come to some harm?'

'Well, that's what Adam thinks, poor young man, but I think he's clutching at straws. Although, of course, it's easier for him to accept that she may have come to harm rather than accept that she may have left of her own free will. But, if he thinks for one minute that she left, he has to accept that she has rejected him, and I don't think he can cope with that.'

'And what makes you so sure she has just left him?' Lovelace asked.

'She used to bring them home. Her men friends.' Mrs Pritchard said disgustedly.

'Did Adam know about these men?' Spencer asked.

Mrs Pritchard nodded. 'Yes, I'm sure he did. Sometimes she'd come home from the pub with a man in tow, even while poor Adam was in the house. But, most of the time, it was while he was out working.'

'What about in the months before Hannah went missing? Do you remember a particular man friend? Someone a little more regular?'

'There was someone,' Mrs Pritchard said. 'I saw him a few times in the months before Hannah left.'

'Is that why you think she left?' Lovelace asked. 'Because there was another man?'

'It makes sense, doesn't it?' Mrs Pritchard said. 'When you play around like she did, then sooner or later, you'll make a connection with someone that forces your hand. I've seen it many times.'

'Do you remember the day Hannah was reported missing?'

'I do.' Mrs Pritchard said. 'I remember it very well. But of course, Adam didn't report her missing that day. He reported it late the next day. She was known to stay out for the night once the drink had taken hold. Adam had come home one evening to find her out but hadn't thought that out of character. When she hadn't returned the following night, he started to grow concerned.'

'Can you remember if either Hannah or Adam acted odd or out of sorts the day Hannah left?'

Mrs Pritchard shook her head.

'Did you see Hannah or her male friend arrive or leave the house on the day she left?' Lovelace asked.

'I saw them both arrive.' Mrs Pritchard said. 'But I never saw them leave. I spent a lot of that day in my garden. So I wouldn't have seen them leave.'

'What about Adam? Did you see him come and go?'

'I saw him come home that evening after work. I heard him pottering around. He came over to my house to help me with a computer problem. I'm not very good with these things, you see. It's a young person's game.'

'How did he seem to you?' Lovelace asked.

'I didn't notice anything different about him. He was the same old Adam. But, of course, he didn't know then that Hannah had left, so I don't suppose I would have noticed anything, would I?'

'I suppose not.' Lovelace agreed. Secretly she suspected that Adam Sinclair had just murdered his wife and her lover and casually came over to his elderly neighbour's home to fix a computer problem before returning home to dispose of the bodies. It was cold and calculated. 'Did you see him leave at all that evening?'

'I'm certain he didn't,' Mrs Pritchard said. 'He didn't leave until his usual time the next morning. I heard his engine start.'

'Has Adam done any work at all to his house since Hannah left?' Lovelace asked. 'Any building work? Any work to the garden?'

'No. Nothing at all. He's rather left the garden to overgrow, I'm afraid. Grief does funny things to people. It seems to have sucked the life out of him.'

Lovelace and Spencer thanked Mrs Pritchard for her candour and sat in the car, listening to the rain beat a steady tattoo on the roof.

'What are you thinking?' Spencer asked. 'That Adam Sinclair came home, found his wife and her lover, killed them, then hid their bodies somewhere before reporting his wife missing?'

'Exactly that.' Lovelace agreed. 'Except maybe he returned to the house during the day and hid away, hoping to catch them at it. He would have known his neighbours' routines. So it wouldn't have been hard for him to get back into his house unobserved.'

'But what did he do with the bodies?' Spencer asked. 'He hasn't left them in the house or the garden.'

'The bodies could be the key.' Lovelace agreed. 'Adam Sinclair has no problem leaving bodies everywhere, so why hide his wife?'

'Because that's a link between him and a victim?' Spencer suggested.

'Probably.' Lovelace agreed. 'But his wife going missing gave him another opportunity. It allowed him to walk into a police station during a national hunt for a serial killer and rub our noses in his genius. He would have loved that, standing among us, secretly revelling in the thrill of the chase.'

'So where next?' Spencer asked.

'The dead mother first.' Lovelace said.

'You think he killed her?' Spencer asked.

'No, I think her death was his trigger. It started this whole chain of events. In nearly all crimes like this, there is a trigger point. Something that starts them off. Death of a mother is high on the list of likely triggers.'

'Okay. The mother it is.'

'And we need to find his sister. If they had an abusive childhood, she might be able to shine some light on Adam's current behaviour. Then we need to speak to Hannah's friends and family and get an angle on her and this mystery fella. Then we must find what links Adam Sinclair to several murdered women.'

'Not much then.'

Lovelace fired up her Merc. 'It's him, Phil. I'm sure of it.'

***

Getting into the house hadn't been a problem. It never usually was. Even those who thought they had done an excellent job securing their home fell short. All the fancy security in the world was only as good as its weakest part, and the weakest part was usually human error. An open window, a large cat flap or a carelessly hidden door key. It didn't take much. In this case, it had been a top window left slightly open.

The problem had been the location of the house. It was overlooked on all sides by neighbouring properties, and getting close enough to break in without being observed proved challenging. But no one noticed delivery drivers these days. A courier of some description visited the average British street every ten minutes in large vans laden with packages. So he donned a cap, slipped a brown box under his arm, and strolled up to the front door. His eyes had scanned the properties to either side, but he saw no movement. There were no cameras, either, and as he made his way to the front door, he realised his actions were now obscured by the placement of several bushes and trees. So although his approach to the house was in plain sight of the neighbours, he couldn't be seen while at the house. Moreover, the road in front of the house was bordered on the other side by fields of wheat which swept up a steady incline to a forest in the distance.

He was perfectly alone and unobserved.

He dropped the package by the front door and strolled around the side of the house to a large wooden gate. It was bolted from the other side, but the bolt was at the top of the gate. He reached over and unbolted it, and closed the gate behind him. Moments later, he found the open window and climbed into the house.

The kitchen was well equipped and modern, with an old-fashioned flue above the cooker. He walked past a long breakfast bar with the remnants of breakfast still in the sink and into the hallway. There was an old table by the front door with an old telephone and a tall coat rack with several jackets hanging from it. He walked around the lower part of the house slowly, enjoying the feeling of power that washed over him.

He climbed the stairs and wandered about the rooms that he found. Then, finally, he made his way into the bathroom. Condensation from that morning's shower routines still lingered on the mirror. Two electric toothbrushes stood in their cradles on top of a glass cabinet. He picked up the pink one and found that it was still damp. He knew from her social media pages that she lived some of the time with her father and at other times with her mother. The toothbrush suggested she had been here today.

He felt his senses surge.

Her bedroom was next to the bathroom. The bed was unmade and dirty laundry had been cast haphazardly across the floor. He walked around the room, touching everything that was hers and holding worn clothing up to his nose so that he could smell her. He pulled strands of long dark hair from a brush on her dressing table and wound them tightly around his fingers.

He climbed into her bed and slowly drew the covers around him. The smell of her assailed his senses until he couldn't contain himself any longer. The urge compelled him. He was about to release the pressure when he heard the front door slam shut. He moved quickly and pulled open the cupboard doors, and climbed inside. His senses tightened even more, and he strained his hearing to listen for clues to what was going on.

Sophie Spencer had paid little attention to the brown parcel on her father's doorstep and had casually dropped it onto the mahogany table as she unlocked the front door and went in.

'Come in. It won't take me a second.'

Two of Sophie's friends followed her into the house and stood in the hallway as Sophie bounded up the stairs to her bedroom. She had left the house in such a hurry that she had utterly forgotten her swimming costume. Sunday afternoons were often spent in an outdoor lido in the next village but given that the weather had taken such a bad turn, they had opted to go to an indoor pool in Oxford. She found her ready-packed kit in a small rucksack at the foot of her bed. She turned and went to open her wardrobe door and then stopped and picked a raincoat off the hangers at the back of the bedroom door. It certainly wasn't the weather for her summer coat!

She bounded back down the stairs and corralled her friends back out of the house, closing and locking the door behind her.

She never saw the figure look out of her bedroom window and watch as she walked down the garden path.

But he saw her.

And he could taste her.

***

They sat in a lay-by in Lovelace's ruby-red Mercedes while Spencer made a few phone calls and researched Adam Sinclair's complicated family history.

'Well, that was more complicated than it needed to be!' Spencer declared as he hung up the phone.

'What do we know?' Lovelace asked.

'Adam's mother was a woman named Janet Weston. Weston is the name of her third husband and Hannah Sinclair's maiden name. Old Mrs Pritchard certainly had that right. It turns out Janet Weston, formally Janet Brown, formally Janet Sinclair, married Hanna's father eighteen years ago. It seems Mr Weston died a couple of years back. Janet Weston died fifteen months ago from cancer, around two months before Hannah went missing.'

'What about Adam's father and Janet's second husband?'

Spencer shook his head. 'Nothing there yet. It's Sunday; there's barely a skeleton crew at the office.'

'Do we know where Adam grew up?'

'That we do know,' Spencer declared proudly. 'Mrs Weston had the good sense not to move house. She was still living in the same house Adam grew up in when she died.'

Spencer reached over and typed the postcode into the car's navigation system. It was fifteen miles away.

'Let's take a look, shall we?'

They pulled up in a nondescript-looking former council estate on the edge of Oxford. The houses were identical, with extensive front gardens mainly laid to driveways. A typical Sunday would see most of the residents out cutting the grass or washing the motors that lined the streets, but such was the weather that few people were out.

'Which one?' Lovelace asked.

'Number twelve.' Spencer pointed to a grey-looking semi-detached house a few yards from the road.

Lovelace pulled up the hood of her coat to cover her hair and stepped out of the car. Spencer retrieved his umbrella from the back seat and launched it into the sky. Together they walked through the rain and up the path to number twelve. Lovelace reached up to the doorbell and pressed. She followed it with a quick rap on the door. They waited a few minutes, but no one came. Spencer walked along the front of the house along a sorry-looking border of dying bushes and peered in through a gap in the net curtains.

'It's empty.' He said as Lovelace followed.

Lovelace peered through the curtains and saw nothing but old faded carpet and peeling wallpaper.

'No one lives there.'

Lovelace and Spencer looked up to see a face looking at them from the front door of number fourteen. The two houses were joined at the centre, and each had a garage on opposite sides between them and their next closest neighbours. The two houses were butterfly images of each other, and they shared a front lawn that was returning to its colour following the hot spell of weather.

'Who are you?' Spencer asked.

'I think the pertinent question is, who the bloody hell are you?' The neighbour said.

Spencer smiled. 'You're quite right.' He reached into his pocket and pulled out his warrant card. 'Detective Sergeant Spencer. This is Detective Constable Lovelace, Thames Valley.'

'I see. Well, you'd better come in then.'

They divested themselves of their wet clothes in the hallway of number fourteen. The neighbour introduced himself as Guy, and he led them into a well-presented and equipped kitchen.

Another man sat at the kitchen table reading the Times and drinking what smelt like strong coffee.

'This is my husband, Mark,' Guy said. 'Can I get you a coffee? Mark, these lovely people are from the police.'

'I heard.' Mark said gruffly. 'I suppose you'd better sit down.'

Mark folded his newspaper and indicated the chairs opposite him. Guy pulled some cups from a cupboard and poured them all coffee.

'What's it all about?' Mark asked.

'Straight to the point as usual.' Guy said, his voice etched with sarcasm. 'You must forgive my husband. He's not religious, but he believes Sundays are sacred.'

Mark shot his partner a look, and then he turned to Lovelace and Spencer and said, 'On the contrary, you must forgive my husband. He loves the drama. He's the original drama queen.'

'Really, Mark, you mustn't be so homophobic.' Guy reached out and laid his hand on Mark's. They smiled at each other, and Lovelace saw the warmth in their eyes.

Lovelace said, 'we're sorry to trouble you on a Sunday. It wasn't our intention. Guy caught us looking through next door's window.'

Mark smiled. 'He would. He's a nosey sod. Guy is the estate's Neighbourhood Watch team. He's the only one in it. And it's not exactly official; he likes to stick his nose into other people's business.'

Guy slapped Mark's hand playfully. Then he said, 'well, he's not wrong. I see everything!'

Lovelace was suddenly reminded of the elderly Mrs Clayton and her snooping on the neighbours. She looked

at Guy and saw how he might be in thirty years, which
made her smile.

'How long have you lived here?' Lovelace asked.

'I grew up here.' Mark said. 'My parent's died years
back and left me the house. They bought the place when
Thatcher sold off all the council houses in the eighties.
Guy's lived with me damn near ten years now, I think.'

Lovelace watched the couple as they talked. Mark was
older than Guy by some ten years, she guessed. His hair
was dark and tinged with silver, and he had a pretty,
boyish face that was beginning to show signs of wear.
Guy was more vibrant. She sensed a youthful playfulness
in him that was infectious. He was an attractive young
man with neatly styled blonde hair and piercing blue
eyes.

'So you knew your neighbours next door?' Lovelace
asked.

Mark nodded. 'Afraid so. Weird lot. The old lady died
over a year ago, I think. House has been sitting empty
ever since. Adam came around a few weeks after the
funeral with a big van and emptied the place. I don't
think he's been back since.'

'The council haven't placed anyone new there?'
Spencer asked.

Mark shook his head. 'Not a council place. Mrs
Weston bought the place with her first husband. She got
the lot in the divorce.'

'So Adam probably inherited the place?'

'Pretty certain he did.' Mark said. 'Him and his sister.'

'I don't suppose you know where the sister lives?'
Lovelace asked.

'Nah.' Mark shook his head. 'I remember when she
left. I can't say I blamed her. Must have been a horrible
place to grow up in.' Mark paused. He preferred to leave
the gossiping to Guy. He didn't like to talk out of turn

about people who weren't around to defend themselves. Then he said, 'do you mind if I ask what this is about?'

'We're following up on Hannah Sinclair's disappearance.' Lovelace said.

'Do you have new information?' Guy asked excitedly.

Mark shot his husband a warning glare, but Guy missed it entirely.

'Nothing like that.' Spencer said. 'It's just a cold case review. We review cases every twelve months or so with a fresh pair of eyes to see if we missed anything.'

'Has she been gone that long?' Mark asked. 'I hadn't realised. I thought she would have popped up for air by now.'

'You think she left of her own free will?' Lovelace asked.

'I don't think anything,' Mark said. 'But it's what people said. That was the rumour that was going around. She was well known for it. She liked a drink and liked her men. I feel sorry for Adam. He was a nice kid, but his mother was awful, and Hannah wasn't much better.'

'How well did you know them?' Lovelace asked.

'I knew their reputation. I left home when I was eighteen and only returned when my folks died. So I knew how they were before, and I knew them after. It wasn't a nice household to bring kids up in. Social services were all over the place for a time. Janet was a terrible drunk. She used to bring fellas home all the time. I reckon they probably weren't very nice to the kids. I'd say that's why Erin ran away when she turned sixteen.'

'Do you think the kids were abused?'

'I honestly don't know.' Mark said. 'Neglected certainly. Adam was always withdrawn. He was a quiet lad anyway, but you could see the darkness in him sometimes. I felt for him when Erin left. He must have borne the brunt of his mother's drunkenness. And the kind of men she brought back weren't the child-loving sort if you know what I mean?'

Lovelace knew all too well what he meant. She had seen it a lot as a beat copper. People could be so cruel.

'What did you make of Adam?' She asked.

'As I say, he was a quiet lad but nice enough. He was bright too. Inquisitive. With the right influences, he could have made more of himself.'

'The mother was married a couple of times?'

'Yeah. I don't remember Mr Sinclair very well. I think he was a nice bloke. Cared for the kids. The second husband I never met, but I knew Bob. Bob Weston, that is. Things got better when he came on the scene. Hannah was his daughter, and she came as part of the package. I suppose it was inevitable that Hannah and Adam would get together. They were old enough if you know what I mean. Hannah must have been about sixteen or seventeen. Adam was a bit younger. They got married when he turned eighteen and left. Bob died a couple of years ago, and Janet went last year. It was very quick. Mercifully so. She fell ill one weekend and died the next.'

'Do you know why they haven't done anything with the house?'

'Which one?' Mark asked.

'What?' Spencer asked.

'There must be two houses.' Mark looked across at Guy with a confused expression.

'Why must there be two?' Lovelace asked.

Guy smiled and said, 'Old Bob Weston managed a farm for his parents. They were a really old couple. They must have been in their nineties easily. He always said he would sell up and move to Spain when they died. Janet was always going on about it, but the old dears wouldn't die. And then Bob died. And then, a few weeks before Janet died, I'm sure she mentioned that she was selling the farm and going to Spain to live out Bob's dream. And then she followed Bob into the next life before she could do anything about it. So, you see, there must be two houses?'

'That's very interesting, thank you.' Lovelace said. 'I don't suppose either of you knows where this farm is, by any chance?'

The two men looked at each and shook their heads.

'No idea,' Mark said. 'I suppose Tom might know.'

'Tom?' Lovelace asked.

'Tom Sinclair.' Mark said. 'Adam's dad.'

Lovelace looked at Spencer with a bewildered expression on her face.

'I just assumed he was dead as well.' She said.

'No.' Mark said. 'I'm fairly sure he's still alive. At least, I'm certain that's who I saw in the Carpenter's Arms a few weeks ago. He was a very distinctive-looking man. Always reminded me of Albert Einstein. I'm certain it was him.'

Lovelace and Spencer thanked the two men for their help, caught a short break in the rain, and returned to Lovelace's car before it started falling again.

'Now that was interesting.' Lovelace said as she started her motor up.

'It was.' Spencer agreed.

'Let's hunt down Tom Sinclair. I reckon he might put us on to the sister.'

'I'm sure he will, but not today. You look knackered.'

'I'm good.'

Spencer disagreed. He could still see the pain etched across Lovelace's face. It was only a few hours since the Night Prowler had tried to take her head off with a hammer, and he could only imagine the thundering headache she must have.

'Sophie's out at a friend's house tonight. So I'll make her bed so you can have that. But for now, Doctor Spencer prescribes a quiet Sunday evening in front of the telly. No arguments.'

Lovelace looked across at her partner and saw the futility of arguing. Spencer's face was resolute. And if she was perfectly honest, her head hurt like hell.

'Okay.' She said and drove them back to Spencer's.

Twenty-Four

Spencer donned a pair of freshly laundered pinstripe trousers and threw on a perfectly ironed crisp white shirt. He slipped two gold cuff links through the ends of his sleeves and deftly did them up. He took a blue tie from his wardrobe and began to sling it around his neck. As he did so, he felt the clasp of his chain that held a silver St Christopher around his neck break, and the charm fell. He untucked his shirt from his trousers and retrieved the jewellery. He held it in his hands so that the light caught the edge of the relief of the baby Jesus on the shoulders of St Christopher. His father had bought the necklace when Spencer had started riding motorbikes. 'He's the patron saint of travellers. Keep him close to your heart, and he'll keep you safe.'

Thus far, he hadn't done a bad job, and in twenty-odd years he'd never come to harm on the roads, but the chain that held the St Christopher had proved less useful, breaking no less than fifteen times. So he draped the St Christopher over the corner of his dressing table mirror and promised to buy a new one when he could.

'Ready to go?'

Lovelace was nursing a steaming black cup of coffee at the breakfast bar. Spencer thought she smelt of freshly picked flowers, and for once, her hair looked as though it was holding fast against its desire to do whatever it wanted.

'I made you coffee.' Lovelace said and nodded toward a full cup of black liquid.

Spencer drank the coffee on the fly and dropped the empty cup in the sink. They were in Lovelace's car five minutes later and fell in with Monday morning's rush hour traffic.

'Where to first?' Lovelace asked.

'I had the office trace Tom Sinclair for us. I have an address for him out in Witney. Let's start there, shall we?'

Mark had been spot on with his description of Tom Sinclair, and Lovelace couldn't help but see the similarity between the old man that stood before her and Albert Einstein. He had a friendly, round face, saggy eyes and a full head of grey hair tinged with yellow at the edges.

Spencer and Lovelace introduced themselves, and the old man stood back from his front door and let them in.

'You must be here about Hannah?' Tom Sinclair said as he showed them through to his small lounge. Spencer and Lovelace sat on a small, care-worn sofa while Tom took a high-backed armchair beside an electric fire across from a small old-fashioned television.

Tom Sinclair's home was the ground floor of a two-story building on a tired-looking council-run estate at the edge of town. He had proven easy for the staff at HQ to find, as only one Tom Sinclair existed on the electoral roll. Lovelace's enduring perception of Tom Sinclair was a man who was living the twilight years of his existence on the fringes of the society he had worked and contributed to his entire life. He existed in as much as he was able and no more. She sensed the old man's lack of financial security, born out by how he lived. Everything was old and unloved. Everything was worn or wearing, and nothing in his small flat couldn't be immediately improved by throwing into a skip. Including, Lovelace thought sadly, Tom Sinclair.

The old man exuded a sense of decay despite his friendly, rounded face. He wore an old sweater and dirty grey trousers. Sitting in his armchair, he reached over to a small coffee table for a packet of cigarettes.

'Do you mind?'

He didn't wait for a reply. Instead, he put the tip to the end of a match and inhaled deeply. The smoke filled the small room.

'We were wondering if you could tell us about your son. About his background?' Lovelace asked.

'Why?' The old man said gruffly. 'What's he done?'

'What makes you think we think he's done anything wrong?'

Lovelace watched as Tom Sinclair looked her over. He was summing her up.

'Because you lot took no fucking interest when Hannah went missing. And now here you are, sitting in my house, asking about Adam's history. That's because you think he's done her in. Am I right?'

A sad old man, Lovelace thought. But not a stupid one.

'Let's just say we're looking deeper into Hannah's disappearance.' Lovelace said.

Tom nodded. 'I thought so. Doesn't surprise me. She was a nasty piece of work. Surprised he didn't put a brick to her head years ago.'

'You think she deserved to be murdered?'

Tom shook his head. 'No. But normal men would call time on the relationship. Walk away. Leave her. But not Adam. He isn't normal. He's twisted, like his mother.'

'Are you normal, Mr Sinclair? Is that why you left Adam's mother?'

Tom smiled.

'Fucking right. She was like Hannah. She was a bully and a drunk. I see a lot of this talk about drunk, nasty men and their toxic relationships, but women can be as bad. Worse even. Men aren't supposed to be victims. Women aren't usually physical. It's all up here…' Tom tapped his head. 'Psychological. But it's just as bad.'

'When did you leave Adam's mother?'

'When Adam was four. I walked away. It broke my heart, but I couldn't take any more.'

'So you just left Adam there? In a toxic environment?'

'I tried to take him. And Erin. I tried to take them both.'

'What happened?'

Tom stubbed out his cigarette and lit another. 'One of her boyfriends happened. I'd started court proceedings to get custody of the kids, and this fella turned up one day where I work and attacked me. Put me in hospital for a month. He went down for GBH or something, and by the time I was fit enough to carry on the court case, Janet had found a new bloke and convinced the court she was a good mother. So they granted her full custody with occasional visiting rights to me. I saw them a few times as they were growing up, and then they stopped visiting. That was until Erin was sixteen, and she turned up on my doorstep with nothing but the clothes she was wearing, begging me to take her in.'

'And did you?'

'Of course I did. She stayed with me for a couple of years before we managed to get her a council place.'

'Didn't Janet try and get her back? She was still responsible for her until she was eighteen.' Lovelace asked.

'Glad to see the back of her, I reckon. She was competition. And she was young and pretty. Her fellas were more interested in Erin than they were in Janet. With her out of the way, she was the Queen of the Hill.'

'What about Adam?' Lovelace asked.

Tom suddenly looked sombre. Lovelace could see the guilt written across his wizened old face.

'Erin's three years older than Adam. I couldn't do anything to help him when he was little, and I couldn't help him when Erin left. I think it probably got worse when Erin escaped. He must have taken the brunt of Janet's temper and drunkenness.'

'You said Adam was twisted, like his mother. What did you mean by that?'

'Erin told me stories about some of the things they used to do to Adam when he was little. Cruel things. Like locking him up in a small room under the stairs. Erin said she came home from a friend's house one night to find Adam standing in the middle of the garden with no clothes on in the freezing rain because he'd said something to upset one of Janet's boyfriends. They stood drinking in the kitchen, mocking him. Erin went to get some warm clothes for her brother, and the boyfriend held her by the throat against the wall and threatened to rape her. She ran away shortly after that. But Adam never left. He started to act out. He started copying some of the things Janet's boyfriends would say. Nasty things. And then he'd start spying on Erin, trying to catch her dressing or in the shower. It all got a bit too creepy for her. I reckon that by the time she left, he was past hope. He was as twisted as his mother.'

'But things changed?' Lovelace asked. 'Didn't Janet get married for a third time?'

'That's right.' Tom said. 'She married Bob Weston, Hannah's dad. I never knew her second husband. He lasted a couple of years before running off with another woman. But Bob was a good man—a hard man but fair. You needed to be tough to cope with Janet, but it seemed like he did a good job. He controlled some of her excesses. She drank less and stopped having affairs. She was getting old, and Bob brought with him some stability. Emotional and financial.'

'Was he a wealthy man?' Lovelace asked.

'So people said. He ran his parent's farm, I think. But he died before they did, poor sod. They must be dead by now, I should think.'

'I don't suppose you know where this farm is, do you?' Spencer asked.

Tom looked across to where Spencer sat and shook his head. 'No. It was a big farm, though. Loads of land.'

England was full of big farms with loads of land, Spencer thought, and his glance at Lovelace showed that she was thinking the same. Still, he wondered if a land registry search or the Wills of the deceased Westons may pull up the information they needed. He'd start a search for that later.

'What can you tell us about Hannah?' Lovelace asked.

'He brought her around a few times.' Tom said. 'He must have been about seventeen. He started coming around to see me after Janet married Bob. Then he started bringing her.'

'You didn't like her?' Lovelace asked, detecting a slight edge to his voice.

'She reminded me of Janet. The way she spoke to him. The way she was with him. It was like my life all over again. But he seemed to love her.'

'Do you think she loved him? Lovelace asked.

'She controlled him. I think she loved the power over him. And he was a meek lad. So quiet. He would never speak up, never defend himself.'

'Did you know that Hannah had affairs?'

'I did. Erin told me. I had words with Adam a few years back. I told him she would never change and that he needed to leave her, but he couldn't. Just like he could never leave his mother, they tied him to them with an unbreakable bond.'

'But you think he could murder her?'

Tom nodded. 'Yes, I do. Adam's mother never left him. That unbreakable bond works both ways. If Hannah had tried to leave, he would have killed her. She made the monster, she and Janet. He was chained to them for life and beyond.'

'Do you know if Hannah had tried to leave?'

Tom shook his head. 'No. I don't know. I think Erin suspected it. She's closer to Adam than I am. She still feels very guilty for leaving him the way she did.'

'Thank you, Tom, you've been very helpful.' Lovelace stood as if to leave. 'Before we go, I don't suppose you could tell us where Erin lives?'

'I can do better than that,' Tom said. He got up from his armchair and drew back the net curtain that hung across his front window. 'Right there. Number twelve.' He glanced at the clock on the wall. 'She'll be back from dropping the kids off at the school any minute.'

***

They sat in Lovelace's car while they waited for Erin to return from the school run.

'I get a better feeling about this every time we talk to someone about Adam Sinclair.' Lovelace said.

Spencer agreed. 'He's a good fit. All the red flags are there. All we need to do now is confirm that he enjoyed killing small animals as a child and loved dressing up in his sister's underwear, and we've got him bang to rights.'

Lovelace shot Spencer a look that suggested he wasn't far off the mark, but his sarcasm did highlight an important fact. There wasn't a shred of evidence suggesting that Hannah Sinclair had been murdered or that Adam Sinclair was the Night Prowler. And even if Adam had murdered his wife, that was still a giant leap to him being a serial killer. So there had to be a link between Adam and his victims. And there had to be some bodies somewhere that belonged to Hannah and her mystery boyfriend. And who exactly was the boyfriend, and why had no one noticed he was missing? The more they dug, the more detritus they had to sift through.

'It would help if we knew where Bob Weston's farm was.' Lovelace said out loud but more to herself.

'It would.' Spencer nodded. 'But even then, if the farm is as big as Tom Sinclair maintains, finding a couple of bodies there will be a hell of a struggle.'

'What if there are more bodies?' Lovelace asked.

Spencer shot her a quick look. 'Go on…'

'Well, Adam's mother died last year, and Hannah was murdered soon after. And from that, Adam launches into a serial killing frenzy with a level of skill and expertise that would suggest he's been active before.'

'Wouldn't we have noticed a trail of dead bodies in the recent past?'

'Only if we linked them together. And what if there weren't that many bodies? One or two, maybe. Like an early trial run, but without many victims?'

Spencer thought about that for a moment. 'I can see that. A young Adam Sinclair, growing up in a household full of abuse and matriarchal violence, takes out his frustrations on other women. Women who aren't his mother because she hasn't left him, and he can't break the unbreakable bond. His mother is untouchable.'

Lovelace agreed, 'Adam Sinclair is a young teenager, surrounded by abuse and violence and maybe even sexual abuse. His emotions are wild and untamed. Tom says that Erin was concerned about Adam's weird interest in her. He would spy on her and try and catch her in the shower.'

Spencer took up the story. 'Then Erin leaves, and Adam needs to feel powerful, but his sister's no longer there, so he starts to spread his wings. He starts spying on other women. Maybe girls at school or other women in the street. And slowly, his offences escalate. But to what? Sexual assault? Rape? Murder? He's a young man. A stupid young man. We would have caught him.'

'Unless,' Lovelace said, 'something, or someone, came along who pressed pause on all that.'

Lovelace looked at Spencer, who smiled. 'Enter Hannah Weston, soon to be Hannah Sinclair.'

Lovelace nodded. 'So just before Adam's offending reaches a crisis point, he stops. Hannah controls him and contains the worst of his character, just like Bob Weston did for Janet. He finally gets all the attention he needs from the right person. He's emotionally and sexually satisfied. He no longer needs his fix. Then last year, his mother died, and the unbreakable bond broke. Adam would start to spiral. His mother has escaped his vengeance. He probably realises that all his pain and anger stems from her, but now it's too late. He can't do anything to stop her, to get justice for himself. And then Hannah declares she is going to leave him, or he finds out she is planning to leave, and he finally snaps, and his rage comes to the fore, and everything he has learned in the past he now applies as an adult, and there's no stopping him. The spree begins.'

Spencer sighed. 'As good as that all sounds, there's just no proof. It's pure speculation.'

Lovelace smiled. 'There will be, somewhere. We have to find it. But I'm right, Phil. I know I'm right.'

Spencer was about to try and reign in Lovelace's unbridled enthusiasm when a young woman in her early

thirties put a key into the house they were watching and
stepped inside. She struggled a few moments with a
small child in a pushchair, giving the two detectives the
time they needed to reach the door.

'Erin Sinclair?'

'No.' She said curtly.

'But you are Erin though? Tom Sinclair's daughter?
Adam Sinclair's sister?'

'You must be the Old Bill. You'd better come in.'

They followed Erin through her small home and into
the kitchen. She pulled the child out of the pushchair,
shoved a bag of crisps in its hand and watched as he
waddled off.

Erin's face bore the scars of an unhappy childhood.
She looked older than she was, with greasy, untidy hair
that fell awkwardly about her shoulders. Her eyes were
dull, and her lips were dry and sore. When she spoke,
her voice was husky, and her teeth bore the signs of a
forty-a-day habit. Then, as if to confirm this, she pulled
a plain packet from her pocket, withdrew a cigarette and
lit it. Then, she reached over the sink, pushed open the
window, and made a lame attempt to blow the smoke
outside.

'Dad said you'd been sniffing about.'

'We're reviewing Hannah Sinclair's disappearance.'
Lovelace began.

'Dad said. Reckons you think Adam's done her in?'

'Do you think it's possible?' Spencer asked.

'Nah,' Erin said dismissively. 'He hasn't got the bottle.
He's wetter than a wet weekend. He hasn't got the balls.
Pretty sure Hannah kept them on her bedside table!'

She laughed at her joke. Then, seriously, she said,
'Adam's not the sort. He's not violent. Hasn't got a
violent bone in him. I laid a couple on him when we
were kids; he'd just take them. He'd walk off and go and

sulk in the garden. But he'd never say anything. Never do anything. Mum used to smack him about something rotten. And her fellas. He just took it all. Never rose his hand to defend himself once.'

'Why did you leave?' Lovelace said abruptly.

Erin looked at Lovelace. She looked angry. Then she said, 'a couple of my mother's boyfriends got a bit friendly. Mostly, I kept them at bay, but one or two threatened to rape me if I didn't put out, so I left. I wasn't going to chance my luck. I had a couple of close calls and reckoned I had played my luck as far as it could stretch. I felt terrible, though, for Adam. He had no one to look out for him. No one to care for him.'

'Did you care for him, Erin?' Lovelace asked.

'Of course. Why'd you say it like that?'

'Did Adam's behaviour ever become inappropriate?' Lovelace asked.

'A couple of times,' Erin admitted. 'He was a teenage boy. They can be weird, and there was no father figure to teach him how to behave. He liked to watch me when he thought I couldn't see him. He did like to watch people. He liked to hide in my bedroom and watch me undress. The times I caught him, he got one hell of a slap, I can tell you.'

'Did you not tell your mother?' Spencer asked.

'Fuck no! She'd have cut his dick off and fed it to him. Nah, like I said, I felt bad for leaving him, but I needed to get out. For my own safety.'

'What about Hannah? Did you like her?' Lovelace asked.

'She was all right, to start with. She was nice to Adam. She looked after him. I think she genuinely cared for him. Bob was a nice bloke. After that, everything seemed to calm down. We all started talking again. Even Mum was nicer.'

'But?' Lovelace prodded.

'I know my brother,' Erin said. 'He's a moody little bugger. Must be properly hard to live with. And Hannah wasn't exactly the easiest person to get on with. She liked to drink a bit, too. And she liked her men.'

'Adam knew she had affairs.' Lovelace said. 'Why do you think he didn't leave her?'

'He couldn't. He wasn't the leaving sort. She controlled every aspect of their lives together. He'd have been lost without her. He told me they had an open relationship.'

'Do you think Adam had other partners?' Spencer asked.

'Fuck no.' Erin replied. 'Not unless he paid for them!' She laughed again.

Lovelace said, 'Do you know if Hannah was going to leave Adam?'

'So that's your thinking, is it?' Erin said, drawing on her cigarette and letting the fumes balloon towards the ceiling. 'You think my little brother did her in to stop her from leaving?' She paused while she dwelt on the thought for a moment. 'Fair play to him if he did. It would be the first fucking balsy thing he's ever done!'

'So you think it's possible?' Lovelace asked.

Erin threw her cigarette out of the window. 'I guess you can only push people so far. And when push comes to shove, I reckon we're all probably capable of murder.'

Lovelace sat in her car and started the engine. She looked across at Spencer, who drew the seatbelt around him and clicked it into place.

'I know what you're thinking,' he said.

'Do you? What am I thinking?'

'You're thinking,' Spencer said, 'that the profile of the man we're after would probably fit the kind of man who liked to hide in bedroom wardrobes and watch women undress.'

Lovelace pushed the car into gear and sped away from the kerb. It looked like Spencer did know what she was thinking after all.

Inside the house, Erin pulled the curtains to one side and watched as the two detectives climbed into a ruby-red car and drove away. She felt her little boy tugging at her trousers and turned to see that he had finished his crisps. She took a chocolate bar from her pocket and gave it to him, and he wandered away contented.

Erin reached into her other pocket and pulled out her phone. She unlocked it, found the entry in her contacts list and dialled the number. It answered after the fourth ring. She spoke into the phone; her voice cracked with unease.

'Adam, what the fuck have you done?'

Twenty-Five

Lovelace drove for several miles before stopping in a small lay-by. She bought two dirty coffees from a burger van and two greasy bacon rolls, and the two of them leant on the bonnet of her car and watched as dark clouds raced in the sky above their heads. The storm that had raged for the last day or so had abated, but the wind still blew till the trees started to bend, and the air was cool and crisp.

'Where to next?' Spencer asked as he took another bite of his roll.

Lovelace considered the question for a moment. 'We should take a closer look at Hannah Sinclair. Speak to her work colleagues and friends. If we're right, she planned to leave with her mystery man. We need to get an angle on that. We need to find out about him. Who he was. Someone must miss him.'

'I can call the station,' Spencer said. 'We should be able to get a list of all the people reported missing at the time of Hannah's disappearance. There can't be that many, and it would be a fair assumption that he was a local man.'

Lovelace shook her head. 'I wouldn't want to assume that. He may have been from out of the area. Spread the net wider. Check the national database.'

'That might throw up hundreds of names,' Spencer said solemnly. 'It would help if we had a name for the man or a description.'

Lovelace agreed. 'Hannah must have confided in someone about her plans. There must have been someone in her life she was close to. Do we know where she worked?'

'I remember reading something in her file about that. An estate agent in Oxford, I think. I can find out when I ring the office.'

'Good idea,' Lovelace said as she sipped her coffee before throwing the tepid liquid into the hedge. 'Do you know, I was thinking about Adam's past. About his past offending. There must be something there too. He's killed before, Phil, I know it. Either someone else was imprisoned for it, or the case was never solved. It's just sitting there waiting for us to find it and link it to Adam.'

'But where to start looking?'

'I'll call Graham; get the boys to dig around a bit.' Lovelace said. 'We can pinpoint the time fairly accurately. It will be sometime after Erin leaves home until Hannah arrives. That's a three or four-year window from when Adam was thirteen until he was about sixteen or seventeen. Given his age, he won't have been able to drive. At best, his crimes would have occurred within three miles of his home. So that narrows down the field quite considerably.'

Spencer took a sip from his coffee before agreeing with Lovelace's critique and sending the contents of his cup in a similar direction.

'I'll make a couple of calls,' Spencer said. He opened the passenger door to the Merc and sat down. Lovelace pulled her mobile phone from her pocket and rang Graham. She strolled along the lay-by while they talked, holding one hand over her other ear to drown out the noise of the passing traffic. By the time she had finished and sat back in her car, the heavens had opened, and the rain came down in stair rods, pounding the car's roof.

Spencer looked out of the windscreen and sighed. 'I guess that's the summer over. I wonder what it's like to live in a country where the weather is always the same?'

'Dull.' Lovelace said. 'Any news?'

Spencer nodded. 'I have an address for the estate agents that Hannah worked for. I should have a list of names from the Missing Person's Database for when Hannah went missing. They're going to e-mail the names over to me. Just two men were reported missing in the Thames Valley Area twenty-four hours after Hannah's disappearance. I stretched that to seventy-two hours to make sure we picked him up. That's six men in the Thames Valley Area for us to look at. If we can get a name or a description from one of Hannah's friends or colleagues, I'm pretty sure we should be able to identify him.'

Lovelace nodded. 'Let's hope someone missed him.' She said. 'Graham's got Stanton and Luton looking back at past cases that resemble ours within a three-mile radius of where Adam grew up. That might take a bit more time.'

'I don't think we have much time left.' Spencer said, and Lovelace noticed a furrow gather on his brow.

'What do you mean?' She asked.

'We just opened the door to the lion's cage, walked in, and smacked a sleeping and contented killer over the head with a big stick. He's going to wake up pissed. We have no idea how Adam Sinclair is going to react.'

Lovelace started the car and turned up the fans to clear the fogging on the windscreen. Spencer was right. Now they had begun digging; it was only a matter of time before Adam Sinclair became aware of it. She remembered Adam's father saying he and Erin had grown closer recently. Erin didn't think for one second that her brother could murder and probably spoke to him shortly after they had left. How would he react? Would he panic? Would he make a mistake? Or would he enjoy the game? For some killers, it was a sport to be played. They all accepted being caught eventually, sometimes relishing the thought as much as they relished the kill. Notoriety was everything. He'd be someone. For the first time in his life, Adam Sinclair would be the name on everyone's lips. There was a danger that he would throw caution to the wind and step up his offending in one final sweep of terror. Was Adam Sinclair the type of man to go out in a blaze of glory?

Lovelace didn't know, and the thought bothered her.

***

'Adam, what the fuck have you done?'

Silence.

'The police have been here. Asking loads of questions about Hannah. They think you've killed her.'

Adam Sinclair held the phone to his ear and, with his left hand, swept his fingers through his mop of blonde hair.

'What did you say?' He asked.

'I told them you couldn't hurt a fly. You couldn't, Adam, could you? You didn't do anything, did you?'

'Of course not. I asked them to look into it. I told you. I go to the police station all the time. They're probably just reviewing old cases.'

'Do you think?'

Adam noticed a slight sigh of relief in his sister's voice. She hadn't been sure. She had doubted. Good. He liked the mystery. It empowered him.

'Sorry, I had to ask. The Old Bill can make you think all sorts of things. Be careful, Adam. If they think you did it, they'll try and find evidence to suit them.'

'There is no evidence,' Adam said, 'I never did anything. They can look all they like. They won't find anything.'

'Okay. Good. Listen, it's my birthday on Friday. Are you coming for a drink? The kids would love to see you.'

And so it went on, the dull, inane chatter that drifted nowhere. It bored him. It was depressing. People were depressing and sad in their silly lives that meant nothing to no one. He answered each question as they came in his usual way, but his mind was racing.

They knew. They were coming. The game was on.

He said goodbye and hung up the phone. He slipped it into his coat pocket and took a deep breath.

The clock was ticking. There wasn't much time left. He'd need to act soon. There was still work to be done. There was still something he needed to do.

He looked over to the dressing table and looked at his reflection. They had consistently underestimated him. They always had. But he had been the Man. He had wielded his power over them, and they never knew. He had been the power. They had never feared him, but death had walked in their shadows. He was Death. And he was coming for them.

He reached over to the side of the mirror and picked up the St Christopher that hung from the edge. He wrapped the broken chain around his fingers and slipped the jewellery into his pocket.

He liked nice things. He wanted to own them.

And now he wanted to own her.

***

They drove through Summertown and followed the navigation system's instructions until Samuel Wright and Co., Estate Agents' offices, appeared. They were a mile from the town centre in a busy little thoroughfare that thronged on either side with shoppers, buses, and bicycles hustling for what little space there was. The estate agents was a relatively large Georgian terraced building that stretched the length of one side of the street with an array of fashionable shops on its ground floor. There was a chemist to one side and a second-hand book shop to the other.

Spencer and Lovelace danced through the pointy edges of a dozen umbrellas and entered the building.

'May I help you?' She was an older woman, heavily made up with bouffant hair, lightly coloured with eyes that shone a brilliant green and a crisp, well-educated voice.

Spencer and Lovelace flashed their warrant cards, and the woman said, 'Mr Wright, some people here would like to speak to you.'

Mr Wright was younger and entirely bald but with a well-bronzed head. He still looked youthful, Lovelace thought, and he moved across the floor like a man half his age.

'These people are from the police,' the older woman whispered, as though to have them in the building was an affront to the building's reputation.

'The police?' Mr Wright said with no attempt to lower his voice. 'And what may we do for you?'

'We're following up on the disappearance of Hannah Sinclair.' Spencer said. He watched as the name rippled around the office.

'I see. Yes. A sad business. Perhaps you'd like to come through to my office.'

They sat in a plush room at the rear of the office. It had large windows that looked out into the office, and the door was propped open. By the way the carpet had not been worn, it looked like the door was never closed.

'Please, take a seat.' Mr Wright waved them down onto two comfortable-looking chairs while he sat at the other side of a large mahogany table. 'May I offer you coffee?'

Three coffees were duly served by a young assistant who smiled sweetly, offered sugar and biscuits and then drifted out again.

'So, any news on Hannah?' Mr Wright asked. 'Has she turned up yet?' Then, 'No, of course not. Stupid thing to say. If she had turned up, you wouldn't be here, would you?'

'Do you expect her to turn up?' Spencer asked.

'Well, we did. That was the gossip that went around the office.' And then, as if to explain himself, 'Not that we gossip, of course. But you know how people are. And then the office is mainly women… but men can be as bad. I suppose it's human nature to speculate and guess, isn't it?'

'And what did people speculate?' Spencer asked.

'Well, she had a bit of a reputation. She liked to party, even on school nights. Sometimes it was impossible to get any work out of her until lunchtime. But she was a lovely girl. Great saleswoman. She's been missed.'

'Tell us about the gossip,' Lovelace asked. 'What were people saying?'

'Have there been any developments?' Mr Wright asked. 'It's been over a year since she left. No one paid much attention then. No one came and asked questions. Her husband came and took some of her things and said he'd reported her missing, but no one ever came.'

'We're just trying to understand a bit more about Hannah. What kind of person was she? Was she the sort of woman to just up and leave for no reason? When she went missing, it was well known that Hannah Sinclair had relationships with other men, and in the months before her disappearance, it was understood that there may have been a significant other man. Do you know anything about that?'

Mr Wright nodded. 'Yes. I see. The rumours certainly went that way. A man came here once or twice to take Hannah to lunch. I thought it was her husband until he came to collect her stuff. I suppose after that, I sort of just believed what people were saying about her. We all just accepted that Hannah had left with her new man.'

'Did you ever catch his name?' Lovelace asked. 'Could you describe him?'

'I'm not very good with names, I'm afraid. Or faces, come to that. He was in his forties, athletic looking. Simon or Steven or something like that. I didn't take much notice of him, I'm afraid. It was over a year ago.'

Lovelace looked crestfallen.

Mr Wright saw the disappointment on her face and said, 'but Nat will know, I'm sure. I think they went out together a couple of times. I'll get her.'

Mr Wright left the office and strolled to one of the desks nearest the window. He spoke to a young woman who sat there, glanced across at Spencer and Lovelace, and then gathered her belongings from the desk. She followed Mr Wright back to his office.

She was a tall young woman who towered over them. She had long dark hair that fell behind her shoulders and wore a well-pressed business suit.

'You're here about Han?' She asked. Her voice was soft and gentle with a hint of the southeast in its tones.

'That's right.' Lovelace said. 'Did you know Hannah very well?'

Mr Wright carried a chair from the larger office, and Nat sat down. He returned to his seat across from them, and all eyes fell on Nat.

'We used to go out clubbing. Han and I went to school together. We pretty much started here at the same time.'

'You must have known her very well?' Lovelace asked.

'She was my best friend. We've been through everything together.'

'What was Hannah like?'

'She could be frosty if she didn't like you. She didn't suffer fools gladly. She had a fearsome temper. But if you were friends, she'd kill for you. She'd do anything for you.'

'Did you know her husband?'

Nat looked across at Mr Wright and then back at Lovelace. 'Is Hannah okay? She's not… she's not dead, is she?'

Lovelace reassured her. 'We haven't found Hannah. We don't know where she is, but we are trying to find her.'

'Why?' Nat asked. 'Why now?'

'We regularly review open cases. With fresh eyes. We're trying to build a picture of Hannah to see if she's the kind of person who would just run away or whether we should be more concerned.'

'Is that why you're asking about Adam? Do you think he might have hurt her?'

'It's always a line of enquiry,' Lovelace said matter-of-factly. 'In most cases, we look to the partners first. Family members, friends. Adam is convinced Hannah has come to harm. What do you think has happened to her?'

Nat looked reticent. She gathered her thoughts and said, 'I wouldn't have thought Hannah would run away. Not initially. Don't get me wrong; I don't think she had a happy marriage. Adam was weird. Creepy. I never liked him. He had a reputation at school for being a bit of a perv. But Hannah liked him. He was like a toy to her, something she could control. And she could be pretty horrible to him. Physically and mentally. He was properly under her thumb. And she liked to play away. She enjoyed other men. She had been like that for as long as I've known her. But then she changed.'

Lovelace sat up. 'In what way? How did she change?'

'She met someone. He was a nice bloke. He treated her well. I think she fell in love for the first time.'

'Did you ever meet this man?' Lovelace asked.

Nat nodded. 'We went out for drinks a few times. I'd never seen Han so happy.'

'So when Hannah went missing, you didn't think it odd?'

Nat shook her head. 'The two of them fantasised about running away together and living on a beach in Thailand or something. So when Han didn't come to work one day, that's where we thought she'd gone. And when her boyfriend didn't come looking for her, we took that to mean that she hadn't gone missing, that they had run away together.'

Or they were both dead, Lovelace thought.

'It is odd, though,' Nat continued.

'What is?' Lovelace asked. 'What's odd?'

'She was my best friend. I figured she'd cool off for a while and then let me know she was all right. I thought if she were on a beach somewhere, living the life of Riley, then sooner or later, she'd invite me. But she never did. Don't you think that's odd?'

'I didn't know Hannah.' Lovelace said. 'But you did. Do you think it is odd?'

Nat raised a hand to her mouth. A tear welled in the corner of one eye, and she stifled the urge to sob.

She nodded, and her eyes started to stream. 'Yes. Yes, I do. It's odd. She would have called me; I know she would.' And then, in a desperate way, she asked, 'She's dead, isn't she? Someone's killed her, haven't they?'

Lovelace pulled her chair closer to Nat and laid an arm around her shoulders. 'We don't know,' she said softly. 'But we think so. It would help us enormously if we could find her boyfriend. The one she wanted to run away with. Do you know who he was? What was his name?'

Nat sobbed. 'I didn't know him. Not very well. Han kept him quite close to her. She wanted him all to herself. But his name was Stefan.'

Lovelace hugged her tightly. 'Do you know anything else about him? Was he married? Where did he work?'

'He wasn't married. Divorced, I think. No kids. That's all I know.'

'Thank you, Nat, you've been really helpful.'

Nat sobbed again. 'Oh, god, you don't think he killed her, do you? I can't believe I thought she just ran away with him. What if Adam was right all along? I'm a terrible friend.'

Lovelace said, 'we don't know what has happened to Hannah. Not yet. But we will, I promise you. You can't blame yourself. You couldn't possibly have known. But I promise you, if any harm has come to Hannah, we'll make the person responsible pay.'

Ten minutes later and they were sat back in Lovelace's car.

'That went better than expected.' Lovelace said.

'It certainly did.' Spencer agreed. 'Look at this.'

He opened his e-mail on his phone and showed it to Lovelace. It was a list of the six men who had gone missing in the Thames Valley Area within seventy-two hours of Hannah Sinclair's disappearance. The third name caught Lovelace's attention, and she saw Spencer smile out of the corner of her eye.

'Stefan Chamberlain, forty-two, Fairford. Oxon.'

'Coincidence?' She asked.

Spencer shrugged. 'Let's go find out, shall we?'

Twenty-Six

Detective Inspector Alison French sat at her desk at Aldgates police station and let out an audible sigh. DI Frampton looked up from his desk and watched as his colleague rubbed the sleep from her eyes.

'Everything okay?' He asked.

French held several sheets of paper in her hand and waved them. 'Surveillance reports on Constable Lovelace. They make for great bedtime reading.'

Every day, around lunchtime, the surveillance team from West Mercia Police compiled a report and e-mailed it to DI French. Every day she went through the reports in minute detail, looking for something that might tie the infamous constable to the murder of Mark Pitts. So far, the reports had drawn a blank. Since the surveillance had begun, Lovelace's activities had been chiefly concerned with investigating the Night Prowler case. She had stayed a couple of nights at the home of DS Spencer, but the surveillance team had reported that there seemed to be no romantic relationship there. Lovelace had either slept in a spare room or on the sofa. The only cause for concern had been the evening that Lovelace had been attacked. Earlier that night, Lovelace had evaded her followers on the A40 while riding a high-powered motorcycle. The team had attempted to keep up, but she had been too fast. They only reconnected with her when Spencer made a flurry of 999 calls, drawing them to a village on the edge of the Cotswold Hills.

Had Lovelace spotted her tail? French rubbed her eyes. It was possible. Off-duty coppers were often cautious when out and about. It paid to be alert. But with Lovelace, she couldn't be sure. Was she expecting to be watched? If so, by whom?

French turned to Frampton and asked, 'where do you think she was going the night she was attacked?'

Frampton had read the reports. He shook his head. 'I don't know. I used to ride bikes in my younger days. It was a good way to relax, to blow the cobwebs away.'

'In the middle of the night?' French questioned.

'It's a peaceful time to ride.' Frampton said. 'The roads are quiet, and you can see what's coming from miles away. You can ride fast and free.'

French wondered if that was it.

'What are you thinking?' Frampton asked.

French didn't know what she was thinking. She was confident that the woman in the CCTV footage was Lovelace, and she was equally convinced that Lovelace was the woman who had spent the evening with Pitts before his murder. But Pitts' murder had been exceptionally brutal. It had all the hallmarks of a revenge killing. It almost smelt like a warning.

'What if she was out that night looking for the Night Prowler?' French asked. 'What if that's her raison d'etre? The daughter of one of England's worst serial killers looking to avenge the sins of her father?'

'That's quite far-fetched, Ally. There's no proof.'

'But psychologically, it works.' French added. 'Her childhood must have left scars. And it certainly fits her career path.'

'And mine and yours.' Frampton said. 'Why did you become a copper?'

'I wanted to help people.' French replied. 'And bring bad people to justice.'

'Me too.' Frampton said. 'I wanted to catch villains and lock them up. And sometimes we don't always get the bad ones, but I don't lure them down dark alleys and cut their balls off, and I'm pretty sure you don't, either.'

'And yet neither of us has Lovelace's history. What if she considers herself to be the personification of Justice, dealing out punishments to those that think they have got away with it?'

'But the Night Prowler hasn't got away with it. Yet. We don't know who he is. He hasn't escaped Justice; he's just not been brought to face it.'

'So maybe Lovelace goes out to try and find him before we can. Maybe she wants to end his reign of terror before he kills again.'

Frampton shrugged. 'Maybe.' He said, unconvinced. 'But right now, we've no proof of that. It's all purely speculation. Until she does something to suggest that, you've got nothing.'

French had to admit that was true. They had nothing. And time was running out. She only had a few days of surveillance left before it was withdrawn.

She glanced out of her office window and watched the rain as it fell onto the street outside.

Time was running out. The question was, for whom?

***

'Andrew Chamberlain?'

'Yes. Who's asking?'

Spencer and Lovelace showed their warrant cards. 'I wonder if we could talk to you about your brother, Stefan?'

Andrew Chamberlain was a neatly dressed man in his early fifties with light grey hair and a neatly sculptured beard cut close to the nape of his face. His eyes were the lightest shade of blue and sparkled with interest. His face gave no other emotion away. Lovelace guessed that Andrew Chamberlain was a man who didn't express his feelings publicly.

Chamberlain glanced at his watch. He stepped out behind the small counter of his bookshop on a small back street in Fairford, slipped the "Open" sign over to read "Closed", and locked the door.

He returned and sat on his small chair, slipped a bookmark between the leaves of the book he was reading, and looked up at the two detectives.

'I must say that was very quick,' he said, 'I only reported him missing a year ago.'

'Why did you report him missing?' Spencer asked.

'Oh, I don't know,' Andrew said. 'Perhaps it had something to do with the fact that he went missing. You know, in the sense that I saw him one day, and I haven't seen him since.'

'I understand that must be distressing for you....' Lovelace began.

Andrew interrupted her. 'Do you? Do you understand?' He asked, and still his face showed no emotion. 'He wasn't a set of keys that I dropped and couldn't find. He was my brother, and one day I never saw him again, and no one cared a damn. No one came to look for him or ask any questions. It was like he didn't matter. But he bloody-well mattered to me.'

'We're asking now.' Lovelace said calmly.

'Now's too bloody late.' Andrew said, and for the first time, his voice cracked.

'It may have been too late then.' Lovelace said, and Spencer gave her a warning look that she ignored.

'What do you mean?' Andrew asked.

'You look like an intelligent man, Mr Chamberlain, so I'll spare you any prevarication. I'm sorry that no one came and looked for your brother when you reported him missing, but DS Spencer and I are here now, and we care. We're also following a line of enquiry that suggests your brother was dead when you reported him missing. We believe he may have been murdered.'

Andrew Chamberlain took a deep breath, composed himself, and let the air out. Lovelace watched as the tension in his shoulders relaxed.

'I wondered, you know.' He began slowly. 'He wasn't the sort to go off without saying a word. You hear about people falling into rivers and canals when drunk, but he wasn't much of a drinker. And he was a good swimmer. You fall into that sort of thing around here. There are lots of lakes. He was a bloody good swimmer. Much better than I ever was. But it's the not knowing that gets you. It eats you up and haunts you every waking hour and minute you try to sleep. Do you know what happened to him?'

Lovelace shook her head. 'Not yet. But we will. With your help, we may get that peace for you.'

Andrew nodded slowly. 'Knowing he was dead would be easier, as silly as it sounds. Easier than not knowing. Of course, I'd prefer it if he had run off, for his sake. But I think I always knew that was a vain hope.'

'Can you tell us about Stefan?' Spencer asked.

'He was a writer,' Andrew said. 'He had a fair bit of success in the early days. Not so much in recent years, but he made a good living. Young adult stuff. He was beginning to venture out into adult fiction, not the dirty stuff, fiction for adults. As opposed to kids' fiction. He'd just signed a three-book deal with a big house. I think that's why I knew he was dead. He was the kind of writer who couldn't stop. If he'd run away, he would have finished his books and had them published, and he would have carried on writing. It's just who he was. Writers never retire. They die.'

'When did you notice he was missing?' Spencer asked.

'We were going to have breakfast together on Friday morning. He had some big news he was going to share with me. Whenever we had news to share, we would have breakfast of smoked salmon and scrambled eggs with a glass of Champagne. I know it seems very decadent, but it was a family tradition. But he never turned up. He never answered my calls, and I never saw him again.'

'Do you know what he was going to tell you?' Lovelace asked.

'I suspected. It had nothing to do with the book stuff, as he had already told me about that. I suppose he might have sold the movie rights, but I think it was to do with a girl.'

'A girl?'

'A woman, actually.' Andrew said. 'I counselled caution. She was married, you see. Nothing good ever comes of that sort of thing. Just a lot of pain, but I felt he was smitten.'

'Did you know the woman?' Lovelace asked.

Andrew shook his head. 'No. I never met her, although he talked about her a lot. Actually, that's not entirely true. She came to his place one weekend, and I saw her from a distance. He was playing his cards very close to his chest, you see. He didn't like me to meet his girlfriends until he was sure they would hang around for a bit.'

'Did you know her name?'

'I'm afraid not.'

'Would you recognise her if you saw a picture of her?'

Andrew thought about this for a moment. 'Yes. Yes, I believe I would.'

Spencer pulled out his mobile phone and unlocked it. He scrolled through several files before finding the one he wanted. It was a photograph that Adam Sinclair had supplied when he reported his wife missing. He enlarged the picture and showed it to Andrew.

He glanced at the photograph and squinted his eyes. Then he took a pair of glasses from a pouch on the desk, balanced them on his nose, and gave the picture another look.

'Yes. That's her. I'd swear by it.'

Spencer smiled at Lovelace.

'That's really helpful,' Lovelace said. 'But it kind of confirms our fears, I'm afraid.'

Andrew took his glasses off and laid them on his desk. 'I thought it might. You think you know what happened to Stefan?'

'We do.' Lovelace said. 'I'm afraid I can't say any more at the moment, and we'd appreciate it if you wouldn't say anything to anyone just yet. It's a live investigation, and we want to be sure we get the right person and all the evidence we need.'

Andrew nodded. 'I understand. But you'll let me know the second you do?'

'We will.' Lovelace said. 'I promise.'

'You do make a lot of promises.' Spencer remarked once they had returned to the car. 'What if you can't keep them.'

'I will.' Lovelace said. 'We know what happened to Hannah Sinclair and Stefan Chamberlain and who did it to them. All we have to do is find their bodies and stop Adam.'

'What if we can't stop him in time?' Spencer asked.

'We have to, Phil. I have to. I have to stop him, and I intend to do exactly that.'

***

Irene laid a cup of coffee before DCI Graham and dropped two paracetamol onto his desk.

'How's the pain?'

Graham looked up. He'd never known pain like it, although it wasn't the biggest issue. He couldn't concentrate or focus on anything for more than a few minutes before having to rest his eyes. His balance had gone, too, as though he'd had one too many drinks, but he hadn't had anything to drink for ages. He scooped up the paracetamol and washed them down with a mouthful of coffee.

'Something's wrong, Irene. I'm worried.'

He looked old, Irene thought. Old and tired. The fire had gone out in his eyes, and the great man she had once known was fading before her very eyes.

'I'm going to call the doctor.' She said, and Graham offered no protestations. Whatever was going on inside his head was coming to the fore, and there was no stopping it.

'I think that's a good idea,' he said, slurring his words slightly.

He picked up his phone as it began to ring. Lovelace.

He listened as she ran through what they had found so far. They had identified the man Hannah Sinclair had been seeing in the weeks before her disappearance. He had disappeared at around the same time. It was progress. Good progress. She believed Adam Sinclair had murdered them both and disposed of their bodies. Probably on an unknown farm. A farm they needed to trace. It all sounded very plausible. It was good work.

'I want a warrant to search the Sinclair's home.' Lovelace said.

Graham rubbed his head. 'Based on what evidence?'

'It's him, sir. There must be evidence somewhere. There must be something in his house.'

'I can't go to a magistrate and ask for a warrant based on a hunch. I need something substantial. Something that links Sinclair to his wife's disappearance or the Night Prowler killings. At the moment, you've got nothing. I'll never get a warrant to search Sinclair's house based on little more than your feeling. I need more, Lucy. Much more.'

He heard her sigh. It echoed around his ears.

'Okay, sir. We'll keep digging.'

Silence.

Had she hung up? He couldn't tell. He couldn't hear anything except a loud buzzing.

Irene was back. She was holding his coat. Talking. Saying something that he couldn't make out. He stood up, and the flash blinded him. It streaked across his eyes, and his legs gave out beneath him.

Irene again. Dearest Irene. Irene was there, holding his head in her hands. Irene was always there.

And then she wasn't.

Twenty-Seven

'He won't go for the warrant. We need more.'

'I didn't think he would,' Spencer said. 'But it was worth a shot.'

They were driving out of Fairford past the airforce base. Lovelace had taken a slight detour to drive around the vast perimeter fence that circumvented the runway. It was one of the longest runways in Europe, and one of the only runways outside of continental North America equipped to take the Space Shuttle in the event of an emergency landing.

It was quiet today, and the large hangers huddled under a low cloud, keeping their secrets out of sight.

'What links Adam Sinclair to the Night Prowler murders?' Lovelace asked as she steered her car away from the town, back towards Oxford.

'Nothing.' Spencer said. 'The victims have nothing in common. They all worked in different industries in different parts of the county. The only common factor is that they didn't know one another, and none knew Adam Sinclair. They were strangers to one another and him.'

The one thing both knew was that it was rare for victims not to be known to their murderers somehow. Stranger killings were mercifully rare but notoriously difficult to solve.

Lovelace shook her head in frustration. Why couldn't she get an angle on it? 'How he picks his victims is the key,' she said. 'It's not by chance. He chooses them. But how?'

'What if it is by chance?' Spencer countered. 'What if he passes them in the street and follows them home? He watches them, waits until they go out, and then breaks in?'

Lovelace pondered that for a second. It was plausible, she supposed, but she didn't like it. It left too much to chance, and she didn't take Adam Sinclair for a chancer. He was a plotter and a planner. He was always prepared, and he never made mistakes. Somehow she saw Adam Sinclair target a victim and stalk them from a distance, always staying in the shadows, picking his moments carefully and strategically.

'What does he do for a living?' Lovelace asked.

Spencer pulled up Sinclair's profile on his phone. 'He works for a security company in Oxford. They install alarm systems and so on.'

Lovelace remembered their interview with Laura Hampshire in her little cottage on the edge of the Cotswold Hills. After she had reported the burglary at her home, she had a security company come around and fit a CCTV system into her home.

'Guardian.' She said out loud.

'What?'

'Does he work for Guardian? They're a security company that installs cameras and burglary alarms.'

Spencer shook his head. 'No. Not Guardian. Ventura Security Systems.'

Lovelace thought about it for a second. It had seemed like a promising start when it had occurred to her, but now she thought about it, Laura Hampshire had her security system installed after the visit by The Night Prowler. She'd reported no visits since then.

'Where are they based?' Lovelace asked.

'Their Head Office is in Headington.' Spencer said. He tapped the postcode into the car's sat-nav. 'It's not too far.'

They made the journey in quick time. Lovelace pulled up outside a small-looking building on the edge of an industrial park. Spencer had called ahead as a precaution. Adam Sinclair was out on a job and wasn't back in the office soon. He was pleased. The last thing they needed was Adam running interference before they could find something that tied him to the Night Prowler. Quietly Spencer nursed the idea that Adam Sinclair was probably already cleaning his tracks. If there was anything, and he was as careful as they believed, he'd be an idiot to leave incriminating evidence where it could be found. He had a horrible feeling that Adam was in the process of sanitising his life. Time was most definitely running out.

They opened the door to Ventura Security System's reception and found it empty. It was an unmanned reception. Instead, a telephone sat on a plain white table with a folder full of names and numbers open next to it. The instructions on the wall directed Lovelace and Spencer to find the name of the person they were there to see and dial their extension. Lovelace went to the first name and tapped the four-digit extension number into the phone.

A few minutes later, a man in his forties dressed in black slacks and an off-white shirt opened the door to their left and examined their warrant cards.

'Come through.'

They followed the man along a small corridor as he stopped at each intersecting door and swiped his access fob over a small pad with a red light. Once the light had gone green, he pushed the door, and they followed him to the next. Eventually, they came to a small office with nearly a dozen desks, each with an array of monitors set in an arc around the operator who sat staring at the screens with a headpiece clipped over their heads and a microphone curled around their face.

'Welcome to the beating heart of Ventura Security.' The man said as he led them to an office at the far end and beckoned them to sit on two comfortable-looking armchairs. Lovelace and Spencer sat down, and Colin Waverly, CEO of Ventura Security Systems, sat opposite them.

The room was less of an office and more of a breakout room, and the walls were littered with motivational soundbites.

'May I ask what this is all about?' Waverly asked.

'We're following up on some routine enquiries about a member of your staff.' Spencer said.

Waverly didn't bat an eyelid. 'I see. You should know that all our staff are security vetted. It's part of the service we offer our clients. Everyone here has a Criminal Records check every eighteen months or so.'

'I have to say,' Lovelace said, 'the building's much bigger on the inside than it looks on the outside. You wouldn't know this is all in here.'

'That's the idea,' Waverly said. 'Sometimes the best form of security is to make people think there's nothing worth stealing. A decrepit farmhouse in the middle of nowhere is less appealing than a huge house along a tree-lined, well tarmac'd road with a gold gilded electric gate barring your way. Part of our remit is to make thieves look somewhere else. I have to say; we're rather good at it.'

'Do you do many private homes?'

'None at all.' Waverly said. 'We fit entirely with the commercial sector. We do alarms, security systems, CCTV, scanners, the lot. And from here, we offer twenty-four-hour surveillance.'

'And what does Adam Sinclair do for you?' Lovelace asked abruptly.

'Adam?' Waverly asked.

Spencer nodded. 'That's right. Adam Sinclair. He does work here, doesn't he?'

'Yes, he does. Adam's one of our fitters. He fits all the security systems and electrics, that sort of thing.'

'What's he like?' Lovelace asked, and Waverly looked at her curiously.

'He's a diligent, hard-working young man. He's a bit quiet with a tendency to moodiness, but I have no complaints.'

'Does he work alone or as part of a team?'

'A bit of both.' Waverly said. 'Depends on the size of the job. Adam's been here since he left school. He knows his stuff. Better than just about anyone here. We tend to put him on delicate jobs and service work. Most of the time, he's on his own. I think he prefers it like that. Look, what's this about? Is it about his wife?'

'What do you know about that?' Lovelace asked.

'Not a lot. We heard she'd run off. Adam was fairly broken up about it, but I couldn't help but feel it was the best thing in the long run.'

'Why's that?' Lovelace asked.

'She used to hit him, or at least that's what people said. He often sported bruises. I didn't know her myself. I saw her once or twice at Christmas parties and that. She liked to drink a lot. It could turn a bit vicious after a while. She wasn't pleasant company when she was like that.'

'And how has Adam been since her disappearance?'

'Quite withdrawn for a time. We offered him compassionate leave, but he carried on working instead. Probably for the best. It's better to keep busy.'

'And recently?' Lovelace asked.

Waverly shrugged. 'Same as always. A bit moody. Quiet. Happier to be left alone mostly.'

'What do you know about a company called Guardian?' Lovelace asked.

'Not much. They're not a competitor. They do mostly residential stuff. Household security, that sort of thing.'

'Your paths never cross?'

'No.'

Lovelace sat forward on her chair. A thought just occurred to her. She asked, 'What sort of clients do you work for?'

'All sorts. Schools, doctor's surgeries, hairdressers, banks. You name it, we've probably got a client in the industry.'

'Hairdressers? What about a company called "Snip Snip"?'

'Well…' Waverly hesitated. 'I really shouldn't divulge that information. Client confidentiality and all that.'

'We could come back with a warrant.' Spencer said.

'I don't think that will be necessary,' Waverly began. 'Most of them advertise that they're our clients, so it's hardly top secret information. What name did you say?'

'Snip Snip.'

Waverly left the room and returned a few moments later with a laptop. He tapped away at the keys for a second, then looked up and said. 'Yes. They're one of ours.'

'What about Pendleton Banks?' Lovelace asked.

'Oh, yes. They're one of ours. One of our biggest clients.'

They spent ten minutes going through the names of the employers of some of the Night Prowler victims, and, barring the Parkes, everyone was linked to Ventura Security Systems in some way.

'Thank you, Mr Waverly. That's been extremely helpful. Just one more thing. Do you know if Adam Sinclair was involved in any installations at these places or been back to them as part of his service work?'

Waverly shook his head. 'No. There's no way of telling, not from the paperwork, at least. I could ask if anyone remembers Adam at these clients, but I'm afraid it wouldn't be much more. Sorry.'

Lovelace felt the disappointment acutely. The evidence was still somewhat circumstantial and might not convince a Magistrate to grant a warrant to search Adam's home. Although there was a link, it finally proved she was on the right track, but it just might not be enough.

'Should I be concerned?' Waverly asked. 'I have a duty of care to my clients. If there's anything about Adam that I should know, please tell me.'

Lovelace was about to speak when Spencer jumped in ahead of her. 'There's nothing to know at the moment. This is just a routine enquiry. You'll be the first to know when we have anything important to tell you.'

'We should have told him,' Lovelace argued as they returned to her car.

'And tell him what?' Spencer countered. 'That Adam Sinclair is The Night Prowler and a vicious sexual predator with a penchant for single women who live alone and, what's more, uses his position in your company to find his victims?'

'Something like that,' Lovelace agreed.

'Spencer looked at his young protege and sighed. 'You have high ideals Lucy, but that would be a silly thing to do. Apart from that, Adam Sinclair would likely sue us for slander; any future court case would probably fail because we accused him of a crime with no evidence to back it up.'

Lovelace unlocked her car, and the two sat down.

'You can be too sensible sometimes, Phil.' Lovelace said.

But he was right; she knew that. Her phone started ringing the second she started her car. She waited for a second for the car's in-built telephone system to pick up the connection before she answered.

It was Stanton. 'Where are you?' He asked.

'On the trail of Adam Sinclair. How are you getting on with our cold cases?'

'That can wait.' Luton said, and the two noticed an inflexion in his voice.

'What is it? What's wrong?' Lovelace asked. She was terrified that they had found another body.

'It's Graham. He's collapsed. They've taken him to the John Radcliffe.'

The John Radcliffe Hospital was five minutes from where they were. Lovelace had seen the signs for it as they drove past.

'We're on our way.'

***

'What happened? Is he okay?'

Lovelace and Spencer found their colleagues in a visitor's room on the second floor.

'We're waiting to hear now.' Luton said.

'What happened?'

'We think he had a stroke. He'd been looking a bit peaky all day. Irene was about to take him to a doctor when he collapsed.'

Irene was sitting in a large armchair reading a months-old magazine. She looked up when her name was mentioned.

'He was slurring his words and complaining of a terrible headache. I've been trying to get him to see a doctor for ages, but you know what men are like. They leave everything to the last minute.'

'He was conscious and talking when they loaded him into the ambulance.' Luton said. 'He's being looked at now.'

'I thought he looked odd all week,' Lovelace said. 'I thought it was the stress of the case.'

'We all thought the same,' Stanton said. 'It wasn't just you. We all should have said something.'

'Well, there's no point dwelling on the what-ifs,' Irene said, folding her magazine closed and standing up. 'He's an awkward, moody bugger and wouldn't have listened to you. I'm going for snacks. Does anybody want anything?'

Spencer opened the door. 'I'll come with you.' Then, to Lovelace, he said, 'Call me if you hear anything. We won't be long.'

Lovelace ran her fingers through her hair and tried to bring it under control, but it successfully resisted her attempt and fell about her head in a manner that suggested it didn't care about style. Finally, Lovelace sank into the armchair that Irene had just vacated and gave out a big sigh.

'I'm sure he'll be okay,' Luton said lamely, pulling up a chair next to Lovelace and sitting down. 'He's a tough old egg.'

'Egg's crack.' Lovelace said. 'Especially older eggs.'

'He's not that old,' Stanton said as he paced the room.

'Old enough to have a stroke.' She countered.

'It's not that rare in younger people.' Luton said. 'But he's in the right place. So let's wait and see what the Docs say.'

They sat awkwardly for a few minutes, then Lovelace looked across at Luton and said, 'Are you in charge now? Of the investigation, I mean.'

'The powers that be are waiting on news about DCI Graham before deciding how to move forward. For the time being, I'm in charge. Where are we with Adam Sinclair?'

Lovelace ran through what they had discovered about Hannah Sinclair's boyfriend and the potential link she and Spencer had found that tied Adam Sinclair to most of the Night Prowler's victims.

'That's good work.' Luton said.

'Good enough for a warrant?' Lovelace asked.

'It's still circumstantial. You can't prove that Sinclair ever met any of the victims, even if he did do any work at their place of business. And you can't prove that he did any work at their offices. No more than you can for anyone else who works for Ventura Security.'

Lovelace had feared that he would say that.

'If there's any evidence, it will be at Sinclair's home. I'm certain that's where he murdered his wife and her lover.'

'I agree.' Luton said. 'But now I'm wearing the boss's hat, and I have to say I don't think we'll get a warrant based on that.'

'What about the farm? Hannah's dad's farm. Have we found that?'

Stanton shook his head. 'Not yet. It's a peculiar one. We've searched the Will's register and found nothing with Bob Weston's name. No Westons died in the last couple of years and left their son and heir a huge farm. Or to Hannah Sinclair, for that matter.'

'That is odd,' Lovelace agreed. 'Perhaps they didn't leave the farm to Bob Weston?'

'Bob Weston never left a will either,' Stanton said. 'He died intestate. He had a bit of money set by, and it all went to Adam's mother, save for a few grand to Hannah. But no farm.'

'And yet both Bob Weston and Adam's mother spoke about inheriting the farm.' Lovelace scratched her head. 'It's odd. But I bet your last dollar Adam knows where it is.'

Spencer and Irene opened the door, deposited snacks onto the small coffee table in the middle of the room, and handed out tepid-looking liquid in plastic cups to everyone. Lovelace tasted hers and found it sweet and bitter but not as bad as she expected.

Everyone took a seat, and the room fell to quiet.

Lovelace broke the silence. 'No news on the farm.' She said, and Spencer cocked his head in the familiar way she had grown to love.

'Nothing?' Spencer asked.

'Not under the Weston name.' Stanton said.

'Perhaps they weren't called Weston.' Irene declared, biting into an iced bun.

Everyone looked at her.

'What do you mean?' Luton asked.

'My dear late husband was a Pratt,' Irene said. 'But he wasn't always a Pratt.' She paused and was about to say something about her late husband being a Pratt but thought better of it. People didn't often get her dark humour. 'He grew up as a Hemshaw but was adopted as a baby. When he came of age, he tracked down his birth mother and reverted to Pratt. I would have preferred Hemshaw.'

'It does explain why we can't find the farm.' Stanton said.

'Okay,' Luton started, looking directly at Stanton. 'Go back to the Registry office and get a copy of every will registered in the last three years and find that bloody farm.'

'They may not have left a will,' Spencer said.

'Look into that, too.' Luton ordered.

'What if the farm was outside of Oxfordshire?' Lovelace ventured.

Luton looked at Lovelace, and the weight of responsibility suddenly felt heavy on his shoulders. 'We'll have to hope they were an Oxford family. If we need to look further afield, we can do that later.'

'Did you get anywhere with the cold cases?'

'Actually, yes.' Luton said. 'Stanton?'

Stanton puffed up. 'So I did what you asked and went back fifteen years or so in and around the location of where Adam Sinclair grew up.' He walked over to his case, which was leaning against the wall and retrieved some papers. 'Here. Take a look at these.'

Lovelace spread the paperwork among the snacks on the coffee table.

'This,' Stanton said, tapping his finger on the photograph of a young woman in a summer hat, 'is Stephane Walker. She was murdered in her bed almost fifteen years ago. Suspicion fell on her boyfriend for a while but never went anywhere. No one was ever arrested; eventually, it went cold. I spoke to one of the detectives on the case; he's been retired for a few years. He remembers the murder well. There had been a spate of intruder rapes in the area, and they were bracing themselves for a death. So it didn't surprise them when they found Stephane. What did surprise him was that the rapes stopped, and no more killings occurred. They were certain someone was spiralling out of control and were gearing up for a major investigation, and then it all just stopped. There was no rhyme or reason to it.'

'When did they stop?' Lovelace asked.

'About the time Adam was sixteen.' Luton said.

'A year or so after Hannah and her father moved in with the Sinclairs.' Lovelace noted. 'We could safely assume that Adam and Hannah started a sexual relationship around the time of Stephane's murder.'

Spencer said, 'That's a big assumption. But if Adam started getting attention from a young woman in a way he hadn't got before, it would certainly explain why his offending stopped suddenly.'

'She would have satisfied him for a while.' Lovelace continued. 'The urge to rape would have subsided. The need to kill would have been contained, at least for a while. But it never goes away entirely. He would have felt the urge occasionally, which would have grown in intensity yearly. He's raped and killed, and he's got away with it. It would have fed his superiority complex. He would begin to believe himself invincible and uncatchable. It was only a matter of time before he was triggered, and it all started again.'

'His mother's death?' Spencer asked.

Lovelace nodded. 'Yes. That's the most powerful trigger. Adam may have harboured thoughts of murdering his mother, and while she was alive, that dream, that fantasy, was always a possibility. Her dying would have ripped that from him, so his attention moved to his wife. We know she wasn't nice to Adam, and he probably entertained similar thoughts about her. He probably tolerated her men friends because he felt he was the one with the power she didn't know he possessed. He was a killer and could kill her whenever he liked.'

'And then,' Spencer said, 'just like his mother, she was going to leave him and take away his opportunity to wield that power.'

'It would have been the final straw,' Lovelace agreed. 'He couldn't let another controlling woman leave his life before answering to him. So he kills his wife and her lover, and his descent into hell begins.'

'It's all very plausible.' Luton agreed. 'But we need proof. We need some evidence.'

'We need a warrant.' Lovelace declared, and Luton nodded.

'Okay,' he said. 'I'll make some calls.'

Luton stood up and left the room.

Lovelace looked at Stanton. "I need to know where that farm is,' she said. 'I'm certain the bodies of Hannah and her lover are not at the Sinclair's home. They have to be at the farm.'

Stanton agreed. 'I'll start working on it now.'

He picked up the papers from the table, poured them into his bag and left the room.

Lovelace looked at Spencer. He noticed the care lines stretch across her face. She was tired.

'He's going to kill again, Phil. He must know we're looking at him. We have to stop him.'

Spencer smiled. 'You will,' he said calmly. 'You will.'

Luton re-entered the room. He didn't look happy.

He shook his head. 'The magistrate wouldn't go for it. She said we were on a fishing trip, and she wasn't about to put her name on a witch hunt.'

'Fuck.' Lovelace said bluntly. 'What the fuck do we do now?'

'We wait,' Luton said. 'He'll make a mistake. Then, when he does, we'll be all over him.'

'By then, it will be too late for someone.' Lovelace said. 'Someone's going to have to die before we catch him. We can't just stand here and do nothing. There has to be something we can do….' She left the thought hanging in the air.

Perhaps there was something she could do?

Twenty-Eight

'What the hell is taking so long?' Lovelace grumbled. She glanced at her watch. They had been waiting in that small room for nearly four hours. Irene had gone out to find a doctor almost two hours ago but had been sent back and told to wait.

Spencer kept coming and going with refreshments, and Luton spent most of the time leaving the room to make phone calls. The temporary role of Senior Investigating Officer of The Night Prowler case came with some serious responsibilities and, what Luton found most annoying, some serious accountability. It was no wonder Graham had had a stroke, he thought, as he picked up the third call from the Police and Crime Commissioner in as many hours.

The clock was pushing on nine o'clock in the evening before a tired-looking young doctor opened the door to the room and stepped inside. He looked at Lovelace and then at Irene. 'Which one of you is Irene Ackerman?'

Lovelace looked at Irene, who stood up. 'I'm Ms Ackerman.'

The doctor looked at the three others in the room.

'It's okay,' Irene said. 'You can speak freely in front of them. They work for Graham.'

The young doctor took a chair and sat down. 'Very well. As you know, Mr Graham was rushed into the emergency room earlier with a suspected stroke. He was conscious and talking to us, and it was obvious that something was upsetting his ability to speak.'

Lovelace sat down on a chair near the doctor. She braced herself for bad news.

'We scanned Mr Graham's head and can confirm that he did not have a stroke.'

'Not a stroke?' Irene asked.

The doctor shook his head. 'No. Not a stroke. But the scan did show up a large mass on his brain about here..' he drew a line on the side of his head to indicate where he thought the tumour might be. 'It's the size of a golf ball.'

Irene drew a hand up to her mouth. 'Cancer?' She asked.

'We can't be sure. We've rushed Mr Graham's blood off for analysis and are now setting up theatre to operate. Once we have the tumour out, we can investigate it more thoroughly.'

'You're operating now?' Lovelace asked.

'Yes. The consultant believes that any delay may well prove fatal. Had Mr Graham come to us as soon as he showed symptoms, we may have been able to slow its growth, but as it is now, it's beginning to press heavily onto the brain. So if we don't operate quickly, it could easily kill him.'

'Can we see him?' Irene asked.

'Mr Graham is conscious and asking to speak to you, Ms Ackerman. He's signed the consent forms for the operation, but apparently, you have Power of Attorney?'

'That's correct,' Irene said. She looked at the three detectives, who, in turn, looked at her. Then, by way of explanation, she said, 'Inspector Graham had a health scare a few years back. It was nothing serious but it made him wonder about his future security. You see, we're both single and with no living relatives, and should we end up in hospital with no way of communicating our desires, who would speak for us? So we chatted about it for a while and gave each other Lasting Power of Attorney should either of us be unable to speak for ourselves. We had no one else, you see.'

'If you would like to come with me.' The doctor held out his arm and guided Irene to the door. 'I'm afraid we can only allow one visitor for now. You'll have to wait until Mr Graham is in recovery.'

Lovelace sat back down. Spencer perched on the side of the table, and Luton picked his phone up on the second ring.

'Yes sir, we've just heard. They're rushing him into theatre now….' The door closed behind him.

'I don't like hospitals,' Lovelace said, 'the last time I was in one, they were grafting skin over the burns on my arm.' She instinctively reached up and stroked her arm as though the memory had ignited the heat.

'That must have been quite hard for you.' Spencer said.

'I was young. My skin healed quite well. Just a few scars. They're nothing compared to the mental ones.'

'Do you ever talk about it?' Spencer asked.

Lovelace shook her head. 'No. We had counselling. I suppose it must have done some good as I think I've done a pretty good job of keeping myself together.'

'If you ever want to talk. About anything. I'm always here.' Spencer said.

Lovelace smiled warmly. 'That's very kind. And good to know, thank you.'

'Tell me…' Spencer began, and Lovelace held her breath. She hated questions that started like that. They were never good.

'Why do they call you Lefty Lovelace?' He asked.

Lovelace laughed, and the tension fell from her shoulders.

'Okay,' she said, 'but it's going to cost you a bottle of gin.' She took a deep breath and braced herself for the mocking. 'When Uncle Mike took my sister and me to Japan, we were enrolled in an English-speaking school filled mostly with children of American soldiers. They had a workshop on site where we were taught, basic mechanics. You know, pulling apart old cars and stuff like that. On the very first day, I tried to tighten up a bolt, and I undid it instead, and the teacher, god damn the man, said, "No, no. Lefty Loosey, Righty Tighty." And I instantly became known as Lefty Lucy.'

Spencer laughed. 'Oh, that is good!' He said. 'That's cheered me up no end.'

'Well, I'm glad you find it funny.' Lovelace said, smiling. She liked it when Spencer smiled. It brightened his face. It reminded her of Sophie. The two were very much alike. 'When I was sixteen, I became known as Loosey Lucy.' She added.

Spencer watched the eyes of the pretty young constable he had been so fortunate to be partnered with. There was so much going on behind those eyes he didn't know where to start.

'Now that sounds like there are some tales I'd like to hear!'

Lovelace put on a demure face and a sweet, youthful voice, 'I couldn't possibly imagine what you mean.' She said. And then, 'But it will cost you a damn site more than one bottle of gin to get those stories out of me!'

'It's a deal,' he said.

Irene came back into the room looking more worn than when she left.

'How is he?' Lovelace asked.

'Worried, of course. As we all are. He's going under now. He looked very old.'

'I'm sure the operation will be a success.' Spencer said, but the platitude felt lame even as he said it. They were all intelligent people; they knew the risks that Graham was facing. And that was all just the beginning. His life would change forever; they only hoped it was for the best.

Irene looked at the clock on the wall. It was getting late. She looked at Lovelace and Spencer and said, 'The consultant said the surgery could take at least a few hours. There's no reason for you two to stay. I'll remain here, in case I'm needed. It would be best if you went home. Get some rest. I think we would all feel better if you concentrate your energies on catching The Night Prowler.'

Lovelace drove them home through the rain. She pulled up outside Spencer's house under the orange glow of a street lamp.

'Sophie's in tonight, then.' Spencer said, noticing the faint glow from his daughter's bedroom window. 'Do you want to come in? I can make up the couch?'

Lovelace declined. 'Not tonight. I think I need my own bed. But thank you. Say hi to Sophie for me.'

She waited as Spencer exited the car and jogged nimbly down his path. She watched as he turned the key in the lock and disappeared inside. Perhaps she should have gone with him? She would have liked the company. And Sophie was nice.

But there was something she wanted to do, and there was no way Spencer would let her do it if she told him. But she couldn't tell him. There were some things you couldn't tell people, no matter how close you got to them. She didn't want him to be disappointed in her.

She sighed. She didn't like getting close to people. It complicated things. It made things more complex. She didn't need complicated; she needed easy. It was easier when you kept people at arm's length. You couldn't hurt them then. And there were things she needed to do. Things that Spencer wouldn't approve of.

She drove slowly through the lanes, back towards the orange glow in the sky that huddled over the city. She didn't need her sat-nav; she knew exactly where she was going.

Lovelace pulled up outside Sinclair's home and turned off her car. No lights were on in the house, and no vehicle sat on the drive. The nearest street lamp was far enough away for her to approach the house under the cover of darkness. The home of Mrs Pritchard had a light on in the downstairs hallway, but other than that was completely dark. She sat in her car while the rain beat a steady rhythm on the roof and watched the neighbourhood for signs of activity. She didn't want to get halfway up Sinclair's drive only to find a young couple making out behind a bush.

When she was satisfied that the area was clear, she opened the door of her car and stepped out into the night. She drew the hood of her jacket over her head, ducked down into the wind, and strolled casually up Sinclair's drive. She knew from experience that only people who acted furtively aroused suspicion. Those that acted normally were rarely bothered by a second glance. She walked up to the side gate as though it were the most normal thing in the world and pulled down the handle. Fortunately, it was unlocked, and she closed the gate behind her, breathing a sigh of relief as she went.

She carefully navigated Sinclair's garden while waiting for her eyes to grow accustomed to the low light. It was a small garden that dog-legged around the back and spread out into a small lawn. A small patio was laid just behind a set of French windows, and a collection of rattan furniture sat looking squat and unloved to one side. Lovelace followed the path around the house until she reached a small door. She tried the handle and found that it was locked. The French Windows were locked, too, but she felt that with a bit of persuasion, they might well force open. They were old windows and did little to resist Lovelace's attention. After five minutes, the catch fell open, and she slid the windows apart.

She stepped inside the Sinclair's home and took a moment to compose herself. She could feel her heart thumping in her chest. Every bone and every muscle screamed at her that this was a bad idea, but she felt compelled to go on. Adam Sinclair needed to be stopped, and she was the only one that could do it. Following rules had always been a problem for her. She had struggled with authority and regulation for as long as she could remember, and she was ill-inclined to change now, especially as she was on the trail of a sadistic killer.

The means justified the end, and the end meant introducing Adam Sinclair to Justice, one way or another. She steeled herself and stepped further into Adam Sinclair's front room.

She needed to find something, however small, that linked Adam Sinclair to the Night Prowler. It didn't need to be much, just enough to compel a magistrate to issue a warrant so they could tear Adam's world to pieces. But where to start?

She began slowly moving among Adam's belongings. She had a small torch, no bigger than the size of a pencil, which gave out a weak light. She didn't mind that. She didn't want to alert the neighbours to her presence. Or Adam, should he return home while she was still inside his house. It had occurred to her that it probably wasn't wise to be caught in the home of a potential serial killer in the middle of the night, and at the back of her mind, she couldn't help but wonder if he was out there somewhere, stalking his next victim.

The thought bothered her, and she redoubled her search.

The front room proved a barren hunting ground. Nothing of note could be found except for a few ornaments and a television. The kitchen was the same. Nothing.

She stole quietly up the stairs. The faint light of her torch guided the way. There were three rooms off the landing at the top of the stairs, one of which was the bathroom. She checked inside the bathroom cabinet and found nothing but toothpaste, soap, and several medication bottles. She checked the labels. They were just ibuprofen and paracetamol.

The first bedroom bore the hallmarks of the dumping ground of a man living alone. It was full of boxes of paperwork, old bank statements, discarded delivery boxes, and the detritus of a lonely life. Lovelace went through the paperwork looking for something…. But what? Whatever it was, she didn't find it. She held out vain hope that she would find the farm's location that she was sure he was using to hide the body of his wife and her lover, but she saw no related documents. She worried that anything that may tie Adam Sinclair to the Night Stalker murders would be found at the farm, not in Sinclair's home.

But still, she searched.

At the same time, Spencer poured himself a large glass of red wine and sat on one of his comfortable armchairs. He slipped his shoes off and let them fall to the carpet. Upstairs, he could hear the gentle rumblings of Sophie's music as the bass gripped the walls and the soft melody swept more graciously around his ears. He wasn't big on modern music, but it sounded nice. He closed his eyes and thought about Lovelace.

Beautiful, enigmatic, mysterious, intelligent, forthright and wholly magnetic, Miss Lucy Lovelace.

He couldn't help but feel that when he was with her, he was in the presence of someone special. It wasn't dirty old man lust or anything like that. He truly believed that she was something different, unfathomable, and the more he tried to fathom her, the less he felt he knew her.

There were secrets inside Lovelace that he doubted he would ever know. But she was a force. A powerful young woman who was about to set the world on fire but only…. But only what? What bothered him?

He sipped his wine and felt the ruby liquid coat the back of his throat. She was like the mythical wood nymph in that the closer you got to see her, the harder she became to see.

He picked up his mobile phone and rang her.

Lovelace was elbow-deep in Sinclair's underwear drawer when her phone rang. It buzzed and vibrated quietly. She never had it on loud. She hated being summoned by electronic equipment.

'Phil?' She said quietly, her voice humming in the dark.

'Lucy?' There was a pause. 'Lucy? Where are you?' The hairs on Spencer's neck stood up. Why the fuck was she whispering? An image of a scared Lovelace hiding in her wardrobe while the Night Prowler stalked her in the night beyond gave him chills.

'I can't talk right now. It's not a good time. Call me later.'

'Lucy, don't hang up. If you hang up, I'll trace your phone and be wherever you are in twenty minutes.'

'Fuck.'

'Lucy?'

'I'm in Sinclair's house.'

Spencer stood up. When he spoke, his voice was angry. Lovelace could feel the timbre to it. 'What the fuck are you doing in Sinclair's house?'

'Looking for evidence,' she said, matter of factly. 'He needs to be stopped, Phil.'

'Not like this.' Spencer said. 'Get out of his house, Lucy. This isn't the way.'

'What is the way, Phil? He needs to be stopped.'

'And we'll stop him, Lucy. You and I. Together. But properly. I can see it in you, Lucy—the pain of your father and the loss of your mother. I understand. I understand what pushes you on, but you know this isn't right. People like Adam Sinclair must meet Justice, but only through the process of the law. It's what separates us from savages.'

Spencer heard the sigh.

'Lucy.'

'Of course, you're right, Phil. What am I thinking?'

'Think quickly, Lucy, because not only could you ruin your career if you're found in his house, you shouldn't forget that Adam Sinclair is a fucking vicious piece of shit who wouldn't hesitate to kill you if he finds you there.'

Spencer paused as he heard a loud thud come from upstairs.

'Lucy, get out of the house. Stay on the phone with me. I want to know you're safe.'

Spencer left his front room and climbed the stairs. Sophie's door was ajar, and the music no longer played. Instead, he met an ominous wall of silence.

'Sophie?' Spencer called.

Lovelace heard the change in Spencer's voice. She paused as she was about to descend Sinclair's staircase.

'Phil? What is it?'

Spencer pushed his daughter's bedroom door open and stepped inside. It was empty.

'I don't know. I can't find Sophie. I thought she was in the house.'

'You thought?'

'I never saw her. Her music was on. She often does that. Sometimes I won't see her for hours or until she wants to drink my wine. But the music's stopped, and her room's empty.'

'Maybe she went to the bathroom?'

'Maybe.'

Spencer turned and pushed the door open to his bedroom, and stepped inside. He looked around his room for something he couldn't quite put his finger on. And then he saw it, or rather, he didn't see it. He didn't see his St Christopher hanging where he had left it earlier that day. He knew, too, that Sophie would never move his things. Not ever.

'Lucy, I think he's here. The fucking Night Prowl……'

Lovelace never heard Spencer end the sentence. She heard something else. Something that froze her to the core. She listened to an electric stun gun being applied to exposed skin and the thud of a body hitting the floor.

Silence. Lovelace waited, her heart in her mouth. Then the voice came.

'Hello, Lucy.'

'Sinclair….'

'What are you doing in my house, Lucy?'

Shit.

'I work in security, Lucy. Did you not think I might have brought some of my work home? I have some of those internet cameras disguised as ornaments around the house. I get alerts when they are activated. So imagine my surprise when I saw you, not twenty minutes after I saw you drop Sergeant Spencer at home.'

'If you hurt him, I'll kill you,' Lovelace said calmly.

'Yes, I believe you would, but fear not; he is merely unconscious. No, I tell a lie; he's waking up. Wait there.'

Lovelace heard the stun gun being applied again, and Spencer groaned in the background.

'There, that should keep him out for a bit. It's one of my own inventions. Bloody difficult to buy in this country but incredibly easy to make if you know how. It's a bit stronger than your average Tazer. It should keep Spencer asleep for a bit.'

Lovelace had a sudden thought that filled her with dread. Sophie. Dear Sophie!

'What have you done with Sophie?' She asked.

'Oh, nothing. Yet. She's beautiful, isn't she? Yes, very pretty. I'm afraid it's not looking too good for her.'

'You won't get away with this, Adam; we'll get you for this. You can't get away with it. It's over.'

'Yes. Yes, I suppose it is. And I never expected to get away with it. Not forever. Now all I need to do is work out my legacy. How do I want to be remembered? These things are important, you see. Image is everything.'

'Let the girl go, Adam. I'll put in a good word for you with the judge. We'll make things easy for you.'

'No, I don't think so. You see, that's just not going to happen. I'm looking at a whole life term for what I've done, and once you've found the proof, there'll be no denying it. And I can't go to prison for longer than life, and we don't hang people these days, so it makes no difference whether the girl lives or dies. No difference at all.'

'Don't hurt the girl, Adam, or I promise you I'll inflict something worse than death on you.'

'I expect you'll try. Goodbye, Lucy.'

The phone went dead, and Lovelace stood at the top of the stairs in suspended animation.

Then the wall started to flash blue.

Lucy returned to Sinclair's bedroom and drew back the curtain. His bedroom overlooked the front of the house, and she watched as three police cars came to a fierce stop on his driveway, their blue lights ablaze. She recognised one of the cars as being from armed response, and she watched as the occupants climbed out and milled about the street. A few seconds later, an unmarked car drew up, and the occupants were joined by two plainclothes officers who had climbed out of a vehicle parked across the street. Lovelace couldn't remember seeing the car when she arrived. So they must have followed her. Shit.

'DS Wainwright, DC Hampton. West Mercia Police. DI French?'

'Yes.' French said. 'Thanks for your call. Where is she?'

'She went into that house about twenty-five minutes ago. We've been watching the back. She hasn't come out yet.'

'Good. Good job, lads. Sergeant?'

A uniformed officer with a grey beard, three stripes on his arm and bright yellow Tazer strapped to his left leg came over. 'Ma'am?'

'Get your men to cover the back. She'll probably make a break for it. Be warned that she is considered a dangerous suspect capable of extreme violence. Be extra vigilant. And make it known that she is a serving Police Officer with Thames Valley and knows our drills. Show her no favouritism, Sergeant.'

The look on the Sergeant's face suggested that he had no intention of showing her any favouritism. A crook's a crook. They all get the same.

He was barking his orders when the front door to Sinclair's home flew open, and Lovelace stepped out.

Sergeant Grey drew his Tazer to high port and levelled it at Lovelace.

'Police officer with a Taser! Stay where you are! Don't move.'

Lovelace kept walking, her hands held aloft in the most unthreatening way she could find.

'I'm afraid I can't stop,' Lovelace said as she slowly walked down the driveway. 'It's life and death. I need to go to my car.'

'Stand fucking still, or I'll discharge my weapon!'

Lovelace thought of Sophie.

'I'm sorry, I can't. I have to go.'

'This is your last warning! Stop, or I'll fire.'

'I'm not going to stop, and if you fire that weapon, a young girl will die. Don't do it, Sergeant.'

Lovelace kept moving slowly towards her car.

'Sergeant!' DI French screamed, and at that moment, Sergeant Grey loosed his weapon at Lovelace, and the powerful barbs drove into her body and delivered an incapacitating shock.

She hit the ground in a daze and promptly fell upon by half a dozen hands which drew her arms behind her back and cuffed her. They hauled her to her knees, and French approached. Lovelace looked up.

'You Tasered me, you fucking bitch.'

French nodded. 'You were warned,' she said, 'and now you're nicked.'

Lovelace paced her small cell restlessly. She was like a trapped lioness with the smell of her prey upon her senses but whose claws had been clipped and the sharp edge of her teeth dulled by her own mistake.

She had been brought to the local station, checked over by the force medic, processed at the Custody suite and locked into her cell.

But most of all, she was furious with herself. She had failed. She had failed Spencer, and she had failed Sophie. It had been a mistake to break into Sinclair's house, and now Sophie would most likely pay for that mistake with her life. She knew, too, that DI French could keep her locked up for twenty-four hours. Twenty-four hours in which she could do nothing to help Sophie. The fury boiled her blood, and she kicked the cell door in frustration. She was trapped. There was nothing she could do. She hadn't felt this powerless since…

The image of her father and sister flashed across her mind. They were sat in an upstairs room of their house while the fire raged about them. She knew then that she would die but couldn't stop it. She was helpless to prevent the disaster.

Once she had recovered and the burns had started to heal, she had vowed that she would never find herself in that position again, and here she was, utterly powerless. Only this time, it was Sophie she was sure would die.

DI French opened the door to the custody suite and stepped inside. DI Frampton followed close behind. The desk sergeant looked up.

'Good morning.'

'Morning, Sarge,' French said. 'How's our client been?'

'She hasn't sat down once. She's paced her cell like a trapped cat.'

French glanced at the clock on the wall. It had just gone seven o'clock in the morning. Lovelace had been in the cell for a little over eight hours. They had sixteen more before applying for an extension or releasing her. They had enough evidence to charge her with breaking and entering but little else. As it stood, there was no way they would be granted an extension. They had no concrete evidence tying Lovelace unequivocally to the Pitts' murder.

French glanced at Frampton. 'Think she's stewed enough?'

Frampton nodded.

The custody Sergeant opened the door to Lovelace's cell, and French stepped inside. Lovelace stopped pacing.

'Morning, Lucy. I think it's time we had a chat, don't you?'

The three of them sat in a small interview room. Frampton passed Lovelace a cup of coffee and a brown paper bag. 'Sausage and bacon. We thought you might be hungry. It's from a burger van up the road, not the canteen, so it's probably edible.'

Lovelace declined them both. 'You need to let me out. Now.'

'I think you need to answer a few questions, don't you?' French asked. She reached over to a small recording machine and pressed "Record."

'Interview with Detective Constable Lucy Lovelace, present are DI French and DI Frampton. Lucy, I must caution you that you are still under arrest, and while you have the right to remain silent, it may harm your defence if you do not mention something when questioned that you later rely on in court. This interview is being recorded and videotaped, and you may request a copy once the proceedings are over. Do you understand?'

'Just get on with it,' Lovelace said. She sat back in her chair and folded her arms.

'Lucy, you've been offered representation and declined it. Would you like to rethink that choice? You should have your lawyer present.'

Lovelace shook her head. 'No. I'm good. Get on with it.' She knew all too well that requesting a lawyer would take time, and that was a luxury she couldn't afford. Sophie was in danger, and she needed to get out quickly. Besides, she was confident she knew the law better than a lawyer and certainly better than the two detectives sat opposite her. Their only power was time, and she needed to get that back.

Lovelace sat forward. 'Did you go to Phil's as I said?' She asked. 'Tell me what you found. Is Phil okay?'

'Following the information you supplied, a fast response team was sent to Sergeant Spencer's home. He was rushed to hospital and is currently being monitored by the doctors.'

'Monitored? Why? Is he okay?'

'Sergeant Spencer was treated for burns to his neck, and the doctors believe that the shock he was exposed to upset the rhythm of his heart, so they're monitoring it closely.'

'And Sophie?' Lovelace asked, knowing full well the answer she was going to get.

French shook her head. 'So far, we have found no trace of Sophie Spencer.'

'Then let me out.' Lovelace demanded. 'I can find her. You have to let me go.'

DI Frampton sat forward. He bent his head to one side and asked, 'why do you think you can find her when others can't? The combined powers of three police forces have joined in probably the largest man-hunt in Oxford's history, so what makes you think you can do what they can't?'

'You need to trust me, and you can't hold me forever. What harm would it do to let me out now?'

'Trust you?' French asked. 'Tell me, Lucy, whose house were you in when we arrested you?'

'It belongs to a man called Adam Sinclair.'

'We've done a bit of research, Lucy. We understand from your colleagues that Adam Sinclair is the prime suspect in the Night Prowler investigation.'

'Is there a question in there?' Lovelace asked.

French nodded. She had been warned that Lovelace would be difficult. She was intelligent and well-educated and knew how the interview process went. However, breaking her down wasn't going to be easy.

'Okay.' French said. 'Did you have a warrant to enter the Sinclair property?'

'No.'

'Did you have Adam Sinclair's permission to be in his house?'

'Why don't you fucking find him and ask him.' Lovelace said.

'Answer the question,' Frampton urged.

'No. Find Sinclair and ask him.' Lovelace challenged.

'What were you looking for?' French asked, shifting the direction of the interview slightly.

'Evidence.'

'Evidence of what?' French asked.

'Evidence that ties Sinclair to the Night Prowler case.'

'What kind of evidence?'

'A memento from one of the victims. Or the location of the farm.'

'Oh, yes, the farm. We understand that the working hypothesis is that Adam Sinclair murdered his wife and her lover and has them buried at this farm that he may or may not have inherited?'

'That's right. If Sophie's alive, he'll be holding her there.'

'For your information, following evidence given to us by Sergeant Spencer, a warrant was issued to us by a magistrate, and a search team has been going over Adam Sinclair's house all night. They've found nothing.'

Lovelace sighed. She had feared that. They were still no closer to Sinclair and, as such, further away from Sophie.

'What were you going to do with any evidence you found?' Frampton asked.

'Use it against Sinclair, of course.' Lovelace said.

'How?' French asked. 'Any evidence you may have found as the result of an illegal search would have been inadmissible in court. It would have been useless to us.'

'I would have found a way to use it. To get the evidence we needed.'

'And if you couldn't?' French asked. 'What would you have done then, Lucy?'

Lovelace looked at the two detectives and realised there was more to this than she had believed. There was another agenda that she couldn't quite see yet. French was bouncing around the edges carefully, probing the boundaries with loaded questions but not giving her hand away for a second. What cards was she holding, Lovelace wondered.

Carefully, Lovelace said, 'I want justice for the victims. And I want to save Sophie.'

'Who's victims?' French pounced on the ambiguity. 'The Night Prowler's or your father's?'

Lovelace sat back in her chair and said nothing.

'Tell me what you think justice is, Lucy.' French asked, shifting the conversation again but staying on topic.

The question piqued Lovelace's interest. Where was this going?

'What do you mean?' Lovelace asked. 'Justice is justice.'

'I disagree,' French said. 'Justice is a concept. People's perception of justice differs. For example, in some societies taking the hand of a thief is considered justice, while we in the West may consider it barbaric and in no way representative of justice. Some may consider a terrorist killed by his own bomb as poetic justice or a child murderer trapped in his cell and stabbed to death as justice. I was wondering what you considered justice. How would you deliver justice to The Night Prowler?'

Lovelace said nothing. She knew a trap when she saw one but was interested in seeing it sprung.

'Can you answer the question, Lucy?' Frampton asked.

Lovelace sat forward. 'I'm a police officer; it's my job to bring people to face justice. How that justice is manifested is not my job. That's for society to decide.'

'You consider yourself an instrument of the law, then?' Frampton asked.

Lovelace nodded. 'If you like.'

'But by breaking into a suspect's home, you've gone outside the law and rendered the law superfluous to your own needs.'

'Sinclair needs to be stopped.' Lovelace said defiantly.

'Did Mark Pitts need to be stopped, Lucy?' French asked.

'Who?'

DI Frampton opened a folder she had brought to the interview and laid a mugshot of Mark Pitts on the table. 'Mark Pitts. Do you recognise this man, Lucy?'

Lovelace picked up the photograph and looked at the man.

'No.' She said.

'Are you sure?' French asked. 'Look at the photograph again, Lucy. Are you sure you've never met this man before?'

'I don't need to look at the photograph.' Lovelace said. 'I have a copper's memory for faces. I've never met him before. Who is he?'

'His name's Mark Pitts. He was a small-time crook. Drugs, theft, violence. And rape. And someone lured him down a dark alley last week and murdered him. They stabbed him and cut off his genitals and displayed him like a grotesque mannequin.'

'Revenge?' Lovelace asked.

'Or someone seeking their own form of justice.' French added pointedly.

Lovelace picked up the tone of French's comment and watched as her dark eyes watched hers with interest. Lovelace showed no emotion. Her eyes gave nothing away. She held French's gaze for a few seconds and then looked back at the photograph of Mark Pitts. Now it was getting interesting.

'Where were you on the night of the 7th, Lucy?' Frampton asked.

'At home in bed.' Lovelace responded instantly.

'You don't want to think about that for a second?' Frampton prompted. 'Think carefully.'

'No need.' Lovelace said. 'I had an early night. I began my new job as a Detective Constable on the morning of the 8th. I was woken early to begin work on the Night Prowler case. So I know exactly where I was.'

'Can anyone corroborate that?' Frampton asked. 'A boyfriend or a girlfriend?'

'I was alone.' Lovelace said succinctly.

French reached into her folder and withdrew another photograph. It was a still shot from a CCTV camera. She laid the photograph on the table before Lovelace, who watched French's eyes carefully. She saw them shine expectantly. Lovelace avoided looking at the photograph. Whatever was on it was considered important to French. Lovelace steeled herself to be careful. She didn't know where this was going but knew she needed to tread carefully.

'I'm now showing Constable Lovelace a CCTV image taken on the night of the 7th of this month from an Off Licence on Temple Street, Oxford.' French said. She tapped the photograph while holding Lovelace's stare. 'Would you look at the photograph, please, Lucy.'

Lovelace pulled the photograph closer to her with the tip of a single finger. She paused and then looked down at the image. It was a grainy image, clearly blown up from the original and digitally manipulated to show a clearer picture. Lovelace felt her pupils dilate and the corner of her mouth rise almost imperceptibly. She caught it quickly and buried the emotion before it gave too much away, but looking back at French, she could see her smiling. French had seen the recognition streak across her face.

Lovelace pushed the photograph back.

'Do you recognise the woman in the photograph, Lucy?' French asked.

'No.'

'Are you sure? Look at the photograph again, would you?'

'I don't recognise the woman in the photograph.' Lovelace said, not looking at the photograph.

'Well, that's interesting,' French continued, 'because I think the woman in the photograph is you, Constable Lovelace.'

'It isn't.' Lovelace said.

'It's not a perfect image, I grant you,' French said. 'But it's you. It's the only image of the woman who spent the evening in Pitts' company. The woman in question carefully avoided all the other CCTV cameras in the city, almost as if she knew exactly where they were and how to avoid them. Much like a police officer would. Like you would.'

'It's not me. I was in bed.'

'But you can't prove that.' French said.

'I didn't realise then that I would need an alibi; otherwise, I would have been sure to get one sorted.'

'You didn't think you would need one,' French said, 'because you thought you'd been clever enough to avoid identification. But you didn't know about the camera in the Off Licence.'

'Why would I want to kill this Pitts bloke? I didn't know him.'

'Why did you break into the Sinclair property, Lucy? As a police officer, you knew it would do you no good.' French paused and watched Lovelace's face for clues, but now she saw nothing but a wall of steel. Lovelace had closed the door.

'We think you have some kind of justice complex, that you look to avenge those you feel the law has let down. We think you lured Pitts into that alley, stabbed him, and displayed him in the way you did to show that justice had been served. There's no other reason for displaying him like that. We also think you broke into Sinclair's home to find him and to kill him, to avenge those he has hurt. You're a vigilante, Lucy, and there's no place in our society for people like you.'

'No offence intended, Inspector,' Lovelace said, smiling, 'but I think you're full of shit.'

French smiled back. 'We've shown your photograph to Pitts' friends who were with him on the night of his murder. They recognised you, Lucy, and are prepared to stand up in court and testify that it was you that they saw with Pitts shortly before he was killed.'

Lovelace sat forward on her chair. 'Let's say for one minute that that was true. That it was me with Pitts that evening. That's not proof I murdered him. Prove it, Inspector, or release me.'

'Very well. Interview terminated.' French reached over and switched off the recording. 'You can return to your cell, Lucy, while we find that proof.'

Lovelace didn't argue. There was no point. She would gain no purchase with DI French. She had set her stall and showed her hand. Now she had to play it, and she had to play it well. Lovelace knew there was no way French would find the evidence she needed, and all she had at the moment was pure supposition. The evidence was circumstantial at best. The clock on her custody would run out in a few hours, and Lovelace would be back in the game. She just had to hope that Sophie would live long enough for her to find her.

In the Custody Suite, Frampton drew French to one side.

'She's right, Ally. Putting her with Pitts on the night of his murder is one thing, but proving she killed him is another.'

French smiled. 'I know. But did you see her face? When she saw herself in that photograph? Did you see it?'

Frampton nodded. 'I saw it. She recognised herself, all right. But it's not enough. Now we need to prove it.'

Thirty

The clock ticked interminably slowly. Twenty-three and a half hours had passed since Lovelace had been tasered and arrested leaving the Sinclair house. Twenty-three hours in which she had a prime opportunity to relive her mistakes and curse herself, over and over, for letting Sophie and Phil down.

Sinclair was going to pay, and she could feel the fight rise within her as her custody clock ran out.

French unlocked the cell door and escorted Lovelace to the custody suite, where a new desk Sergeant bore down on her. French was alone. DI Frampton was even more noticeable for his absence.

'Evening Inspector,' the desk Sergeant said, shifting himself on his stool to better see his computer screen. 'So what are we doing here then?'

'We're bailing Miss Lovelace for four weeks, pending further enquiries.'

'Very well. Any bail conditions?'

'Miss Lovelace is to have no contact with any police officer with involvement in the Night Prowler investigation and absolutely no contact with an individual named Adam Sinclair.'

They hadn't found him, then, Lovelace thought. Sinclair was still at large. That gave her some hope. It gave Sophie hope.

The desk Sergeant ran through the bail conditions, and Lovelace signed a black box that sat in front of the screen. When the paperwork was completed, Lovelace was handed back the few items she had had on her person when she was arrested. There were two mobile phones, a work one and a personal one; a purse containing a few notes and several credit cards; and a ballpoint pen.

'Where are my car keys?' Lovelace asked. She had driven to the Sinclair house the previous evening once she had dropped Spencer off, and she was sure she had them on her when she was arrested.

French held them aloft. 'We took the liberty of retrieving your car from outside Mr Sinclair's home. We don't want you going back there. Your car's in our car park.'

She handed the keys to Lovelace.

At the back door to the police station, French handed Lovelace a large brown envelope.

'What's this?' Lovelace asked.

'Official notice of your suspension as a Police Constable from Thames Valley Police. Effective immediately. You're hereby suspended from all duties, on full pay, subject to a disciplinary investigation into your conduct. You'll receive written notification on when your disciplinary will be held.'

Lovelace knew it was coming and felt indifferent to it. The police had served their purpose. It was time to move on. But first, she needed to deal with Adam Sinclair.

French said, 'you're forbidden to have any contact with any of your colleagues or to attempt to contact them in any way. And don't go planning any foreign trips.'

Lovelace smiled. French unlocked the door and opened it. It was dark outside. Lovelace stepped out into the fresh air and turned to face DI French.

'You've kept me for nearly twenty fours hours out of spite and because you could, not because you should. A young girl's life is in danger, and if she dies, I'll hold you personally responsible.'

French looked deep into Lovelace's eyes. She wasn't sure what she saw in those eyes, but it scared her.

'Take care, Lucy.' She said and closed the door behind her.

Lovelace found her car and started the engine. She turned the heating up and waited for the air to warm.

She was out, and the game was on, but where to start?

Her work phone began to vibrate. She looked at it blankly, not recognising the number. Then, after thirty seconds, it rang off. In the last twenty-four hours, she had received a phone call from the same number on the hour, every hour. Lovelace picked her phone up and dialled the number. It answered immediately.

'About fucking time.' The voice said.

Lovelace held her breath for a moment. She recognised the voice. Adam Sinclair.

'I've been tied up,' Lovelace said matter-of-factly.

'I know. They caught you in my house. That was very silly of you.'

'Shit happens.'

Sinclair laughed, and his laughter ripped at Lovelace's soul.

'If you've hurt the girl, I'll kill you.' Lovelace said.

'Now, there's no need to be like that.' Sinclair replied, offended. 'For your information, the girl is perfectly well. She has a small bruise over her left eye, and if she doesn't stop bloody crying, I'm going to blacken the other one, but other than that, she's fully intact. For now.'

'Leave her alone, Adam. She's innocent. Take me. Let her go and take me.'

There was a long pause when Lovelace could only hear Sinclair's breathing.

'I was hoping you would offer that,' he said. 'I didn't want to suggest it myself. It seems so much more fitting if you make the offer. I'm so pleased you agree.'

Lovelace felt her heart pound deep within her chest. It pounded so hard she could hear it.

'So you agree? Me for the girl?'

'I agree.' Sinclair said. 'Drive Westbound on the A34 past the Botley Interchange for a few miles. There's a lay-by. In the lay-by is a Blue Ford Mondeo. The boot's open. Inside the boot is a pair of handcuffs and a blindfold. Get in the boot, put the hood on, and cuff your arms behind your back.'

'That seems excessive.' Lovelace said.

'It is,' Sinclair agreed, 'But I know you, Lucy. I know who you are.'

Lovelace saw the image of her father flash before her eyes. He had said something similar to her when they last met. But they didn't know her at all. They had no idea what she was capable of.

'I saw a movie once where something similar happened.' Lovelace said. 'What makes you think I'm going to agree to that.'

'The Vanishing.' Sinclair said. 'I've seen the film. Actually, there were two films, a Dutch version and a Hollywood version. They had wildly different endings if I remember.'

'Which ending will I get?' Lovelace asked. She remembered that the Hollywood version had a happy ending. The Dutch version was very dark.

'You'll never know unless you agree to my terms.'

'And if I don't?'

'You have an hour, Lucy. An hour to get in the boot. If you don't, the girl dies.'

Lovelace pondered the situation. It wasn't good, but she didn't see any other way. Sinclair had all the cards, and she had nothing to offer but herself.

'Okay. I'm on my way.' She said at last.

'Oh, and Lucy. I'll be watching. Drop your mobile phones out of the window before you get here. If you don't comply, the girl dies. Don't tell anyone where you are going, or the girl dies. If you don't turn up, the girl dies. If I suspect you are up to anything, I'll walk away, and the girl dies. Do exactly as I say, Lucy or the girl dies.'

'Okay, Adam, I get it. But how do I know that Sophie is still alive or that you'll let her go if I comply.'

'You don't,' Sinclair said softly. 'You have one hour, Lucy. The clock's ticking.'

The line went dead.

Lovelace took her mobile phones and threw them out into the car park. She put her car into gear and drove out of the station. The night was quiet, and the sky was heavy with dark, thunderous clouds that streaked across the heavens. As she approached the Botley Interchange, she saw the familiar outline of Seacourt Tower, just below the highway, silhouetted in the night sky. For a moment, it was lit up as lightning flashed behind her, and then it was plunged back into darkness, once more dipped into an orange mist that hugged the city.

She slowed as she drove past the Interchange, and after a couple of miles, the lay-by came into view. Sure enough, a Blue Ford Mondeo was sitting there, waiting.

Lovelace pulled in behind it and got out. There were few people on the road, and there was little light for her to see by. She was surrounded by a dense thicket of trees that seemed to crowd around her. Somewhere in those trees, she knew that Sinclair would be watching.

She opened the boot of the Mondeo. She felt no fear. She never felt fear. Fear was of no use to her, and Sinclair was the one that needed to be afraid. If Sophie was dead, she intended to kill him. If that wasn't Justice, she didn't know what was.

Slowly she climbed into the car and closed the boot behind her. She pulled the hood over her head, clasped her hands tightly behind her back, and slipped on the handcuffs. They were modern police issue, and she wondered where Sinclair had got them from.

When she had finished, she lay in the most comfortable position she could find and waited. And waited, and waited.

She heard the thunder roll about in the outside world, and now and then, a lorry trundled past the lay-by causing the car to vibrate and move. But still no one came.

She was about to give up and try and extricate herself from the cuffs when she heard footsteps approach. The light inside the boot came on as the door opened, and she saw a figure outlined through the hood. The figure reached down, and she felt a sharp scratch on her arm as a hypodermic syringe was inserted.

She felt her senses dull almost immediately, and she fought against the drug as it coursed through her veins, but whatever he had injected her with was a powerful substance that ultimately won the battle of wills. Despite her struggle, she felt the darkness overwhelm her, and her eyes closed, and she fell fast asleep.

***

She woke with a bad taste in her mouth and a blinding headache. She tried to get up, but she was restrained at the wrists. They were still behind her back, but now they were secured behind some kind of framework.

She blinked and tried to get her eyes to work, but she was still groggy, and her vision swam before her.

'Here, drink this.'

A hand held out a bottle of water.

She looked at the owner of the hand and saw Adam Sinclair look down at her.

'Sorry. It has a bit of a kick. I've given you something to take the edge off, but it will take a few minutes.'

Lovelace leaned back on the frame that held her up and waited for the blurry vision to settle down. The next time she opened her eyes, things had improved. She took a long moment to take in her surroundings.

She was being held in what she guessed was the cellar of the farmhouse they had been looking for. It had a musty smell and was dark save for a single bulb that hung from the ceiling. Adam Sinclair stood watching her.

In the other corner of the cellar sat Sophie. Her arms were tied behind her, and she looked like she had been crying. Her eyes were red and puffy, and Lovelace saw the look of pain and despair etched deep in her expression.

'You said you'd let Sophie go.' Lovelace growled.

'I lied.' Sinclair said. 'I must admit I do not need her, but she's cute. I'm sure we'll have a very pleasant date. Well,' he said, and he laughed, and once again, the laugh reached into Lovelace's soul and tore at it. 'When I say we'll have a pleasant date, it won't end well for her.'

'You bastard.' Lovelace felt the word escape her before she could reign it in. She needed Sinclair calm - for now.

'It was never about her.' Sinclair explained, 'it was about you.'

'Me? Why Me?'

'Because you're Jack Lovelace's daughter. You'll be my final kill. I'll succeed where your father failed, and I'll be the most famous serial killer in Britain's history. The Night Prowler and the tragic slaying of Lucy Lovelace.'

He laughed again.

Lovelace looked across at Sophie. 'Are you okay? Has he hurt you?'

Sophie sniffed and shook her head. 'No. I mean, he hit me, but he hasn't hurt me. Not like that. Is Dad… dead?'

Sinclair turned on Sophie and scowled at her. 'I fucking told you I didn't kill him,' he screamed. 'Why don't you fucking women ever listen?'

Lovelace ignored Sinclair. 'Your Dad's fine, I promise.' She held Sophie's eyes and tried to exude comfort and security. 'It's going to be all right, Sophie, I promise.'

Now Sinclair turned on Lovelace.

'You think so, do you? Have you any idea the position you're in?' He moved over to where Lovelace was sitting and knelt before her, pushing his face within an inch of hers. 'Because it doesn't look too good from where I'm standing.'

Lovelace looked deep into the eyes of Adam Sinclair and saw her father. They were cold eyes, loveless and empty. There was no compassion there, no warmth and no humanity. She had seen evil like that before and vowed to track it down wherever it hid and destroy it.

'I'm not frightened of you, Adam. I feel sorry for you.'

He laughed again.

'Oh, please, you're killing me!'

'It's not your fault. I blame your mother.'

Lovelace watched for the reaction in Sinclair's body language. He seemed to soften slightly.

'You know nothing about her.' He said softly. He got up and walked over to Sophie.

'I know she abused you. I know her boyfriends abused you. You had a horrible childhood, Adam. It wasn't nice. And it wasn't fair to you. Such a young and defenceless little boy.'

Adam knelt before Sophie and ran his hand down her cheek, brushing away a tear.

'Mother could be cruel, but I loved her. She only ever wanted the best for me.'

'Is that why she hit you? When she was drunk?'

'She was a different person when she was in drink. She was so kind and loving when she was sober.'

'But she wasn't sober very much as you got older, was she, Adam?' Lovelace watched as Sinclair ran his fingers down Sophie's neck. Sophie shuddered and tried to turn away.

'She had different blokes every night of the week. Some were okay. Some were nasty. As my sister, Erin, got older, they started showing more interest in her than my mother. My mother hated that.'

'What about you, Adam? What did they do to you?'

'Nothing,' he snapped. He stood up, stuck his hands in his pocket, and turned to face Lovelace. He looked like a lost little boy in a play of his own writing but who had forgotten his lines.

'Did they beat you, Adam? Did they touch you? Did they make you touch them?'

Adam cupped his hands over his ears and shouted, 'Shut up! Shut up! Shut up! Stop talking. You don't know what you're talking about.'

'Did it get worse when Erin left, Adam?'

The fury in Sinclair's eyes burned fiercely. 'Fucking bitch left me. She left me with them. She left me with her.'

'You hated your sister, didn't you, Adam? And you hated your mother. Do you hate all women, Adam?'

'I don't hate women. Only those that remind me of her.'

'Who?' Lovelace asked. 'Your mother? Janet?'

Sinclair started to prowl the cellar. Lovelace could see the conflicting emotions battle it out in his mind. He was beginning to unravel.

'You took back control, though, didn't you, Adam? How did that make you feel?'

Adam stopped and looked at Lovelace. What did she know?

'You started with your sister, didn't you? Watching her. Spying on her. It made you feel strong. It gave you power over her. Did you watch your mother, Adam? With her boyfriends. Did that give you power, Adam? Did it excite you?'

'Yeah, I watched them. And girls at school. I'd watch them, and they never knew. They never saw me. I could see them in the changing rooms or at the swimming pools. I'd follow them home, and they never even knew.'

Lovelace sat up and felt the handcuffs rub her skin. Sinclair began to prowl again.

'But you didn't stop there, did you, Adam?' Lovelace prompted.

'I started going out at night when it was dark, and no one could see me.' He sat down a few feet from Lovelace and smiled. 'They were the best times. You could be whoever you wanted to be at night, and no one could see you. No one could judge you. I wandered the streets for hours, looking in people's windows, watching their shadows on the curtains. Sometimes I'd see people's images as they changed for bed or got out of the shower. Sometimes I'd hear them screw. It gave me power.

'Then, one night, I climbed into a woman's garden and tried the door. I don't know why I did that. I think I'd seen her in the day… she reminded me of Mother. I wanted to get close to her, so I went back when it was dark and tried the door. It was open. They often were back then. So I went in and had a look around. She was asleep. I went in and stood at the foot of her bed and watched her sleep. I felt so powerful. I can't describe how it made me feel.'

'Did you take anything, Adam? That first time?'

Sinclair looked at Lovelace. 'Yeah. There was a small trinket on her bedside table. I took it. How did you know?'

'Because you take memories. It's not enough to abuse these people, but you must take a piece of them for yourself.'

Sinclair growled. 'I didn't abuse her!' He shouted.

'Not like that, that's true. Not to begin with. Who was the first woman you attacked?'

'Some little bitch. I don't remember her name. I followed her off the bus one evening and watched as she got undressed for bed. I don't know why I did that. I hadn't intended to. There was this urge. I couldn't control it. But I didn't kill her.'

'Not that time, no. And there were others, weren't there, Adam? Once you had done it once, it became easy to do it again and again. You couldn't stop yourself, could you? And then you murdered Stephane Walker.'

Sinclair laughed. 'Stupid bitch caught me standing at the foot of her bed and started screaming. I didn't know what to do so I hit her and couldn't stop. I hit her so hard I broke a finger. But she had seen me so I had to kill her. You can understand that. I had to kill her. I couldn't let her live.'

Lovelace watched Sinclair as he relived the moment he murdered his first woman. She could see the buzz it gave him.

'How did it make you feel, Adam? Killing a woman with your bare hands? It aroused you. You raped her as she died, didn't you?'

Sinclair smiled at the recollection. 'It gave me power. I had the power.'

'Power you didn't have at home?' Lovelace asked.

'It made me a somebody,' Sinclair mused. 'I went home that night, a man. No one knew what I had done, but for days I felt they could smell it on me: the sex and the death. I was sure they knew. I was sure she knew. But no one came for me. I got away with it.'

'That enhanced the thrill of the kill. Getting away with it. But you stopped. Why did you stop, Adam?'

'Hannah.' He said softly, and for the first time, Lovelace detected a note of regret in his voice.

Sinclair got up and sat next to Sophie. He laid his hand on the inside of her leg and ran it up as far as it would go. Sophie was thankfully wearing dark trousers, but Lovelace saw her tense up as Adam moved his hand further up her leg.

'Hannah. You remind me of her.' He said, looking coldly into Sophie's eyes.

Sophie said nothing. She held her breath.

'You loved Hannah, didn't you, Adam.' Lovelace continued, searching for a way to distract Sinclair from his intentions with Sophie. 'And she was the first woman who loved you back, wasn't she? The first woman to show you love and attention. The first woman who listened to you.'

'Mother brought back Bob one evening, and it was like he never went away. He was able to control her worst excesses. He brought out the best in her. She was almost nice. And he brought Hannah with him. One night Hannah came to my room, and we made love. I'd never had it like that before. I had always taken it from women, and here was a young woman giving it to me freely, like she wanted to. It took the edge off. I would have killed again, you know. I even knew who I was going to kill. I'd planned it to the minutest detail. I was going to take a weapon with me this time, something small but hard. I took a hammer from the shed. I didn't want to break another finger. It hurt too much. And then Hannah came, and she kept coming, and we fell in love.'

Sinclair kept his hand on the inside of Sophie's leg, and his gaze never left her eyes. Sophie kept very still, but Lovelace could see the tension in her shoulders. If he attacked her now, there was nothing she could do.

'But Hannah wasn't what you thought she was, was she Adam? She controlled you just like your mother used to.'

'Not at first.' Adam said. 'It was good at first. We got married and bought a house. It was good. But she was never happy. She was always after more and hated that I had no ambition or drive. I was happy like that, but she wanted more. Then she started to drink and stay out late with her friends. I could smell the men on her when she got home, so one night, I followed her and watched her.'

'You took back control in the only way you knew how.' Lovelace said.

'I watched her with other men. She fawned over them. I was there when she gave sexual favours in back alleys. I watched her with them.'

'How did it make you feel, Adam? Seeing Hannah with other men?'

'I thought I'd be angry, but I wasn't. It gave me power over her. I knew, but she didn't know that I knew, and that gave me all the power I needed. And she always came home to me. Always. She could never leave me.'

'So you returned to your old ways? You started again. You started spying on women when you knew they couldn't see you? You couldn't resist the urge, could you?'

'It was easy,' Sinclair said. 'I worked all over Oxford and saw them, but they never saw me. They never noticed me. No one ever noticed me, but that worked in my favour. I found out their names and followed them on social media. I found out where they lived and broke into their homes when they were out, which made me feel strong. Sometimes I waited until they came home, *and they never knew I was there.* But the urge kept getting stronger and stronger.'

'And then what happened, Adam? What happened that set you off again?' Lovelace asked. She watched as Sinclair moved his hand from Sophie's leg and ran his fingers through her hair.

'Mother died.' He said.

'Why did that change things?'

'It took away my power. My power was always over her.'

'The women you kill. Stephane Walker and the others. You were killing your mother.'

Sinclair cupped his hand around the back of Sophie's head.

'You attacked and killed women that reminded you of your mother.' Lovelace said.

'Women would look at me like shit. They would talk down to me. They always thought they were better than me. Just like she did.'

'But then she died,' Lovelace continued. 'She escaped you. You couldn't kill your mother any more because she was already dead.'

'Then they started to remind me of *her.*'

'Hannah?' Lovelace asked.

Sinclair moved his face to within an inch of Sophie's. 'You smell like her,' he said, 'you remind me of her.'

'She's not Hannah, Adam. She's done nothing to hurt you.'

'You're all the same,' Sinclair growled, and Lovelace noted the change in the timbre of his voice.

'Hannah was going to leave you, wasn't she?' Lovelace pressed, trying to keep Sinclair focused. 'Just like your mother, she was going to escape you. But you had it in your power to stop her in a way that you couldn't with your mother.'

'She started to bring the same man home a few times. She hadn't done that before. And she started to change. She was even less attentive to me; sometimes, she was cruel. But she started taking more care of herself, doing herself up better before she went out. She started spending money on good clothes and perfume. I knew something was wrong. So I started tracking her phone and monitoring her calls. I drove to work one morning and parked my van in a small lay-by where no one would notice it, and I walked back to the house and let myself in. She came home with him at about lunchtime. They fucked in my bed. I heard them. I watched them. And they talked about leaving. About running away. Running away from me!'

'You couldn't let that happen, could you, Adam? So they had to die.'

Sinclair looked back at Lovelace, and she could see the monster smile back at her.

'He had his back to me as I came out of the wardrobe. Hannah saw me. I zapped him, and he went down like a sack of shit. She fought like a banshee, but I fought harder. I hit her so hard that the side of her head caved in. It was over in seconds, but I had the satisfaction of knowing she knew it was me. I had the power again. I left the bodies in the house, went back to work, and returned as normal that evening. I got the bodies out of the house that night, brought them here, and buried them.'

'But the urge never dulled, did it?'

Sinclair shook his head. 'It never goes away. It never stops. I'm glad it's over.'

'But it's not over yet, Adam. There are two ways this can end, and it doesn't have to be a bad way.'

Lovelace watched helplessly as Sinclair ran his free hand over Sophie's white shirt. Sophie gritted her teeth and stifled the scream that gathered in her lungs.

'What happened with Molly Parkes?' Lovelace asked.

'I had never intended it to be her,' Sinclair said as his fingers toyed with the buttons on Sophie's shirt. 'I saw her from her neighbour's window. I knew the moment I saw her that I needed her. I had to have her. She was just like Hannah was when we first met. I needed her. I needed to be with Hannah again. So I waited until they left, and I broke into their home. I found the girl's room. She smelt like Hannah.' Sinclair pushed his nose into Sophie's skin and sniffed. 'She smelt like you.'

Lovelace could sense that Sinclair's emotions were beginning to simmer. She was running out of time.

'What happened then?'

'They came home. The woman found me in their pantry, so I zapped her. I reached the man before he knew what was happening and hit him with the hammer until he stopped breathing. Then I did the woman. Then

I went to look for the girl. I could see the green light on the telephone in the hall, and I almost bottled it. I nearly went straight out of the back and away from the house, but I figured I had a small amount of time before the police came, so I went up the stairs to look for her. I found the girl in her parent's bedroom, but it wasn't her. It wasn't the girl I was looking for. It gave me quite a shock. But I still couldn't hear any sirens, so I kept looking. Finally, I found her in an airing cupboard. She didn't even scream. I injected her with the same stuff I gave you. It knocked her out pretty quickly, but I guess that's because she was so small. I tried it once on a woman and expected it to work as on the show "Dexter," but it didn't work that quickly in real life. I had a bit of a fight for a minute or two until the drug took effect. It nearly spoiled everything. That's why I had you tie yourself up before I injected you. I had to be sure it had worked.'

Sinclair grinned at the memory.

'She was ever so light. I dropped her over my shoulders and carried her across the fields. I was almost back at my van before I heard the sirens.'

There was a deathly silence as Sinclair relived what happened next in the dark recess of his mind.

'You lot could never catch me.' He said, at last, and he turned and grinned at Lovelace. 'I even went to the police station all the time. I handed myself to you on a plate, and you never looked twice.'

'We've got you now,' Lovelace argued, and she watched as Sinclair's grin stretched and convulsed into a laugh.

'Not quite.' He said. 'I'm not quite done yet, but I imagine I soon will be. And I don't mind that not really. I always knew it would come to an end. But it will end my way,' he said, pulling Sophie closer. 'It will end my way.'

Lovelace watched helplessly as Sinclair pulled Sophie along the floor. Her arms were restrained behind her back, and she screamed as the bonds dug deep into her skin as the frame that held her pulled her back. Sinclair climbed on top of her prostrate figure and clawed at the buttons that held her clothing together. Sophie writhed in fear and desperation, but as small as Sinclair was, she was no match for his power. She screamed and fought, but Sinclair dominated her.

'You're pathetic,' Lovelace screamed, 'you're a small, pathetic little man who can only get his kicks from attacking defenceless young girls. You should be ashamed of yourself; you're no man. You're weak.'

Sinclair stood up from Sophie and turned on Lovelace.

'Will you shut the fuck up!' He balled. He walked over to a small table that sat along the far wall. He picked up a small hammer with a rounded edge and a clawed back and returned to where Lovelace was seated. He pointed the hammer at Lovelace and began waving it around. 'I'm going to fucking kill you if you don't shut up.'

'You haven't got the balls,' Lovelace spat. 'You're nothing. I'm a real woman, not a girl, and you're too simple to choose me over a child. You're not a man. You're not even a boy. You're nothing.'

Lovelace watched as the fury rose behind his eyes.

'You can't talk your way out of this,' Sinclair said, 'you can talk all you like, but it won't change anything. The police aren't coming. No one's coming. There's no cavalry waiting over the hill to come to your rescue.'

'I'm not waiting for anything,' Lovelace said calmly. 'I don't need rescuing. I don't need the cavalry.'

'Then why do you keep fucking talking!' Sinclair asked.

'To give myself time.' Lovelace replied.

'Time for what?' Sinclair asked.

Lovelace slipped her hands from behind her back and held them aloft.

'To undo my cuffs, you fucking moron.'

In a flash, she reared up, grabbed Sinclair behind the head, and pulled him closer to her while driving her forehead towards the bridge of his nose. She heard the crack as his nose broke, and he fell backwards to the floor, writhing in agony.

Lovelace sprung to her feet and kicked the hammer away from where Sinclair had dropped it. She stood over him as the tears cleared from his eyes.

'Get up.' Lovelace demanded.

'Fuck off,' Sinclair replied as he wiped the blood away from his mouth.

'Get up and face me like a man, you pathetic piece of shit.'

Lovelace's voice was calm and relaxed.

'No.' Sinclair said.

It was Lovelace's turn to laugh. 'You really are pathetic.' She said and aimed a powerful kick to the side of his head. She watched as the light went out of Sinclair's eyes as his head bounced off the concrete floor.

Lovelace undid the binds that held Sophie and took her into her arms. She held her like that for several minutes while Sophie's sobbing ebbed away.

After a while, Sophie looked up and said, 'Is he dead?'

Lovelace watched as Sinclair's chest rose and fell in a steady rhythm.

'No. But he's going to have a sore head.' She said gently.

'I wish he was dead.' Sophie said, and Lovelace appreciated the sentiment.

'He'll get what's coming to him, I promise,' Lovelace said. 'Come on. Let's get out of here.'

They climbed out of the cellar and into a large unfurnished kitchen. Dust littered every surface, and grime stuck to the windows. Lovelace and Sophie made their way to the door and pushed it open.

It was light outside. Several hours had passed since Lovelace had climbed into the back of the car, but the sun was still low in the sky, and the early morning freshness had yet to blow away in the slight breeze.

'How long was I asleep?' Lovelace asked, taking Sophie by the hand and leading her across the courtyard to an old cowshed that looked like it had seen better days.

'Ages.' Sophie said, 'He brought you in and then disappeared for a few hours.'

'Probably waiting to see if I'd brought help.' Lovelace said.

Sophie stopped and looked back at the farmhouse. Lovelace followed her gaze. It was a large, Victorian building with huge chimney stacks that reached out into the sky.

'Shouldn't we have tied him up or something?' Sophie asked.

Lovelace shook her head. 'We'll be long gone before he wakes up. He won't be able to follow us.'

The words came back at her like a boomerang and hit her full in the side of the head as she watched the door to the farmhouse fly open and Adam Sinclair stumble out, looking drowsy but fully mobile.

'Shit.'

Lovelace took in her surroundings quickly. She chastised herself for her complacency. Sinclair had a much harder head than she gave him credit for, and now he was striding across the courtyard at them, holding a twelve-bore shotgun in his hands. There was still some distance between them and Sinclair, but she couldn't afford to let him get closer. She had seen the damage a shotgun could do up close, and it didn't bear thinking about. She grabbed Sophie's hand and pulled her down the side of the cowshed.

She heard the crack as Sinclair pulled the trigger, and they both instinctively ducked, but the shot ran high and punched a hole in the side of the barn, showering them with debris.

'Run, Sophie!' Lovelace screamed as she let go of her hand, and the two of them ran as fast as they could away from Sinclair. As they made it to the far end of the cowshed, Sinclair made it to where they had first stood. He aimed the gun casually at the two young women and fired.

Lovelace felt the air tremble as the shot flew past, but Sinclair's aim was poor, and it went past them harmlessly.

The farm was a sprawling estate of abandoned and derelict barns and outhouses, and everywhere Lovelace looked, she could see a dozen places where they could hide. Still, Sinclair was no fool, and she didn't fancy their chances of remaining hidden for long. What they needed now was distance and a lot of it. The gun became incrementally more harmless the further away they got from it.

They could hear Sinclair's footsteps as he approached, and Lovelace recognised the unmistakable sound of the shotgun being cocked and reloaded.

'You can run, Lucy. But I will kill you in the end.' Sinclair cried out.

'We need to get as far away from him as possible,' Lovelace said, looking calmly into Sophie's eyes. She saw the fear look back.

'But he has a gun!' Sophie cried, and the wall beside them exploded as shot flew into it.

Lovelace grabbed Sophie again, and they ran as fast as they could across the open courtyard to the next barns. They made it to safety and out of sight just as Sinclair loosed another round at them.

'He has to re-load,' Lovelace explained. 'It gives us a small opportunity.'

They ran down the side of the barn and out beyond it to where the farm boundary began, and a hundred acres of arable farmland spread out before them as far as the eye could see. Then, in the distance, Lovelace saw what she was looking for. A large wood sat in the folds of two hills and skirted almost three-quarters of the farmland. She knew they could evade Sinclair for hours if they could get to the woodland. Or get into a position to fight back.

'There!' Lovelace cried. 'Head to the woods.'

Lovelace looked back at Sophie and saw the panic in her face.

'Listen,' Lovelace said reassuringly. 'It's not a proper gun. It's a shotgun. The shot inside the cartridge separates when it leaves the gun and gets wider and wider the further it goes. So the further we get from it, the safer we'll be. You just need to run.'

Sophie nodded. 'Are you sure?'

'If you get hit at a distance, it will be a flesh wound, nothing more—a scratch. If you feel it, keep running. Don't stop until you reach the trees. And Sophie, if I can't keep up for any reason, don't wait for me. Keep running.'

They were up and over the fence in seconds, and Lovelace was pleased to see that Sophie's youth told in her favour as she began to edge away from her. They were halfway across the field when Lovelace heard the shot. Sinclair had taken time to aim this time, and she felt pain as some of the shot drove into her shoulder.

The second shot came fast on its heels, but they had managed to increase the distance between them, and the shot flew past them harmlessly.

Lovelace dared not look behind her. She kept running as she saw Sophie reach the tree line.

And then she felt her ankle slip on the uneven ground, and her speed caused her to fall in a heap barely a hundred yards from safety. She made to get up, but the pain shot up her leg and felled her again. She watched in horror as Sophie began to come back to help her.

'No!' Lovelace screamed at the top of her voice. 'Stay there!'

Another shot ran out, and Lovelace was relieved to see Sophie return to safety.

Lovelace lay back on the floor and looked up at the sky. This wasn't the way she had expected this to end, but she took comfort in the fact that Sophie was safe. She had at least saved Sophie.

She sat up as Sinclair approached. He was carrying the gun with the end held at her head.

'Make a single move, and I'll blow your head off.' He said as he neared her.

'You're going to anyway, so why don't you just get on with it.' Lovelace replied.

'No. I want you to beg. I want you to fear me. I want to hear you scream.'

Lovelace laughed. She laughed so hard that tears began to well up in her eyes.

'What the fuck is so funny?' Sinclair asked angrily.

Lovelace wiped a tear away. 'You are, Adam. You are. I'm not afraid of you, and I'm not afraid to die. I won't be one of your victims. I'll be the heroic young woman who gave her life to save another, while you will be the miserable piece of shit suffering the rest of his life away in prison. So fucking shoot me, or fuck off.'

Lovelace stared at Adam, and he stared back. He was confused. It wasn't supposed to be like this. She was supposed to be afraid of him. So why wasn't she afraid?

'Hurry up, Adam. I haven't got all day.' Lovelace goaded. She closed her eyes and waited for the end.

Sinclair slowly moved the gun up to its shooting position and nudged the stock into the crook of his shoulder. The last few shots had left their mark, and he could feel where the skin was bruised. But this would be the last time. The last shot. He pulled his eye down to see the line better and gently began to squeeze the trigger.

It came at once. All the noise and the shouting. A dozen men in black fatigues raced across the field unobserved until they were within a hundred yards. They were all screaming and shouting demands.

'Armed Police!'

'Put the fucking gun down, or we'll shoot!'

'Armed Police put the gun down!'

'Put the gun down! Put the gun down! Put the gun down!'

Too much noise! Too much shouting. Sinclair raised his weapon until it was pointed at Lovelace's head, and a single, powerful shot from a Heckler and Koch streaked across the field and slammed into Sinclair's chest, knocking him to the floor.

Lovelace felt Sophie's presence and reached out for her.

'I thought he was going to kill you,' Sophie cried.

'So did I.' Lovelace admitted. 'I guess it wasn't my day today.'

The paramedics came a little while later and carried Lovelace off the field and into the back of a waiting ambulance. A second one had arrived for Sinclair but had been put on hold while the Air Ambulance was called.

DI French held the back of the door open as Sophie climbed in.

'Looks like we got here just in time.' French said.

Lovelace looked at her Nemesis and smiled. 'How did you know where to find us?'

'We didn't.' French said. 'Not at first. But I took a punt on you. As you asked, I decided to trust you and see if you could find Sinclair when we couldn't. DI Frampton put a tracker in your car when we collected it from Sinclair's house. We found it abandoned in a lay-by near the Botley Interchange. We were a bit stumped at first. Then we ran the number plates of cars that had triggered our Number Plate Recognition software that had used that stretch of the road to see what we could find. Some random old Ford Mondeo had triggered the cameras at one end but didn't trigger the ones at the other for nearly eight hours. That's a long time to drive, barely five miles.'

'So you tracked the Mondeo?'

'Sort of. It was registered to this farm, so we took a gamble and came here looking for you. And here you are.'

Lovelace smiled again. 'Thank you, Inspector. You saved my life.'

'Think nothing of it, Lucy. Of course, we won't mention that you've broken the conditions of your bail, but we'll let that one go.'

For the first time since Lovelace had known French, she saw her smile.

French began to shut the door.

'Will he die?' Lovelace asked.

'I don't know,' French said. 'They're working on him now.'

'Don't let him die,' Lovelace said. 'I want him to suffer in jail for the rest of his life.'

French nodded and shut the ambulance door. She hadn't expected that. That didn't fit. She shook her head.

Lucy Lovelace confused the hell out of her.

Thirty-One

Two weeks later.

The summer storms abated, and drier weather pushed the clouds over the horizon until the country was bathed in wall-to-wall sunshine.

Graham was sat in a wheelchair on the grounds of his small home in Woodstock. A large parasol had been erected on the lawn, and he had been manoeuvred into position so that he was in the shade with his back to the sun. Irene sat beside him and poured him a cold drink from a container to her side. She was dressed in a loose-fitting cotton dress and wore a summer hat. Her hair curled beneath it, and Lovelace thought she looked a dozen years younger.

Charlie wore a long, flowery dress that hugged her figure and showed her off perfectly. She sat between Graham and Spencer, drinking red wine from a large glass.

Spencer sat across from Graham and raised a glass of white wine to his lips. Despite the warm weather, he was immaculately dressed in perfectly ironed black trousers and a crisp white shirt. His only deference to the heat was in the way he rolled up his sleeves and loosened a button from around his neck. Lovelace watched him with growing affection.

Behind him, Sophie was lying on the lawn, basking in the sun like a chameleon. Her skin was beautifully bronzed, and her long dark hair cascaded down her shoulders. Lovelace felt her heart hum with affection. She would have died a dozen deaths for Sophie but was infinitely pleased it hadn't come to that.

Despite her best attempts, Lovelace had failed to manage her hair, and it fell from her head in waves of unrest and disorder. She wore a pair of white cotton trousers and a plain white top that showed off a toned midriff. She still had some remnants of her youth about her, and she intended to enjoy it while it lasted. She reached out to the table before her and raised a glass of wine to her lips.

Sophie got up from the floor and joined them as they sat around the table.

'It's so hot,' she exclaimed. 'Can I have a glass of wine?'

Spencer poured her a small glass, then relented and filled it up.

'I heard that Sinclair will make a full recovery.' Spencer said. 'As I understand it, he won't contest the charges.'

'It would be hard to, given what they've found.' Graham remarked.

Following Sinclair's arrest, specialist search teams began a forensic search of the farmyard and its barns. They found Hannah Sinclair and her boyfriend in a shallow grave in the house's gardens. In the two weeks since then, they found four more bodies. They were currently undergoing DNA testing to identify them. Among Sinclair's possessions at the farm, they found personal items belonging to all the Night Prowler victims and a hundred more artefacts they had yet to find owners for. Sinclair's night-time activities had been vastly understated.

'I suppose he'll get a whole life tariff?' Irene asked.

'No more than he deserves,' Lovelace said. 'I expect he'll join my father at HMP Black Rock.'

The island prison off the western coast of Scotland had opened its doors, and the first prisoners were being settled there already.

'When does your father go?' Graham asked.

'Next week.' Lovelace stated matter of factly. 'But let's not talk about him,' she said gently, 'what about you? What's your prognosis?'

'The tumour turned out to be benign, thankfully. I ought to make a full recovery.'

'Back to work, then?' Spencer asked. 'They've put Luton in as lead investigator with the Major Investigation Team. Stanton follows him around like a lap dog!'

Graham chuckled. 'They'll do very well, but in answer to your question, I won't be returning to work. I'm taking early retirement. I think it's time I started taking it easy. I'm going to take a leaf out of Lucy's book, literally, and write a book. I think I've got a few in me.'

'I'll introduce you to my agent if you like.' Lovelace said. 'She keeps banging on at me to write another.'

Graham reached over and took Irene's hand in his. 'And Irene has done me the honour of agreeing to be my wife.'

Lovelace gushed. 'That's wonderful news! I'm so pleased for you both! I didn't know you two were a thing.'

'We weren't.' Irene admitted. 'I suppose when you nearly lose someone, you realise how much you love them. I can tell you it was a shock to us both.'

Sophie caught Lovelace's eye and looked away sheepishly. Lovelace had seen the look, and it warmed her soul. Charlie saw it too.

'What about you, Lucy?' Charlie asked. 'What are you going to do? They'll have your job in the end.'

Lovelace took a long sip of her wine. Finally, it was time for explanations. The people around her deserved to know. But where to start?

'They already have it,' she began slowly. 'I resigned. They still want to convene a disciplinary, but I won't go. Being in the police served its purpose, but it's time to move on.

'That's not the first time you've said something like that to me,' Graham said. 'I'm intrigued to know what you mean.'

Lovelace smiled. Graham had lost none of his edge. She reached into her bag, sitting by her feet and pulled out a large brown envelope. Inside was the paperwork concerning her involvement in the Mark Pitts murder investigation. It was common knowledge among officers in the Thames Valley that Lovelace was the prime suspect. They had all seen the photograph of the woman taken from a CCTV image outside an Off-Licence on the night of the killing. They all agreed that it was Lucy Lovelace.

Lovelace laid the photograph on the table. Irene picked it up and passed it along to Graham, who passed it along the table until it reached Sophie.

'Everyone is convinced the woman in the photograph is me.' Lovelace said.

'It looks like you,' Spencer said.

Charlie agreed. 'It really does.'

'It isn't.' Sophie said firmly. 'I mean, it looks like you, but it isn't.' She laid the image back on the table.

'No,' Lovelace said, and she grew even more fond of Sophie. 'It isn't me.'

'Then who is it?' Charlie asked.

Graham cleared his throat. 'It's your sister, isn't it?' He asked. 'The woman in the photograph is Zoe Lovelace.'

Lovelace nodded. 'Yes. I think so.'

'When French showed me that photograph, I felt my stomach rise into my mouth.' Graham continued. 'It nearly knocked me over, but then I remembered the conversation we had in my office when I told you that I was the one who rescued you from the fire. It wasn't you I rescued; it was Zoe. Then there was the confusion with Molly Parkes. Young girls very often look very alike. You and your sister still look alike?'

'To an untrained eye, looking at a grainy image from a CCTV camera, then yes, we could be confused with one another,' Lovelace admitted.

'Did you know she was in the UK?' Graham asked.

'No. I suspected it when we went to visit my father in Long Lartin. I was sure of it when DI French showed me the photograph.'

'But why is she here? And what is her involvement in the Pitts' murder?' Spencer asked.

Lovelace paused while she poured herself another glass of wine. 'She's here to get my father out of prison. I'm not sure why she killed Pitts, but I could hazard a guess.'

There was silence as everyone watched Lovelace attentively. Then, slowly, she started her story.

'Zoe was always daddy's little girl. I was always mummy's girl. My mum and I would play together, read together and cook together. We did girly things, creative things. But Zoe and my dad did something else. They had a special bond. It was a bond I never truly understood, and as much as I craved my father's attention in how he showered Zoe with it, I never got it. They had a secret connection, and I was never invited in.

'She was cold, too. Sometimes I was afraid of her, but I couldn't figure out why. She is almost a year older than me, and I always thought that was why they were close. She was the firstborn. There's a special connection there that other children never have. But she never had that connection with my mother. It was almost like my dad understood Zoe. When he looked at her, he saw himself or a younger, female version of him. She had no empathy. No care. No love. I think my father recognised her sociopathic tendencies and nurtured them, controlled them, and developed them.'

'You think he created a murderer?' Spencer asked.

'Not all sociopaths are murderers.' Lovelace said. 'There's much research now into how some people seem to perform at a higher level than others, and much of it is down to some level of sociopathy. One of the defining characteristics of a sociopath is an inability to feel emotion, guilt, or remorse. Zoe had that by the bucket load. It's what separated us the most. I feel things acutely, while she feels nothing. She's cold-hearted in the strictest sense of the term.

'Then, as we were growing into teenagers, my father's activities caught up with him. And then it caught up with us.

'We watched as he stabbed my mother to death in the kitchen of our home. He knew the end was coming, and I'm sure my mother confronted him about it. He snapped and grabbed a knife lying nearby on the worktop and stabbed her. I screamed and screamed. It was the most traumatic experience of my life, but Zoe just stood there and watched. It looked like she enjoyed it.'

'So then dad took us to a room upstairs and locked us inside while he doused the house in petrol, but when it came to it, he couldn't do it. He just held us and cried. I think he was crying for himself and maybe Zoe, but I don't think he felt much for me. But he couldn't do it. He couldn't start the fire.

'So Zoe got up, casually lit a match, and threw it into the hallway. It went up with a hell of a screech. The smell was toxic, and the smoke filled our lungs. Zoe just

returned and laid down beside Dad, and we waited to
die.

'And then you came.'

Everyone looked across at Graham. It was the first
time anyone knew of their connection.

'Me and DI Sutherland were right on your father's tail.
We were watching the house when we saw the windows
on the top floor blow out. We didn't think much about
what we were doing. We just streamed in looking for
you. Jack put up a bit of a fight, but Sutherland was
once the British Army's heavyweight boxing champion
and knocked him out with a single punch. We picked
you girls up and got you out as the fire properly took
hold. Somehow Jack managed to get himself out by the
back door. He walked into the arms of armed officers as
they were setting up a perimeter.'

Lovelace felt the scars on her arms pulse with the
memory.

'Uncle Mike took us out of the country almost
immediately. I never told anyone about what Zoe had
done, but never trusted her again. We grew apart. She
never really spoke to me, but I watched her carefully. I
now knew what she was capable of, and she knew I
knew. I always thought she would come for me, but she
never did. But I realised early on that she would one day
need stopping and that I would be the only one that
could stop her. The greatest trick the Devil ever played
was convincing us he doesn't exist, which was Zoe's
most precious gift. She hid her darkness well. But I knew
it was there. I could see it. I could see what she was
becoming.

'So I started to copy everything she did. When she
learned a foreign language, so did I. I learned more. I
knew I needed to be better. When she started learning to
shoot, I joined an American Cadet force in Japan and

became a better soldier. When she went to study law, so did I. Every turn she took, I followed, and I became better than her. She learned to fly, and so did I. She took up kickboxing, and I became the girls' under eighteen cage fighting champion. With every step she took, I was two steps ahead of her.

'Then, when she was about fifteen, she hooked up with a young man from a Yakuza family. I think she made it happen that way. He wasn't much, to be honest, and I think she used him to get her foot in the door. Within a few years, she became one of their most trusted Lieutenants. People were terrified of her. And she was bloody good at it too.

'She went to Hong Kong to study law at a university there, set up an office in a known Triad neighbourhood, and started to rattle some cages. I don't know much about what she did in Hong Kong, but she got stuck into her criminal life. As far as I can tell, she created a powerful Triad/Yakuza relationship and dominated gang activity from Tokyo to Beijing and southeast Asia. She was becoming unstoppable.'

'What did you do?' Charlie asked.

'I confided in Uncle Mike and told him my plans. He always suspected that Zoe wasn't quite right but put it down to the trauma of our childhoods. I explained what I knew about Zoe and what I had done to counter her, and I told him I knew that I would have to kill her one day. He agrees with me but thinks Zoe will try to kill me first. He and my aunty live in fear that one day Zoe will come for them, and there's nothing they can do to stop her.'

'That's why you said the police had served their purpose,' Graham said, 'and why you said you never took up the sponsorship deal to fight professionally. You had got what you needed. You had become better than Zoe. You didn't need more.'

'Exactly. I came to England to get away from Zoe's influence. I studied law at the best university in the world and joined the police as a beat copper. There was no point in taking graduate entry. I didn't want to lead. I wanted to learn. The only way to learn is from the ground up, so that's where I went. I don't think there's much more I can learn. But I will have to face Zoe sooner or later, and I have a feeling that's coming soon.'

'Do you think she came to England to kill you?' Spencer asked.

'No. She came for Jack Lovelace. When she's done whatever it is she's going to do with him; then she'll come for me.'

'I don't understand about Mark Pitts?' Charlie asked.

'I'm only guessing, but Zoe won't come all this way and not open communication channels with local criminal gangs. I guess she contacted the crime family that Pitts was involved with as part of that networking plan. Pitts' history with women would have offended her. I think she murdered him and displayed his body in the way that she did as a warning to others. Zoe Lovelace was here, and she was to be obeyed. That kind of fear only comes if you get your hands dirty. She would have left them certain of what she was capable of.'

A strange silence descended on the small gathering. They could feel the storm coming, and it frightened them. Zoe Lovelace was a formidable opponent. She was going to take some stopping.

'So what do you do next?' Graham asked.

'They're sending my father to HMP Black Rock in two weeks. I'm going to shadow him and see what happens.

It's too much of a coincidence that she's here now. She'll make her move soon, and then I'll know what to do.'
Lovelace raised her glass of wine and said, 'until then, I intend to get pissed with my friends and enjoy the sun!'

They all raised their glasses into the air.

'To friends!'

Spencer held his glass aloft a little longer. 'To good friends,' he said softly, 'who will always be here for you, Lucy, whenever you need us.'

Lovelace looked around the little gathering and at the man with a hole in his head, a young woman with more holes in her body than nature intended, another middle-aged man with a heart problem and a beautiful young girl with a warm heart and no idea of the pain that life could bring.

And she never felt happier.

Support Indie Writers

Thank you very much for reading my book. I am an independently published author, meaning I write, produce, edit, market, advertise and publish my work. Like most Indie authors, I do this while working for a living. Unfortunately, self-publishing, as it is otherwise known, makes few writers any money. It costs most of us more in advertising than we can ever hope to make in royalties.

The music world reveres Indie Musicians. People travel hundreds of miles to listen to new Indie bands, buy their records and download their songs. As a result, support for Indie Musicians is enormous. Because of this, the music world benefits from fresh sounds, voices and music, uninhibited by what the leading labels believe will sell the most.

The same cannot be said of Indie Writers. People often say writers self-publish because they are not good enough to find an agent or publisher. The truth is much simpler. The publishing world is highly competitive, with huge expenses and small margins. An agent or publisher takes a massive risk when taking on a new and unknown author, so, more often than not, they don't. A new author needs time and room to grow and blossom. It may be years before their work turns a profit. Agatha Christie didn't become a household name until the publication of The Murder Of Roger Ackroyd in 1926, eight years and five books after she had finished writing her first novel.

It is far easier, more profitable and safer to pay already famous people considerable advances for books they know will sell. So it is no surprise that the most widely read crime novels today are by celebrity authors, be they TV chefs, TV producers and quiz show hosts or musicians.

I'm not saying don't buy them! I read them myself. But for every book you read by an established or celebrity writer, buy a book written by an Indie Author. Discover new worlds, stories and adventures unmolested by what people think will work and delivered to you with passion. It may be rough around the edges - we don't have a team of editors mulling over our every word or a marketing team thinking of the best way to sell it. But it's honest, and it's passionate, and it's created with love.

Then leave a review. It costs nothing. A one-star review with text is worth ten five-star reviews without. It doesn't have to be much. A simple 'I liked it' will suffice. And tell people. Tell your workmates, your neighbour and your postman. Tell everyone you meet all about the book you just read. Be the reason an Indie author goes viral and gets a long-coveted publishing deal.

Maybe one day, you will be able to say that you were there at the beginning.

Gary Burroughs, March 2023

Read the next Lovelace adventure!

**HMP BLackRock
By GS Burroughs**

A Classic Whodunit wrapped in a modern-day thriller.

As a young man, Ethan Mackay's mother was brutally murdered by a convict freed on parole. Motivated by a powerful sense of social justice, Ethan Mackay is now one of the world's wealthiest men. Billionaire philanthropist and prison reformer Mackay now runs half a dozen private prisons across the UK. HMP BlackRock is his most ambitious plan yet.

On a small jagged rock, thirty miles off the Scottish coast, lies the island of BlackRock, now one of the most sophisticated and secure Super-Max facilities anywhere in the world. Designed to hold Britain's most evil men and women, BlackRock is the place where evil goes to die. No one sent to BlackRock will ever leave. The locals have named it Devil's Island…

Proud to show off his achievements, Ethan Mackay hosts a prison tour, inviting his primary backer, Sir Malcolm Lambert MP and most vocal critic, Esther Friedman, a columnist for The Times, to a carefully planned visit.

Also on the island is Lovelace, daughter of the infamous Jack Lovelace, the Cherwell Valley Strangler, who has flown to the island to visit her father. However, when the helicopter that flies her to the island develops a technical fault, and a brutal winter storm cuts them off from the mainland, Lovelace is forced to join the VIP tour and is given a room at the Governor's Residence, The Mansion House. She joins Mackay's PA, Grace Mahone, the island's governor, Johnathon Preece and his enigmatic wife, Elouise, as they take refuge from the storm.

However, not everything, or everyone, is as they seem, and secrets thought hidden begin to be exposed.

By the following morning, one of them is dead. But the killer hasn't finished yet…

Will anyone survive HMP BlackRock?

Made in the USA
Monee, IL
19 July 2023

39584219R00277